Praise for *New York Times* bestselling author

MARIA V.
SNYDER

'Filled with Snyder's trademark sarcastic humour, fast-
paced action and creepy villainy, *Touch of Power* is a
spellbinding romantic adventure that will leave readers
salivating for the next book in the series.'
—*USA TODAY* **on** *Touch of Power*

'The descriptions are vivid and draw you into the rugged
journey across the mountains. You'll want to follow
their voyage into the next book.'
—*RT Book Reviews* **on** *Touch of Power*

'This is one of those rare books that will keep readers
dreaming long after they've read it.'
—*Publishers Weekly, starred review,* **on** *Poison Study*

'Snyder delivers another excellent adventure.'
—*Publishers Weekly* **on** *Fire Study*

'A compelling new fantasy series.'
—*SFX* **magazine on** *Sea Glass*

D0784592

Also by New York Times bestselling author
Maria V. Snyder

from
MIRA BOOKS

STORM GLASS
SEA GLASS
SPY GLASS

Healer series

TOUCH OF POWER
SCENT OF MAGIC

from
MIRA INK

The Chronicles of IXIA

POISON STUDY
MAGIC STUDY
FIRE STUDY

Inside Series

INSIDE OUT
OUTSIDE IN

MARIA V. SNYDER

SCENT OF MAGIC

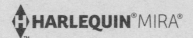

HARLEQUIN® MIRA®

All the characters in this book have no existence outside the imagination of the author, and have no relation whatsoever to anyone bearing the same name or names. They are not even distantly inspired by any individual known or unknown to the author, and all the incidents are pure invention.

All Rights Reserved including the right of reproduction in whole or in part in any form. This edition is published by arrangement with Harlequin Enterprises II B.V./S.à.r.l. The text of this publication or any part thereof may not be reproduced or transmitted in any form or by any means, electronic or mechanical, including photocopying, recording, storage in an information retrieval system, or otherwise, without the written permission of the publisher.

This book is sold subject to the condition that it shall not, by way of trade or otherwise, be lent, resold, hired out or otherwise circulated without the prior consent of the publisher in any form of binding or cover other than that in which it is published and without a similar condition including this condition being imposed on the subsequent purchaser.

Harlequin MIRA is a registered trademark of Harlequin Enterprises Limited, used under licence.

First published in Great Britain 2013
Harlequin MIRA, an imprint of Harlequin (UK) Limited,
Eton House, 18-24 Paradise Road,
Richmond, Surrey, TW9 1SR

© Maria V. Snyder 2013

ISBN 978 1 848 45221 3

58-0513

Harlequin's policy is to use papers that are natural, renewable and recyclable products and made from wood grown in sustainable forests. The logging and manufacturing processes conform to the legal environmental regulations of the country of origin.

Printed and bound by
CPI Group (UK) Ltd, Croydon, CR0 4YY

SCENT OF MAGIC

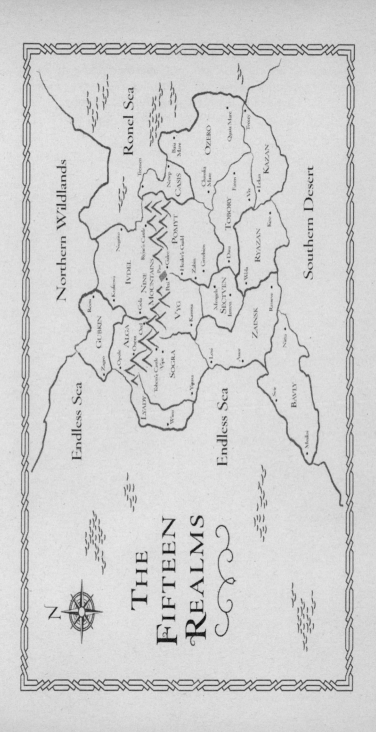

THE
FIFTEEN
REALMS

N

Ronel Sea

Northern Wildlands

Endless Sea

Endless Sea

Southern Desert

OZERO

Quoia Mare

Basa Mare

Bornen

KAZAN

Chreska Mare

Newp

Fazen

OASIS

Wa

Ucheo

POMYT

Nisep

Reixa's Castle

Relew's Castle

TOBORY

Negotan

Gola

Pita

Galev

Diwa

Kolfowa

IVDEL

Kkeo

Healer's Guild

RYAZAN

Zalan

NINE

MOUNTAINS

Gershbon

Weda

VYG

Kasema

SECTVEN

Mergal

Isswot

Roen

Oyole

ALGA

Onava

Oset

Opel

ZAINSK

Ratnew

Zego

SCGRA

Lesal

Amar

Nella

Teketek Castle

Vape

BAVLY

LYADY

Yiguta

Ser

Witen

Medar

For Mom.
You started me on this path long ago by reading me books
every night, by taking me to movies and to the theatre.
Thanks for always supporting my dreams.
I may be a gypsy, Mom, but it's all your fault!

CHAPTER 1

"I'm dead," I said to Kerrick.

He kept his flat expression, and I knew I'd get more co-operation from the cave's stone walls. Too bad for him that I didn't need his approval. But it would be nice if we worked out an agreement at least.

"No one knows I survived. It's the perfect opportunity for me to go undercover, and—"

"No. It's not safe," he said.

"Why not? No one will be looking for me. I could slip in—"

"What about Danny and Zila? They're going to need you to teach them how to be healers." Kerrick added another branch to our small fire.

We had stopped to rest in a narrow cave. Kerrick and I'd been traveling at night and sleeping during the day to keep a low profile since we still remained in Tohon Sogra's realm. We were close to what had been the Realm of Vyg's western border. After the plague had killed two-thirds of our population nearly six years ago, many of the Fifteen Realms resembled broken toys, with tiny pieces of their populations scattered far and wide.

Unfortunately Tohon had decided to sweep up those pieces

to form one realm, or rather one kingdom. A good idea until you realized Tohon, the powerful life magician, was also a deluded megalomaniac whose army included a battalion of dead soldiers. Yes, dead. Tohon had discovered how to re-animate the dead.

"Danny and Zila don't need me yet. They're too young," I said. "Danny probably won't develop healing powers until he's closer to fifteen, which won't be for another year or two. Zila has six or seven more years."

"Still, it makes the most sense to rendezvous with Ryne in Ivdel as planned. We'll need to gather his men and then join forces with Estrid so we can stop Tohon's army from advancing into Pomyt."

"For you," I agreed. "Not me." Before he could argue, I added, "Besides, I gave my word to Estrid—"

"Which was voided when you *died,* Avry." He sat next to me and pulled me in close, wrapping an arm around my shoulder.

I leaned against him, breathing in his scent of spring sunshine and clean earth. Every time we talked about my death, he'd sought my touch as if he still couldn't believe I'd survived. Considering the plague had a hundred-percent fatality rate and it had indeed killed me a week ago, his actions were understandable.

However, a giant Peace Lily had brought me back to life. The ramifications of that action were...huge. Which was why I needed to figure out exactly what happened and what it meant for the rest of the Fifteen Realms. Or what was left of them.

I dropped the topic. For now. Kerrick and I had just admitted our feelings for each other. We had seven more days until we reached Peti, and I didn't want to spend that time arguing with him. So much better to do…other, more intimate activities while we rested.

We approached the outer edge of Peti near dawn. Stopping in a thick copse of trees, Kerrick reached out with his forest magic to search for ambushers, marauders or mercs. His magic was a gift from the forest, and through that connection, he sensed other people. Or rather, he felt the irritations and annoyances that the forest considered intruders to its home.

When I held Kerrick's hand, I also connected and experienced the unique bond he shared with the forest. I wondered if my eye color changed from sea-green to a darker green when his magic zipped through my body. Kerrick's eye color changed to match the forest. Since it was the middle of spring, the surrounding greenery was thick and lush, an emerald carpet.

When I had first met him, his eyes were russet with flecks of gold, orange and maroon. The warm colors belied his personality at the time. He had been as cold and distant as the snow-capped peaks of the Nine Mountains.

But not anymore.

He caught me staring and smiled. It transformed his face from unreadable to…happy. Which still surprised me. I had been used to him gazing at me with annoyance, anger or exasperation, and these pleasant looks threw me.

He waited.

I shook my head and returned to studying the town. It was near the foothills of the Nine Mountains. Even from this distance, it appeared that most of the buildings had burned down. No signs of life.

"Do you think the marauders got to Peti?" I asked. Since it was the closest town to the main pass through the mountains, it had been a popular place to stop before making the treacherous crossing.

Even after the plague, Peti had managed to survive. But without law enforcement, large groups of marauders had formed in the foothills. They would attack populated areas when they ran out of food and supplies. They'd killed, looted and burned without mercy.

"Probably before Tohon got to them," he said.

Tohon had swept through the foothills and killed all the marauders, leaving their bodies for us to trip over. He had *claimed* he was cleaning out the undesirables that had infected his kingdom. I considered Tohon's abominations—his dead soldiers. Why wouldn't he turn those marauders into more mindless, obedient troops? I asked Kerrick.

"He wanted us to find them. So we would rush to the pass and right into his ambush."

I shuddered. The memory of the dead carrying me away still haunted my sleep along with Tohon's voice beckoning me. The forest didn't consider those things intruders because they weren't alive. According to Kerrick, the living green ignored the damage they inflicted since it couldn't sense any life nearby. Which meant the dead could sneak up on Kerrick. An unpleasant thought.

"Let's check out Peti before we find a place to rest," Kerrick said.

As expected, no one lived among the burned ruins. A light breeze swirled the ash. Our boots crunched on broken glass. Peti was bigger than I had thought. As we drew closer to the center, we encountered a few brick factories and businesses that had survived the fire. The flames had missed the heart of the town. With the marauders gone, people could return and build anew.

Except Peti was in the Realm of Vyg. Even though it was

near the eastern border, this area was technically occupied by
Tohon's army. Kerrick and I had dodged a number of his patrols on our way here.

Kerrick found another small cave for us to hide in until
nightfall. I understood the need to be hidden from sight and
protected from an attack. However, I would have liked to
camp under the sky for our last day together.

We set up our bedrolls and lit a small fire to drive off
the chill and cook a simple meal. Sitting on opposite sides, I
broached the subject of my future plans.

"No," Kerrick said without considering anything I'd just
said.

"I'm not asking. I need to talk to my sister. To explain—"

"No. It's too dangerous."

"I'm not asking," I repeated because he tended to think he
was in charge. "Besides, I was on the run for three years. I
know how to get around without encountering trouble. And
I can defend myself." I pulled one of my throwing knives and
pointed it at Kerrick. "And I know how to walk through the
woods without making noise, so I'll stick to the forest. Plus
my healing powers can be used—"

"I know," he growled.

I suppressed a smile, remembering blasting him with pain.
He'd deserved it. I'd been trying to escape from him and his
companions, but he wouldn't let go. And he called *me* stubborn. He was the most obstinate person I knew. Worry flared.
Would he drag me to Ivdel with him?

"No one knows I'm alive," I said again. "No one is looking
for me. No more bounty hunters, no mercenaries or Tohon's
dead." And best of all, no Tohon. The man who'd threatened
to claim me, and I knew, if push came to shove, he could with
one touch. I hugged my arms close to my body.

"But what about the patrols? And Estrid's holy army? Or

Jael? She killed Flea and tried to kill us. If she sees you…"
Fear cracked his stony expression for a moment.

"She won't. I'll wear a disguise."

"But your sister is Jael's page. If you get close to Noelle, she'll know."

"Then I'll make sure Noelle's alone."

"But what if she still hates you? She'll tell Jael you're alive."

He had me there.

I thought fast. "Then I won't approach Noelle until after you and Ryne arrive with his army." Hopefully in time to help Estrid defeat Tohon. Without Ryne, there was more than a good chance Tohon would overrun her defenses and add all of us to his ranks of dead. "I'll do reconnaissance and fact-gathering. I promise." I sensed a softening. "Tohon told me he has spies in Estrid's camp. I might be able to find them."

"No. You lie low, blend in and don't call attention to yourself. Learn what you can from watching and listening. Don't ask questions." Even though he was clearly unhappy, he continued. "You'll need a good disguise. Go to Mom's in Mengels, she'll—"

"But she's days out of the way, and I don't want anyone to know I'm alive."

"If you don't follow my *suggestions,* then I'll just follow *you.*"
And he would.

I kept my expression neutral. "Why Mom's?"

"Before the plague she helped women who had run away from their abusive husbands. Her inn was known as a safe house for these women, and she would give them a new look, a new name and find them a safe place to live." He held a hand up. "She'll keep all your secrets. You can trust her. That's why everyone calls her Mom."

"All right. Any other *suggestions?*"

"Don't work in the infirmary. I know it'll be tempting, but

find a job that lets you be invisible. Like a maid or a kitchen servant."

"Okay. Anything else?"

"Stay away from anyone you recognize or know. Belen's still there." Kerrick's face paled. "You should tell Belen. He can help."

"No, he can't. Come on, Kerrick, you know he's a rotten liar."

"Easy for *you* to say. He's not going to rip *your* arms off." He hugged his arms to his chest.

"He's not going to hurt you," I said. Or would he? Belen was the Poppa Bear of our group, and we had become close friends. The thought of him mourning my death almost changed my mind.

"Have Prince Ryne tell him. I sacrificed my life for his, so he owes me one." Ryne had had the plague and I'd healed him by assuming the sickness.

Unfortunately for the six million people who had died, the plague killed healers as well, so we'd stopped healing plague victims until we could determine another way. But once the population panicked and rumors spread that we refused to help people…it had turned ugly fast. Long story short, I was the last healer alive until Danny and Zila's powers woke. If they did.

"How long are you going to play dead?" Kerrick asked.

"As long as I can. It's a good strategy."

"For you. I'm the one that's going to have to deal with Belen, Quain and Loren."

"I'm sure Ryne's keeping them busy with his genius military tactics that will stop Tohon." Which was the reason I'd given up my life for him.

Kerrick relaxed his arms and moved to sit next to me. He pulled me close. "At least I won't have to act like I'm sad and missing you."

"You mean you'll go from moody, sullen and distant, to moody, sullen, distant and sad? The guys won't suspect a *thing*," I teased.

"Don't start." He tangled his fingers in my hair. "You were the reason for all those…"

"Temper tantrums? Grumpiness? Irritability?"

He tilted my head until I gazed up at him. A dangerous glint shone in his eyes. "You didn't make it easy."

"True, but neither did you."

"True." A hint of a smile. "I guess we're meant to be together."

"Surprisingly," I agreed.

"Not to Belen. Once he forgives me for lying to him, he's going to gloat."

Belen had been his loyal friend, bodyguard and all but his older brother ever since Kerrick was born. It made sense that he could read Kerrick better than anyone.

"When did he figure it out?" I asked.

"Well before I did." Kerrick gazed at the fire. "I think he made a comment after you escaped and I saved you from the mercs."

An odd time. Kerrick had been furious at me. "And when did you…agree with him?"

"My feelings started changing after you healed Belen and we were at Mom's." He returned his focus to me. Cupping my face with his other hand, he said, "You had me tied in knots. You saved Belen's life, and I wanted to kill you and thank you at the same time. And during those nights when we didn't know if you'd live or die, I went from being angry to worried to frustrated to scared all within a single heartbeat. If you had died, I would have killed you."

"You know that doesn't make sense, right?"

"Nothing about that time made sense."

"You kept me from dying. Did you know that?"

He tilted his head in surprise. "No. How?"

"You gave me the energy to heal myself. If you hadn't stayed with me and held my hand, I would have gone into the afterlife."

"And here I thought it was Mom's tonics."

"Good thing the Lamp Post Inn is on the edge of the forest."

"That's why I like it. I can still access my power there. That and her desserts are the best in the Fifteen Realms."

"I'll make sure I try some when I'm there."

All humor fled his face. "But I won't be there to watch your back."

"Then I'll have to be extra careful."

"Promise?"

"Yes." I leaned forward and kissed him. He was right. What I planned to do was dangerous, but these were dangerous times. And I needed to become Noelle's older sister again before I resumed being Avry the healer. Plus my decision allowed me the freedom to just be a regular person. Someone unnoticeable, who blended in and didn't attract Tohon's attention.

When we reached the border road between Vyg and Pomyt that night, Kerrick had a few last-minute instructions. "Stay in the forest on the east side of the border. Better to go through Pomyt Realm than to get caught in the middle of any skirmishes in Vyg. You'll be safer traveling in the daylight."

I nodded, even though I knew to stay out of Vyg and to avoid Zabin until I was disguised. He needed to tell me. Plus if he didn't lecture me, I'd worry he was following me as he had when I'd surrendered to Tohon. His forest magic had camouflaged him, and I'd never seen him until he appeared without warning in the garden.

Kerrick had been livid since he'd seen me kissing Tohon.

Under the influence of Tohon's life magic, I hadn't had a choice. His powers had filled me with an unnatural desire and smashed my willpower to dust. After Tohon had left, and still reeling from Tohon's display of dominance, I'd been grabbed by Kerrick who had then confessed he'd be upset if Tohon lured me away.

"Avry, are you listening to me?"

"Yes. Vyg bad. Pomyt good."

"Avry." His aggravation was clear.

I smiled. He was rather handsome when he was annoyed. Before he could launch into another lecture, I handed him Flea's juggling stones for Belen, the letter and necklace for Noelle and the pouch full of Quain and Loren's favorite herbs for them.

"But—"

"It'll help with the ruse that I'd died."

"How do I explain the extra time it took for me to catch up to them?"

"You're supposed to be grieving, so it should be obvious even to Quain why. But if anyone asks, just give them that stony stare and they'll back right off." I met his gaze. "Yes, that one."

"I'm not happy about this," he said, but he handed me a pouchful of coins. "There should be enough in here for a couple months."

He wrapped me into a fiercely protective hug before kissing me. His magic shot through me. If I were a plant, I'd have grown roots.

I pulled back before I changed my mind and stayed with him. "I'll see you in Zabin."

"You better."

Squeezing his hand, I said goodbye and headed southeast.

When I glanced back, he remained where I had left him, watching me. I shooed. He hefted his pack and turned north.

Although we were apart, the woods vibrated with his magic. A tingle zipped along my skin whenever I touched a leaf or brushed against a bush. Kerrick was keeping track of me. When I rested the next day, I kept my hand on the ground. That evening, his magic disappeared abruptly. Which, I hoped, meant he had reached the pass through the Nine Mountains and didn't mean he'd encountered trouble.

A sharp ache of loneliness consumed me along with a horrible feeling that I'd never see him again.

KERRICK

Kerrick hefted his pack, heading north toward the main pass of the Nine Mountains. But after a few steps, he paused and glanced back. Avry had disappeared from sight, but thanks to his magical connection, he felt her passage through the woods. Unlike other intruders in the forest, she didn't irritate the foliage and wasn't deemed a nuisance to the living green.

No, she saved those special qualities just for him, driving him crazy with her stubbornness and risky schemes. He should follow her. Despite her promises to be careful, these were perilous times. Tohon and his abominations aside, mercs and gangs still roamed what was left of the Fifteen Realms.

The thought of losing her again sent sharp needles of pain into the center of his heart. He rubbed his hand over the stubble on his chin. The scent of vanilla filled his nose, and the memory of stroking Avry's neck came unbidden. Avry's new scent since the Peace Lily saved her life. Before she had smelled of honey and the lemon-scented soap she favored. While it was an interesting side-effect of her recovery, Kerrick didn't care why it had happened. She was alive, that was all that mattered to him.

The desire to rush after her pulsed in his chest. He could send Ryne a note, telling the prince to meet him in Zabin. Ex-

cept Avry wouldn't be happy and he had no legitimate reason
to change their plans to gather troops in Ivdel before marching south to aid Estrid. That would alert Ryne. And, for now,
Kerrick knew that if everyone believed Avry dead, especially
Tohon, she would be safer. Unless she tipped her hand.

He sighed. Best to meet up with Ryne as quickly as possible
so they could deal with Tohon once and for all.

It took him a day to reach the road up to the main pass. Although it was spring and many of the other passes had opened,
they were more difficult to climb. Kerrick weighed the risks.
Tohon would expect him to go to Ivdel. If Kerrick headed
east across Pomyt and used the Milligreen pass, the journey
would be about twenty-two days. But if he crossed the main
pass, it would take him closer to seventeen days. Unless he
ran into one of Tohon's ambushes.

The smart move would be to go the longer, safer route. Except Tohon might expect him to do just that and have that pass
blocked. Milligreen was narrow and twisty, creating plenty
of hiding spots, while the wider main pass gave him more
room to maneuver.

In the end, speed won over all the other factors. Kerrick
increased his pace, hoping to traverse the nine ridges in five
days. His connection with Avry stopped when he stepped
from the tree line. Worry for her flared. He concentrated on
his progress to keep his imagination from running wild. It
was all he could do at the moment.

After he crossed three ridges, he relaxed a bit. Surely Tohon's men wouldn't come this far to ambush him. By the fifth
day, he descended the Nine Mountains and entered a lush val-
ley in Ivdel Realm.

He breathed in deep, letting his tight muscles relax. The
smells of pine and the sea mixed into a familiar scent. It'd been
three years since he'd been in the northern realms. The Realm

of Alga…home was twelve days to the west. His brother, Izak, and Great-Aunt Yasmin still lived in the Algan Palace in Orel.

Ryne's castle was located about the same distance in the opposite direction. Kerrick turned east. Regret that he wouldn't be able to check in on what remained of his family settled deep inside him. He'd send them a letter once he reached Ryne's.

Someday, he'd return to Alga with Avry. After Tohon's defeat and the Fifteen Realms restored. Kerrick had to believe that in order to keep fighting.

With his thoughts on Avry, he paralleled the east/west path below the foothills of the Nine Mountains. Keeping to the forest, he sensed a few other groups of travelers but avoided them even though the northern realms had been living in relative peace for the past two years.

He didn't encounter any trouble until the eighth day of his eastern trek. Kerrick heard a sound that made his blood turn to ice. A throaty growl full of menace. He reached farther out with his magic. Aside from birds, rabbits and squirrels, the forest surrounding him was empty of larger predators.

Another growl sounded. It was louder and closer. This time Kerrick recognized the creature. An ufa. He pulled his sword and backed against a thick trunk, debating if he should climb the tree before the ufa attacked. He nixed the idea. Ufas had sharp claws to match their razor-sharp teeth.

Leaves rustled. Why couldn't he sense it? Kerrick pulled power, blending in with the mottled browns and black of the trunk. But his scent gave him away. A large ufa broke through the bushes, heading straight for him.

Images from another attack flashed in his mind. The memory of burning pain and the sound of ripping flesh as teeth punctured his throat caused sweat to pour from his body. *Not again*.

Kerrick pointed his sword at the beast, but it stopped a

foot from the blade's tip. The ufa was as long as Kerrick was tall. Gray brindled fur covered solid muscle. It stared at Kerrick with cold dead eyes. Horror welled. Tohon was one sick bastard.

More rustling announced the arrival of another five dead ufas. They always traveled in packs. They fanned out, blocking any chance for escape. Not as if he could outrun one, let alone six.

Kerrick tried to influence the vines growing nearby, hoping they would tangle in the ufas' legs, but the forest didn't sense the ufas as a threat, even as they moved through the underbrush. Dead flesh nourished the living green and was an accepted part of its ecosystem. And the tree canopy above him contained nothing but healthy strong limbs.

With no other recourse left, he gripped the hilt of his sword, hoping to take a couple out before they finished him.

CHAPTER 2

I reached the outskirts of Mengels fourteen days after I left Kerrick. Bypassing Zabin had been tedious. I'd spent more time hiding than walking. The High Priestess Estrid's holy army patrols covered more ground than before. Plus she had increased the frequency of their sweeps.

The noise of her squads' passage through the forest had made it easy to avoid them—it just took longer. But their ineptitude worried me greatly. There was no way they would be able to perform any stealth military tactics without giving their positions away. Tohon's troops would cut right through them. They needed to learn Kerrick's trick of moving in the woods without making a sound.

Outside the Lamp Post Inn, I wrapped my hair into a tight knot. It had grown a couple inches since Mom and her daughter, Melina, had dyed the blond strands back to my natural auburn color and trimmed it. Now it hung straight to the end of my shoulder blades.

I donned a pair of eyeglasses that I'd found. It made everything a little blurry but not enough to hinder me. Then I pulled the hood of my cloak over my head. While the spring days had been warm, the nights cooled fast enough that I wouldn't draw unwanted attention. I'd decided to enter the inn during the evening rush when the arrival of one more person wouldn't be unusual. I'd rent a room where Mom could help me with a better disguise when she had time.

A good plan, except only a few people arrived. Anxiety grew. Mom always had a full house. Well, the days I'd been here she had. Perhaps this was her off-season.

When I pushed into the common room, I jerked to a stop. The reasons for the small turnout sat at the bar and occupied most of the tables. Estrid's red-robed acolytes had invaded the inn.

I would have retreated, but a few of the acolytes spotted me standing in the doorway. If I left, it would be suspicious. So I strolled over to the bar to inquire about a room. Waiting for the bartender to finish with another customer, I scanned the inn's common area.

A blaze roared in the hearth. Mom had covered the rough wooden tables with bright tablecloths, and cushions softened the chairs. Pastel paintings of flowers hung on the walls, and the mantel displayed Mom's teapot collection. Despite the relaxed decor, tension thickened the air.

The door to the kitchen banged open. Mom stood on the threshold brandishing a spoon and fussing at one of the servers. Wisps of her pure white hair had escaped her bun. Stains coated her apron, and she looked years older even though I'd last seen her four and a half months ago. Not good.

She spotted me but didn't react. "What can I do for you?"

"I'd like to rent a room."

Mom glanced at the acolytes sitting at the bar. One man nodded to her. She pointed her spoon toward the tables. "Have a seat. I might have an open room, let me check."

Oh, no. I retreated and found a small table in the back right corner out of the direct firelight. My thoughts swirled with questions. When had Estrid invaded Mengels? Should I just bolt and hope for the best?

A server I didn't recognize took my order. In fact, I didn't know any of the waitstaff. More than a few acolytes eyed me with interest. Swords hung from their waists. Which was a new twist. The acolytes I'd seen before hadn't been armed. Well, not visibly. I wondered if these devotees would try to "recruit" me as they had my sister.

Noelle had been living on the streets of Grzebien when Estrid's army had arrived to "help" the plague survivors, whether they'd wanted it or not. Along with a group of other street rats, Noelle had been rounded up and sent to a training camp.

The scars on my back burned with guilt as I remembered Noelle swinging a mallet at my head and accusing me of abandoning her. She'd been ten when my mother and younger brother, Allyn, had sickened with the plague and died, leaving her alone. At the time, I was in Galee working as an apprentice healer. Noelle said she'd sent me letters begging me to come home, but I never received them. I suspected my mentor, Tara, had intercepted them.

That still wasn't an acceptable excuse. Or the fact that, since the plague swept with such speed, I wouldn't have gotten home in time. Noelle was right. I'd abandoned her, and I needed to make amends.

Since my every move was being scrutinized by the acolytes, I ate my meal without tasting it.

Mom arrived with a slice of strawberry pie. She set it down in front of me.

"I didn't order—"

"A skinny little thing like you can afford to have dessert."

And just for a second, I caught a gleam of recognition in her eyes before she returned to brisk innkeeper.

"I do have a vacancy. How long are you planning to stay?"

"One night."

"Just you?"

"Yes."

"When you're finished, I'll show you the way." She left.

Kerrick was right. The pie was delicious. Too bad I couldn't really enjoy it. Not with Mom acting so strange. I hoped I'd have time to talk to her before the acolytes ambushed me. Because even looking through the blurry lenses of my glasses, there was no missing the nods and speculative stares that passed between them.

Mom led me to a tiny room on the first floor. Relief loosened a few knots in my stomach when I spotted the window between a narrow bed and a tall, thin armoire. I yanked off the spectacles and rubbed the ache in my forehead. While she lit the lantern on the night table, I closed the door and leaned against it.

"Tell me this isn't as bad as it looks," I said.

"It's worse." Grief leaked through the bland persona she'd adopted.

"Melina?"

"Taken." She sat on the edge of the bed as if her legs could no longer hold her. "As you will be."

No surprise. "Now?"

"Middle of the night. They have keys to all the doors, so you need to leave right now."

"Do they recognize me?" I asked.

"No. They think you're a lone traveler and an easy target."

"Tell me what happened?"

The story sounded too familiar. Estrid's troops had arrived to help. They'd conscripted all the young people and "converted" as many as they could, turning them into true believers of the creator.

"My rooms are filled with acolytes, and Chane, the one in charge of Mengels, is staying here, as well," Mom said.

"The big guy at the bar?" I asked.

"Yes. He says if I cooperate, I'll see Melina again."

"Do you know where they took her?"

"Up north. They need soldiers to fight King Tohon's army. They're planning to recruit in all the towns in Sectven Realm." Mom twisted the end of her apron. "I don't know what I'll do if she's killed in battle."

"She won't be. I'll make sure she's safe."

Mom glanced at me. "I can't ask—"

"You're not. I'm offering. Besides, I saved her before, and I'm not about to let her get hurt again."

She straightened her apron. "How can I help?"

I debated. Kerrick had instructed me to find a job that made me invisible. If Estrid's acolytes recruited me as a soldier for her army, then I'd be one of dozens. And one uniformed soldier looked much like another. Except I'd be watched as a potential flight risk and wouldn't have any freedom. Their squads needed to learn how to move within the forests without giving away their positions or they'd be slaughtered. It was something I could do if I managed to convince them they needed my help.

Mom waited for my answer.

Kerrick wouldn't be happy. Good thing he wasn't here to lecture me.

"I need a better disguise." I explained to Mom about my death and about the Peace Lily's role in my survival, just in case something happened to me and Kerrick. "However, you cannot tell a soul I'm alive."

"Of course not, dearie. I protect my girls," she said with a spark of the Mom I'd remembered.

I outlined my plan.

"Goodness, such a to-do. You're heading straight into trouble. I hope you know what you're doing." She left to fetch a few supplies.

I hoped so, too. While I waited for her, I arranged the room to aid with my plans. Mom returned with a basin, dyes, towels and a tray laden with other materials, including a couple jars filled with flesh-colored goo. At least that was what it looked like.

"I can't lighten your hair since they've seen it darker, but I can dye it so it's more red than brown." She gestured for me to sit. "Make sure you always wear it up or pulled back. It will help make you look older."

She worked fast, and soon my hair was wrapped tight in a towel. Opening one of the jars, she dipped her fingers in and then smeared the goo over my face and neck. Then she attacked my eyebrows with tweezers, plucking without pause. She dyed the thin arcs she left behind.

"This is going to hurt," she warned me before brandishing a syringe. "Hold very still."

I almost jumped from my seat when she pricked my bottom lip. Bracing for the stab of pain to my upper lip didn't make it feel any better. My lips throbbed as if I'd bitten them very hard.

"Watz tat or?" I asked through swollen lips.

"It's venom from a lannik snake. It'll make your lips fuller for now." She considered. "Usually it wears off in six months, but it might not last that long for you."

"Ight ot?"

"Healers heal faster, right?"

Our bodies healed about ten times faster. I nodded. It was easier than talking.

"Don't worry, you'll get used to them. Now let's get the lightener off your face."

Mom washed my face, combed and braided my hair so the braid circled my head like a rope. She sprinkled something wet over my nose and cheeks before blotting at it with a towel.

With a satisfied smile she flourished a hand mirror, turning it until a stranger stared back at me.

"Freckles?" My now pale skin sported an array of freckles.

"They match the hair color. I used an ink that should last six months, and your natural skin color shouldn't return for at least four months. I'll put together a package of supplies for you to take along, so you can reapply if needed. And you'll need a new name and realm to go along with the disguise." She stepped back and regarded me. "Not bad, dearie. With the spectacles on, no one will recognize you."

The glasses had given me a headache. Conscious of my lips, I formed my words with care. "I can't wear…long."

"Not to worry." Mom rummaged through her supplies and produced a pair of glasses with silver wired frames. "These have plain glass."

She helped me adjust them so they fit.

"Smart," I said.

Sadness filled her eyes. "No, I'm not. If I'd listened to the rumors, I could have sent Melina away before those red-robed devils arrived."

"Where would you have sent her? Not north or west, Tohon is invading those realms as we speak. Estrid has the north and east occupied. South?"

Pausing in the middle of cleaning up, she gaped at me. "No. Travelers from the south have told me such horror stories about a Skeleton King in Ryazan Realm."

"Skeleton King?"

"He has gathered a following and they're armed with the bones of their enemies."

"Are you sure? That sounds far-fetched."

"If it was only one or two travelers, I'd dismiss it, but many people have been fleeing from Ryazan. And they all say the same things."

Just what we needed—more trouble. "Then you couldn't have sent her anywhere, Mom. No place is safe anymore."

No place is safe. My words to Mom replayed in my mind as I waited on top of the armoire. There was just enough room for me to sit cross-legged. Watery moonlight illuminated the lump under the bedcovers, but my hiding spot remained in the shadows.

A breeze rustled the leaves in the forest outside my open window. The fresh scent of living green reminded me of Kerrick. I half expected him to climb into my room. But nothing stirred or caused the insects to halt their nightly chirping.

The thin handles of my throwing knives dug into my damp palms. My cloak hung inside the armoire, and I wore my black travel clothes. Three years on the run from bounty hunters and mercenaries had taught me patience.

To pass the time, I thought about a new name and realm. Since my skin color now matched the people born in the northern realms, I decided I would be from Gubkin. It was tempting to pick Alga, but when Prince Kerrick of Alga showed up with Prince Ryne of Ivdel, there was a slight chance someone would try to introduce us. Plague survivors always sought out others from their former realms.

As for a name...I chose my mother's name, Irina. A wave of grief swelled. I'd never had the chance to say goodbye to her or Allyn. Noelle had buried them in the mass graves and left Lekas. I'd arrived home to an empty house. My father and older brother, Criss, had died in a mine collapse before the plague struck. Four members of my family gone. I swallowed the tears that threatened. I would not lose Noelle, too.

The sudden quiet warned me. Shuffling footsteps outside approached my window. I shifted into a crouch and concentrated on the sounds. Two acolytes moved to block my escape. Then the lock on my door clicked and two robed figures entered. One moved toward my bed while the other stood before the now closed door.

Only four? Or did they have more waiting in the hallway? Did it matter? Not really.

I threw a knife at the person guarding the door—thunk—and then a second—thunk—pinning the sleeves of his robe to the wood. One down. I leapt off the armoire and landed on the acolyte near the bed. He fell with a solid thud. Just to be safe, I touched the back of his neck.

Power swelled from my core, and I channeled it into him, zapping him into unconsciousness. Not many people knew healers had that ability, and the acolyte wouldn't remember what hit him. I doubted his partner even saw the action as he struggled to free himself.

Now for the two outside. I dove through the window, hit the ground and rolled. A cry of surprise sounded nearby, but I gained my feet and dashed into the woods. They chased after me. As soon as I reached a thicker area, I slowed and moved through the forest the way Kerrick had taught me.

My passage matched the natural sounds of the woods. Unlike my pursuers, who crashed through as if running from a pack of ufas. I found a hiding spot. They cursed as they stumbled into trees, and the fabric of their robes caught on thorns. I muffled my breathing as one came quite close to me.

He yelled at his companion to stop making so much noise. They paused and listened, then decided to split up to cover more ground. Big mistake. I waited until they were far enough apart, then I stepped behind the acolyte who had yelled.

Touching the back of his neck, I zapped him. He jerked in surprise before collapsing.

His companion's noisy passage was easy to track. I caught up to him and pulled my stiletto. Instead of zapping this one, I pressed the tip of the blade against his throat. "Looking for me?"

He froze. "Uh."

"Don't do anything stupid," I warned as I yanked his sword from his belt and tossed it aside. "Follow my orders and your head will remain attached to your thick neck. Understand?"

"Yes."

"Good. Let's go." I grabbed the collar of his robe.

"Where?" he asked.

"Back to the Lamp Post Inn."

He paused. "You're crazy."

"So I've heard." I poked him with my blade. "Now move."

When we reached the front of the inn, I instructed my captive to go inside first. Drawing in a deep breath, I stayed behind him as he pushed open the door. This could be a very big mistake. I steadied my nerves by concentrating on being confident like Loren and cocky like Quain.

While we were still in the shadowy threshold, I peeked around my guy. The common area was rather crowded for the middle of the night. I counted five. All armed.

The leader, Chane, rounded on my acolyte. "What's going on? Where is she?" he demanded.

"Uh."

My captive wasn't the most loquacious. I moved next to him but kept my stiletto pressed against his skin.

"I found him lost in the woods." I tsked. "Poor thing should know the forest is dangerous at night."

Swords appeared in four hands within seconds.

However, Chane studied me. I copied him. He was as tall

as Belen but not as wide. Although I didn't doubt strong muscles lurked underneath his robe. His nose looked as if someone had sat on it, and his brown hair had been cut military short. A soldier despite the acolyte's garb. He appeared to be around Loren's age—about thirty-five.

He broke the silence. "You're either incredibly stupid or…"

"Or what?" I asked.

"Or incredibly stupid."

"Now, now. Play nice. I didn't kill any of your men. And I could have easily disappeared. I still can," I said with a bravado I didn't feel.

He motioned to one of his men. "Hent, check her room." Then he returned his attention to me. "Okay, I'll play. What do you want?"

"It's more about what *you* want. You sent your colleagues to ambush me. I assume you have a good reason?"

A slight smile tugged at the corner of his mouth. "I just wanted to talk."

Yeah, right. "Okay. So talk."

It took him a moment to cover his surprise. "Just like that?"

"You're looking for bodies for Estrid's army. Right?"

"We're missionaries, spreading the creator's message of peace and educating the—"

"Save the speech for someone who is gullible enough to fall for it. Fact is, I'm interested. You know I'm skilled. Four of your guys couldn't catch me. I can fight for Estrid, but I don't want to be a draftee, devotee or anything else ending in *ee*."

Understanding shone in his eyes. He relaxed until Hent returned from my room with the acolyte I'd pinned to the door. Two small rips marked the sleeves of his robe. He clutched my knives in tight fists, glaring at me.

"We can't wake Tyson," Hent said.

Every gaze focused on me. "He'll be fine once the drug wears off."

"What did you use?" Chane asked.

"Trade secret."

"And my other acolyte?"

"Sleeping in the woods."

He paused for a moment before gesturing to the bar. "Let's have a drink and discuss your…terms."

I waited.

"Consider it a cease-fire. No one will attack you. I give you my word."

"And you are?"

"High Priest Chane of Ozero Realm."

High Priest? An impressive rank. "What are you doing in Mengels?"

He laughed. "Spreading the word. I can be very persuasive."

I glanced at his men. They still held their swords at the ready. "Uh-huh."

"They're overprotective." He signaled them, and all but Hent sheathed their weapons.

He stared at me as if waiting for the opportunity to throw my knives at me.

Chane noticed. "Hent, give me those."

With reluctance, Hent handed him the two throwing knives. Chane placed them on the bar, then he inclined his head at me, waiting. I released his man and slid my stiletto back into its holder on my belt. He pulled a stool out for me, then settled on the one next to it as if we were old friends getting reacquainted. But his gaze turned cold when he focused on my ex-captive. "Otto, fetch us some wine."

The man rushed to obey.

"So, Miss…?"

"Irina of Gubkin Realm." I perched on the edge of the stool.

"You've traveled a long way."

I shrugged. "The northern realms are quiet compared to what's happening on this side of the Nine Mountains."

"As I understand it, you're looking for a higher-ranking position in the High Priestess's army. Why didn't you approach the officers up near Zabin?"

"They weren't smart enough to catch me while I crossed through their territory."

Otto placed two glasses of red wine on the bar and retreated to the other end.

Chane swirled his wine. "But I haven't caught you either."

"That's why you need me."

"That doesn't make sense."

I swallowed a mouthful of wine. "I've been in Vyg. I've seen Tohon's…special troops." I let the horror and revulsion show on my face. No acting required. "You *need* me."

He considered. "Word from the High Priestess is that those creatures are a rumor. A tactic to spread fear in our army."

I stared at him, doing my best to match Kerrick's flat expression.

"The information about them came from a dubious source," he tried.

"Then you are calling me a liar." And also Belen, Quain and Loren. If Belen were here, he'd squash Chane so the rest of his body matched his nose. I snatched my knives and stood.

"Wait. I apologize. It's just so…implausible. I know Tohon's a powerful life magician, but for him to be able to animate the dead is…unbelievable."

I could have explained how Tohon injected them with an unknown substance and then froze their bodies in a stasis so they didn't decay. The combination of the mystery drug and magic gave them a fake life. Why it worked, I had no idea. However, that was much more than I planned to reveal to Chane.

Instead, I said, "You would have an easier time recruiting soldiers if you showed the people what Tohon's capable of. Then you wouldn't have to resort to late-night abductions and rounding up street rats."

He peered at me as if he had misjudged me. "How do I know you're not a spy for Tohon?"

"Because if I was spying for him, I would have let you kidnap me. Then I would be like all the rest you've conscripted—a nameless, faceless soldier able to blend in with ease. He probably has a dozen spies in place already. Tohon's no fool."

When he didn't respond, I said, "This has been a colossal waste of time. I'm leaving."

"Where are you going?"

"To join Tohon's forces. Might as well fight for the winner." I headed for the door. Would they try to stop me?

"Irina, wait," Chane said.

I turned, expecting to see sharp blades pointed at me. Instead he sent Otto to fetch him parchment and ink.

"Finish your wine," he said.

Still wary, I settled back on the stool. After Otto returned, Chane wrote a letter of introduction.

"Give this to Major Granvil," he said, handing it to me.

I scanned the letter. Even though there were a few compliments about me, three words stood out as if they'd been written in bright red ink. *My aunt Estrid*. Chane was her nephew. I almost groaned out loud. So much for keeping a low profile.

KERRICK

The dead ufa pack kept their positions as if waiting.

Waiting for what? Kerrick stretched his senses to the maximum distance and felt the unmistakable vibrations of a galloping horse. *A potential ally or more trouble?* With six ufas poised to attack, it couldn't get any worse.

He kept a firm grip on his sword as he speculated on the approaching rider. It could be Tohon, coming to gloat over Kerrick's imminent death. But why would he travel all this way when he was busy preparing for war? Because it was exactly what Tohon would take the time to do.

After all, Kerrick and Avry had snatched Ryne from Tohon, denying him his revenge. Ryne's military savvy posed a very serious threat to Tohon's plans to become king of all the realms.

The ufas didn't flinch as the horse slowed and entered the clearing. Kerrick recognized the rider. Although lines of strain marked her face and her long blond hair was frizzy and unkempt, she had the same sad smile he remembered from school.

"Cellina, fancy meeting you here," Kerrick said.

"We've been waiting for you," she said.

"We? Is Tohon here, as well?"

"No. It's just me and the dead mutts." She gestured to the ufas, crinkling her pudgy nose in disgust.

"Was this your idea?"

"Nothing about this is my idea, Kerrick."

"Yet, you're here."

"Tohon is a hard man to refuse. He's forced me into a very difficult position."

Lyady Realm had been invaded by Tohon last year. To ensure the president's cooperation, Tohon had taken his daughter, Cellina, with him.

"I'd feel bad, but your position is better than mine at the moment," he said.

"True."

"How did you find me?" he asked.

"The pack was given your scent. Instead of guessing which pass you'd take, we crossed the Nine Mountains and found a place to wait east of the Milligreen pass."

"Smart."

"Tohon's plan. Just like these mutts. Dead ufas are easier to train and more loyal than the living ones. They won't attack you until I give them the signal."

The four scars on his neck burned as his heart rate jumped. "Is giving them the signal part of Tohon's plan?"

"Yes. I'm to report every detail of your death and dismemberment to him. I've also been ordered to bring home a souvenir."

Stunned, he stared at her.

"Your sword, Kerrick. Don't be so morbid."

He swallowed. "Hard not to be." He braced for the signal, but she remained quiet. Sensing her ambivalence, he said, "Cellina, come with me to Ryne's."

"I can't."

"Why not? We'll protect you."

"I know you'll try."

"We'll succeed. We saved Ryne and the children."

"But not your lady love."

"She chose her fate."

Cellina sat straighter in the saddle. "So did I."

"There's no reason for you to return to Tohon now." But as he said the words, he realized she must still be in love with him. Either Tohon's life magic had influenced her, or she'd never recovered from her school crush. In his younger days, he would have scoffed at the notion. However, he'd learned love didn't follow logic at all.

"You don't have to do this," he said.

She clutched the reins tighter. The horse moved a few steps to the side, smelling her fear. "I can't disobey him."

In desperation, he stepped away from the tree. The ufas growled and snarled but didn't move. Kerrick pointed his blade at the ground, slowly approaching Cellina. Sweat soaked his shirt and burned in his eyes. But he kept his gaze on her.

He stopped with two feet between them. Her lips pinched tight together as if she'd whistle, but no sound escaped. Yet.

Kerrick offered her the hilt of his sword. "Take it."

CHAPTER 3

I arrived in Zabin around midmorning a week after I'd left Mom's. The town was completely overrun with Estrid's acolytes and soldiers. When I'd been here with Kerrick, there had been only a few red robes. Now, it appeared as if the streets were covered with blood. A bad omen.

And the feel of the town had changed. Before, unease rippled just under the surface of the populace. Now, outright fear fogged the air.

My dark gray cloak no longer helped me to blend in. Plus, the day would be too warm for my fur-lined garment. Summer was only three weeks away. I removed my cloak and packed it into my knapsack, put my glasses on, then strode through town as if I belonged. But it wasn't long before a group of five soldiers stopped to question me.

Showing them Chane's letter, I asked where I might find Major Granvil. They glanced at each other with suspicion creasing their collective foreheads.

"This letter could be a forgery," the female lieutenant said, passing around the paper to her team again.

I suspected this could take all day. To speed it up, I asked, "Why don't we ask the High Priestess? I'm sure *she'll* recognize her own nephew's signature," I bluffed. The last thing I wanted was an audience with Estrid.

But my comment had the desired effect. At the mere mention of her name, they blanched. I offered them a more palatable suggestion. "Or we can all find Major Granvil and let him decide on the authenticity of the letter." Plus it would give me an escort so I didn't have to do this song and dance all over again.

The lieutenant agreed. I suppressed a laugh as they surrounded me. What did they think I'd do? We walked through the center of town. While the market appeared crowded, I noticed there were fewer stands selling goods than before. I wondered if the nice lady who sold me my cloak and boots remained in business.

We left the town proper. The buildings thinned, and soon farm fields stretched into the distance to the north and east. Except no crops had been planted. Tents, campfires and training areas filled the landscape. It appeared to be the bulk of Estrid's army. She had a few training camps throughout Pomyt, but it seemed she had concentrated her forces here.

I spotted the grand manor house east of the city's heart. It had been built on a hill and overlooked Zabin and the surrounding lands. When I'd been a...guest of Estrid's, I'd stayed there while I'd cared for her wounded. A decent-sized infirmary occupied the ground floor and the caregivers had been quick learners.

A pang of remorse touched my heart. I should be saving lives right now and not playing dead. I did promise Estrid I would return to help with the injured after I healed Ryne. Not the best decision, but I'd thought I'd be dead. Actually, I wouldn't mind working for her. Despite her strict rules regarding having fun—as in, not having any—she really cared

about her soldiers and acolytes. Unlike Tohon, who only cared
for himself.

I planned to honor my promise to her eventually. Noelle
first. Glancing at the manor, I wondered if Estrid was still living there with her granddaughter and Jael. Did Noelle have
a room there, as well?

The lieutenant's voice jerked me from my musings. "Major
Granvil's company is just ahead. His tent is the big one with
the battle-ax painted on it."

Leaving her companions outside, we entered. Major Granvil, a captain and a female lieutenant had gathered around a
table with maps spread out before them. A few had fallen to
the dirt floor. The major leaned back in his chair. His long,
lanky legs stretched out in front of him. Concentrating on
his companions, he stroked his bushy unregulation mustache.

While the lieutenant waited for the major to acknowledge
our presence, I listened to the discussion.

"...two squads from Dagger Company disappeared in Vyg's
sector five."

"Something big is going on over there."

"We can't risk any more scouts."

"Send Ursan and his jumping jacks, they'll find out what's
going on."

"Too dangerous. The only squad that's been successful on
the other side of the border has been Belen's."

"And why is that?" Major Granvil asked his officers.

No one answered.

"I know why," I said into the silence.

The lieutenant sucked in her breath at my audacity. And
the major turned his full attention on me. Most people would
have been intimidated by the force of his gaze, but after facing
Kerrick's wrath and Tohon's ire, the major didn't scare me at
all. Unimpressed, I stared right back at him.

"And who the hell are you?" Major Granvil demanded.

"She's…uh…High Priest…er…sent. Here, sir." The lieutenant thrust the letter into his hands.

The major scanned the document and then tossed it onto the table. His officers bent their heads to read it.

"Um…sir, is the signature authentic?"

"Yes, Lieutenant. You're dismissed."

She snapped a salute and bolted from the tent.

Once again the major studied me. White streaked his short black hair and peppered his mustache.

"Now, why would Chane send you to me?" he asked.

"Perhaps because I know the answer to your question," I said.

"Please, enlighten us."

I ignored the hint of sarcasm in his tone. "Belen's successful because he knows how to move through Vyg's forest without making a sound. I'm sure he taught his squad how to, as well."

"And you know this…how?"

"Because I've been through those woods recently, and all the other squads made so much noise, I easily avoided them, which I'm sure Tohon's soldiers did, as well."

"You know Belen?"

"I met him once."

"So why didn't Chane send you to him?"

"Belen already has those skills, he doesn't need my help. You do. I can train your scouts and special squads. Actually, I'm surprised no one has asked Belen to teach more of you."

"He's been busy." The major fiddled with his mustache. "Why should we trust you?"

I pointed to the letter.

"Chane's a good kid, but he can be tricked."

"I've seen the other side, Major." I shuddered as the memory of the dead filled me with horror. "You need all the help you can get or Tohon's going to decimate you."

"And I'm thinking you're not the type to scare easily."

"No, sir."

He gestured to the female lieutenant. "This is Lieutenant Thea. Her platoon includes the special squads for our company. You can coordinate with her. Now…" He drummed his fingers on his leg. "What do we call you?"

It was a rhetorical question, but I answered it anyway. "General Irina has a nice ring to it."

He laughed and stood. "There's only one general in this whole outfit, sweetheart."

"And who is he?"

"*She* is General Jael. Not only does she command the army, but the very air. And she has a nasty temper. I'd suggest you stay far away from her."

Worry for my sister swirled. Jael had taken her on as a page. They were together every day.

The major extended his hand. "Welcome to Axe Company, *Sergeant* Irina."

"How about Lieutenant Irina?"

"Let's see what you can do first, and then we'll talk."

I shook his hand. "Deal."

Lieutenant Thea eyed me critically. She matched my height, which was a bit of a surprise since, at five feet eight inches, I was on the tall side for a woman. Her no-nonsense demeanor hid her opinion about me. I had the feeling she wasn't the type to make a quick judgment.

"First stop, the supply tent." She led me to a huge canvas structure that was more like a building than a tent.

I was given two sets of the daily uniform—basic green camouflage fatigues—they were very smart to change from red—

with the sergeant stripes stitched onto the upper sleeves, a thick leather weapon's belt, a pair of brown boots manufactured for rough terrain, a backpack also camouflaged, underclothes and a dress uniform, which consisted of a button-down collared shirt, jacket and a skirt all in the same bland khaki color. The dress shoes had a two-inch heel.

"Heels and a skirt?" I asked Thea.

Humor sparked in her blue eyes, but it didn't reach her face. "The dress uniform must be worn when meeting with high-ranking officers, priests and priestesses. I doubt you'll have need of it."

"Thank the creator!"

This time she smiled, but it only lasted a second. Back to business, she asked, "Weapon of choice?"

I glanced at her belt. She wore a sword on her right hip and a dagger on her left.

"I don't need anything."

She gestured to me. "That stiletto won't be enough to defend yourself."

I brandished a couple of my throwing knives. "How about these?"

Thea shrugged. "They're only good if you know how to use them."

Aiming for the center post, I buried four in a neat row.

"That's handy."

"Keeps the gentleman callers away."

Another fleeting smile. I considered it a minor victory.

"I'll show you to your quarters."

I grabbed my knives and followed her. We walked past tents and around training areas. At first the camp looked as if it had been haphazardly planned, but as Thea pointed out the various platoons, a pattern emerged. Each company had been grouped together.

My quarters ended up being a tent occupied by two other female sergeants.

"Your roommates are also assigned to my platoon."

"How many soldiers do you command?"

"I have fifty-six. Five squads of ten soldiers with one sergeant commanding each squad." She cocked her head. "And you."

I dumped my uniforms onto the empty cot.

"Bed linens can be found in the storage locker." She pointed to the large trunk at the foot of the cot. "Get dressed and I'll introduce you to the other sergeants." She left.

As I changed into the fatigues, I wondered how the other sergeants would react to my sudden…assignment. Stuffing all my things into the trunk, I locked it, then tucked the key into my pocket.

Lieutenant Thea waited for me outside. "My platoon is in training right now. We're not on patrol duty for another two days. Will that be enough time to teach them?" She led me to one of the open areas used for practice.

"Not all of them." I considered. Since I'd never taught anyone the skill, I wasn't sure how long it would take. Or if I could. I suppressed the doubts. Too late to worry about them now. "I might be able to train one squad if they're quick learners."

"And if they cooperate." Thea gave me a tight smile that almost resembled a grimace.

"Because I'm new?"

Thea raised a finger. "That's one of the three things against you. The others are that you're a young female and that you haven't earned your place here. All of my sergeants have been promoted up through the ranks. Not *assigned* a rank."

I understood two of the three. "Female? General Jael's in charge, and the last time I checked, she's a young female."

"She's also the High Priestess's daughter-in-law and an air magician."

"And I'm not."

"Correct. Plus we need to rebuild our population. Women of childbearing years are already in short supply, and my lady sergeants are older."

I caught on. "They don't want us getting killed in battle."

"Yep. It's all about our future survival."

"But if we don't stop Tohon, we won't have a future."

"These guys are quite confident we'll win." Thea stopped at the edge and watched the men practice. "They have to be, in order to do their jobs."

I studied the fighters. Most had stripped off their shirts in deference to the afternoon heat. Some of them held wooden swords while others fought with knives. The clangs of metal blades sounded as a few used real weapons. Sweat coated muscles and stained their sleeveless undershirts.

After a few minutes, Thea whistled and three men and two women broke from the knots of fighters and headed toward us.

As they approached, I wondered if the male sergeants in Estrid's army had to be over six feet tall and solid muscle, because these guys made Kerrick seem small—something I'd thought only Belen could do. I glanced at Thea.

"Don't let them intimidate you," she said under her breath.

Too late.

When they reached us, they saluted the lieutenant.

"At ease, Sergeants," she said.

They dropped their hands, but their tight postures were far from relaxed. All wore their hair buzzed short, even the women. All glared at me. And their nonverbal message was clear. *Go away, stranger. You don't belong here.*

I fought my desire to step back, reminding myself that I'd faced down Kerrick. But there were five of them. Kill. Me. Now.

Thea introduced me. "Sergeant Irina, this is Sergeants Liv, Ursan, Odd, Saul and Wynn."

"Nice to meet you," I said.

They remained silent and unfriendly.

Thea's voice took on her no-nonsense tone. "Major Granvil has assigned Sergeant Irina to our platoon to help with our special operations training."

"We don't need help," Sergeant Ursan said.

His named sounded familiar—something about jumping jacks.

"That's not your decision, *Sergeant*. It's the major's," Thea said. "Your squad will be the first to start the training."

Wrong move. Yes, she was his commanding officer, and he'd obey her orders, but his whole demeanor shouted I'd get more cooperation from Tohon's dead. I had to get all the sergeants on board or the lessons with their squads would be a frustrating and fruitless waste of everyone's time.

"Sergeant Ursan, you said your squad doesn't need help. Is that correct?" I asked.

"Yes."

"Then how about we work out a deal?"

A flash of interest sparked in his brown eyes.

"How about you give me the opportunity to prove to the five of you that I know something worth learning?"

"And in exchange?"

"Full cooperation."

He glanced at the other sergeants. They nodded.

"Agreed," Ursan said.

We shook hands.

"When would be a good time?" I asked Thea.

"Now. And I'll be observing."

"Great." I scanned the area. "Is there a section of the forest reserved for training and free of Death Lilys?"

"Yes," Ursan said. "Do we need any weapons?"

"No. But you'll need your shirts."

He paused for a moment and shot me a look. I wasn't sure what he thought, but I knew he was intrigued despite himself. Good.

They collected their uniforms. Instead of strapping on their swords, they just tucked their utility knives into their belts. Thea pulled Ursan aside and said something to him. He nodded but kept his gaze on me.

We headed to the woods north of Zabin. Familiar territory for me as I had bypassed the city through this area a few weeks ago.

When we reached the edge of the forest, I turned to the five sergeants. "We're going to play a game of hide-and-seek. You hide and I'll seek. Standard rules apply."

I pressed my lips together to keep from smiling at their outraged expressions that clearly said, *grown-ups don't play kids' games*.

Thea's voice remained emotionless when she said, "Sergeant Irina, please go over the rules with them. I'm sure it's been… a while since they've engaged in this activity."

"Of course. I count to a hundred while you go hide in the woods. You can only stay in one hiding spot for thirty minutes before you need to find another. You can move at any time and, if you hear me approach, feel free to change positions. If I find you all, I win. If I don't find you all by sunset, you win. Any questions?"

Everyone glanced at the sky. We had about two hours until sunset.

"Sounds pretty straightforward," Thea said. "Let the game begin."

They grumbled but trudged into the woods as I turned my back on them and counted.

When I reached one hundred, I yelled, "Ready or not, here I come."

Thea stared at me as if I'd grown a second head. "I hope you know what you're doing."

"Don't worry, Lieutenant." I saluted her before entering the lush greenery.

I drew in a deep breath. Oh, yes. The Queen Seeker was back!

I stepped into the shadowy half-light. Streams of sunlight cut through the forest canopy. Without thought, I touched the leafy branch of a bush, seeking Kerrick's magic. Disappointment stabbed deep.

Moving without matching the forest's song, I crunched deeper into the underbrush. When I'd gone about a hundred paces, I stopped.

"Okay, Sergeants," I shouted to the surrounding trees. "You've heard me tromping around. Now I'm going to go silent."

I concentrated, listening to the sounds. An off note came from my right. I headed in that direction and surprised Sergeant Liv. After that, it didn't take me long to find Odd, Saul and Wynn. Not that I was bragging, but if I could locate Belen, Quain and Loren, who'd all had training, I could find these sergeants who hadn't.

Ursan proved to be harder to find. He possessed some skill, and I had to wait until he moved to another hiding spot to discern his general location. Once there, I lost him again. I made a few loops until I remembered what Kerrick had done to throw me literally off his scent.

I returned to the original place I'd zeroed in on. Then I looked up, spotting the sergeant sitting on the tree's lowest branch. Ursan jumped off and landed next to me. His expression unreadable.

Before I could say *found you*, he stepped close to me. Now he let his anger show along with the blade in his hand. How did I miss that?

"Who the hell are you?" he demanded.

KERRICK

Kerrick offered the hilt of his sword to Cellina. From atop her horse, she met his gaze. If she signaled the pack of six dead ufas behind him, he would be torn apart.

"Take it," he repeated.

"No. You're going to need it." Cellina whistled.

The high-pitched sound pierced his heart, releasing a surge of fear-fueled energy. Grabbing the hilt of his sword, he spun. The closest ufa launched straight at him. Kerrick sidestepped and slashed down with all his strength, decapitating the creature.

The rest pounced. Kerrick lopped off another head before they closed the distance, knocking him to the ground. His weapon flew from his grasp so he punched and kicked as his world filled with gray fur, sharp claws, growls and the rancid odor of decay.

When an ufa clamped its teeth around his neck, Kerrick fought with pure desperation. He grabbed the beast's jaws, cutting his fingers on its teeth, and pulled the jaws apart.

"Heel." Cellina's loud command sliced through the ruckus.

The ufa on Kerrick yanked its mouth from his grasp and bounded over to sit with its pack mates behind Cellina. She had dismounted and now held his sword.

Kerrick jumped to his feet, preparing for another round.

"Relax. I wasn't going to let them kill you." She gestured to the pack. "I needed you to fight them so I can lie convincingly to Tohon that you're dead."

"You could have told me," he rasped.

"Then you wouldn't have fought so hard." She approached. "Here, grab the hilt."

Despite her claims, Kerrick didn't trust her. "Why?"

"Tohon's magic will sense your blood on your sword, helping to support our ruse."

Kerrick glanced at his hands. Blood dripped from multiple cuts. As he reached for the sword, he wondered if he could take the weapon and kill Cellina before she could signal her ufas. His fingers closed around the leather. Meeting her gaze, he released the weapon.

"Last chance for you to come with me to Ryne's," he said, knowing the next time they encountered each other would probably be on the battlefield.

"Last chance for you to get out of here before I change my mind," she said.

He gave her a two finger salute and resumed his trek east.

Kerrick's energy faded after a few miles. Kneeling next to a stream, he washed the dried blood, ufa slime and sweat from his face, neck and arms. His hands shook with a delayed reaction from the fight.

That was too close. He hoped Cellina's reprieve meant she might be a potential ally in the future. Pushing to his feet, he continued east.

A loud crash sounded behind him. Kerrick spun, grabbing for his sword. His fingers wrapped around an unfamiliar hilt.

"My bad," Quain said, returning the copper statue that had

fallen to the marble floor, turning it so the dent was no longer visible. He glanced at Kerrick's hand. "Expecting trouble?"

"Depends. Why are you here?" he asked.

Quain and Loren, or as Belen liked to call them, the monkeys, had been...not quite avoiding him since he'd arrived at Ryne's castle four days ago, but they'd been keeping out of his way. They had acknowledged Avry's absence with grief-stricken expressions. Ryne had warned them prior to Kerrick's arrival, but they had hoped, with Kerrick's magic strengthening her healing powers, she would have survived the plague.

"Prince Ryne is looking for you," Quain said. The lantern's glow shone on his bald head.

"What does he want?" Kerrick planned to help speed up the departure preparations. Every day spent here gave Avry another day to encounter trouble.

"Don't know, but he said right away."

Kerrick suppressed his annoyance as he headed toward the prince's office. Ryne probably wanted another detailed explanation of the ufa attack. He realized he still held the sword's hilt and relaxed his grip. Cellina had taken the sword his father had gifted to him when he'd graduated from boarding school. Before the plague had killed King Neil and most of Kerrick's family.

He concealed the shudder that ripped through him when he thought of the ufa pack. Kerrick would be content to never see another ufa in his lifetime. But the fact Tohon was training and using them meant Kerrick would likely encounter them in battle.

Worry for Cellina swirled in his stomach. He hoped she'd be able to lie to Tohon. The life magician was quick to anger and could easily murder her with one touch.

Quain followed Kerrick into Ryne's spacious office. Large windows allowed in plenty of sunlight. Oversized armchairs

Maria V. Snyder

ringed the huge black slab of obsidian that served as Ryne's desk and conference table. Loren lounged in a red-and-gold-striped chair but sat up straight and eyed Kerrick warily. A few silver hairs shone among Loren's short black hair. At thirty-five he was the oldest of Kerrick's gentlemen and balanced Quain's youth and inexperience nicely. Otherwise, Kerrick would have lost his patience with Quain long ago.

A memory tugged. Avry had accused Kerrick of being moody, sullen and distant. And from the way Quain and Loren had been acting around him, he guessed they thought the same. He smoothed his expression and approached.

Ryne was bent over a map of the Fifteen Realms. Kerrick waited, studying his friend. Ryne's dark brown hair fell forward almost covering his hazel eyes. Thin and five inches shorter than Kerrick, his pleasant and average appearance belied his cunning mind.

Tapping the map with a stylus, Ryne said, "I think if we send in waves of smaller units, we could soften Tohon's troops up before hitting them with a bigger force."

"Sounds like something you should discuss with Estrid," Kerrick said.

Ryne looked up at his tone. "I know you're all about action, but there has to be a great deal of planning beforehand or we won't succeed. Why are you so anxious to leave?"

"Summer is a few weeks away. It's prime time for Tohon to launch an attack. We should be there," he said.

"Tohon won't attack *until* we're there."

"That doesn't make sense."

"It does to Tohon," Ryne said. "The Nine Mountains are an effective barrier. If he conquered Estrid's army before we arrived, then he would have to cross the mountains to get to us. We'd litter the passes with ambushes, and it would make it harder for Tohon to succeed."

"We're safe here, so why don't we stay and see what happens?" Quain asked.

"I said it would be *harder* for him to succeed, not that it would stop him. We don't have the resources or manpower to fight him." Ryne glanced at Kerrick before continuing. "Besides, Avry promised Danny we'd heal our world. That includes *all* fifteen realms."

There was a moment of silence as the men mourned their friend. Kerrick hated deceiving them, but he understood the need. Tohon could have spies among Ryne's soldiers. Plus, he had promised Avry not to tell a soul that she lived, including Ryne. Kerrick would honor his word.

"When are we leaving?" Kerrick asked.

"When we're ready," Ryne said.

"What did you want to see me about?" He tried not to growl in irritation.

"Have you talked to Danny and Zila about Avry yet?"

Instantly wary, Kerrick said, "I thought you—"

"I warned them when we left you that she might not survive the sickness, but they need to hear what happened to her from you."

"Ryne, I—"

"It's not a request. Talk to them before we leave."

"Yes, sir. Anything else?"

"No."

Kerrick left. Hard enough dealing with the monkey's gloomy moods, but he felt almost sick thinking about upsetting the kids. No sense putting it off. He strode to the wing where they had been staying.

Not wanting to scare them, he drew in a calming breath before entering their room. A woman sat with Zila in her lap, reading her a book. Danny was at a desk, hunched over a wooden puzzle.

According to Avry, these two might develop healing powers. Tohon had injected them with the Death Lily's lethal toxin, but they'd survived the poison. Two among dozens of children who had been killed by Tohon's experiments.

"Can I help you?" their nanny asked.

"Kerrick!" Zila jumped down and flung herself at him, wrapping her thin arms around his legs. The eight-year-old's bushy brown hair had been wrestled into a braid.

Danny kept his distance. "We heard you'd arrived, but Prince Ryne said you needed some time and we should wait."

How diplomatic of him, Kerrick thought wryly. He glanced at the young woman hovering nearby. "Can I talk to them?"

"Oh. Sure." She headed toward another door. "I'll be in Zila's room if you need anything," she said to the kids. "Anything at all." She shot Kerrick a warning look before leaving.

Danny rolled his eyes. "She's overprotective." His black hair was neatly trimmed, and he was an inch taller. No surprise, since at thirteen he was just starting puberty.

Delaying the inevitable, Kerrick asked them how they liked living here.

"Oh, it's fun," Zila said. "Prince Ryne visits us every day. He plays chess with Danny and wins every time."

"I'm getting better," Danny protested.

She ignored him. "There's heaps of books everywhere."

"You don't know how to read," Danny said.

"I do, too. Berna's teaching me."

"Berna?" Kerrick asked.

"Our nanny."

"Ah. Do you like her?"

"She's okay for a girl," Danny said, crossing his arms.

"She's the nicest person I know." Zila chewed on her lower lip. "Well, the second nicest. Avry's the first." She peered up at Kerrick with big olive-colored eyes. "Where's Avry, Kerrick? Prince Ryne said you'd tell us what happened to her."

He crouched down so he was eye level with the two kids. Trying to break it to them gently, Kerrick explained how Avry died from the plague. Seeing Zila's pretty eyes flood with tears was worse than being knifed in the gut.

"So if we become healers, we shouldn't heal anyone with the plague?" Danny asked. His voice warbled, and the tip of his nose turned red.

"You won't find anyone," Kerrick said. Although there was a possibility Tohon would use the information he'd learned from working with the Healer's Guild to create another strain. But this wasn't the time to express his worries. "There hasn't been a case in over two years. Prince Ryne had been frozen in a magical stasis to keep him alive until I found a healer." He gave them a wry smile. "I didn't think it would take me so long."

Danny kept up his brave front and returned Kerrick's grin.

But Zila burst into loud sobs. "You killed her," she shouted, then ran from the room and slammed the door.

Kerrick and Danny exchanged a glance.

"She's eight," Danny said. "Her reaction is understandable."

The nanny poked her head in, asking what happened. Kerrick told her.

She scowled at him. "They're children. If I'd known what you were here to talk about I'd have stayed with them."

"They hardly knew her." Kerrick tried to defend himself as Berna hurried from the room after Zila.

Danny gazed at him with a pained expression. "She rescued us from Tohon." He gestured to the room. "We went from lab rats to being spoiled rotten. Doesn't matter how much time we spent with her. She's…" He swallowed. "She will always be special to us."

"Yeah. I get that," Kerrick said. "Sorry."

Berna returned flustered and red-faced as if she had been running. "Zila's disappeared. Don't just sit there, help me look for her."

When Berna turned her back, Danny rolled his eyes. "Berna gives up too fast," he whispered to Kerrick. "Come on, this shouldn't take long."

Kerrick followed the boy from the room, marveling at the boy's ability to shift back and forth from a child to a young man in moments.

However, Danny would be wrong about the search. It would extend for hours, enlisted dozens of seekers and covered the entire fifty-room castle without success.

A new worry swirled in his chest. If they couldn't even find an eight-year-old, how would they fare against Tohon's army?

CHAPTER 4

Ursan flourished his knife, threatening me. "Talk, or I'll start cutting off body parts."

"Yours? Or mine?" I kept my voice steady despite my insides twisting into goo. "It's an important distinction."

Grabbing my left hand, he pressed the blade against my wrist. Blood welled as the sharp steel cut into my skin.

"I see." I craned my neck to meet his gaze a good six inches above me.

He was as solid as an oak tree. He even had muscles in his neck. A square-shaped head added to his sturdiness. His intent to harm shone in his eyes. I would have been terrified, except he held my hand. Skin contact was all I needed to defend myself. Except if I shocked him, then what would I do?

"I'm Irina of Gubkin Realm. I volunteered—"

"Bullshit. You're one of Tohon's magicians." He drew in a deep breath. "I can smell it."

Oh, no. He was a magic sniffer. I cursed my rotten luck. The day had just been too easy.

"He sent you to spy on us." Ursan's knife cut deeper.

I hissed in pain. "Why would I offer to help train your men if I worked for Tohon?" I sensed a softening. "He'd want me to *sabotage* your efforts, not aid them."

"But you're not an ordinary girl, are you?" Ursan sniffed my hair. "Not a water mage or air…" Another snort. "I smell forest magic and life magic." His grip tightened. "Only one life magician in the Fifteen Realms, which means you've been with Tohon."

I thought fast. "And there's only one forest mage left. And they're on opposite sides."

"Prince Kerrick disappeared. No one knows where he is. He could be dead or Tohon's prisoner."

So Ursan knew Kerrick was a forest mage. I wondered what else he knew. However, this had gone on too long. I made a quick decision and zapped him. He grunted but failed to let go. Sending another blast, I forced him to his knees. What was it with these big guys? Didn't they feel pain? The third assault loosened his grip on the knife. I yanked the weapon from his hand, then released him.

I stepped back as he sank onto his heels, panting and sweating.

When he regained his composure, he asked, "What magic is that?"

My initial instinct was to lie, but all he had to do was notice the already healing cut on my wrist to figure it out. "I'm a healer."

A variety of expressions crossed his face. From surprised to suspicious to confused and then back to suspicious. "The healer with Prince Kerrick also disappeared."

"Obviously, there's more than one healer." I waved my left hand. "I can prove it to you in a few hours."

His confusion returned. "Why are you here?"

"Tohon lifted the bounty on healers and I was sick of hiding." I shrugged. "I wanted to help."

"Why aren't you helping in the infirmary?"

Good question. Did I have a good answer? "Healers are still not welcome."

"Not around here. That other healer was here for a few weeks last year. She saved a bunch of lives. We owe her."

Nice to know I'd been appreciated. "It's still a big risk. And one I'm not ready to take."

He gestured to the forest. "Who taught you how to go silent?"

"No one. I've been on the run for four years. I've learned a few things." I glanced around. The light was fading fast. "What are you going to do?"

"Me?"

I laughed at his shocked expression. "Yes, you."

Ursan stared at me. "I'd thought you'd…disappear."

"Then you thought wrong. I'm tired of running and want to help. I'd rather teach your squad for now. But if you want to expose me…I won't stop you." Handing him his knife, I waited.

He clambered to his feet and once again towered over me. The desire to cut and run pulsed through me for a second, but I steadied my nerves.

"All right," he said. "We'll do it your way *for now*. But if I see you doing anything suspicious, I'll drag your ass to the major. Understand?"

"Yes."

"Good."

As we headed back, I said, "Lieutenant Thea knows you're a magic sniffer. She asked you to sniff me out, right?"

"Yes, but not many do. We don't want too many people to know just in case Tohon sends one of his magicians undercover." He gave me a pointed look.

"It's a good strategy. I'm sure Tohon has spies in camp."

"You're sure as in you *know*, or you're sure as in you *think?*"

Now it was my turn to give him a pointed stare.

"Yeah. Dumb question. No doubt he has spies."

We joined the lieutenant and the other sergeants a few minutes after sunset. All five of them turned to us. I kept quiet just in case Ursan changed his mind.

"She found me," he said. "We'll begin training my squad in the morning."

The lieutenant said, "What took you so long?"

Ursan grinned. "I cheated."

Thea failed to see the humor. "Explain, Sergeant."

"It's war, sir. Rules don't apply."

I followed Sergeants Liv and Wynn back to our tent. They lit a lantern and stared at me as if assessing the enemy. I stretched out on my cot, glad to relax for the first time all day. They remained standing.

"You're a little young to be a sergeant," Wynn said. Her frown contrasted with her round face and small nose.

"More than a little. She's just a baby." Liv smirked, flashing big square teeth. Her light brown hair resembled a fine fuzz and had been clipped so short the hair couldn't lie flat.

Liv noticed the direction of my gaze. She ran a hand over her head. "Lice. If you manage to get sent out on missions, you'll be shaving your head, too. Long hair's a bitch to take care of when you're a *real* soldier."

"You haven't been promoted from a grunt." Wynn pointed to my face. "Too pale."

Resigned to the interrogation, I pushed up on one elbow. "You don't have any people from the northern realms here?"

"We do. But we've been training outside for months." She pulled her collar down and showed an impressive tan line, visible even in the soft lantern light. "So what's your story, Baby Face?"

"Just what Lieutenant Thea said, I've been assigned to train—"

"Yeah, yeah." Liv waved a hand. "Who cares about that? Not us. You show up from nowhere with this uncanny skill. There has to be a reason."

I considered my options. These two seemed to have adopted the whole hardened-soldier persona. But was it all swagger or a true indication of their characters?

"I came down here to see a bit of action," I said.

They snorted in amusement.

"She's cute when she's trying to be tough," Wynn said.

"You're going to see more than a bit, Baby Face," Liv said. "There's more to being a sergeant than sneaking around the woods. Think you can handle it?"

"Yes." No sense selling myself short.

Wynn's demeanor turned speculative. "That's rather bold."

"Yes."

Liv and Wynn exchanged a glance.

"She's training the jacks tomorrow," Liv said to her friend. "If that doesn't send her away, nothing will."

"Oh, yeah." Suddenly in a good mood, Wynn slapped my shoulder. "Good luck with that." She strode from the tent.

Liv followed her but glanced back when she reached the flap. "Come on, Baby Face. It's time for the sergeant's fire."

We first headed to the mess tent for supper. It was noisy and hot under the canvas. Many of the soldiers sat at long wooden tables, but a few had settled on the ground. While waiting in line, I searched for an empty spot and found none.

After filling our trays, Liv and Wynn led me back outside.

"Those guys are pigs," Wynn said. "They've lost their table manners during the plague years."

"And they stink, too," Liv added. "After sweating all day

in the hot sun, they're not going to waste time bathing when they have to do it all again tomorrow."

"They'll only clean up when ordered," Wynn said in disgust.

Before we reached one of the many campfires scattered over the fields, Liv turned to me. "That's the sergeant's fire. We eat, talk, gossip, discuss strategy and discipline. But no matter what the topic is, what we discuss at the fire *stays* at the fire. Understand?"

"Yes."

The three other sergeants—Ursan, Saul and Odd—had already settled down with their meals. When we approached, conversation ceased. They kept their impassive expressions as I sat next to Liv and Wynn to eat my supper.

Conversation eventually resumed. The bland food was of the standard meat-and-potatoes variety. At least it was warm. I listened to the comfortable banter. It sounded as though the five of them had been working together for a while. A pang of longing touched me.

I missed *my* guys. Missed the monkeys arguing. Missed Belen's teasing. Missed Flea's lopsided grins most of all. He shouldn't have died. Sudden fury welled, and I realized that it might be near impossible for me not to strangle Jael when I saw her again. She had tried to kill all of us, but only succeeded in taking Flea's life.

When the topic turned to the patrols disappearing in Vyg, I paid closer attention.

"Tohon's protecting something in sector five. We need to send more scouts," Odd said.

"We will, once Belen returns from sweeping Vyg's southern border," Liv said.

"But that'll take weeks!" Odd tossed another log onto the blaze. Bright orange sparks leapt into the air.

Ursan gave me a contemplative look after Odd's comment.

"It's vital we keep Tohon out of the southern realms," Liv said.

"Why?" Odd asked.

"So we're not battling him on two fronts, you idiot!"

"What's Tohon waiting for?" Wynn asked. "He's amassed an army in western Vyg and has control of Kaisma, but so far has only sent patrols farther north and east."

A good question. And no one offered an answer. Why would he wait? The weather was favorable. If he hurried, he could strike before Ryne arrived. Unless he wanted Ryne and Estrid to team up. Tohon never lacked for confidence. He might be planning to eliminate them both in one massive sweep.

Or, he might be creating more dead soldiers. They probably needed time to train. Perhaps that mystery drug was grown in Vyg.

"What's in sector five?" I asked the group.

"We don't know," Liv said. "Haven't you—"

"I meant, what part of Vyg is in that sector? Are there towns? Forests? Any natural resources like a quarry?"

"Oh." Liv glanced around. "It's north of the center of Vyg. Near the Nine Mountains."

"The area is forested," Ursan said. "But there are a number of abandoned mining towns up there."

"There's your answer," I said. "He's protecting one of those mining operations. Probably ore so he can manufacture more weapons."

"The Nine Mountains are full of ore," Ursan said. "It would be smarter and safer for him to mine behind his lines in Sogra."

"Plus he has control of Lyady Realm," Odd said. "And has captured the president's daughter to ensure their cooperation. Lyady's steel mills are still in operation as far as I know."

He had a point. I considered. "What else is mined in that area besides ore?"

Odd said, "The arms merchant in town claims his weapons are crafted from the liquid metal found at the bottom of the Nine Mountains. He mentioned there's a shaft in Vyg that goes deep under the mountains."

His comment caused a riot of laughter.

"You were conned," Saul said. It was the first time he'd spoken since I'd arrived. He appeared to be the type of person who was content to just listen.

I would have agreed with Saul, but Odd's statement triggered a memory. Kerrick had purchased my stiletto and throwing knives from a merchant in Zabin. Probably the same one, since he'd claimed my weapons had been crafted from liquid metal, as well. And Kerrick had nodded as if it meant something to him. Perhaps I should pay the merchant a visit when I had some free time.

Tohon's hand stroked my back, igniting a trail of fire along my skin. His other arm wrapped around my waist, trapping me against him.

"Do you really believe teaching your little trick can defeat my army, my dear?" His throaty chuckle vibrated in my chest.

I tried to squirm free, but his magic flooded my senses. Desire tingled as heat spread from my insides out, turning my willpower into goo.

"You think you escaped, but you haven't. From the very first time I touched you, you've been mine. I've already claimed you, my dear."

My heart fluttered as a wave of intense pleasure rolled through me. Something jolted my cot, and I snapped awake.

Wynn stood over me. "That must have been quite a dream, Baby Face. Lots of writhing and moaning. Who was the lucky man? Or was it a woman?" She smirked.

I sat up, rubbing my face. "Just a nightmare."

"Ah, too bad. Do you get them often?"

Debating how much to tell her, I hesitated but then decided since we shared a tent, she and Liv should know. "Every night."

"That stinks."

An understatement. Before she could question me further, I stood, changed and grabbed a quick breakfast before heading over to the forest training area to meet Ursan's squad. They stood at attention at the edge of the field. Two rows of five young men known as the jumping jacks. Despite their cockiness, I sensed an undercurrent of hostility from them.

I glanced at Ursan. "Jumping jacks?"

"Remember that move I pulled on you?"

"When you jumped down from the tree?"

"That's our squad's signature style for ambushing the enemy," Ursan said.

"You were jackknifed, sweetheart!" a soldier called from the ranks, and they all laughed.

One look from Ursan silenced them. He had their respect, but I didn't. Fair enough, for now.

I turned to the group. "Who called me sweetheart?" No one moved. "What? Too chicken? Come on, reveal yourself."

A soldier in the front row stepped forward with a challenging smirk. I crossed my arms and scrutinized him for a long moment while I wrapped my fingers around the handle of one of my throwing knives.

"You're not my father or my lover," I said, causing a ripple of snickers. Boys.

I pulled my knife and threw it at the center of his belt, hoping I put the right amount of heat behind it. I didn't want to hurt him.

He yelped as the tip of the blade pierced the leather far enough to keep the weapon in place. Staring at me in shock, he opened his mouth, but snapped it shut when I walked up to him.

I gripped the handle of the knife. "If you call me *sweetheart* again—" I yanked it out "—I'll aim *lower*. Understand?"

"Yes."

I waited.

"Yes, Sergeant."

"Good. Return to your position, soldier." I scanned the others. A combination of surprised, impressed and admiring expressions met my gaze.

"Does anyone else wish to call me sweetheart?" I asked.

No one said a word.

"I believe you proved your point, Sergeant," Ursan said. "Let's get started."

I spent the rest of the day teaching the jumping jacks how to move in the forest. Not exactly sure if I could explain the technique in my own way, I taught it the same way Kerrick had shown me.

A few, like Ursan, caught on quick. Others struggled but eventually mastered the technique, and a couple had no sense of rhythm at all. They would have to return tomorrow for more practice.

Lieutenant Thea arrived in midafternoon to watch the session. She consulted briefly with Ursan before leaving.

The next day I worked with Ursan's two remaining men while the others practiced their new skills. This time Major Granvil visited and asked for a demonstration.

I picked the four best students to accompany me and the major. We walked deeper into the forest until I found a suitable location.

"All right, gentlemen, I want you to take a noisy stroll away from us. Then on my command, go silent. Your goal is to return one at a time and get as close to Major Granvil as possible. He'll signal when he hears you. Understand?"

"Yes, Sergeant," they said in unison and with a little too much enthusiasm.

"Go."

They tromped through the bushes as if they'd get extra points for noisiness. No doubt scaring away all wildlife. Major Granvil regarded their retreating backs before pulling his gaze to me. "I'd thought they'd give you a hard time."

"They tried."

"And?"

"They're smart, Major. They quickly learned this technique can save lives." I drew in a breath and projected my voice over the din. "Gentlemen, go silent!"

The crunching, snapping and rustling died in an instant.

"They could have just stopped moving," Major Granvil said. He stroked his mustache.

I agreed. "That's why I asked them to return. Listen closely, Major."

He scanned the woods, turning in a slow circle. Although I had picked the best, they still needed practice. Small sounds, off notes and rustlings reached me. I tracked the first soldier. He had gone wide and planned to approach from our left.

When the soldier was about four feet away, the major heard him and called out his location. Major Granvil's voice remained steady but couldn't completely mask his surprise.

The next two soldiers were caught a few feet farther away, giving the major a sense of security. The last man looped around us. He showed more patience than the other three, moving when the major moved and stepping with care.

I examined a berry bush so I wouldn't give the soldier away. He crept up behind the major and grabbed his shoulders. The major jerked but didn't cry out. He turned and shook the smiling soldier's hand.

We returned to the exit point. Lieutenant Thea and Sergeant Ursan waited for us with the rest of the jumping jacks in the field next to the woods.

"That was very impressive," Major Granvil said. "Sergeant Ursan, I want you and your jacks to check out sector five on your next patrol."

"Yes, sir," Ursan said.

"No," I said. "They're not ready."

"Explain, Sergeant."

"They need more practice."

"How much more?"

"A couple days, at least." Although I would have been happier with a week. "And I should go along."

The major stroked his mustache while he considered. "All right, two more days, but you're not going, Sergeant Irina. I need you here to train my other squads."

He cut me off when I tried to argue, and left with Lieutenant Thea.

I spent the next two days working with the jumping jacks and Thea, who'd wanted to learn the skill, as well. At the end of the second day, I gathered them around me for some last-minute advice.

"While most people won't hear you, you still need to avoid the Death Lilys. They will sense you no matter how quiet you are. Bypass them altogether, but if you're desperate, Peace Lilys smell like vanilla, and Death Lilys have a faint aroma of anise. Also Death Lilys hiss before they snatch you, so you have some warning."

"I thought both types of Lilys smelled like honey and lemon?" one of the soldiers asked.

"They do, but when you get closer—"

"You're dead," Ursan said. "The Death Lily will spit out your bones once it eats all your flesh. Don't go near them at all."

I bit my lip to keep from correcting him. It only consumed those who died immediately from the toxin it injected into them. Some were spat out and died later from the poison, and a few, like me, lived through the experience. Those survivors developed healing powers.

Instead, I said, "If you encounter a squad of Tohon's dead soldiers, the best way—"

Ursan interrupted me again. "We don't believe the rumors about them, Sergeant Irina. It's a scare tactic."

"And you should be scared, Ursan. I've seen them. They're real and hard to stop."

"You've seen them, and Belen claims to have fought them, but no one else has. Not another soul." His implication clear.

"It's a good strategy to keep them hidden until the battle starts. The shock and revulsion caused by their arrival will give Tohon's men an advantage. Think about it."

But Ursan wouldn't budge. "Word from General Jael is that Tohon managed to convince Belen that these impossible things exist to spread fear through our ranks."

"Do you really think Belen would be so easily tricked?"

"All I know is Belen's loyal to Prince Kerrick, not the High Priestess."

"What about me? Have I been tricked, as well?"

"Yes."

And he couldn't trust me. "You'll discover the real truth soon enough, and when you encounter the horror, cut its head off. It's the only way to stop it."

Ursan and his jumping jacks left for their patrol the next morning. Wearing camouflage and barely discernible in the predawn light, the eleven men melted into the forest. I stood at the edge and listened. They had improved over the past four days. I hoped it was enough.

An odd feeling lumped in my chest. It was as if I had healed them, and now the jacks were headed for danger. So far, no one had returned from that sector. If all went well, they'd be back in ten days.

To keep from brooding over the jacks, I concentrated on training Sergeant Wynn's squad. Since I'd arrived, I'd worked eight days straight. But I finally had an afternoon off on the ninth day.

Exhaustion dragged at my limbs, but I needed to do a little exploring. Walking through the camp, I scanned faces, searching for Melina. She could have been sent to another training camp or was out on patrol, but I'd promised Mom I'd look after her. I'd figure out how I'd keep my promise once I found her.

I also searched for my sister, Noelle, although I knew she'd most likely be with Jael. From a distance, the general's tent near the manor house blended in with the others surrounding it. All the same size, color and shape. Except Jael's tent buzzed with activity and red-robed acolytes. I settled in a shady spot on a rise to watch the action, noting who entered and who left.

A familiar figure ducked through the flaps. Recognition shot through me like a cold lance. Noelle headed east, walking fast. Only my promise to Kerrick kept me from following her. She disappeared from my sight, then returned with a major in tow.

My heart pumped like I had just run up the Nine Mountains. After a few moments, my pulse settled, but each time Noelle appeared, it quickened. From what I'd seen, I'd guess Jael sent her to relay messages and fetch officers, acolytes, food and supplies.

When the sunlight faded, Jael and Noelle left together and headed toward the manor house. No surprise that Jael wouldn't sleep on a cot outside when an opulent room and four-poster bed waited for her inside.

Jael's graceful strides matched her royal bearing. Even with a sword hanging from her belt, she appeared to be more like a queen than a general. Noelle stayed two steps behind her. She had pulled her long black hair into a knot, making her look older than her fourteen years. Or was it fifteen?

I realized with a jolt that she had turned fifteen a month ago, which made me twenty-one. My birthday had been completely forgotten—too busy struggling to keep away from Tohon's touch when I'd been his prisoner.

When Jael and Noelle entered the building, I debated. With the infirmary on the ground floor, another soldier walking around wouldn't be too noticeable. But if any of the infirmary workers recognized me, my cover would be blown.

Instead, I made another sweep of the camp, noting the position of the companies and platoons. There was a large, enclosed complex in the northeast corner. The fence around it had been built with what appeared to be two-story oversized barn doors attached to thick posts. I peeked in through the small gap next to a post. Inside the enclosure was a sprawling collection of barns, sheds and a farmhouse. Why would it be fenced off?

Unable to deduce the reason, I grabbed supper and joined the other sergeants at the fire. With Ursan, Liv and Saul on patrol, there were only three of us. I asked Odd about the complex.

"That's for the prisoners of war," he said.

"I didn't see anyone."

"They were probably all inside. They wear these bright yellow jumpsuits so they're real easy to spot. We don't have many POWs yet. The High Priestess values life, so I'd expect we'll be ordered to capture our enemies instead of killing them when possible. The enclosure has plenty of room," Odd said in a dismissive tone.

"Unlike General Jael," Wynn said. "She has no qualms about killing the enemy and wishes to attack Tohon first, but the High Priestess won't give her permission."

"She's stepped up the patrols again," Odd said. "How much do you want to bet she'll disobey the High Priestess's orders?"

"I'll bet a week's pay the colonels won't let her. They're still loyal to the High Priestess," Wynn countered.

Her comment stirred a memory. When Jael had tried to kill us, she'd mentioned not wanting to tip her hand to Estrid. I wondered if that meant she planned to gain the army's support? Not that a ruthless leader wouldn't be a good thing against Tohon's troops, but if she defeated Tohon, that would put Jael in a very powerful position.

"How long will the colonels be loyal?" I asked.

Wynn acted as if I'd insulted them. "They obey the High Priestess's commands. General Jael is just a messenger."

"A messenger who can suck all the breath from a man and kill him. I think that adds a little incentive to switch loyalties, don't you?"

Odd laughed. "She has you there. And, I, for one, would appreciate a more aggressive move. All this slinking around, fact gathering and waiting is driving me crazy. I'm craving some action."

Ursan's jumping jacks returned twelve days after they'd left. It was the last day of spring, and a few soldiers felt their timing was a sign of the creator's favor. The knots in my stomach loosened when I counted eleven men. In high spirits, the jacks told the other soldiers about near misses and their various adventures.

Major Granvil called Ursan and Lieutenant Thea into his tent for a debriefing. I followed, and no one commented on my presence.

"We encountered a few of Tohon's patrols," Ursan said. "But we avoided them as ordered. It was—" he glanced at me "—easy, sir."

"Then why are you two days late?" Granvil asked.

"We discovered a factory in full operation in sector five. It was well guarded and so was the constant flow of wagons that brought supplies and delivered large metal containers before leaving, loaded with cargo hidden under tarps. We couldn't leave until we had determined what they're manufacturing."

"Go on."

"I sent a few team members to follow the wagons with the cargo. A couple tracked the wagons with the containers, and the rest watched the factory. We were only able to glimpse inside, but the beta team managed to snatch one of the cargo items. Although I'm not sure it was the only item being manufactured or not. The wagon team then rendezvoused with us, and we returned to camp."

"Don't keep us in suspense, Sergeant."

"The containers then headed to a quarry north of the factory. The team was unable to get close enough to determine exactly what was being extracted from the ground. And the item…" Ursan reached into his pack and withdrew a short fat circular metal pipe. He handed it to Major Granvil.

Granvil examined it before giving it to Lieutenant Thea. She flipped it around, but shrugged and tossed it to me.

My initial impression of a pipe was correct, except both ends flared out in a cone shape, leaving the middle narrower. The edges were thicker and had been rolled, so it wasn't sharp.

About four inches high and ten inches in diameter, it didn't resemble anything I'd seen before. I handed it to Ursan.

"It pulls apart," he said. He demonstrated, breaking it into two halves. "Like a manacle cuff or a gauntlet." Ursan stuck his forearm inside. "You can cinch it tighter, but only so much. You'd have to have really thick arms for it to be of any use."

The word *thick* triggered a connection. Horror welled as I realized what the cuff was for.

They were neck protectors for Tohon's dead soldiers. If we couldn't decapitate them, they would be impossible to kill.

KERRICK

"No. Shift your weight to the balls of your feet," Kerrick said to the young man. "Then move." He clutched two of Flea's juggling stones—one in each hand. It helped to keep him from screaming in frustration at the young men and women who had been assigned to his squad.

"Once more, same drill," he ordered.

Ryne had given Kerrick, Loren and Quain each a squad of eight soldiers to command. They would take point and ensure the passage was safe for the rest of the battalion. In order to be effective in their job, Kerrick and the monkeys had to teach all twenty-four how to move in the forest without making noise.

Ryne would have liked the entire battalion trained before they'd left for Zabin. All eight hundred of them. It sounded like a huge amount, but was considered small for a battalion. Not many people had been willing to leave the northern realms. And Ryne would never force anyone to sign up. Either way, Kerrick wasn't going to have the patience or the time to train them all.

Kerrick listened as the squad finished the exercise. *Not terrible.* After five days, they'd finally caught on. Now all they needed was practice. He squeezed the stones. Ryne had been prepping and planning for the past seventeen days, and Kerrick wanted to strangle him.

It has been forty horrible days since he and Avry had parted ways. Once he knew she was safe, then he could concentrate on training and scouting. But that wasn't going to happen anytime soon. So he sucked in a deep breath and sent his squad into the forest to try again.

At the end of the day, the squad gathered around him as he critiqued their efforts and dispensed advice.

"That's it for today, gentlemen," he said, dismissing them.

"Excuse me, sir, but we're not all men," one of the women said. She stood with her hands on her hips as if challenging him.

"Sorry, it's a habit. I meant no offense."

She blinked at him in surprise. "Oh. Okay." She followed her teammates to the mess tent for supper but glanced back at him before ducking inside.

"She likes you," Quain said as he joined Kerrick.

"Shut up." Loren punched his friend on the arm.

Quain didn't flinch. With wide shoulders and thick muscles to match his occasional thick head, Quain was as solid as Belen. However, he was a foot shorter than Poppa Bear.

"Why? I'm just stating a fact. Doesn't mean anything," Quain said.

"To you, but—"

Kerrick interrupted Loren. "While I'd love to chat with you, I'm late."

Loren smirked. "Got another tea party to attend?"

"Yep."

"Don't forget to bring Mr. Bunny a carrot." Quain sniggered.

"Good idea. Thanks for the tip." Kerrick strode to the castle, leaving the monkeys behind.

He avoided everyone as he headed to a tiny dining room beside the kitchen. Zila and Danny were already waiting for him. Smiling, he joined them at the small table. Far better than eating in the mess tent with dozens of sweaty and smelly soldiers.

Zila beamed at him and described her day in minute detail. As he listened to her, he remembered how she had managed to avoid being found that night he'd told her about Avry. Little imp had slipped back into her room soon after they had all left to search for her. Kerrick had figured it out only after the entire castle had been torn apart and he'd put himself in Zila's place. He'd found her sound asleep in her bed.

Ever since then, he'd been taking his evening meal with both kids. For him, it was the best part of the day.

When Zila finished listing all the books she'd read that afternoon, Danny jumped in before she could start with another topic. "When is the army leaving?" he asked Kerrick.

"Soon. We're almost finished with the preparations." He hoped.

Danny twisted a napkin in his hands. "I want to go with you." Before Kerrick could reply, he rushed on. "I can help. Do stuff like fetch water for the troops, fix armor, work in the infirmary. Whatever they need. I'd be safe behind the front lines. Please?"

Kerrick's first instinct was to say no. However, he'd learned…or rather, Avry had taught him…that just because he said no didn't mean the other person would listen. She certainly hadn't.

Instead, he considered Danny's request. The boy might develop healing powers, which would make him very valuable. Tohon was aware of Danny and Zila's potential, and he had to know they were staying here. Would they be safer with Kerrick and Ryne? What if Estrid discovered their potential? Or Jael?

Flea had only been a year older when he had joined Kerrick's group. *And look how that turned out. You couldn't keep him safe.*

Danny stared at him, waiting for an answer.

"I'll talk to Ryne." He held up a hand before Danny could celebrate. "Don't get your hopes up. His decision is final."

Later that night he discussed Danny's request with Ryne in his office.

"No. He's safer here," Ryne said.

"Tohon—"

"I'm leaving an elite squad to guard them. They'll be fine."

"Even if Tohon sends his dead after them? And a couple of ufa packs?" Kerrick shuddered at the thought.

"You're the first to see the ufa pack. It may be the only one he has. Tohon probably doesn't have the time to create more and train them. Estrid's been harrying his troops." Ryne tapped his fingers on the table. "Still, it would be even safer to have them staying at an unknown location. How's that?"

"Danny won't be happy, but I will."

Ryne smiled. "Good. Now about the point squads—"

The door opened, and one of Ryne's guards poked his head in. "Sorry to interrupt, but there's a messenger here from Krakowa."

Krakowa was in northern Ivdel near the border with Gubkin Realm.

"What's the message?" Ryne asked.

"He won't tell me. Only you."

It was a bit unusual. Most messages didn't need to be given directly to the prince.

"All right, let him in," Ryne said.

Kerrick gave him a questioning look. Ryne motioned for

him to stay. He stood behind the prince with his hand resting on the hilt of his sword in case the messenger had been sent by Tohon.

The man hardly glanced at Kerrick. His pale face was drawn, and he looked as if he hadn't slept in days. Bowing to the prince, he waited for permission to speak.

"Go on, man, don't keep us in suspense," Ryne said. "What news do you bring?"

"Terrible news, sire. The northern tribes have invaded Krakowa."

Kerrick leaned forward. *Did he just say the tribes had invaded?* Ryne drilled the man with rapid-fire questions. When? How many? And so on. But Kerrick couldn't focus on the answers. If the northern tribes were on the warpath, then they had bigger problems than Tohon.

CHAPTER 5

I took the two halves of the metal protector from Ursan and fitted them around my throat. Even at its tightest setting it was a little big, but it covered my neck. "Still don't believe Tohon has reanimated the dead?" I asked.

"It's a piece of armor," Ursan said. "No big deal, we all wear armor in battle."

"Around your neck?"

"It's too awkward, but not unheard of."

"Uh-huh." I glanced at Major Granvil. Did he understand the danger? Did he understand Tohon could send his well-protected dead soldiers and there'd be nothing we could do to stop them?

"The High Priestess and General Jael have ordered us to stifle all rumors about impossible creatures," he said. "The creator would never allow such things to exist."

I looked at Lieutenant Thea. Did she believe this bull? Her expression remained neutral.

Interesting how the army's belief in the creator was invoked only when convenient. They didn't act like true advocates. In fact, the soldiers behaved more superstitiously than devout. At least they stayed casual about the religious aspect. I didn't worry about being turned in for not being spiritual enough.

Piety wasn't a requirement to be a soldier, unlike with the acolytes, whose devotion had to be pure.

"I hope the High Priestess has an explanation prepared." And a strategy. I pulled the neck protector off and handed it to the major.

He dismissed us. As we walked back to our tents, I considered the situation, trying not to panic. It seemed odd that Estrid hadn't believed Belen about the dead. From the few times I'd met her, she'd come across as intelligent and practical. Unless she didn't know. Belen and Jael had been in school together along with Kerrick, Ryne and Tohon. Belen might have told Jael, believing she'd inform the High Priestess.

Why wouldn't Jael pass along the information? She'd spent six years in boarding school with Tohon, attending magic classes with him and Kerrick. She should know what Tohon was capable of and how his warped mind worked.

Unfortunately, I was also well acquainted with Tohon's magic. His voice continued to haunt my dreams, his magic tricked my body into desiring his touch. I shuddered. No. I wouldn't be claimed.

When Ursan rushed off to join his celebrating jacks, Lieutenant Thea turned to me. "Speaking hypothetically, how would you kill a soldier who is already dead?"

"Decapitation."

"And if they're wearing a metal collar?"

I searched my memories back to when I'd had the misfortune of encountering them. My skin crawled just thinking about their cold flesh and lifeless gazes. They obeyed simple commands and could be trained, so some intelligence must still exist. "You could try crushing their heads so they can't follow orders."

She fingered the handle of her sword. "Hard to do with a metal blade."

"Mallets and hammers would be better. But would still require some effort and time. You'd have to be pretty strong to break the skull."

Thea grimaced.

"A crossbow bolt might pierce the bone," I mused aloud. "But the archer would need excellent aim, and one bolt might not be enough. A knife in the eye might—"

"That's enough, Sergeant. I get your point."

"That we're screwed? Hypothetically, of course."

"Of course."

Thea had raised an important question. We needed a counter-offensive to fight the armored dead. Hard to plan when no one believed it would be necessary. Belen needed to know. He could inform Prince Ryne and Kerrick when they arrived.

"Lieutenant, when is Belen's squad due back?" I asked.

"In a couple days, why?"

"Can you tell him about the neck armor?"

"Why can't you?"

"Last time I talked to him, he threatened to tear my arms off," I lied. Belen would never hurt me.

She shook her head. "Did you insult his prince?"

Yes. Many times. "Something like that."

Thea stared at me so long, I wondered if I was in trouble.

"I hope someday that you'll tell me who you really are, Sergeant. Ursan doesn't cover for anyone, so you must be very special." She strode away.

So much for my disguise. At least she didn't threaten to expose me. A minor comfort.

The next day was the first day of summer. I resumed the silent training under a bright sun. The leaves rustled in the warm humid breeze. This time, I taught both Sergeant Saul's squad and the Odd Squad, which was Sergeant Odd's men… or rather, boys. They had to give everything a nickname. Liv and Wynn's squads were out on patrol. Ursan and his jacks helped, so the lessons went faster. Around midday a familiar voice stopped my heart.

"Sergeant Ursan, General Jael wishes to see you. Now," Noelle called into the woods.

As the message was relayed, I crept closer to my sister. She scanned the trees in impatience. Standing in a patch of sunlight, she reminded me of our mother. She had the same long black eyelashes and light blue eyes. Allyn had also favored our mother while my older brother, Criss, and I resembled our father—reddish-brown hair and green eyes.

The skin between Noelle's eyebrows puckered as she frowned. "General Jael is not a patient woman, Sergeant."

Was there a hint of fear in her eyes? Instantly concerned, I stepped from my hiding spot.

She rounded on me and I froze. That was stupid.

"Where is Ursan?" she demanded.

"He's on his way." I pitched my voice lower than normal.

"Good."

"Why does the general wish to see him?" I asked.

"That's none of your business, Sergeant," she snapped, then ignored me.

I should have been happy she didn't recognize me. Noelle was supposed to believe I was missing and presumed dead. Yet, I couldn't stop the disappointment and pain from spreading. My little sister had changed so much over the past three years. At age ten, Noelle had cared for our mother and Allyn while they died from the plague, leaving her all alone for the first time in her life. So I shouldn't have been surprised by her behavior when I'd tried to rescue her from Estrid's training camp five months ago.

Ursan arrived and they left. I debated following them. Jael probably wanted more information about his scouting mission. Plus I doubted I could get close enough to the tent to overhear anything important. I returned to my group.

That night around the sergeant's fire, I tried to act casual as I inquired about the summons. "Did the general congratulate you on your successful mission?" I asked Ursan. He had been unusually quiet, letting Odd do all the talking while Saul listened as usual.

"No." Ursan cleaned his leather scabbard with saddle soap.

"What did she want?" Odd asked.

Ursan glanced at me for a second before he said, "Intel on the enemy patrols we encountered. Locations, numbers, that sort of thing."

"Why not get all that from the major?" Odd asked.

Ursan shrugged. "Don't know."

"What did she think about that armor you found?"

"How do you know?" Ursan glanced at Odd with a neutral expression, but the muscles in his arms tensed.

I sensed trouble, but kept my mouth shut.

Odd grinned. "The question should be who *doesn't* know. Come on, Ursan, you know nothing in this camp stays a secret for long. Plus, it's no surprise Tohon would want to protect his troops. Just seems strange for him to be manufacturing new equipment when there's a ton of stuff lying around."

"Oh, yeah, it's everywhere. Just the other day I tripped over a shield," Saul teased.

"I meant each realm had at least one armory." Odd's tone bordered on huffy. "Before the plague there were thousands of soldiers in each realm. The dead don't need armor."

I choked on my tea. Ursan glared at me, but soon the conversation turned to other safer topics. All along I wondered what the general had really inquired about.

When it grew late, we headed toward our tents. I pulled Ursan aside and asked him.

"I'm not surprised that you're concerned," he said.

"You didn't answer my question."

He considered. "She's been hearing good things about our training. You know what that means, don't you?"

Unfortunately. "She wants to know more about me."

"Yep."

"What did you tell her?"

"The truth."

I suppressed my fear. Jael knew no other healers had survived the panic during the plague. And the last time I'd seen Jael, she had tried to kill me. I'd buried two of my throwing knives into her in self-defense. One into her upper arm and the other in her thigh. She wasn't the type to forgive and forget. And without Kerrick's help, a second attempt to kill me would no doubt succeed.

"The whole truth?" I asked.

Ursan studied my expression. "No. I left out the healer part."

"Thanks."

"I didn't do it for you."

Uh-oh. Blackmail time. I waited.

"I did it for us." He swept a hand out, indicating the tents, campfires and soldiers. "Right now, we need this training. So I'm being selfish."

"Will you let me know when you decide to stop being selfish?"

"I can tell you right now when I'll stop. Do you want to know?"

"Go on." I braced for his answer.

"When we move from skirmishes to full-out war. Casualties will unfortunately be much higher and more serious than the sprained ankles and cuts suffered out on patrols."

"Fair enough." And another reminder that my time was limited. I needed to talk to Noelle and find Melina.

On my next day off, I walked into Zabin to buy a few needed items. It had been fifty long days since Kerrick and I parted. I calculated the time it would take for him to reach Ryne's castle. Then added the approximate days Ryne would need to assemble his elite troops, plus the fact that a bigger group would move more slowly, especially when crossing the Nine Mountains.

My spirits sank. Kerrick and Ryne probably wouldn't arrive for another week at the earliest and more realistically, not for another two weeks.

The hustle and bustle of the market helped to take my mind off Kerrick. Dressed in my fatigues, I blended into the crowd, and no one gave me more than a passing glance. Handy.

I browsed the stalls, purchasing new undergarments and leather ties for my hair. During Liv and Wynn's last patrol, I had reapplied Mom's lightening cream and dyed my hair again. Mom's estimates of how long my disguise would last didn't quite match for me. My healing powers accounted for the faster recovery.

After I finished my shopping, I paused in front of the weapons merchant's table of goods. I hoped it looked as if I hadn't been planning to stop there. The owner appeared at my elbow. I recognized him from before, but he didn't show any signs that he remembered me.

He launched into a sales pitch for each weapon I touched. Under his easy, affable personality, I sensed tension, as if he chose his words with care. It made sense, considering this town was basically occupied territory and his livelihood could be shut down at any time by Estrid or Jael.

I played along, asking questions about one or another sword

or knife. When he mentioned liquid metal, my heart squeezed harder.

"What's so special about liquid metal?" I asked, keeping the same noncommittal tone.

"It's mined from the bottom of the Nine Mountains and the edge never dulls."

"Never dulls? That's hard to believe."

He demonstrated with two different blades, dragging them along a rough surface. The liquid metal kept its sharp edge. Impressive—reminding me my stiletto was also made from the same metal. I hadn't had to sharpen it yet, but then again, I hadn't used it that much either.

"Why doesn't it dull?" I asked.

He floundered for a second. "Well, it's unique to all the Fifteen Realms. It's also very flexible, lightweight and near impossible to break."

In other words, he didn't know. "Do you have any armor made with liquid metal?"

"That would be useful, especially in these trying times. However, the supply is limited. The mines have been shut down since the plague. I've only a few knives left."

That last bit sounded like a sales ploy. But in the end, I bought a small dagger with a boot sheath so I could hide the weapon.

On my way back to camp, I spotted Belen leaving Jael's tent. No mistaking the bear of a man who towered over everyone. The sudden desire to run up and hug him pulsed in my veins. Instead, I changed course so I'd avoid passing him.

Belen's return created problems for me. After a couple days, the camp gossip must have informed him about the silent training. He showed up during one of our sessions, no doubt curious.

At first, he watched or, rather, listened to the exercise. None of the men learning the technique heard his near soundless entrance into the woods, which, considering his size, always impressed me. I knew right away. After traveling with him for three months, I could detect his subtle movements.

He waited until after we had finished for the day to appear as if by magic from a clump of bushes. Two members of the Odd Squad cried out in surprise. I used the distraction to fade into the forest.

"Not bad, gentlemen," Belen said in his friendly baritone. "You need more practice, but not bad at all."

They stood a little straighter at the compliment.

Belen glanced around. "So where's this Sergeant Irina that I've been hearing about?"

I kept still, hoping no one saw where I'd disappeared. The men exchanged looks as a murmur rippled through the two squads.

Ursan came to my rescue. "She's out on a special assignment. Can I help you?"

"No need, Sergeant," Belen said. "Just wanted to compare notes. When she returns, can you tell her I'd like to talk?"

"I'll let her know. Will you be around for a while or are you heading out soon?" Ursan asked.

Standing next to Belen, Ursan didn't appear to be as tall or as muscular. Belen had a few inches on Ursan and was thicker. Lines of fatigue creased Belen's face, and he sported a few cuts and bruises. He rubbed his big hand over the black stubble on his jaw. His hair had also grown. The ends brushed the collar of his shirt.

"I'm staying for a couple more days," Belen said.

"Another patrol?"

"No. It's personal, Sergeant. I need to find my friends. They've been gone too long."

Belen hid his emotions, but I knew Poppa Bear must be

beside himself with worry over us. He'd protected Kerrick since childhood. It had to be hard not knowing what had happened while we'd been in Sogra, rescuing Ryne from Tohon.

Then it hit me. Belen needed to be told Ryne and the others were safe. Otherwise, he'd search Sogra and Vyg for us. And he'd get caught and killed.

How could I give him this information without revealing myself? I considered my options as Ursan, Belen and the others left the forest, returning to the camp. I could send him an anonymous note, or start a rumor. But would he believe them? It was worth a try. If he decided to leave regardless, I would stop him.

After waiting a few more minutes, I headed back. When I reached my tent, Ursan stepped from the shadows.

"That's the third time I've covered for you," he said. "You owe me some answers."

I glanced at his hands, checking for weapons. None. Relaxing slightly, I crossed my arms. "For what questions?"

"Why did you hide from Belen?"

"Didn't Lieutenant Thea tell you?" I couldn't keep the surprise from my voice.

"She doesn't confide everything."

Interesting. I'd thought he was her go-to guy for advice. Was this a test? "I had a run-in with Belen a few years ago and would like to avoid another encounter."

"But he knows your name." Understanding lit his expression. "You used another name then."

I gave him a tight smile.

"I'm tired of guessing. Tell me who you are. You owe me," he said.

That was the second time he'd said I owed him, and this time it pissed me off. "Two squads disappeared without a trace in sector five, Sergeant. Yet you and all your jumping jacks returned alive and well from that very sector. I'd say we're even."

He opened his mouth, but I said, "Think about it."

"I have. It was too easy getting there and back. It could have been all a ploy to get us to trust you."

"And look at how well it worked." I didn't bother to suppress my sarcasm. I continued before he could reply. "Are you going to arrest me?"

Ursan frowned but didn't reply.

I pushed past him and entered my tent. Not much I could do if he decided to expose me. I had bigger worries. Like how I would stop Belen from leaving the camp.

Except a couple days later, my problem had been solved. A messenger on horseback arrived, announcing that Prince Ryne's troops would be here in about a week. The gossip zipped through the camp, igniting a variety of emotions.

A majority thought we didn't need Prince Ryne and his elite troops, others welcomed the additional soldiers, while two of us—me and, I was sure, Belen—were ecstatic to hear the news.

Ten days later, Ryne rode into camp. He sat on a huge chestnut-colored horse. Quain and Loren rode just behind him on two piebald mares. They led a small battalion.

I scanned every single one of those faces—approximately four hundred soldiers. My heart thumped up my throat. Just to be certain, I looked a second time, but the results were the same.

Kerrick wasn't among them.

KERRICK

"No. Absolutely not. You can't have them," Izak said.

Kerrick kept his temper…barely. "I'm not asking for your permission—"

"Good, because you won't get it."

Izak's stubbornness matched his own. It was about the only thing the brothers had in common. While dark-haired Kerrick had grown over six feet tall, Izak was five feet ten inches with white-blond hair. Izak's icy blue eyes stayed the same color all year. Kerrick had been the only family member to be gifted with magic, which had always been a source of conflict between them.

"Let me rephrase," Kerrick said in an even tone. "I don't *need* your permission. I—"

"*You* haven't been here in three years. What *you* need is to reacquaint yourself with what's going on in Alga Realm."

He gave Izak a cold stare. "Just what has been going on?"

Izak gestured to the windows. They were in the sitting area of their father's royal suite. When King Neil died from the plague five years ago, Kerrick had inherited the position. However, he had stayed in his own rooms and refused to allow anyone to call him king. But Izak had moved into the

Maria V. Snyder

expansive suite of rooms right away. He also had no qualms about being called king.

"Peace and prosperity," Izak said. "Alga is a safe haven for the plague survivors."

"Because of Prince Ryne, you idiot. Without his help, Alga Realm wouldn't exist."

"And I'm grateful, but I can't let you take my soldiers because of some crazy rumor."

By pure force of will, Kerrick did *not* strangle his brother. Avry would be proud of him, provided she'd speak to him after he failed to show up with Ryne and half his army. The other half was bivouacking in the fields north of Orel, Kerrick's hometown. Ryne had asked him to gather more troops and address the threat from the northern wildlands. He couldn't refuse. It was too important. But he had insisted Quain and Loren go with Ryne, despite their protests. Kerrick knew they would protect Avry once her secret was out.

"They are not yours, Izak. I did not abdicate the throne." He held up a hand, stopping his younger brother's outburst. "It isn't a rumor. If the northern tribes reach Alga, then the peace and prosperity you're so proud of will be gone."

Izak pished. "We can defend against the tribes. The message could have been from one of Tohon's spies. What a great tactic. Lure all our soldiers north while he sneaks in over the Nine Mountains."

"Ryne already ruled that out. The source of the message is reliable, and he detailed hundreds of warriors. The tribal people are ruthless, they—"

"Probably have been decimated by the plague, as well."

Kerrick ceased arguing. It was a waste of time. He strode to the door, yanked it open and ordered one of the guards standing outside to fetch General Zamiel.

"You can't…"

Kerrick waited, but Izak didn't finish. Good. "Before General Zamiel arrives, I've another matter to discuss." He settled into his father's favorite armchair.

Wary, Izak perched on the edge of the desk, crossing his arms. "Go on."

"I brought two children with me. Zila and Danny and their nanny, Berna. The kids are…special. And they're going to need protection while I'm in the north."

"How much protection?"

"A squad dedicated to keeping them safe."

Izak dropped his arms. "That *is* special. What are you worried about?"

"Kidnappers sent by Tohon."

He stood in alarm. "Why did you bring them here? We're closer to Tohon. They'd be safer in Ryne's castle."

Kerrick agreed. However, with this new threat from the north, Ryne believed they'd be better protected in Orel. "You have the pass between Alga and Sogra guarded, right?"

"Of course. And I've a couple battalions along the coast in case Tohon decides to invade from the Endless Sea."

"Tohon's been too busy with Estrid to worry about the northern realms. The kids should be fine," Kerrick said, trying to convince himself.

"I think you and Ryne are being rather naive regarding Tohon."

An odd statement. Izak's demeanor set off a warning, but before Kerrick could question him, the door burst open.

Great-Aunt Yasmin entered with a swish of skirts. She clutched her shawl tight, but her sharp gaze sliced right through Kerrick. *Uh-oh.*

"Three years, Kerry." She held up three gnarled fingers. "You're gone three years and I have to hear about your return from my maid." She radiated indignation, anger and guilt-inducing energy at him.

Izak's smirk died when she rounded on him. "Don't be so smug, young man. You haven't seen your brother in years and you've been fighting with him! What kind of welcome is that?"

"How did—"

She harrumphed. "I'm old, not stupid. Now come here, Kerry, and give your favorite auntie a hug."

Kerrick bent over and gave her a gentle squeeze. She was half his size and all bones. Her white hair had been pulled up into a neat bun. Great-Aunt Yasmin looked pretty good for a ninety-year-old.

She rested her hand on his cheek and smiled. "Ah, Kerry. You've found your heart. Who is she?"

He shouldn't have been surprised. Despite her claim to have no magical abilities, she had a canny knack for reading a person's soul.

"A healer, but she's…gone."

She patted his cheek as if consoling him, but the shrewd gleam in her gray eyes told him she wasn't buying his act at all. Great-Aunt Yasmin stepped away instead of questioning him further.

"What have you boys been arguing about?" she asked.

They exchanged a glance.

"I'm old, not fragile. If it's bad news, *you'd* be better off if I heard it from you and not my maid."

Kerrick explained about the northern tribes invading Krakowa. "I want to take at least half of the Algan army and drive the tribes back into the wildlands."

Surprised, Great-Aunt Yasmin turned to Izak. "Didn't you tell Kerry about the deal?"

Izak's face paled. "How did…? Never mind. Old, not stupid, I know."

"What deal?" Kerrick asked.

Izak stepped back as if expecting a blow. "You weren't here. I did what I could for *our* people."

"He was too young when you left him in charge, Kerry. Don't blame him for panicking and making a deal with King Tohon."

CHAPTER 6

I scanned the soldiers' faces a third and fourth time, hoping Kerrick had decided to arrive at Estrid's camp incognito. It would have been an excellent idea since Jael had no qualms about killing him either. However, no one even resembled him or matched his build.

Disappointment and worry flared in equal measure. Had Tohon's men caught up to him before he'd reached Ryne's? Was he hurt? Captured? Or killed? Despite the danger, I edged closer to the procession as they paraded right past Jael's tent and headed straight for the manor house.

Jael watched Ryne and his men go by with an icy glare. Would she try to harm them? Noelle stood by her side and studied the passing soldiers with a keen interest. Was she looking for me? Did that little smile mean she was happy about my absence?

Belen was far from happy. He strode right up to the procession and blocked Prince Ryne's path. The horse stopped. Smart horse. Belen grabbed the horse's cheek strap and spoke to Ryne.

He had to be asking about Kerrick. I hurried to catch up, but Ryne leaned forward and said something to Belen. It must have soothed him, because he released the horse and walked next to Quain and Loren. From atop their horses, both men gave Belen queasy smiles before returning their gazes to Ryne's back.

They dismounted in the courtyard in front of the manor house and then entered with Belen in tow. I grunted in frustration. Who could I ask about Kerrick? None of the soldiers waiting patiently outside looked familiar. I couldn't just stroll into the building with both Estrid's and Ryne's armies watching.

Frustration welled. I would just have to wait for the camp gossip to reach our company. Or did I? One of the reasons for this ruse was so I could gather information about Estrid's army and operations. Who could I tell this to now? I'd have to reveal myself, and I still hadn't talked to Noelle or found Melina.

I sucked in a breath, settling my racing heartbeat. No need to rush into a decision. News about Avry the healer and Prince Kerrick would reach me, and I'd get a better sense of how to proceed.

Having a plan didn't make me feel any better, so I decided to spend my morning searching for Melina. I walked through Dagger, Cutlass and Garrote's companies' areas, asking a few young girls Melina's age if they knew her. Nothing. Then I swept through the others, scanning faces. No Melina.

On the way back to my area, I heard Ryne's name. Without thought, I stopped to listen.

"…left half of his soldiers behind. The marauders had invaded," a private said.

"Sergeant Vic said they've taken over the northern realms and everyone is dead," another said.

"Then why would Prince Ryne leave, you dolt!" He smacked his companion on the head. "You can't believe anything Vic says."

"I heard Prince Kerrick is working for King Tohon as a double agent," yet another chimed in.

Wild rumors and speculation weren't helping me. I would have to check with a more reliable gossip source, such as Lieutenant Thea or Major Granvil. Continuing on, I wondered how long I should wait before approaching them. Perhaps tomorrow.

Hurried movement caught my attention, and I spotted Noelle running an errand for Jael. I needed to talk to her alone, but she was either out in the camp in plain sight or with Jael. Fingering my stiletto, I considered another option.

"Excuse me, Sergeant," a voice sounded behind me.

I turned around. A very young private snapped to attention. He appeared to be eleven or twelve years old, but had to be at least fifteen—the minimum age to be a soldier in Estrid's army.

"At ease," I said.

He relaxed his stance but ran his hands down his shirt as if nervous. "Uh…are you the one looking for Melina from Mengels?"

"Yes. Do you know where she is?"

He wiped his hands on his pants, leaving damp stains behind. "Uh…can I ask why you want to know?"

"I'm a friend of her mother and I promised to check on Melina."

His gaze darted to the side before returning to me. "I mean no disrespect, Sergeant, but you're new here, aren't you?"

I wouldn't consider two months new, but I nodded.

"I'm guessing you haven't encountered the Purity Priestess yet?"

Uh-oh. I had dodged her and her goons before. "Go on."

"Um…well, as members of the army, we are the creator's weapons and we must be pure of heart and soul. But Melina didn't pass…inspection." His prominent Adam's apple bobbed as he swallowed. "She was sent to the monastery in Chinska Mare to atone for her...misdeeds."

Various emotions swept through me. First, relief that Melina was alive and reasonably safe. Second, outrage that she had been incarcerated for life because she wasn't a virgin. And third, surprise that she hadn't passed. Sixteen seemed too young to me. Regardless of my views, it didn't change my feelings for her. Or the fact that I needed to rescue her... somehow. Yet another worry, and an addition to my already long to-do list.

"Thanks for telling me, Private."

He dashed off.

That solved one mystery. Feeling better about my situation, I found a comfortable place to sit and watched the manor house.

Ryne, Belen and the monkeys emerged after sunset. Shouting orders to his troops, Ryne directed them to bivouac in the fields north of the manor. Loren and Quain guided them to the proper spot while Ryne and Belen were joined by the High Priestess Estrid.

A ripple of sound emanated all around me as Estrid's army jumped to attention at her appearance. She wore a red silk gown with gold brocade glinting in the lantern light. From this distance she looked elegant and younger than her fifty-two years. Ryne offered his arm, and she rested her hand on the crook as they descended the steps.

Her hand remained on his arm as they crossed to Jael's tent. A sign to her troops that they were working together as equals. Impressive. My opinion of her intelligence rose a couple notches.

Followed by a scowling Belen, they entered Jael's tent. I wondered if Ryne had broken the news to him about me. Or perhaps his uncharacteristic demeanor meant Kerrick was missing or worse. The temptation to sneak up to the tent and listen through the fabric pulsed in my chest. Before I could act on my impulse and be caught snooping, I turned away and headed for the sergeant's fire, skipping supper. My stomach already felt as if I'd swallowed a twenty-pound rock.

All five of Lieutenant Thea's sergeants lounged by the fire. No surprise the conversation focused on Ryne's troops. Ursan watched me as I settled between Odd and Liv, his gaze contemplative. The others hardly noticed my arrival.

"…he's holding back," Odd said. "He has to have more soldiers."

"Yeah," Liv agreed. "No way he could have driven the marauders from the northern realms with only four hundred."

"The captain of Falchion Company thought there'd be at least a thousand," Wynn said.

"Oh? Did you just happen to run into Captain Lynton today? Or are you stalking the poor man again?" Liv asked.

Wynn punched her on the arm.

"Why would Prince Ryne hold back troops?" I asked Odd.

"There could be trouble in the north or it could be a strategic thing. Perhaps he's keeping them in northern Pomyt just in case the battle doesn't go well here and he needs to make a fast retreat." Odd shrugged.

He *could* shrug. Trouble in the north meant *nothing* to him, but it made my heart shuffle. *Deep breath, Avry.*

Once my fears settled, I considered his guess. Knowing Ryne, I dismissed the protection for a retreat scenario. Ryne wouldn't waste resources. A strategic move made more sense. Perhaps they were planning to cross the Nine Mountains through the Orel pass and drop in behind Tohon's army. And Kerrick had been assigned to lead them.

It was a nice fantasy. It included Kerrick being alive and well and probably pissed off because he had planned to meet up with me in Zabin. I clung to it for a bit. But it didn't take long for my healer side to worry that he was injured and dying somewhere and here I was, playing soldier.

"...you think, Irina?" Ursan asked.

It took me a moment to realize he was speaking to me. "Think about what?"

"You seem distracted tonight. Something wrong?" Ursan appeared to be the soul of concern, but I knew better.

"Nothing's wrong. Just tired. What did you want to know?"

"We were discussing Prince Ryne," Ursan said. "The last thing we need is some pampered, spoiled prince draining our resources. But I'm curious as to his timing. Don't you think it's rather convenient that Ryne arrives now? He's been missing for over two years, and now he just shows up out of the blue." His expression said what he hadn't—*just like you*.

"He's probably been guarding his realm all that time," Odd said.

"Coming down here is a big risk," Liv said. "He's safer on the other side of the Nine Mountains."

"Irina?" Ursan waited as if I alone possessed the answer.

Before I could offer an opinion, a figure approached our fire. My heart flipped when I recognized my sister.

"General Jael wishes to speak to Sergeants Ursan and Irina. Now," Noelle said.

Not good. "What does she want?" I asked.

"You'll find out soon enough," she snapped. "Let's go."

I stood on weak legs. Ursan had been watching my face, so I smoothed my expression to, I hoped, one of mild curiosity.

Bright lantern light shone through the fabric of Jael's tent. I squinted as I followed Noelle through the flaps. As I had suspected, this was used solely for the planning of a war. Huge conference tables ringed with chairs filled the tent. Maps hung from the walls along with charts and diagrams. Officers sat in groups, discussing important matters. Or, at least, it appeared, by their stern faces and tight muscles, to be vital. Thank goodness I didn't recognize anyone except Jael.

Would she see through my disguise? Noelle hadn't, but Jael's magic might remember me. Jael stood at the end of a small table, talking to a couple of colonels. Noelle waited until she was noticed and then informed Jael of our arrival. The general flicked her gaze to us before she dismissed Noelle. Jael gestured us closer.

Ursan stayed one step behind me, and I felt his body heat on my back. We saluted, although I had to stifle the desire to stab my stiletto through Jael's heart as payback for killing Flea.

Despite the lines of strain in her face, she was beautiful. Her long blond hair flowed down her back. Big blue eyes assessed us with mild interest.

I braced for her to recognize me. Would she cry out in surprise or attack me or order her guards to arrest me? With her, any or all of those reactions were possible.

"I've been hearing good things about you, Sergeant Irina," she said. "Major Granvil is very satisfied with the work you've been doing."

Not sure where this was going, I said, "Thank you, sir."

"Granvil also informed me that Sergeant Ursan and his jumping jacks have been successful employing your training. Would you say they are your best students?" Jael asked.

"Yes, sir."

"Good. I want you to run a training exercise tomorrow afternoon. The teams will be Sergeant Ursan and his jacks versus that whelp Ryne and his chosen few." Jael pursed her full lips in distain.

"Sir?" I asked.

"Yes."

"What is the objective of the exercise?"

"The objective is for one team to sneak up and ambush the other. The whelp believes our army is lacking in certain covert skills, and I want to prove him wrong. I'll be observing so *don't* disappoint me, Sergeant."

"Yes, sir." One positive thing about Kerrick remaining in the north, no one to lecture me about how much trouble I was in right now.

"Excellent. You're dismissed. Sergeant Ursan, a word."

My cue to leave. I saluted and hurried outside into the darkness. Pausing to let my eyes adjust, I wondered what Jael wanted with Ursan. Instead of heading to my tent, I stepped to the side as if waiting for him. The guards stationed by the entrance didn't react. They continued to ignore me.

Leaning closer to the fabric, I strained to hear Jael's voice. Nothing. Either the fabric was too thick or the noise inside was too loud. Would Ursan tell me what she wanted? His *yes, sir,* though, was crisp and loud. Show-off.

I joined him when he strode from the tent. For the first time since I'd known him, he seemed…distressed. He barely acknowledged my presence as I tagged along, and he remained silent the entire trip back.

Just before we parted ways, I asked, "What did the general say?"

"It's classified," he said.

"Was it about tomorrow's exercise?"

Ursan gave me a blank stare.

I sighed. "I want your jacks to be at the training site early tomorrow so we can go over a few things. Prince Ryne's men will be hard to beat."

"How do you know?"

Ah, there was the suspicious Ursan I'd grown to tolerate. "Belen is one of his men."

"Oh." He considered. "How hard to beat?"

Almost impossible if Ryne brought Loren and Quain, but that wouldn't be positive. "More challenging than finding me. But I think the jacks will score a few jackknives tomorrow."

I expected a smile, but he stiffened, shot me an unreadable look and said good-night.

In the middle of the darkened room, Kerrick lay inside a glass coffin. His open eyes were lifeless and without color. I shouted his name and pounded on the glass.

"No need to carry on, my dear," Tohon said, stepping from the shadows. "He can't hear you." He took my hand in his, turning it so my palm faced up. "Besides, you're mine. You've been mine since that first kiss." Tohon pressed his lips to my wrist.

His magic shot up my arm and straight into my core. A wave of sensations radiated out, turning my muscles into a spongy mess. Unable to stand, I sank to the ground. Tohon followed, pushing me flat.

He leaned over me. "You can't hide from me, my dear. I will find you. I promise." Tohon pressed his lips to mine.

Odd's booming voice woke me. My lips tingled from Tohon's kiss, and the image of Kerrick in the coffin wouldn't dissipate.

Odd bounced on the edge of Wynn's cot. "Took me all night, but I've got the good stuff."

Liv threw her pillow at him. "Go away."

He ignored her. "I've sorted through all the wild rumors and gossip and discovered the truth! The tribes from the wildlands have indeed invaded the northern part of Ivdel Realm."

I sat up. "That's horrible."

"Not to worry, Prince Kerrick is leading the rest of Prince Ryne's troops in an attempt to stop them."

"Attempt?" I asked. My relief over Kerrick being alive and well was instantly replaced with worry.

"The tribes are notoriously vicious and effective against larger opponents."

"How do you know?" Wynn asked. "You grew up in Ryazan Realm."

"And we don't have history books in Ryazan?" he shot back.

Before they could launch into an argument, I asked, "How effective?"

"At one point they had control of all the land north of the Nine Mountains. When they found passable routes through the mountains, they attacked the southern lands. They weren't called realms then."

"And?" Wynn prompted.

"An army waited for them. Spotters had seen the tribesmen and warned the southerners. But even outnumbered ten to one, they used the terrain to their advantage. They hid in the foothills and sent small groups out to harass the army before returning to their hiding spots. Using that tactic, they managed to remain in the area for a number of years until more forces arrived and drove them back over the mountains and all the way to the wildlands."

The strategy sounded familiar. I searched my memories and recalled Kerrick mentioning Ryne's elite squads and how they had been successful against a bigger army. I wondered if Ryne learned it from the tribes? And I hoped he'd taught Kerrick a counteroffensive.

"Did you find anything else out?" I asked.

"Do you remember the healer who came through here about six months ago?"

Murmurs of assent. Oh, no, this was it.

"She saved Davy's leg," Liv said. "They were going to cut it off because of an infection. Why?"

"She died saving Prince Ryne's life," Odd said in a dramatic voice.

I guess I should have felt appreciated as they appeared to be upset by my heroic death. But it just made me sick to my stomach.

Wynn and Liv pumped him for details, but he only had the basics. Eventually the topic returned to Ryne's troops.

"They're a quiet lot," Odd said. "I hope that doesn't mean they're scared."

After Odd left, I sent the jacks out to practice. I stood in the middle of the training area and shouted instructions as they ran the drills over and over again. I wasn't the only one nervous. Ursan paced, making it hard for me to listen to the others. And a few times when he was out on recon, I heard him crash through the underbrush.

Before Ryne showed up, I gathered the jacks around me. "Just relax and do what you *know* how to do. Keep it fun. And follow the rules. We're all on the same side."

Ursan flinched when I said that last bit. I suspected Jael had ordered him to cheat. I gave the jacks an hour off to eat and rest. They headed back to camp in high spirits, but I stopped Ursan before he could follow them.

"What's wrong?" I asked him.

"Nothing."

"Yeah, right. Did the general order you to break the rules in order to win?" I demanded.

He seemed surprised by the question. "No."

"Then what's going on?"

Ursan refused to answer. He pushed past, leaving me alone with my swirling thoughts. No surprise Jael was up to no good. But what did she intend? I would have to stick close to Ursan this afternoon and find out.

I stood with the jacks when Ryne and his team arrived, keeping my distance and hoping to blend in with the crowd.

Ryne's team consisted of Belen, Quain and Loren. Four of them against Ursan and his squad. Major Granvil accompanied Noelle, who would fetch the general when the teams started interacting. Granvil read the rules of engagement to all the participants.

Each team would travel in opposite directions for an hour. They couldn't spread out or go in different directions. They had to stay together as they would out on patrol. Not side by side, but close. They couldn't lie in wait for more than fifteen minutes, and those who were "caught" had to return to base where the officers waited. Caught meant being surprised by an opposing team member. If there were still active participants on both sides at sundown, the winner would be determined by the percentage of "kills."

"Sergeant Irina?" Granvil called.

Oh, no. "Yes, sir?" I stepped forward, drawing everyone's attention. My gaze stayed on Granvil, but my skin itched as I felt Ryne and the guys studying me.

"You'll be the intermediary, ensuring everyone is following the rules and dealing with any contested 'kills.'"

"Yes, sir."

"Any questions?" Granvil asked.

Everyone's focus returned to the major. Everyone's but Belen's. His gaze burned into my soul, and I shifted so my back was to him.

"How far can we go?" Ryne asked.

"This large patch of woods is surrounded by farm fields. As long as you stay within the forest, you can travel anywhere."

"Fair enough," Ryne said. Then he looked at me. "How can we be sure Sergeant Irina isn't biased? After all, she trained these men."

Good question. I glanced around, but it seemed no one

wanted to answer him. "All I can give you is my word to be impartial, sir. If you'd like to pick—"

"Her word is enough," Belen said.

Ryne accepted Belen's endorsement without hesitation. But I worried. Did he recognize me? I'd have to avoid him during the exercise. Oh, joy.

Since there were no other questions, Major Granvil sent the teams deeper into the woods. Ryne's team to the east and Ursan's to the west. I stayed behind with the major and Noelle. Nothing would happen for more than an hour, so I didn't need to be out there yet.

Major Granvil chatted with me, asking about the jacks' odds and how the morning practice had gone. I answered his questions but kept track of Noelle. This could be my chance to talk to her. She found a rock to sit on. Pulling a square of paper from her pants pocket, she unfolded and stared at it.

"Excuse me, Sergeant," the major said as one of his lieutenants arrived with a message.

I left them as they talked in hushed tones. Hoping to appear casual, I approached Noelle.

She didn't even glance up when she said, "Shouldn't you be in the woods, Sergeant?"

"Not yet. But when I do go, that's when you should fetch the general." I recognized my handwriting. She was reading my letter! And from the creases, it wasn't the first time. Fear and sadness gripped my throat, making it hard to breathe.

She sighed dramatically. "Can I help you with something?"

I pointed to the paper. "Bad news?"

Noelle folded it so I couldn't see the words. "It's none of—"

"My business," I finished for her. "You're right. I suppose you already talked it over with a friend. Or does the general keep you too busy to make friends?"

"I've a very important job, Sergeant. It's an honor to be

her page. This—" she waved the letter "—is all in the past. It means nothing to me now."

Yet she tucked it back into her pocket, and I caught a glimpse of a silver chain around her neck when she stood. She wore my necklace. The hands pendant our older brother, Criss, had given me before I'd left for my apprenticeship. I had put it in the envelope with the letter.

Hope. Real hope that I might get my sister back spread through me like a healing balm.

As Noelle went to find Jael, I entered into the "war zone." All was quiet. I settled in to wait. Sure enough, I heard the minute off notes to the west. The jumping jacks were traveling northeast, probably hoping to get in behind Ryne's team. I concentrated, but the monkeys couldn't hide from me. To the east, I picked up Loren and Quain's progress. Ryne's passage sounds weren't as familiar. We'd only traveled together once, and I'd been sick with the plague at the time, so my memory was more than a little fuzzy.

Belen, though… Why couldn't I hear Poppa Bear? Perhaps he had stopped. I wished I had Kerrick's forest magic right now. Then I would know everyone's exact position. I touched a leaf, seeking the tingle of his magic even though I knew he was in the north. Nothing, as expected. I breathed in the earthy smell of living green—his scent—to console myself.

A few off notes and sour sounds meant the two teams were drawing closer to each other. But still no Belen. He had been out on patrols these past four months. Perhaps he had improved.

I moved so I could observe the almost silent action. A muffled pip sounded behind me before two large hands grasped my shoulders. I clamped down on my squeak of surprise. I'd found Belen. Or rather, he had found me.

He turned me to face him. I braced for…I had no idea. He stared at me for a heartbeat, then crushed me in a rib-breaking hug for so long I thought I would faint from lack of air.

Easing his embrace, he still didn't let go. "You have a lot of explaining to do," he whispered.

"I know. What are you doing out here? It's against the rules."

"Tell that to the other team. One of theirs has broken away from the main group and I was following him."

Alarmed, I asked, "Which one?"

"Sergeant Ursan."

"Where is he now?"

"Don't know. When I heard you, my priorities shifted."

"Heard me?"

"You can change your hair, your appearance and your voice, but you can't change how you move through the forest. You still sound the same." He smiled. "I didn't believe it when Prince Ryne told me you'd died. And I suspected earlier today, but this confirmed it. Does Kerrick know? Are you going to tell me what's going on?"

"Yes, Kerrick knows. I'll tell you everything later. First we need to find Ursan. He's been acting…strange."

We listened. Our conversation had drawn the jacks south toward us with the monkeys close behind. *Ryne?* I mouthed to Belen.

He used two fingers on his left hand to indicate the monkeys and his right index finger to mark Ryne. Close enough to be within the rules, but too far for my comfort level.

When the forest exploded with the sounds of people running through the bushes, I exchanged an alarmed glance with Belen.

"Part of the exercise?" he asked.

"No."

"Another squad training?"

"No." My mind raced. And I put a few clues together. "It's a distraction."

"To help the jacks win?" Belen asked.

"No. Ryne. We have to protect him."

He broke into a run, and I followed close behind. We needed to get to Ryne before Ursan assassinated him.

KERRICK

Kerrick sat behind his father's immense desk, trying to make sense of the "deal" his idiot brother had made with Tohon. He glanced at General Zamiel, who refused to sit, and his Great-Aunt Yasmin, who had settled into an armchair with a blanket over her legs despite the heat.

"Tell me *exactly* what Izak promised Tohon," he ordered the general.

"Izak could tell you himself, Kerry," Great-Aunt Yasmin said with a note of disapproval in her voice. "I don't know why you had him placed under house arrest."

"It was for his protection," he said, keeping his temper.

"I don't under—"

"From me. So I don't kill him. Understand now?" he asked her.

"Yes." She adjusted the blanket and played with the tassels. "You shouldn't fight with him, Kerry. He's all the family you have left."

He drew in a breath before replying, "I have you."

"I don't count. I have one foot and four toes in the grave."

"You've been saying that since I was seven. You're going to outlive us all."

"Only if you keep running off and fighting—"

"Do you know what Tohon's been doing while I've been away? What he has created?" he asked, keeping his voice even.

"She doesn't, but Izak does," General Zamiel said. "That's why he made that deal and why I supported his decision."

Kerrick met the general's gaze. The man had been his father's right-hand man since he could remember. His short black hair had turned white, and wrinkles etched his face. But he still radiated a powerful confidence, and his sword hung within easy reach. Zamiel had taught Kerrick how to fight. And even though he had lost the last two fingers on his right hand in battle, Zamiel was near impossible to beat. Or he had been. Kerrick wondered who would win if they fought now.

"Which is why I need to know everything that happened," Kerrick said. "Great-Aunt Yasmin, perhaps you'd rather—"

"I'm not moving. I'm old, not frail." She glared at the general. "I can't help your brother if I don't know what's going on."

He took another moment to settle his temper before he said or did something he'd regret. Kerrick had impressed his great-aunt by not throttling his brother when he heard the news about Tohon, but there was still time to disappoint her.

"All right, stay," he said to her. "General, please start from the beginning. How did Tohon's soldiers get past our sentries in the Nine Mountains?"

"Last summer his troops came barreling through the Orel Pass like an avalanche. The mindless intensity of the attack took us by surprise. Once we rallied, we discovered that nothing stopped them. Arrows and swords had no effect."

"Decapitation does," Kerrick said.

"By the time we figured that out, most of my troops were beyond terrified. Frightened men and women make poor fighters."

"Terrified of what?" Great-Aunt Yasmin asked.

Kerrick told her about Tohon's dead soldiers.

She scowled. "You knew about them, and didn't warn Izak?"

"I found out in the winter. Izak should have warned *me*."

"And just how was he supposed to do that?" she asked. "We had no idea where you were for three years."

She was right. So focused on finding a healer, he had neglected his family and duties.

"And the deal?" he asked the general.

"If our army swears allegiance to him and joins his forces, he'd leave the rest of us alone. It was the only way to save the realm. I planned to go with them, but Tohon wouldn't take me."

Kerrick considered. Tohon had needed more soldiers to fight Estrid, so he'd raided Alga, knowing Kerrick had left Izak in charge. But why hadn't he left troops behind? Or taken Izak like he had Cellina? Because Tohon probably figured once he conquered the south, he could easily enter Alga under the guise of bringing back the stolen troops. And once he crossed the Nine Mountains, the rest of the northern realms would be his.

A good strategy, except the tribes had invaded. Instead of following Ryne to the south, Kerrick had come here and discovered Tohon's plan. Unfortunately, he didn't have the resources to do anything about it. All he could do was send a message to Ryne, warning him that Tohon had more troops than they'd estimated.

"Did Tohon sign an agreement?" Kerrick asked.

"No. Just gave us his word."

Which meant nothing. "What exactly did he say?"

"That Alga Realm would remain safe as long as he was king of all the realms."

"Did Izak acknowledge him as king?"

"Yes."

Kerrick suppressed a curse. "Does Tohon know I didn't abdicate?"

General Zamiel smiled. "No. We failed to mention that to him."

"See?" Great-Aunt Yasmin tapped her temple. "Your brother did the best he could in a horrible situation. And he even gave you a way out. You owe him an apology."

Kerrick wouldn't go that far. "How many soldiers did we lose?"

"Fourteen hundred," Zamiel said.

"That's double what we had."

"We combined with Gubkin Realm. Their survivors wouldn't last another winter, so we welcomed them here, along with all the Algan survivors. We figured it was safer for everybody to live and work together in one town. It felt like the days before the plague. Laughter, music, babies being born. At least until Tohon arrived."

"Is Gubkin deserted?" Kerrick asked.

"There are a few gangs still up there, but not enough of them to worry about."

But that meant there was no one left for Kerrick to recruit to help him against the tribes. And with their army gone, Alga would be an easy target if the tribes got past Kerrick. If. With only four hundred soldiers, it was more likely when.

CHAPTER 7

Loud footfalls, panicked yells and curses filled the forest. The noise of the unexpected intruders covered any sounds that might have helped us find Prince Ryne. Belen headed in the direction of Ryne's last known position. I stayed close, listening to the chaos around us.

"…over there…go left…"

"…two more. Move it!"

Someone crossed right behind us. I glanced back in time to see a person dive into the underbrush. His bright yellow jumpsuit clashed against the greenery. Yellow meant something…it took me a moment to make the connection. And then more flashes of yellow confirmed my suspicions. Estrid's prisoners of war had escaped, and their guards were in noisy pursuit. I smelled smoke. Was the POW camp on fire? Breathing in deep, I detected the unmistakable aroma of burning wood.

Belen stopped. "He was here. Should I call out for him?"

"No. His response might tip off Ursan. Plus we don't want the sergeant to know we're on to him." My mind raced. "Wouldn't Quain and Loren stay with him?"

"Depends."

Just then Loren and Quain appeared.

"What's going on?" Loren asked Belen. "Where's Ryne?"

"I'd hoped with you."

"We lost him in the confusion. Guess Sergeant Irina's men needed to cheat to win." Quain scowled at me.

I ignored him. "Your prince's been targeted for assassination. We need to find Ursan and stop him."

"Where are they?" Quain asked, pulling his dagger.

"If we knew that, we wouldn't be standing here," Belen growled.

An idea clicked. "We'll each take a compass point. Belen south, Quain north, Loren west, and I'll take east. Watch the trees, Ursan likes to ambush from above."

The monkeys glanced at Belen, clearly confused as to why I was giving the orders. I hadn't seen a spark of recognition in their eyes, and I didn't have time to educate them.

"Go," he said, turning south.

Quain snapped his mouth shut. He'd have time later to ask questions. As I headed east, worry for Ryne grew. I should have guessed this earlier. After all, Jael had tried to kill me to stop me from healing Ryne. If we stopped Ursan, I planned to assign the monkeys as his permanent bodyguards.

The sounds of the fleeing POWs and guards quieted as the chase moved farther west. I concentrated. A slight rustle came from my right. Scanning the trees, I quickened my pace as another small shuffle sounded. Ryne.

I strained, listening for any movement from Ursan. Nothing. Again I glanced up, searching the lower branches.

Ryne turned in my direction when I drew close. Relief at finding him alive was immediately replaced with fear as Ursan dropped from the tree above the prince's head.

"Watch out," I yelled, pointing.

But Ryne was too slow to react. Ursan landed on him. I raced to them. Sitting on top of Ryne, Ursan held the blade of his knife against Ryne's throat.

"Ursan, don't do it," I said.

"Don't come any closer," Ursan said to me, but he kept his gaze on Ryne.

Ryne peered back at him, looking rather calm for a man in his position.

I stopped and held my hands out. "Ursan, we're on the same side."

"Are we?"

"Yes, we are."

"I have my orders," he said.

Yet Ryne still breathed. "Those orders don't make sense. And you know it. What about the prince's army? When they find out you— Oh. You plan to blame the POWs. Right?"

No response.

"How do you plan on silencing me?" I asked. A few sour notes sounded to my right. I lowered my hands.

This time he met my gaze. "You're a traitor."

"Ah. And I'm an assassin, too. Clever." More muted rustlings disturbed the quiet.

"You weren't supposed to be here," Ursan said.

"And you're not going to kill Ryne," I said.

"I have my orders."

"Then what are you waiting for? Your jacks to arrive? Or for Ryne's men?" I gestured to the surrounding forest. "You know someone's coming."

"If I slit his throat, can you heal him?" he asked.

Odd question. "It depends."

"On what?"

"On how deep you cut, how fast he bleeds out and how quick I can get to him." The sounds of movement grew louder. I counted at least two people heading toward us.

"If he was bleeding to death, would you heal him at the cost of your own life?"

"I already have, Ursan. I think you've figured that out by now."

"Yeah." He smiled and stood. "But I wanted you to admit it." Ursan helped Ryne to his feet.

Ryne brushed dirt and leaves off his back and pants. He frowned at me. "We need to work on your negotiation skills. Generally you don't goad the person holding the knife into hurrying."

"You're still alive. Besides, *you* weren't helping," I said.

"I was keeping out of it."

"Uh-huh. You're welcome."

Ursan made a strangled sound. Belen had wrapped his huge hands around the Sergeant's thick neck. Belen's improved silent skills impressed me yet again.

"Belen, that's enough," Ryne said when Ursan's face paled.

He tossed Ursan to the ground with ease. The Sergeant gasped for breath and gaped at Belen. Probably no one had done that to Ursan before. Loren and Quain appeared from the forest with weapons drawn. They had been the two creeping up on us with more noise than usual for them. Probably to distract Ursan from Belen. Loren gave me a careful look.

"What are we going to do with him?" Belen asked Ryne.

"Nothing. He'll report to Jael that he couldn't get near me."

"What if she orders another attack?" I asked.

"I'm going to have a little chat with Jael. I'll let her know I'm on to her, and have taken steps to ensure Estrid is informed if anything should happen to me."

"Is that wise?" Belen asked. "She can kill you from a distance. Or send someone else."

"She doesn't want Estrid to know what she's been up to, so I'll be safe for now."

"Do you know what she is planning?" I asked.

"Not yet."

"And what happens when she doesn't care about Estrid anymore?" I asked.

"Hopefully, I'll figure out her scheme first. Otherwise, I'll be in big trouble."

In that case, I suspected we all would.

"Loren and Quain, you need to stay with Ryne at all times," I said.

"We don't take orders from you, Sergeant," Quain said. "Your man tried to assassinate—"

"He isn't mine. *My* man has eyes that change color with the seasons."

Loren laughed at Quain's perplexed expression. "Oh, man, you're not very observant, are you."

"Wait," Quain said. "Whose eyes change color?"

His question resulted in more laughter. Once again, Belen pulled me into a hug as Ryne and Loren beamed at me.

It took Quain another minute to put it all together. He grabbed my arms and yanked me from Belen's embrace so we were face-to-face. "You're alive! Does Kerrick know?" he demanded in anger.

The rest of the men sobered in an instant.

"Yes," I said.

"Why didn't he tell us?" Quain's grip on my forearms tightened.

"Because I asked him not to."

"You?" He sputtered. "Why?"

I'd never seen Quain this upset. I explained my logical reasons for going undercover.

"It's a smart strategy," Ryne said.

"But why couldn't *we* know about it?" Quain demanded. "Do you know what you put us all through?"

"I…"

"You don't trust us," Loren said.

"It's not…" Or was it? I couldn't speak.

"In a case like this, the fewer people who know about it the better," Ryne said. "And I think Avry should continue with the ruse, even though it's only a matter of time until the word is out."

Ryne's matter-of-fact statement scared me more than Quain's crushing grip. The news would spread, and soon Tohon would know I'd survived the plague. Then he'd want to reclaim me. Not only as a medical marvel to study, but to make Kerrick suffer. A shudder ripped through me.

"Quain, let go," Belen said. "You're hurting her."

He dropped my arms, pushing me away. "She'll heal."

His cold words were like a slap in my face.

"We'd better get back," Ursan said, joining us. He had recovered but kept a respectful distance. Even though I was pretty sure he'd heard every word.

"Not together," Ryne said. "You and Avry take a different route. And let me do all the talking when we meet up with the others."

I followed Ursan through the darkening forest.

After traveling for a few minutes in silence, he asked, "Why didn't you tell your friends the real reason you played dead?"

"I told them about my sister."

He huffed. "That's not the reason."

"Yes, it is. Don't play these games. You know *nothing* about me."

Ursan kept quiet the remainder of the trip. Jael, Major Granvil and the rest of the jumping jacks waited for us at the starting point of the exercise. It felt as if we'd been gone days instead of hours. Noelle wasn't in sight, and Ryne's group hadn't made it back yet.

"Report, Sergeant," Jael ordered Ursan, her agitation obvious.

"The exercise was interrupted by the escaping POWs, sir. I was separated from my men as I tried to help round them up. Were they all recaptured, sir?"

"Yes. Have you seen the other team?" Jael asked.

"Yes. They kept together during the confusion and are on their way here."

Disappointment flashed for a second before she smoothed her expression. When Ryne joined us, she showed no signs of her earlier distress. They discussed the aborted exercise.

"We can try again tomorrow afternoon," Jael said.

"No need, General," Ryne said. "Your men proved their skills today. I was quite impressed. Sergeant Irina is doing a fine job and I don't want to waste another day that can be used for training." He steered her from the forest with Belen, Loren and Quain trailing behind.

Belen winked at me, but the monkeys hadn't even glanced in my direction.

Major Granvil waited until they left before addressing us. "This was a crazy day, but you proved yourselves. Report for training in the morning, but you can have tomorrow afternoon off. Dismissed."

The jacks cheered and headed back to camp. Ursan and I were about to follow when the major said, "Sergeants, a word."

We exchanged a glance before turning around.

"I'm not an idiot," Granvil said. "Something big happened today, and I'm not talking about the POWs well-timed escape. Tell me."

"It's better if you didn't know, sir," I said.

"Shouldn't I be the judge of that?"

"No, sir. Trust me. All you need to know is that Sergeant Ursan made you proud, and he should be promoted," I said.

"And what about you? Should I promote you, too?"

"No, sir."

"Really? What happened to your aspirations to become an officer?"

I looked at Ursan. "I still need to earn my sergeant's stripes, sir."

"I'm not even going to pretend that I understood that. All right, go."

We didn't hesitate. Without saying a word, Ursan and I bolted from the forest. Halfway back to camp, we slowed. I considered the day's events.

"What will you do if General Jael orders you to assassinate Ryne again?" I asked.

"She won't. I failed. And once Prince Ryne has his talk with her, she'll know I tipped my hand. I'll either be demoted or sent out on a very dangerous mission that has no chance for success."

"Perhaps the major—"

"Generals trump majors," Ursan said.

"True. But do princes trump generals?"

"I attacked him."

"Ryne's not the type to hold a grudge."

Ursan considered. "Isn't he a king? Both his parents died."

"Technically, yes. But he hasn't assumed the title."

"Neither has Prince Kerrick," Ursan said. "Don't you find that odd?"

"Not with Kerrick. He loved his father very much. I think it's still too painful for him to assume the title. Plus he hasn't been home in years."

Ursan remained quiet until we reached his tent. "Prince Kerrick's a forest mage. Which means his eyes change color with the seasons. Right?" he asked.

"Yes."

He stared at me for a moment. "Lucky guy." Ursan ducked into his tent.

I stood there a moment in complete shock. He'd accused me of being a traitor, a spy, and didn't trust me at all. Yet, he'd said that. And what exactly did that mean?

Why did I bring out the worst in people? Even Quain was mad at me, and I didn't think that was possible. If the bald monkey started spouting poetry in the future, I'd bury my stiletto in him.

Wynn and Liv had waited for me in our tent. They had lit a lantern, and both sat cross-legged on their cots. Liv sewed a hole in a pair of her fatigues while Wynn sharpened her sword.

"How did the exercise go?" Liv asked, glancing up.

I told them about the escape but not the assassination attempt.

"Odd," Wynn said. "The POW camp is usually locked down tight."

"Well, that'll give the general another reason to shut it down." Liv cut the thread with her teeth.

"I don't think that's enough of a reason for the High Priestess to agree," Wynn said.

"If they shut it down, where would they keep the prisoners?" I asked.

They exchanged a glance. "Ah, Baby Face. You're cute when you're naive," Liv said. "It's war. What do you think will happen to them?"

"Oh." Jael would kill them.

"It's been one of those…sticking points between the High Priestess and General Jael." Liv packed up her sewing kit. "The general argues that keeping the POWs alive is a drain on our resources and manpower. Once the battle begins, we're going to need everything we have."

Wynn slid her sword into her scabbard. "But the High Priestess values life. I hear they argue about it frequently."

"It should be interesting now that Prince Ryne is here.

He's bound to take the High Priestess's side. Did you see how chummy they were when he arrived?" Liv stood and stretched. "Let's eat, I'm starved."

I followed them to the mess tent, although I didn't have an appetite. Quain's reaction kept replaying in my mind. Ryne had agreed with me. Belen hadn't seemed upset. Then again, Belen only knew about my "death" since Ryne had arrived in Estrid's camp. The monkeys had known back when they'd left me in Sogra, believing my days were numbered.

And I hadn't even learned anything important about Jael and Estrid's army. Some undercover agent I'd been. Ursan sniffed me out that first day, and Lieutenant Thea knew I wasn't who I'd claimed to be. I hadn't talked to my sister. Melina was incarcerated at Chinska Mare, so I hadn't fulfilled my promise to Mom.

Grabbing a tray, I ladled a few scoops of stew and took a hunk of bread. We sat by the sergeant's fire. I picked at my food before giving up and setting it aside. The others debated and gossiped. Their voices flowed around me, but I didn't listen. From the corner of my eye, I noticed Ursan glancing at me, but I wouldn't meet his gaze. Instead, I drew pictures in the dirt with a stick.

I wondered if Belen and the guys were discussing strategy, or my rise from the grave, or something random.

"...Irina? ...Sergeant Irina!"

"Huh?" I looked up.

Odd crouched next to me. "What's wrong?"

"Nothing."

"Uh-huh."

"What do you want?" I asked.

"For you to stop scowling at the ground. Although your picture of leaves is quite...nice," Odd said.

"They're hands." Useless hands.

"Oh…yes, now I see," he lied.

I gave him my best Kerrick stare. "What do you want?"

"My squad is up for training tomorrow. Do you want to schedule the drills for the afternoon?"

Major Granvil had given us the afternoon off. All of a sudden I knew exactly what I needed to do, and what I had been avoiding all this time became clear. "How about we drill in the morning with the jacks?"

"That's fine."

"Good." I stood.

"Where are you going?" Ursan asked me.

"Back to my tent."

"It's early." His suspicion had returned.

I shrugged. "I'm tired." And I had a busy night planned. My back burned with the heat of Ursan's gaze.

When I reached my tent, I cut through to the other side, then slipped under the far wall. Keeping out of sight of the sergeant's fire, I headed to Lieutenant Thea's tent. She wasn't inside, but I found her around another campfire reserved for the officers of Axe Company.

She noticed me standing nearby, and I waved her over.

"What's wrong?" she asked as she joined me.

"Nothing. I just wondered if you talked to Belen about that neck armor."

"No. Major Granvil ordered us not to mention it to anyone."

"Where is it?" I asked.

"In the major's tent. You're not planning anything stupid. Right, Sergeant?"

"You know I'm not really a sergeant."

"You've proven yourself, *Sergeant*."

I smiled. "That's nice to hear. However, my past has caught up to me and soon everyone will know. It's inevitable."

"Should I prepare to cover my ass?"

I laughed. "No. I'm the only one who'll be in trouble."

"What kind of trouble?"

My smile faded. I'd become a target for Jael and Tohon. Scanning the camp, I realized I wasn't the only one. Once the war started, all these soldiers would be targets, as well.

"Irina?"

"Nothing bad. Minor trouble only."

"So, no midnight jail breaks?" she asked with a hint of a smile.

"Not yet."

Thea grinned. It was nice to finally crack her serious demeanor. Too bad I hadn't been joking. She returned to the fire, and I spotted Major Granvil talking to one of his captains. Now or never.

Taking a circuitous route, I approached Granvil's tent from the rear. I lifted the fabric and crawled inside. The walls glowed with the firelight from outside, but there was just enough light for me to see a tall man standing in the middle of the tent as if he waited for me.

"Ursan," I said.

He held the neck armor up. "Looking for this?"

KERRICK

"I can't leave you and Alga unprotected," Kerrick said for the twentieth time.

"We'll be fine, Kerry." Unperturbed, Great-Aunt Yasmin sipped her tea as if they'd been discussing the weather.

After he had talked with General Zamiel, he had spent the rest of the day trying to figure out a way to deal with the tribes without leaving Alga vulnerable. But he'd come up with nothing. Great-Aunt Yasmin had finally dragged him out of his father's office to eat a very late supper.

"You can't do both," she said. "Go lead your army north to fight the tribes." She tapped a finger on the table. "Take General Zamiel, but leave Izak. He's been doing so well."

"Well?" He sputtered. "He—"

"None of that, Kerry. He protected our people. If Izak didn't make that deal, what do you think Tohon would have done?"

Taken the town by force, killed anyone who resisted, and turned the dead into his soldiers. Kerrick wilted under her stern gaze. "I'd rather leave you in charge."

"That's sweet of you, but I think Izak is the better choice."

"I'll agree on one condition," he said.

She straightened. "Go on."

"That he obtains approval from you on all future decisions."

"But, I've got—"

"One foot and four toes in the grave, I know. Doesn't matter."

"Oh, all right, Kerry. I'll sit in as an adviser. Happy now?"

"No."

"What would make you happy?"

"For the fighting to stop, for the tribes to turn around and go home." He shook his head. "It's impossible."

She snapped her fingers at him. "Boo-hooing will not help you. If you think it's impossible, then it will be. Go." She shooed. "Make the impossible possible."

"Yes, ma'am." He kissed her on the forehead before leaving. Ever since he was little, he knew to never argue with Great-Aunt Yasmin.

"No," Kerrick said early the next morning. "It's too dangerous."

"What if Tohon returns?" Danny asked.

"He won't harm you or Zila. You're too important to him. But the tribal warriors don't care who you are, and they have no qualms over killing children."

Danny remained stubborn. "But—"

"No more discussion. You and Zila will stay here with Berna. My brother, Izak, has promised to play chess with you."

"But—"

"I didn't come here to argue with you," he said. "I came to say goodbye. Where's Zila?"

Danny gestured. "She's under the bed."

Kerrick suppressed his impatience. He knelt next to the bed and raised the edge of the quilt. "Zila, please come out."

"Not until you agree to let us come," she said.

"All right, then stay there." He dropped the quilt and sat

on the floor, resting his back against the mattress. He rubbed his face. Three hours wasn't enough sleep, but he needed to get his troops on the road. Time to try another tactic.

"Too bad it's too dark under there to read," he said.

He heard her scootch closer.

"Are there books here?" she asked.

"Just a few thousand or so. Our library has two floors full of shelves and these big soft armchairs that are perfect for reading."

Zila peeked out. Dust bunnies clung to her hair. "Where is it?"

"It's hard to find, but I can show you."

She slid out. "Can we go now?"

"Sure." Kerrick stood and took her hand.

Danny followed them downstairs to the library. Zila squealed and ran around the shelves. Kerrick hadn't been lying about the place. His father had loved books, and he couldn't remember a time where his father hadn't collected them. They even had a printing press.

Grief pulsed in his chest. He missed his father as much today as he had four years ago when King Neil had succumbed to the plague. Kerrick's mother had never seemed to have time for him or his brother, preferring to spend all her time with his sister, Rae. And Rae had pretty much ignored her older brothers. He never really knew her.

Kerrick scanned the library, remembering many late nights spent here with his father. At least Zila and Danny could enjoy it. And he'd show Zila his father's prized possession—the printing press—if he returned.

Standing next to him, Danny crossed his arms. "Well played. Zila won't think about you until you're long gone."

"Did you see the chess set in the corner?" Kerrick asked.

"I'm not falling for it."

"The black pieces have been carved from obsidian, and the white from milk quartz. The kings wear real gold crowns, and sapphires decorate the queens' tiaras. And the board is marble. The pieces just glide over the surface."

Danny took a step but stopped. "I'm still mad at you."

"And I'm still not letting you come along. You might as well enjoy your stay."

After Danny checked out the chess set and Zila found enough books to keep her occupied for hours, Kerrick said goodbye.

He then met General Zamiel, Great-Aunt Yasmin and Izak in the front courtyard. The general had managed to gather a couple dozen volunteers in a few hours. Not near enough to make a difference, but impressive nonetheless. Kerrick had considered leaving Zamiel behind to protect his family, but he knew the old general would view it as an insult.

Kerrick gave them a few last-minute instructions. "If we can't stop the tribes, I'll send a messenger. As soon as you receive word, gather everyone and head for the main pass. Once you cross over, travel south through Pomyt and find Ryne."

"The whole town?" Izak asked.

"Of course."

"It would take weeks to coordinate."

"You'll only have a few hours, so I strongly suggest you get everyone prepared beforehand."

Izak opened his mouth, but Great-Aunt Yasmin put her hand on his arm, stopping him.

"Consider the alternative," she said.

Kerrick didn't trust Izak's ability to imagine how bad it would be. His brother tended to be too optimistic. "Izak, our chances of success are little to none. The smartest thing you could do is to leave now."

CHAPTER 8

"One more exercise, gentlemen, then you have the afternoon off," I said to the assembled jumping jacks and the Odd Squad. "Jacks, go west, while the odds go east. Wait fifteen minutes, then begin. First team to find Belen wins."

Belen had been training Ryne's troops nearby and agreed to help me with this last drill. The twenty men moved through the forest, disappearing into the thick and wet greenery. It had rained last night but had cleared by morning. The scent of living green, sunshine and moist earth reminded me of Kerrick. Longing and concern for him flared; I hoped I'd see him again.

About five minutes after the men left, Belen turned to me. "Ryne confirmed what you suspected. That neck armor Ursan brought us last night is made of liquid metal and all but impossible to crack." Poppa Bear looked as worried as I felt.

"Does he have a counteroffensive?" I asked.

"Not yet. At least we have some warning of what Tohon's up to."

"But none of Estrid's soldiers believe us. They're in for a very nasty surprise." I shuddered just thinking about those dead soldiers, what would happen when they came... No.

I wasn't going to consider that possibility. I was safe behind Estrid's lines.

"Ryne's working on convincing Estrid. He's sending me and the boys out on a hunting mission tomorrow."

"To capture one of the dead?" Unease churned in my stomach.

"If we can."

"Are the monkeys going?" I asked.

"No. They've been taking their role as Ryne's bodyguards seriously." Belen pretended to be shocked by the idea.

I smiled. "Which boys?"

"Ursan and his jumping jacks."

"Why them and not your squad?" I shouldn't have been surprised. Ursan had said Jael would send him out on a dangerous mission as punishment for failing to assassinate Ryne.

"We're hoping Ursan can sniff out the dead. From a distance, it's hard to tell them apart from the living soldiers. Estrid and Jael agreed, but we only get one chance."

Another unexpected development. Ursan had shared his secret with them. I wondered what else he'd told them last night.

After Ursan had taken the neck armor from Major Granvil's tent, I had chased him down and had demanded to know what he was doing.

"Helping you," he had said. "You never would have found it. And you shouldn't be seen entering Prince Ryne's tent. I'll take this to him and explain where we found it and your theories about it."

"I'm going to be revealed anyway," I'd said. "Why wait?"

"Because I'm being selfish. The longer you are Sergeant Irina, the more soldiers learn a life-saving skill. Once you're known as Healer Avry, you'll be stuck in the infirmary."

"I wouldn't call it being stuck. I enjoy healing. It's what I'm supposed to be doing."

"You will eventually. Besides, Prince Ryne agreed that you should continue. And he's a military genius."

"Gee, that's not what you called him at the sergeant's fire."

"I've changed my mind."

"Super." I'd considered. "I guess a few more days won't hurt. But I'm talking to my sister before I'm outed."

"Fine." He'd turned to go.

"Ursan." I'd grabbed his arm and pointed to the bruises on his neck. "Give me your sword or Belen might throttle first and ask questions later."

"Good idea." Ursan had taken off his scabbard and handed it to me.

"I'll leave it in your tent," I had said, then added, "Thanks."

He had nodded before heading toward Ryne's encampment.

"I'd better go, or they'll accuse me of cheating," Belen said, pulling me from my memories.

"Don't make it impossible to find you. The jacks have the afternoon off."

He grinned. "But I have my reputation to uphold."

"If you go longer than two hours, I won't be here."

"Are you training another squad?"

"Yes." Eventually.

Belen stepped away but paused. "Almost forgot." He removed three round stones from his pocket. "There are yours." Belen dropped Flea's juggling stones into my hands.

"But you knew Flea longer, and—"

"I told you before. They're *your* keepers. So keep them close."

I pressed my hands to my heart. "I will."

After almost two hours of creeping around the forest, one of the jacks discovered Belen. He had fallen asleep, and the young man had literally tripped over him. So much for his reputation.

In high spirits, the jacks left to enjoy their time off. I walked back to camp with Belen and Ursan. They discussed plans for their mission.

Before Belen headed to Ryne's encampment, he said, "Avry, Ryne wants to talk to you this afternoon about how you survived the plague."

I glanced at Ursan. He looked shocked.

Belen noticed my concern. "Ryne says we can trust him."

"Swell." I wasn't sure *I* could trust him, despite his actions last night.

"Did Kerrick help you like he did when you saved my life?"

"It's complicated," I hedged.

"She saved you?" Ursan asked.

"Oh, yeah, a merc stabbed me in the guts a dozen times. And she saved Flea from a Death Lily, and healed Loren's leg, and—"

"Seven times, Belen," I said. "You were only stabbed seven times."

"Oh. It felt like a dozen, but then again I don't have any scars to count."

Most people didn't know that when healers assumed an injury, we took everything. Our skin showed the scars, not theirs. Ursan asked for more details. Belen was happy to provide them in gory detail. I muttered an excuse and left them. Before reporting to Ryne, I had something to take care of.

I was halfway to the POW complex when Ursan caught up with me.

"Shouldn't you be planning the mission with Belen?" I asked.

"Nothing left to plan. Intelligence has pinpointed one of

Tohon's squads in Vyg's sector two as a potential target. We leave at dawn, just like a regular patrol," Ursan said.

"Regular? Are you still denying the true nature of those you're hunting?"

"I'm keeping an open mind."

Ah, progress. "Why aren't you enjoying your afternoon off?" I asked.

"What makes you say I'm not enjoying it?"

"It's hot, humid, and you've no idea where I'm going. Oh." I'd blame my sluggish mind on lack of sleep, but the sticky weather deserved some credit.

"Oh? What does that mean?"

I glanced at him. Was he playing dumb? Hard to tell. "Oh, as in, I realized that you're following me to make sure I'm not reporting to my spymaster before talking to Ryne."

"Spymaster? Wow, and I thought being called sergeant was special. Will you introduce him to me?" Ursan teased.

"No. *She's* shy."

"Too bad."

We walked for a few minutes in silence. But then he asked, "Why don't you call him Prince Ryne?"

"Don't you want to know where we're headed?"

"Nope. I've already guessed."

"Really?"

"Why so doubtful? I figured out what you were doing last night."

I couldn't argue. "He's not my prince."

"Yet you sacrificed your life for him."

"He's needed," I said.

"So are you."

"I can save a few lives, but his tactics will defeat Tohon, saving thousands."

"I think you're overestimating his impact compared to our

army. Every day more troops from our training bases arrive. Every day Tohon waits to attack, we grow stronger."

"And so does Tohon's. When you return from your mission with Belen, we'll talk again."

When we drew closer to the POW complex, Ursan said, "You won't get in. They're on lockdown."

"I just want to take a look around the outside."

"You're not going to find out how they escaped that way."

I huffed. "So you can read minds now?"

"No. Just following the logic. And that's one thing I learned about you. You're logical."

"Okay then, Mr. Genius, tell me how we're going to get inside?"

"We ask nicely." He grinned. "The guard at the gate owes me a favor. So let me do the talking."

We arrived at the main gate to the POW complex. Ursan sweet-talked his way through the entrance and into the biggest building. Long and narrow, it appeared to be a converted barn.

"Sergeant Dena is in her office. Second room on the right," a guard said, waving us inside.

The building had been a sizable stable. The rows of horse stalls had been converted into cells. It was at least twenty degrees hotter in here. Dena's tiny space smelled like leather and appeared to have been a tack room. She scanned a limp paper behind a makeshift desk. Her short, curly brown hair clung to her large sweaty forehead.

"Finally. The repairs are going slow in this heat." It didn't take her long to notice our confusion. "Please tell me you brought fresh workers?"

"No," I said. "Our squads were training in the woods yesterday, and—"

"Ah, hell, sister, I don't need you to piss and moan at me, too. I've gotten enough of that crap from a whole list of officers. I'm sorry your training was ruined. We're making sure it won't happen again."

"I'm not here to complain," I said. "I'm just...curious about how it happened. The timing seemed odd. Wouldn't it have been better for them to escape during the night?"

Dena sighed. "I'm too busy to satisfy your curiosity. Go listen to the camp gossip."

"What if I can provide you with fresh workers? Do you have time for me now?"

"The jacks won't be happy," Ursan said.

"I'm not talking about them," I said to him.

"How many?" Dena asked.

"As many as you need."

Dena studied us as if she couldn't quite figure us out. "Okay, but if no one shows up to help, I'm going straight to your commanding officer." She surged to her feet. "This way."

We followed her through the stable's main walkway. Cells lined each side, and I glanced at the few prisoners who occupied them. Many of the men had rolled their yellow jumpsuits down to their waists. Sweat glistened on their chests, even though they lay on their cots. A few peered at us through the bars.

Meeting their curious gazes, I wondered if I'd recognize any of them. I had spent twenty-six days in Tohon's castle; it was possible I had healed one of them or seen them around his vast complex. There were only a couple women, although I really couldn't be sure because all the prisoners' hair had been shorn.

Aside from mild interest, no one reacted to our presence. I didn't see any familiar faces. Dena led us out into a long training ring behind the barn. Soft dirt cushioned our steps as we headed toward the far left corner where sunlight streamed through the half-burned wall that had been part of the back fence of the complex. The training area woods were just a few steps beyond the breach. A group of ash-smeared soldiers yanked scorched boards from the frame, tossing them onto a pile. They moved slowly in the oppressive heat.

"That's where the prisoners escaped," Dena said. "They had pulled a couple boards loose and snuck out one at a time until one of my guards noticed. Then they ripped off the boards and bolted. It was during their exercise time, which is why they escaped in the daylight. At night, they're locked in their cells."

"Who set the fire?" Ursan asked.

"We don't know. Once my guards sounded the alarm, one of the prisoners must have set fire to the wall. Not all of them had escaped at that time, and those who did, we've recaptured."

I studied the damage. "I'm surprised the whole fence didn't burn down."

"Marisol arrived as soon as she smelled smoke."

"Marisol?" I asked.

"The High Priestess's water mage. There's a lake not far from here, and she quickly extinguished the fire," Dena said. "Thank the creator she was nearby."

Marisol's proximity seemed rather convenient. I shared a glance with Ursan as we headed back to Dena's office.

"How many POWs can you handle?" I asked her.

"This building can house three hundred, and we have three others ready for another two hundred each. We could probably squeeze in a thousand." Dena settled behind her desk. "I need another ten workers to give these guys a break."

"All right," I said, then thanked Dena for her time.

Ursan stayed by my side as I walked south through Ryne's small army. The soldiers watched us with the same curious expressions as the POWs. All of Estrid's forces had been avoiding Ryne's, as if ordered to stay away. I wondered how they would fight together if both armies kept their distance. At least no one would notice me entering Ryne's tent and rush to inform Jael.

"Reporting in to Prince Ryne?" Ursan asked in a neutral tone.

I glanced at him, gauging his mood. He didn't appear to be upset, but he wasn't the easiest to read. "If I can find his tent." They all looked the same—a light green color that blended in with the fields. None of them had guards posted outside the entrance either.

"You don't think he's staying in the manor house with Estrid?"

"He's not the type to live in comfort while his troops camp outside. Do you remember which one is his?"

Ursan pointed to a tent. "Do you want company?"

"No, thanks."

"Still don't trust me?"

"Let's just say I'm still suspicious of this…new side of you." I realized we had switched roles. Interesting.

"Fair enough. I guess time will tell." He headed back to our camp.

I approached the tent Ursan had indicated. No hidden guards tried to block my way. No one challenged me at all. Calling a hello, I waited for an answer.

"Come in," Ryne said, drawing back the flap.

It was a relief getting in out of the sun. I expected the tent to be stuffy, but it was cooler than outside. When my eyes adjusted, I spotted Quain and Loren standing on opposite sides of the entrance. Belen sat at a conference table filled with maps. A narrow cot and chest lined the side wall. Major Granvil's tent looked lavish in comparison to Ryne's.

The monkeys wouldn't return my greeting. I hoped they'd forgive me in time. As I sank into a chair next to Belen, he gave me a bright smile.

"Where have you been?" Belen asked.

"Doing a little reconnaissance," I said, then asked Ryne if he could spare a squad to help with the repairs.

"Of course. It will show Estrid's soldiers we can be useful." Ryne sent Loren to relay his orders. "Why did you check out the POW complex? We already know Jael arranged the escape as a distraction."

"I wanted to see who else might be helping her."

"And?"

"Marisol's timely arrival is suspicious. She could be loyal to Jael, but the camp gossip says Jael has been wanting to shut down the POW camp. So why have Marisol save the structure?"

"Maybe Jael's hoping to use it for something else," Belen said.

"Or Marisol could have been there on Estrid's orders." Ryne sat on the opposite side of the table.

"Which means Estrid had prior knowledge of your assassination and didn't warn you," I said.

No one said anything for a minute.

"We can't trust either of them," Belen said.

"Who says I have?" Ryne asked with an impish grin.

"You did go into the forest for that exercise," I said.

"It was all part of my plan."

"Uh-huh. Right."

Ryne laughed. "Now tell us everything that has happened since we parted company."

It took a while to fill them in on the details of my encounter with the Peace Lily and my life as Sergeant Irina. I did leave out a few personal ones about Kerrick and me. Ryne asked a couple questions during my tale, but when I finished, he leaned back in his chair and stared at the ceiling. I helped myself to a glass of water, soothing my burning throat.

"You know what you need to do next, right?" Ryne asked.

I hadn't before, but after spelling it all out for them the answer was obvious. The realization caused guilt to swell. I'd wasted so much time. "Go collect Peace Lily…serum and experiment with it."

"Why?" Belen asked. "The plague is over."

"Because we might be able to use the substance to revive the dead," I said.

"Like Tohon does?"

"Oh, no. Living and breathing like me."

"How do you know it'll work?"

"I don't. That's why I would need to experiment."

"Isn't that how the plague started? With healers playing around with the Death Lily toxin and losing control," Quain said.

"They were trying to discover a cure for the toxin," I said.

"It doesn't matter what the intentions were or what the logic was behind the decision. What matters is that six million people died." Quain gasped in mock horror, then added with deadly sarcasm, "Unless those six million people are *pretending* to be dead."

KERRICK

Kerrick watched as the long line of his army marched past. The soldiers' loud tread grated on his nerves along with their slow progress. He missed Belen and the others. Missed being responsible for only a small unit. They could have covered twice the ground in the same time. His gaze tracked to the end where the supply wagons and auxiliary personnel were guarded by one of Ryne's elite squads—the remaining six squads had accompanied Ryne. With an army this size, food and supplies were vital. Kerrick couldn't let them be stolen or compromised in any way.

They'd been on the road for two days and covered a scant twenty miles. At this rate, they wouldn't arrive at Krakowa for another eleven days. One benefit to the ruckus of four-hundred-plus soldiers was they'd attracted a few stragglers who joined their ranks. The entire army would have to be quieter when they closed in on Krakowa, which would slow them down even more.

As they'd traveled farther from the Nine Mountains, the terrain smoothed and opened up into flat grasslands. The long blades of grass swayed stiffly in the breeze, filling the air with a dry rasp. No rain meant firm ground perfect for walking, but it also meant limited water. And that led to more problems.

Kerrick clutched the reins tighter. The horse shifted under him but remained in place. Ryne had made it sound so easy. Take half his army and drive the tribes back to the wildlands. He hadn't mentioned the squabbles between personnel, the logistics of feeding everyone and digging latrines in hard sun-cooked earth while fighting off hungry packs of ufas—the living kind, thank the forest.

One of his majors rode toward him. Probably to suggest they stop for the night. Ryne had given him four companies with four majors who bickered worse than Kerrick and his brother. They handled most of the day-to-day drudgery but needed him to make all the key decisions and to mediate all their disagreements. Most of the time Kerrick asked General Zamiel his opinion and the general had quickly turned into his primary adviser.

Each major also rode a horse. Kerrick had argued with Ryne against bringing horses. Too noisy. However, he had to admit they made communication between him and the majors easier and faster.

"Prince Kerrick," Major Sondra called. "The scouts have returned."

Finally. He spurred his mount and followed the major to the front of the column. Half his squad had been sent to collect information on the tribes right after Ryne had received the news of the attack. They had been trained by Kerrick, and he'd picked the best for the mission, but he'd worried over their lack of experience.

He spotted the scouts walking their sweaty horses. Counting heads, Kerrick felt a moment of relief. All four had survived. They appeared tired. Dust coated their fatigues and hair.

As soon as he dismounted, Sergeant Jave and the others snapped to attention.

"Relax, gentlemen," Kerrick said, then caught his mistake. "Sorry, Cerise."

She waved off his apology. Once she had realized he treated everyone in his squad the same, she had stopped correcting him.

"Report," he said to Jave.

The sergeant opened his mouth but then closed it as if uncertain where to start.

"Most important first."

"Yes, sir. We confirmed that the tribes have invaded Krakowa, and we have ascertained there are approximately twelve hundred camped around the city's boundaries."

Hell. "All warriors?"

"No, sir. It appeared to be the entire tribe, including children."

Interesting. "Did you see any survivors?"

"Yes. Three days after we left Prince Ryne's, we encountered a number of refugees, traveling south."

"Did you talk to them?"

"Yes. The fleeing citizens told us they had a few hours' warning so they left with what they could carry before the tribes reached the city. We didn't see anyone else after the fifth day."

Not a surprise. "What about within the city? Are there survivors there?"

"We were unable to pierce their outer encampments. But we did loop around them. And, sir…" Jave hesitated.

"Go on."

"There are more tribes arriving. We spotted a line of campfires stretching to the north."

Kerrick kept his emotions in check even though fear washed through him. His army was already outnumbered. "Anything else?"

"Yes. When we returned for our horses, we saw evidence that a large force had passed through the forest south of Krakowa."

"More refugees?" He hoped.

"No. We caught up to them. The tribes are spreading south, heading this way."

Kerrick cursed. What about "most important first" hadn't the sergeant understood? He pressed his balled fists against his thighs to prevent him from shaking the man. After he had lost his temper and hit Avry, he had vowed never to do it again. To anyone. Well, except the enemy. And Tohon. It would be pure joy to feel his fist connect with that man's jaw. But that was a fight for another day.

"How many are coming?" Kerrick asked.

"About a thousand. And they're all warriors."

"How far away are they?"

"Right now, they're about a day from Krakowa. They're moving slowly, as if feeling their way. I'd say about six to eight miles a day. The woods are pretty thick."

"Horses?"

"No."

Finally, one bit of good news. Kerrick calculated the distance and amount of time his army needed to travel in order to meet up with the advancing tribes in the forest that stretched about fifty miles south of the city. Once the warriors reached the grass plains, then Kerrick's smaller force had no chance of stopping them.

With this ungainly group, even if they doubled their speed and increased the number of hours marching, it would be impossible. However, if he split the army into four units, traveling independently, it just might work.

Kerrick called a stop for the night and met with Zamiel and the majors. For once, they all agreed with his plan. They would split the supplies four ways. Two companies would travel wide into flanking positions. The other two would head straight north. Kerrick would scout ahead with his squad and send runners back to each unit to report the tribes' location and a point of engagement.

In the morning, it didn't take long to organize the companies, but there were issues with the division of supplies. Kerrick ordered General Zamiel to handle it. He could be counted on to remain impartial and fair.

He was going over a few last-minute instructions with his majors when Cerise arrived. She waited until he finished before approaching him.

"Problem?" he asked.

"Yes. We found…something in the supply wagons."

"Just spit it out. It can't be any worse than the news you brought me yesterday."

"Uh…" Cerise gestured.

Sergeant Jave dragged two struggling figures closer. Danny and Zila stopped fighting when they met Kerrick's gaze.

"I stand corrected," he said.

CHAPTER 9

"You can't go alone," Ryne said, sounding rather annoyingly like Kerrick. "There've been reports of clashes with Tohon's troops to the southwest."

"I don't want anyone to see me get swallowed by a giant lily. That'll set off too many questions that I'd like to avoid answering," I said.

We sat on opposite sides of his conference table inside his tent. I had Dagger Company's squads practicing the silent training in the forest and had left Sergeant Odd in charge of the afternoon sessions. His Odd Squad trained as much as possible. They were determined to improve in order to jackknife the jumping jacks. With an evil gleam in his eyes, Odd had called it a little payback.

"Then take a few soldiers you can trust," Ryne said.

From his post by the entrance, Quain snorted with derision and muttered, "That rules out everyone here."

I ignored him. "Belen left yesterday with Ursan and the jacks." They were hunting the dead. A shiver brushed my spine.

"What about your lieutenant and a couple of the other sergeants in your platoon?" Ryne asked.

I considered confiding in Thea, Wynn and Liv. Thea already knew enough to guess, and my roommates had suspected I wasn't quite what I'd claimed from the beginning. "All right. I'll talk to my LT."

"The sooner the better," he said. "It would be best if you returned before Belen."

"You're that confident he'll succeed?"

"He hasn't failed me or Kerrick yet."

Or me. I rubbed my stomach. He had stayed between me and the mercs long enough for Kerrick and the others to get into position, sacrificing his life to save me from capture.

"Why should I be back first?" I asked.

"Once Estrid sees the truth of Tohon's depravity, one of three things will happen. She'll either order it decapitated immediately, claiming it's a one-of-a-kind abomination, or she'll cover it up, ordering Ursan to keep it quiet until she can determine exactly what it is, or she'll be smart and involve her top military aides right away and prepare her army for what they'll be facing."

"Doesn't she trust your word?"

"No." He smiled. "And she shouldn't."

"I'm not going to ask." Pushing from the table, I stood. "I'll report back when I'm leaving."

Ryne stopped me when I reached the flaps.

"There's a fourth possibility," he called.

Turning, I waited.

He stared at the wall of the tent as if he could see through the fabric.

"And?"

"That Tohon learns of Belen's mission and launches his attack before we have a chance to find a way to stop his dead."

I found Thea conferring with another lieutenant outside Major Granvil's tent. When she finished, she gestured for me to join her as she headed to the training area.

"Problem?" she asked.

"Do you know the true nature of Ursan and Belen's mission?" I asked.

She gave me a slight nod, looking not at all surprised by my question. "Sergeant Ursan has kept me informed."

"About everything?"

Keeping her voice pitched low, she said, "Yes, Avry. About everything."

Suddenly a few things made sense. Estrid had known about the assassination attempt beforehand. But her failure to warn Ryne meant she either didn't want to tip her hand to Jael, or she didn't trust Ryne. Or both.

I decided it would be best for me to stay out of the political intrigue and focus on my own tasks. At least I didn't have to explain as much to Thea. Taking a deep breath, I made my request.

She remained quiet for so long, I worried she hadn't understood how important this mission was.

"I know you don't believe they exist, but—"

"That's not it," she said. "Wynn and Liv are too chatty. They can't be trusted to keep such juicy gossip to themselves. I think it should be me, you and Sergeant Saul."

"Saul? But he hardly says a word."

"Exactly." She paused when we reached the training area. "When do you want to leave?"

"Tomorrow morning."

"What about the silent training?"

"Sergeant Odd can cover for me."

"Have you cleared this with Major Granvil?"

Oops. I'd forgotten he needed to be informed. "Uh… Not yet."

"I'll take care of it. Find Saul, explain to him what we plan

to do. Then both of you meet me in my tent right after supper. We'll finalize the details of our mission."

Thea hadn't wasted any time in taking charge.

"Lieutenant, I'm happy to follow orders while we're en
route, but once we find the Lilys—"

"Then they're all yours, Sergeant." She waved me off.

I waited until Saul and his squad had finished with their
hand-to-hand-combat drills before approaching him. While
his soldiers returned to their tents, he stood next to the water
barrel. Removing his shirt, he poured water over his head
and upper body, washing away the sweat and dirt. His long
lean muscles were the source of his wiry strength. He also
had the fastest reflexes of all the sergeants in Thea's platoon,
even though he was the oldest at—my guess—close to forty.

Toweling off, he met my gaze. His light blue eyes studied
me with mild curiosity. He gestured, prompting me to explain. I filled him in about the search for Peace Lilys. If he
found the task strange or odd, he didn't show it.

"We're to meet with the LT after supper," I said.

"All right," Saul said.

I couldn't resist asking, "Aren't you curious why we're
going?"

"I'm to protect you. Correct?"

"Basically."

"That's all I need." He smiled.

Later in the lieutenant's tent, Saul surprised us both by un-
folding a map of the area. Despite his apparent lack of interest, he had brought the locations of all the Lilys surrounding
Estrid's army and Zabin.

"This is a classified document. Did you steal this from
Major Piran?" Thea asked Saul.

"I borrowed it, sir."

"Isn't this vital information?" I asked.

"The location of the ones in Vyg are the most important," Thea said. "And every one of our patrols has memorized them all by now."

I examined the map. "This will speed things up considerably."

"We had to make a series of maps as we marched across Pomyt. We lost too many scouts to the Death Lilys," Thea said. She tapped one of the red marks. "Although this doesn't tell us if it's a Peace or Death Lily or how many of them are there."

"That's fine. We'll figure it out once we get there."

"We?" Saul asked.

Both he and Thea looked at me as if I'd gone crazy. "*I'll* figure it out. Okay?"

"Better," Thea agreed.

After we finalized our plans, Saul and I left. He headed to our fire.

When I didn't follow him, he stopped. "Coming?"

"I'll be there in a bit. I've a few things to do."

He nodded and continued. Saul was going to be an easy traveling companion. Ursan would have questioned me, demanding to know what *things,* or just following me. In this case, it wasn't any of his business. I'd put if off too long. I needed to finally do what I'd come here to do.

I watched Jael's tent. It didn't take long for Noelle to leave, running an errand for the general. Following her, I waited for the opportunity to confront her. She kept busy, fetching officers, delivering orders and bringing a tray of food. Every third or fourth time, she'd remain inside the tent longer than a few minutes.

About to give up for the night, I caught movement near the entrance. Noelle headed back to the mess tent. This time she took the food in the opposite direction. I scrambled to keep up as she wove through the camp. Then she slipped between tents, disappearing from view. Dashing after her, I entered the same gap and stopped. The opening led to a secluded spot behind a row of officers' quarters. Moonlight illuminated the space.

Noelle plopped on the ground as if exhausted. I debated. Should I wait until she finished eating? Or approach her now?

"Why are you following me, Sergeant Irina?" she asked.

My heart swelled a bit with pride—she could spot a tail. I stepped from the shadows. "I've been wanting to talk to you, but you're always so busy."

Noelle speared a piece of meat with her fork. "The general's preparing for war. It's not a good time for idle chatter." Her tone implied this wasn't a good time either.

Too bad. "And once Tohon attacks, it's not going to get any better."

"You have five minutes." She scraped her teeth on the fork's tines.

The metallic screech cut right through me as it had the thousand times when we were growing up. I shuddered.

Setting her tray aside, she surged to her feet. "I should have known. You'd never sacrifice your life for another. You're incapable of bravery."

So much for the happy reunion. I had expected this to be difficult, but there had been a tiny bit of hope that she'd forgiven me.

She gestured to my uniform. "And you've been hiding in plain sight. Neat trick. Did you do that when Mom and Allyn were sick? Spying on us until they died? Waiting until I left town before making your presence known to the neighbors?"

"No. I explained it all—"

"In your letter, I know. It doesn't matter. As soon as you

learned about the plague, you should have come straight home to check on us. Family first, Avry."

"You're right. I messed up, Noelle. I made a horrible, self-ish mistake. I'm sorry."

She crossed her arms. "Sorry doesn't cut it."

"Then what can I do to atone for my actions?"

"Contract the plague and die a horrible, painful death." Her tone was nasty.

"Done that. What's next?"

"You're such a liar." Noelle swept past me.

I grabbed her wrist and spun her around to face me. "I have *never* lied to you."

She pointed to the stripes on my sleeve. "What do you call this, *Sergeant?* I'd say impersonating a soldier is lying."

"I meant the real *you,* Noelle. Not Jael's lackey. I've never deceived my little shadow."

Yanking her wrist from my grip, she said, "That person is long gone. She died during the plague. A good thing, too. She was weak and pathetic, begging for help, crying nonstop for days, letting the street rats take advantage of her, hoping to find a friendly...anything. She learned that in order to sur-vive, she needed to kill her old self. To become the complete opposite. And I don't fall for anyone's tricks." She gestured to me. "Besides, I'm going to tell Jael about you. So you should run as far away from here as fast as possible."

"Not going to happen. I'm done running and hiding. When I return from my mission, everyone will know who I am."

"Then Jael will kill you."

I shook my head. "I don't think so. And I'm not afraid of her." Which was true. After Tohon, no one scared me.

Noelle failed to look convinced.

"What else can I do?" I asked.

"Leave me alone."

"No."

"Then I'll kill you." She pulled a dagger from her belt and brandished it. "I call this my little shadow. It kept me alive more than once."

"You'll have to hit a vital organ or a major artery," I warned. "Otherwise I'll heal."

"I've treated the blade with a fast-acting poison."

More impressed than frightened, I shifted my weight to the balls of my feet. When she lunged, I twisted to the side and caught her wrist, trapping her arm against my body. My fingers touched her skin.

"Noelle, stop."

"Or what? You'll hurt me?"

"I can."

"But you won't because you're trying to make amends," she mocked.

"No. I won't because I will *never* hurt you again." I let her go and held my hands out to the side.

"You're not going to give up, are you?"

"No. Because the old Noelle isn't dead. Far from it. She's hiding inside and I plan to coax her out."

"Don't bother." She stabbed her blade into my stomach. Caught off guard, I stumbled back.

Keeping her hand on the hilt, she stayed with me. "How about now? Give up?"

Despite the burning pain eating through my guts, I met her gaze. "No."

For just a second, the old Noelle gazed back. But she pressed her lips together. Yanking the weapon out, she wiped the blade on my shirt. "Next time it *will* be coated with poison. Stay away from me."

"Not going...to...happen," I puffed.

She paused, opened her mouth but snapped it shut. Without glancing back, she left.

Wrapping my arms around my waist, I sank to my knees. Blood soon soaked my sleeves as the world spun around me. Pain clawed at my insides. Sweat dripped and stung my eyes. I huddled on the ground.

My emotions seesawed. Her attack felt more like a reaction to fear than of malicious intent. Fear that I might break through her defenses and she'd start to forgive me. Hating me was easier than forgiving me. I remembered my own hatred when Kerrick had backhanded me. Even after his apology and promise never to do it again, I couldn't trust him. It took time and courage to change my mind.

I decided to view my encounter with Noelle as a positive step. Next time would be better. And I would be prepared for anything, including a poison-tipped dagger. Unless Jael got to me first.

Eventually the pain lessened. I lurched to my feet and returned to my tent well after midnight. Snores emanated from Wynn's and Liv's cots. Fumbling around in the dark, I removed my bloodstained uniform and stuffed it into the bottom of my locker. The wound still oozed, so I wrapped a bandage around my waist before donning my nightclothes. Weak from blood loss and healing, I collapsed onto my cot.

Saul woke me the next morning. Disoriented, I squinted into the brightness. Liv and Wynn were gone. Remembering the mission, I jumped out of bed. I'd overslept! A wave of dizziness sat me back down.

"Are you—"

I waved off Saul's concern. "Give me a minute."

"The lieutenant's waiting."

And probably pissed. "Tell her I'll be right out."

When Saul left, I changed. The cut had sealed shut, but the skin remained red, swollen and tender to the touch. With stiff movements, I packed my bag and slung it over my shoulder.

Thea and Saul stood outside my tent.

"This isn't a promising start to our mission, Sergeant," she said.

"Sorry. I had an upset stomach last night and didn't sleep well."

"I trust you're feeling better?"

"Yes, sir."

"Good. Let's go. We're burning daylight." She headed north, setting a brisk pace.

Saul fell into step beside me. "Problem?"

"Not at the moment." Which was the truth. After being in one place for close to fifty days, the thought of hiking through the forest for a few days energized my steps.

Even though we hadn't discussed it, we all went silent once we entered the woods. Saul and his squad had also caught on quick to the training. No surprise since they had already been a quiet group. Interesting how the ten soldiers within a group all matched personalities with their sergeant. Did the assigning officer do it on purpose, or did the men and women change as they worked with a certain group? I'd have to ask Thea later.

During the day, we encountered a few patrols. We slipped by a couple, but most heard us. Thea needed more practice. However, once they ascertained our friendly status, they moved on.

We stopped for the night before full darkness. No sense stumbling around in the dark, setting up camp. Saul collected firewood while Thea and I built a stone ring to contain the fire. The season had been drier than normal, and the clearing we picked was small.

After we started a little fire, we attracted two different patrols, checking for unfriendlies.

"Shouldn't they be patrolling in Vyg?" I asked Thea.

She had insisted on cooking and was hunched over the pot. "We've plenty of soldiers in Vyg. They're also patrolling east and south of Zabin. We can't let Tohon's army come in from behind."

"Why is Tohon waiting to attack?"

"I've no idea. According to our intel, he has the men and resources. But once he reached the middle of Vyg, he stopped."

"Sector five," Saul said.

Where the liquid metal mine was located. He needed it to protect his dead troops. But shouldn't he have enough by now?

"That was months ago. Why doesn't Estrid take the initiative?" I asked.

"The High Priestess doesn't want all-out war," Thea said.

Right. She'd rather "claim" towns and villages in the name of peace where there was no resistance—just people trying to survive.

"Whatever his reasons, it's good for us," Thea said.

I let the subject drop, and we chatted about mundane things. Thea was born in Casis Realm.

"Compared to the warrior priests back home, the High Priestess's rules are minor annoyances," Thea said. "I think we're the only realm that actually benefited from the plague."

Surprised by her comment, I asked, "But the plague killed so many. Surely you lost family and friends."

She stared at the fire. "Probably. I was taken from my family when I was four to be raised by the priests. Training and lessons dominated my life. I had no time for friends."

Saul looked impressed. "Assassin?"

A smile flickered. "Scared?"

"Only if you say yes."

"Not an assassin," I answered for her.

"Why do you say that?" Thea asked.

"You're too noisy in the forest."

Another rare smile. "You're right. I was training to be a bodyguard for the cardinals."

"That's still impressive," Saul said.

She shrugged. "I didn't finish, but I've learned a few tricks."

"Handy," I said.

"It keeps the gentlemen callers away."

I laughed while Saul looked confused. "How did you end up in Estrid's army?"

"Someone needs to bring the survivors together. I'd thought I'd lend a hand."

We asked Saul about his past, but he was reluctant to share anything besides the fact he was born in Tobory.

When it grew late, I stood, stretched and smoothed out my bedroll. "Should we set a watch?" I asked Thea.

"Yes. Take the first shift. Wake Saul in two hours, and I'll go last," Thea said.

"All right." I checked my belt, making sure my knives were secured, then scanned the forest for a good spot.

"Why do you do that?" Saul asked.

"I'm looking for—"

"Not that." He pointed at my hand. "Touching the leaves."

Without thinking, I had grabbed a bush, hoping to feel Kerrick's magic. How to explain it? "I'm seeking a connection."

"To the forest?" Saul asked.

"Yes."

He accepted it without asking further questions. Saul and Thea settled in for the night, and I made a sweep around our camp, checking for intruders before I found a location to watch and listen.

Once again I fingered a leaf. No tingle vibrated through

my fingers. I hadn't lied to Saul. To me, connecting to the forest meant linking to Kerrick. Loneliness etched a familiar groove into my heart. Worry for Kerrick flared along with the real possibility that I'd never see him again.

We found the first clump of Lilys the next day. Four giant white flowers grew between two massive oak trees. I sniffed the air. The scent of honey and lemons dominated. I wouldn't pick up the slighter scents of anise or vanilla until I was closer.

I removed my pack and handed it to Saul. His queasy expression matched Thea's. Even though I explained to them about my immunity to the Death Lily toxin, they hadn't truly believed me. Approaching a Lily went against a lifetime of avoidance and fear.

"Relax," I said. "This shouldn't take long."

I walked toward the flowers, and the clean smell of vanilla greeted me. All four were Peace Lilys. Perfect.

When I reached the base of the closest flower, I placed my hands on a thick petal, hoping it would recognize or remember me. The plants' roots were all connected. But nothing happened. I tried the next one, then the other two. Same thing. Nothing.

"Now what?" Thea asked.

"We try another set," I said.

We consulted Saul's borrowed map and headed farther north to a clump. Again, it contained all Peace Lilys. Again, they refused to open or acknowledge me.

"Should we return?" Thea asked.

"No. We need to locate a Death Lily so I can find out what's going on."

Saul and Thea exchanged a glance. One of those she-lost-her-mind-and-should-we-humor-her? looks.

"You can go back," I said. "There is one Death Lily for every hundred Peace Lilys, so it might take a while."

They stayed with me. We found one the next day in a clump of Lilys northeast of Zabin. The Death Lily hissed when I approached. Its petals opened as its vines reached for me. Large seed pods hung below its fibrous leaves. Knives and swords couldn't cut through any part of the plant, but I wondered if a weapon made of liquid metal could.

The speed of the Lily still surprised me, even after being snatched a number of times. Softness scooped me up, then instant blackness as the petals clamped shut. I braced for either pricks in my arms or for it to spit me out.

Last time I'd been in a Death Lily, it had rejected me, claiming I tasted bad. I'd been in the last stage of the plague and had hoped it would take away my pain.

However, this time two sharp thorns pierced my upper arms as the Lily shot its toxin into me. Peace flowed over me, and my consciousness floated from my body, along the plant's roots and into its soul. Through this connection, not only was I able to see outside the Lily, but I felt its emotions and basic thoughts, as well.

Recognition and joy emanated from the plant. Also approval over my new taste. From my encounters with the Lilys, I sensed the Death Lilys and Peace Lilys were two separate beings spread over multiple plants.

I inquired about the Peace Lilys, asking why they wouldn't open for me. *I need its sacks,* I thought. *It's important.*

It didn't know, but it showed me a cluster of Lilys west of our location, urging me to go there.

Why?

Find what you need.

And before it could expel me, I asked why the Peace Lily saved my life when I'd died from the plague.

No save.

Yes, it did. Why?

Instead of answering, the Lily removed the thorns. My awareness snapped back into my body as it dumped me onto the ground. Feeling heavy and awkward, I remained there for a minute. Once I recovered from the transition, I realized I held two orange sacks in my hands.

The Death Lily had given me its deadly toxin. I'd no idea why. The soft round casing of the sack was durable, and I could squeeze it without popping it. Tohon had used a metal needle to extract the poison. He had injected it into children, theorizing that the survivors of the toxin would become healers. His hypothesis had been accurate, but at the deplorable cost of dozens of young lives.

I felt a measure of satisfaction that I'd been able to kill Tohon's Death Lilys, and to rescue the only survivors of Tohon's experiments, Danny and Zila. At least they were safe and sound in Ryne's castle.

I lumbered to my feet and joined Saul and Thea. They'd waited a safe distance away. Saul handed me my pack.

"Well?" Thea asked. "What happened?"

Tucking the sacks into a pocket of my bag, I debated how much to tell them. "It directed me to another cluster west of here. Saul, can I see the map?"

He handed it to me.

"Why there?" Thea asked.

"It believes I'd get a response from a Peace Lily there." I unfolded the map, searching for the spot. There was a mark due west of our location, but it was a few miles over the border in Vyg.

"Did you find it?" Thea asked.

I showed her.

"No can do. Time to go back to camp."

"It's not that far into Vyg. We'll be safe," I said.

"Major Granvil ordered us to stay out of Vyg."

"All right. When we get to the border, I'll go in alone."

"Are you disobeying a direct order, Sergeant?"

"Yes, sir."

She glanced at Saul.

"I'll go in with her," he said.

I sensed her indecision and tried another tactic. "We don't need to tell Major Granvil. I'm sure he'll just be happy that the mission was a success."

"And when we encounter one of Tohon's patrols and are captured or killed?" Thea asked.

"Then violating a direct order won't seem that bad in comparison," I joked.

Saul laughed.

Thea scowled. "I don't think you're fully aware of the danger, Sergeant."

My good humor disappeared. "I'm *well aware* of the consequences, Lieutenant. More than anyone. If this mission wasn't vital, I wouldn't risk our lives."

She stared at me for a moment. "First sign of an enemy patrol—"

"We're out of there," I agreed.

"So you can sneak back?" Saul asked.

"Hush." I slapped him on the arm. This wasn't a good time for him to be chatty.

Thea didn't look happy, but she grabbed the map and took point, heading west.

Once we reached the border with Vyg, we slowed and kept alert for Tohon's troops. We encountered no one from either side. It took us two days to reach the cluster that the Death Lily had indicated. We found them in the late afternoon. There were a number of Lilys bunched together just like the vision the plant had shown me, but there was one Lily that stood apart. It grew between two tree trunks and seemed familiar.

Focusing on the ones I'd seen, I approached them. The scents of anise and vanilla filled the air, indicating three Peace Lilys and one Death. When I reached them, nothing happened. Not even the Death Lily twitched when I touched it. Frustrated, I pulled my stiletto. It had been made from liquid metal and might inflict damage. But I just couldn't bring myself to harm the Lilys.

Instead, I tried the lone Lily. A faint scent of vanilla tickled my nose. Another Peace Lily. Expecting it to remain immobile, I was surprised when it dipped its petals toward me.

Finally! I waited for it to grab me, but it kept bending until the top of the flower brushed the ground. The petals opened and deposited a naked man.

I froze in shock for a moment before kneeling down next to the immobile figure.

Recognition pierced my heart, and I gasped.

Flea lay there. It appeared he'd been perfectly preserved except his clothes had dissolved. His skin was bone-white, and his open eyes were dull and lifeless. Still dead.

Fresh grief swelled. When I closed his eyes, a spark shot through my fingertips. A second later, an ice-cold hand grasped my wrist with surprising strength. I stared at Flea's now open eyes. Had the movement been a reflex? Or had he been turned into one of Tohon's dead? Fear rose as his grip turned painful.

KERRICK

Standing behind a leafy barberry bush, Kerrick watched the warriors. He counted men and noted weapons, seeking weaknesses. The four units of his army were moving into position—two to the south, one to the west and the other east. It had taken them six days, but they had been able to reach the forest in time to set up an ambush. Kerrick had used his forest magic to camouflage his skin and clothes to blend in with the lush foliage so he could spy on them. The living green was irritated by all the intruders—at least eleven hundred by his count.

The pale-skinned warriors wore white cotton sleeveless shirts and baggy white pants. Colorful sashes around their waists kept them from looking like ghosts against the greenery. Even their long hair braided down their backs was pale yellow.

They carried a thick short sword on their hips and had a dagger tucked into their sashes. The sword's two-foot-long blade was oddly shaped. It started out straight but then widened and curved at the bottom. The end looked as if it had been chopped off. He guessed it was a dadao sword. Kerrick had heard about them but had never seen one.

Regardless of the name, it appeared deadly and ideal for close-quarter fighting. Which was surprising considering the tribesmen acted as if they were very uncomfortable with their location. They jumped at every little noise and kept craning their necks to peer up into the treetops.

The wildlands were flat and wide-open. And Kerrick remembered learning that the tribes followed the herds of snow ufas nicknamed snufas as they migrated. A distant cousin of the ufa, the snufa was the size of a bull with long deadly horns and white shaggy hair. The tribes hunted them with spears. Besides eating the meat, they also used their pelts for tents and clothing. Of course, those heavy garments would be useless in this warmer climate.

While the tribesmen had the advantage of numbers, Kerrick's troops had experience with fighting in the woods. He hoped it would be enough.

Kerrick returned to their temporary headquarters near the edge of the forest to consult and coordinate with his four majors one last time. They had erected a small tent for their use.

"The tribesmen will be settling in soon," Kerrick said. "The moon will be just bright enough tonight. When the leaves shake, that'll be my signal to launch the attack. By the time they realize what's going on, we should have the upper hand."

"Uh, Kerrick," Danny said from behind him.

He rounded on the boy. "Shouldn't you be helping feed the soldiers?"

Standing just inside the tent's flaps, Danny swallowed. "We're done. Cold rations take half the time to serve." He held up a handful of beef jerky. "I brought this for you."

"Sorry." Kerrick took the jerky and studied the boy.

Danny and Zila had been helping with the cooking in Major Sondra's unit since they'd been discovered. Although Kerrick had wanted to send them back to Orel immediately, he couldn't spare the men and horses at that time. However, tonight they would be sitting on a horse along with two guards at a safe distance away from the fighting. If Kerrick's army failed, he would signal them and they would take off to warn Izak.

"What do you need?" Kerrick asked him when he didn't leave. Despite disobeying him, Danny had proven useful these past six days. Danny reminded him of Avry—a good and bad thing.

"Shouldn't you make sure the tribesmen plan to attack us? Maybe they're not looking for war, but for food or warmth."

Major Volker snorted with amusement. "The tribesmen are always looking for war, son."

"But that was *before* the plague. Maybe they changed."

Volker gave Kerrick a pointed glare. Kerrick didn't like the stout man but did admire his military savvy. He was about to explain to Danny the reasons for the ambush, when he reconsidered.

Instead he asked, "What are you suggesting?"

"That we send in someone with a white flag of truce and find out what they're doing here," Danny said.

"Ridiculous," Volker said.

"If they're here to fight, then we lose the element of surprise. It's our biggest advantage," Kerrick said.

"So you're just going to kill them without learning more? What if they're here for another reason?" Danny asked.

"The tribes don't travel south unless they're on the warpath, son. Our history books are filled with their heinous acts," Volker said in a condescending tone.

"Sometimes history books are wrong." Danny appealed to Kerrick. "Look at what everyone said about the healers refusing to heal those with the plague, but it turned out to be all wrong."

And that did it. Kerrick had been about to agree with Volker, but Danny made a valid point.

"If the army is already in the attack position, we can react right away if the response to our flag of truce is negative," General Zamiel said.

Kerrick agreed, despite knowing the majors wouldn't be happy at all.

Striding toward the warriors' camp, Kerrick wasn't happy about the situation either. If, by some miracle, Danny had been right and the tribes weren't on the warpath, then this encounter would save many lives. It was worth the effort.

Even though the majors wanted to send one of the soldiers, Kerrick volunteered to go. It made the most sense. After all, he could use his forest magic to escape, but not his sword. He'd left it nearby, tied to a vine so he could retrieve it from a distance with his magic.

The forest's displeasure over the sheer number of intruders hummed in Kerrick's veins. Through his connection with the living green, he sensed the locations of all those irritants. At least his army had reached their positions with only minor rustling. They waited for his signal.

Now or never, he thought. The tribesmen had settled down for the night. Holding a white handkerchief in his right hand, he approached the outer guards. Kerrick stopped when two of the warriors spotted him. He spread his arms wide, showing them he was unarmed.

They pulled their swords and scanned the forest behind him. The man on the left yelled a warning, and soon Kerrick was surrounded by six armed warriors. More shouts and loud crunchings meant the rest of the warriors were being roused. Uneasy, Kerrick sent his magic into the vines growing near their feet and into a tree with a broken limb just in case.

He waved the handkerchief. "I'd like to speak with your leader."

His circle of guards escorted him to a tall muscular man. Kerrick hadn't noticed how slight the others were until he met their leader. The man rested his hand on the hilt of his dadao. The blade seemed longer than the ones carried by the others. Ice-blue eyes stared at him with such coldness, Kerrick felt a chill brush his skin.

"Who are you?" the leader asked in a thick accent.

"I'm Kerrick of Alga Realm. And you?"

"Noak. Why are you here?"

"To ask you the same thing."

"You cannot stop us."

Kerrick ignored that. "You don't belong here."

Noak's expression didn't change, but Kerrick's heart filled with an icy dread.

"No one here now. You all...gone."

"Not all. Our people fled when you arrived," Kerrick said.

The leader huffed. "Not like before."

"A sickness has taken many, but those that remain—"

He waved. "Ours now."

"No, it isn't. However, we might be able to work something out. To share—"

"No. We stay. You die." Noak gestured.

The warrior to Kerrick's right swung his dadao. Kerrick dropped to the ground. Pulling magic, he blended with the forest floor, then sent the limb crashing down nearby. The slight distraction allowed him to encourage the vines to tangle around the warriors' ankles and yank them off their feet. Then he shook all the leaves nearby, signaling his waiting army.

Keeping the surrounding warriors off balance, Kerrick heard his men approach and doubled his efforts. He just needed to survive a few more minutes. Kerrick snaked along the ground, remaining on his stomach.

Just when he grasped his sword, a pair of white snufa-skinned boots blocked Kerrick's way. He glanced up and met the leader's cold gaze. The man could see him despite his camouflage. And his big sword was pointed at Kerrick's throat.

CHAPTER 10

Flea met my questioning gaze. His light green eyes crazed with confusion and alarm. But most important, life shone from them. He hadn't been turned into one of the dead. I released the breath I'd been holding as joy filled me.

"Wh—" croaked from his unused vocal cords. "Who?" He looked over my shoulder. He squeaked, dropped my arm and scooted away in panic. He was going to bolt.

"Back off," I said to Thea and Saul as I dove for Flea, tackling him. I sat on his chest and grabbed his bare shoulders. "Flea, it's me. Avry."

"No." He struggled.

"Stop or I'll zap you with my healing powers."

He paused, and I hurried to continue. "I taught you how to juggle."

"You don't look—"

"I'm wearing a disguise."

"No." Shaking his head, he muscled me off and tried to stand.

Loath to cause him pain, I clung to his waist and dragged him back to the ground. "Kerrick and Belen rescued you from the stockade."

He hesitated.

"Kerrick gave you the name Flea because you're fast and hard to catch," I said.

Confusion still swirled in his gaze.

"Belen calls Loren and Quain the monkeys."

Flea yanked my shirt sleeve down, revealing my healer tattoo on my right shoulder—a circle with hands radiating out so that they resembled the petals of a daisy from a distance.

Instead of relaxing, his agitation increased. "Jael!" He scrambled to his feet and scanned the area.

"She's not here. We fought her off." *And you died*—but I wasn't going to add to his distress right now. I stood, brushing dirt off my pants.

"Where's Kerrick? Who are they?"

"Thea and Saul. They're with me."

"What's—" He finally noticed his lack of clothing. Color flushed through him, and he covered himself with his hands. "What's going on!"

I glanced back. "Saul?"

"On it." Saul dug through his backpack and pulled out a pair of pants. The sergeant approached Flea as if the boy could jump as high and as fast as his namesake.

Thea and I turned our backs, giving Flea some privacy. The bright daylight had faded, and it would be dark soon.

"Now what?" Thea asked me.

I considered. Flea needed a few hours to adjust and hot food. His ribs protruded farther than his shrunken stomach. Calling him skeletal would be an understatement.

"Okay," Saul said.

Flea wore Saul's extra set of fatigues. I bit my lip to keep from smiling at how much the uniform's sleeves and pant legs had been rolled up. A belt cinched tight kept his pants from falling down. The extra material was bunched around Flea's waist. The desire to hug him bloomed in my chest, but I kept firm control of my emotions. Flea still acted shaky and uncertain.

Searching my memories, I recalled the cave we had stayed in the night after we'd given Flea to the Lily. It was a couple miles away from here. Stricken with grief at that time, no one had any energy to travel far. I was surprised I even remembered the way since I had shuffled behind Kerrick with tears blurring my vision.

I suggested we overnight in the cavern, so we could build a fire without risk of discovery.

Flea gave me an odd look.

"I still dislike caves," I said. "But it's our best option at the moment."

Thea agreed.

Before Flea could protest or ask questions, I said, "And I'll explain everything to you once we're there."

Thea gestured for me to lead the way. By nightfall, we'd reached the cave. The stone walls seemed to settle Flea's nerves. We built a fire, cooked a hearty stew and set up our bedrolls. Since one of us would be on watch throughout the night, Flea could sleep in mine.

As if by unspoken agreement, we ate dinner in silence. When everyone had finished the meal, all three gazes turned to me.

"Time to explain," Flea said.

"Yes, *Avry,* please do," Saul added with a smirk.

Keeping my secret had ceased to be a priority. Flea was alive!

"Avry, quit staring at me with that goofy smile and start talking," Flea said.

I told him about Jael's attack. He seemed to handle the news of his death well. But when I mentioned his burial, he interrupted.

"Wait," he said, suddenly alarmed. "Am I going to get sick from the toxin and die again?"

"No. We thought we gave you to a Death Lily, but it was really a Peace Lily." I noticed his queasy expression. "Yes, it was my idea to feed you to the plant. I was acting on pure instinct. And, considering I'm actually talking to you right now, I'm not sorry!"

Flea flashed me his lopsided grin. Unable to resist, I wrapped my arms around him and squeezed.

After a minute, he said, "Uh, Avry. I can't breathe."

I let him go and continued with the story, including Ryne's rescue, but not my own resurrection.

"I knew you'd heal Prince Ryne," Flea said. He brightened. "And Quain owes me two silvers for winning that bet."

"He'll be happy to pay," I said, laughing.

Thea and Saul had kept quiet during the whole explanation, but now Thea gazed at me with a shrewd look. Uh-oh.

"What's the *real* reason you wanted the Peace Lily serum?" Thea asked me.

"I told you, to test if it stops—"

"Are you sure that's why Prince Ryne wants it?" Thea glanced at Flea.

"What else… Oh." I understood her insinuation. "Ryne doesn't know about him." But he was well aware what the Peace Lily had done for me. Unlike Thea, Saul and Flea.

Was Ryne hoping the serum not only countered Tohon's dead but brought them back to life?

"It doesn't matter now," I said. "The Peace Lilys won't open for me." We would have to come up with another way to stop Tohon's dead.

"Do you think the Peace Lily will bring others back to life?" Thea asked.

"I've no idea."

She stared at the fire. "I guess there's only one way to find out."

Offer them another dead body and see what happened. I shuddered at the image.

"Where's Kerrick?" Flea asked into the silence.

"In the north," I said, explaining.

Worry creased his young face. Even gaunt, Flea resembled a typical sixteen-year-old. A few hairs peppered his chin and his light brown hair hung in his eyes. But an old soul met my gaze. He'd grown up on the streets, thieving to survive. Kerrick and the others had all but adopted him.

"Kerrick will be fine," I said, although I wondered who I was trying to console. Me or Flea? "He's probably bossing everyone around, driving them crazy." And before he could ask more questions, I updated him on the whereabouts of the others. "I hope Belen is back by the time we return." Poppa Bear would be ecstatic to see Flea again. He had suffered the most.

Saul offered to take first watch. I tucked Flea into my bedroll despite his protests, pulling the blanket up to his neck.

"You'll just have to suffer through an inordinate amount of mothering," I said. "There's no help for it. Oh! I almost forgot." I dug into my pack, removed the three juggling stones and dropped them into his hand. "These are yours."

He examined them. "But I only found one."

"Belen kept searching for you. And when he found the others, he carved his name and Kerrick's into one and the monkeys' into the other. He gave them to me before I left to rescue Ryne. He called them my keepers." I smiled at the memory. The stones had traveled far since then. I'd given them to Kerrick to return to Belen to support the ruse that I'd died, and Belen gave them back.

Flea pushed up to one elbow. "And you didn't grind out Kerrick's name? Or toss it at his head?"

"It was tempting."

He studied my expression. "You didn't scowl when you said Kerrick's name. Don't tell me you're friends now!"

"We're not friends." I remembered Kerrick's intense kiss when he showed me he wanted to be more than friends.

"You're smiling again. Does that mean…? Are you two…?" Flea couldn't even say the word. "Don't tell me."

"I won't."

He groaned. "Now I owe Belen two silvers." He flopped back onto the bedroll.

I fixed his blankets again, but he didn't stay put for long. He sat up and juggled the stones.

"They're evenly balanced," Flea said.

Snatching one out of the air, I ignored his squawk of outrage and pointed. "Sleep now." I waggled my fingers. "Or I'll touch—"

He returned to a reclined position. "That's not fair."

"Too bad. So sad."

Flea's grin turned into a huge yawn. He piled the rocks next to him. "Avry, why is your name with mine?"

I glanced at Thea; she appeared to be asleep, but I wasn't going to take the chance. "I'll tell you later."

"Promise," he mumbled, half-asleep.

Smoothing his hair away from his eyes, I promised.

As Flea slept, I kept checking on him, ensuring that he still breathed. Unlike Flea's, my sleep was restless. Tohon haunted my dreams as his magic poisoned my heart. When Saul woke me for my watch shift, I gladly vacated his bedroll.

Guarding a hidden cave entrance didn't require much skill. With a bright moon illuminating the forest, I made a few sweeps but found nothing. Then I settled on top of a boulder. I listened as the nocturnal animals shuffled through the underbrush, stalking their prey. The familiar and comforting sounds lulled me into a light doze.

A sour note to the west startled me. I grabbed my stiletto, pulling the weapon from its sheath as another odd sound reached me. Straining to locate the source, I held my breath. Two or three people headed this way, moving fast. I debated. Should I wake Saul and Thea? Or wait until I confirmed if the patrol was friendly or not? Or hope they passed us by without discovering us?

Before I could decide, the intruders slipped into view. Three of them wearing Tohon's basic uniform—dark brown pants, shirt, leather armor and boots. They passed my hiding spot without any indication that they had seen me. However, they were traveling in the same direction we needed to go. East toward Estrid's camp and her main force.

Time to wake Thea. I dropped to the ground. And froze.

More noise sounded to the west. It was subtle at first, then amplified and spread. I guessed the group contained at least a dozen, but kept increasing my estimate as they approached. Pressing against the boulder, I waited.

Soon a few figures crossed my line of sight. Armed with swords and daggers, they wore a dark green collar, stretching from chest to chin. I watched as more and more soldiers marched past. No one glanced in my direction. Other than the noise of their passage, which wasn't that loud considering their numbers, they were silent. No whispered conversations, coughs or grunts. No signs of life at all. A parade of the dead.

Cold fear snaked through me. I gripped the hilt of my stiletto even though I wanted to run away or melt into the boulder where they couldn't reach me.

By the time the last one passed, I had counted over two hundred of them. I raced into the cave and woke everyone.

"They're headed for Zabin. We need to warn our troops,"

I said. Shooing Flea off my bedroll, I shoved it into my knapsack. "Saul, get water to douse the coals. I'll fold your—"

Thea stopped me. "Relax, Irina…er…Avry. We have patrols out. They have probably already spotted the invasion and warned our camp. We've been training for this for months." She glanced around. "Finish packing. We'll follow this company, and make sure they don't try to get around our forces."

It didn't take us long to get ready. Before we left, Saul gave Flea one of his daggers. Thea took point. Even in the semi-darkness, it wasn't hard to find their trail. Broken branches, leaves and boot prints marked their path. Which wasn't as large as I'd expected, considering the size of the company. The dead traveled light.

We crossed the border into Pomyt as the sky lightened. An hour after dawn, we encountered our first surprise. Another trampled path, indicating a second force was headed toward Zabin.

"Which one do we follow?" I asked Thea.

"The left one."

"Why?"

"They're going northeast. There's a chance that group could bypass our patrols and loop in behind us."

"And that wouldn't be good?" Flea asked.

"No. You don't want the other army to get in behind you," Thea explained. "Let's go."

After an hour Thea skidded to a stop. She held up a hand, indicating silence. The sounds of the army dominated—we had almost caught up. And perhaps we'd gotten too close as a few off notes reverberated from both sides of the path.

Just as Thea signaled a retreat, shuffles sounded behind us. I had a split second to realize we were surrounded before Tohon's soldiers burst from the bushes. So focused on following the army, we'd walked right into an ambush. Fear sizzled in my blood, igniting my heart rate. The thought of being captured by the dead almost sent me into a full-out panic.

But instinct kicked in, and the four of us turned back to back, facing the ring of armed men. My pulse eased quite a bit when I noticed they weren't wearing metal collars, and their gazes held life instead of death. I counted ten of them.

They kept their positions as one man stepped forward. The tip of his sword pointed at the ground despite Saul and Thea holding theirs in an attack position. The thick muscled sergeant studied us for a moment, then said, "You're not a standard patrol, that's for sure. Which might explain why you're in this sector. Did you get lost?"

No one replied.

"You're not supposed to be here, so no one should miss you." He paused as if considering the situation.

His comment implied he knew Estrid's patrol schedule. Spies in her camp were a given, but I had thought the patrol locations had been secured.

"Surrender and you'll be our first prisoners of war, or die." He acted as if it didn't matter to him which option we'd choose.

If I'd been with Kerrick and Belen, I would have laughed at the offer. They could handle ten armed men. However, I wasn't so confident in Thea and Saul's abilities. Plus, the desire to protect the newly living Flea pulsed through my chest. I'd surrender if it meant saving his life.

"Flea, do you know how to wield a sword?" Thea asked.

"Yes, sir," Flea said with a little too much enthusiasm.

"Saul, your first task is to get Mr. Flea a sword," Thea said.

"Yes, sir."

"Thea, you can't—"

"Trust me, Irina. Just like I've trusted you," she said.

She had me there. I shoved my stiletto into its holder and

pulled two throwing knives, one for each hand. "Flea, do you remember that trick I played on you with the kissing spider?"

"Yes."

"All right, that's enough," the sergeant said. "Last chance."

"We will not surrender," Thea said simply. Before the sergeant could reply, she yelled, "Now!"

Thea and Saul surged forward. I took aim, sending one knife into the sergeant's upper arm and the second one into the thigh of the man to his left. The ring of metal on metal, curses and the smell of blood soon filled the air as Saul and Thea engaged. I had enough time to throw two more knives before the soldiers closed in.

Switching to my stiletto, I parried a sword thrust, but my weapon was no match against a longer blade. The soldier knocked my attack aside with ease. My stiletto flew from my grasp as the point of his sword poked my chest.

I spread my hands out. "I surrender."

"Turn around and get down on your knees," he said. "Hands behind your head."

Following his orders, I knelt. The clank of manacles sounded as he pulled them from his belt. When he grabbed my left arm to cuff my wrist, I grasped his fingers with my free hand. I zapped him, sending a painful burst of my power into him, overloading his nervous system. With a strangled cry, he collapsed onto the ground. One down.

I glanced at the others. Thea held off three men, including the sergeant. Although injured, he fought with a fierce determination along with two others. Her skills with a sword were impressive. Saul fought three, but he was obviously struggling. Flea had obtained a sword and held his own against one opponent. One man lay in a heap on the ground. Two down.

Stepping behind one of Saul's attackers, I touched the back of his neck, found the sweet spot with my thumb and zapped him. The man arched back in surprise, then crumpled to the ground. Three down.

A loud clang sounded as Flea unarmed his opponent. "Avry," he called. Flea aimed the point of his sword at the man's chest. The soldier held his hands up as if in surrender. I rushed over and touched the back of his neck. Four down.

Saul unarmed another and punched him. The man grunted and fell back. Five down.

Flea had joined Thea, and by the time I reached them, they had knocked two more out. I zapped them just in case. Seven down.

One of the soldiers grabbed me from behind. He placed his knife's blade on my throat and ordered my companions to stop. They ignored him. I clasped his wrist and sent my magic into him, hurting instead of healing. He jerked and fell to his knees, dragging me down with him. With another blast, he slumped over. I removed the knife from his nerveless fingers. Eight down.

By the time I'd finished, the sounds of fighting had died. Saul, Thea and Flea stood among the prone forms. Ten down. They looked rather smug and none the worse for wear. Although, I checked Flea despite his protests, making sure he was well.

I zapped the last three ambushers to ensure they would remain down. We grinned at each other for a few moments, catching our breath.

"How long will they be out?" Thea asked.

"They'll be unconscious for three to four hours," I said.

She nodded. "That'll give us enough time to catch up to the main group."

"But shouldn't we report back?" I asked, thinking another run-in might not end as well.

"Not until we determine where they're going and what they're planning to do."

"What happens when these guys wake up?" Flea pointed with the sword.

"If they're smart, they'll return to their base," Thea said.

"And if they're not?" Flea asked.

"They'll chase after us," I said.

"*If* they can find us." Saul smiled.

He could smile. He didn't have to worry about keeping Flea safe. I opened my mouth to retort—

"Relax, Mom. We'll protect him," Thea said.

"I can take care of myself," Flea protested.

"He's handy with that sword," Saul added.

Memories of his vacant stare and blue lips flashed in my mind. Jael had sucked the life from Flea without touching him. I looked at each of my companions, seeking their undivided attention. "Not all dangers are physical. And if the dead soldiers we're following discover us, all your skills will be useless."

Saul and Thea exchanged a glance as if they were trying to decide if they should humor me or not.

Flea caught what he probably thought was a mistake. "Wait. Did you say *dead* soldiers?"

"A lot has happened since you died, Flea," I said.

"She can explain her theories to you later," Thea said.

Theories? I gave her a Kerrick look—flat and cold.

"On one level, I know you're telling the truth, but on another I just can't wrap my mind around it. Can you understand that?" she asked.

I could.

"Let's go before the enemy gets too far ahead of us," Thea said. "I don't want to trigger another ambush, so this time we'll slow down and stop frequently. Watch for my signal."

We stayed close to her, pausing when instructed and listening for sounds of an attack. As the day wore on, I noticed the path we'd been trailing thinned. The light noise of the soldiers' passage was punctuated from time to time with a strange rumbling noise that vibrated through the soles of my boots. The sounds eventually diminished until I could no longer hear them. Then their tracks faded. We stopped.

"Did we miss a turn?" I asked.

"No way. The path was clearly marked," Thea said.

Thinking about Ursan and his jacks, I glanced up into the treetops. No movement aside from the light breeze rustling the leaves. No signs of anyone hiding up there either. With that many, at least a couple of their weapons would glint in the sunlight.

We continued northeast for another hour, but saw nothing to indicate anyone had passed this way.

Over two hundred dead soldiers had disappeared.

KERRICK

Noak stepped back and gestured for Kerrick to stand. The sounds of fighting filled the forest around them. His army had engaged the tribal warriors, but Kerrick didn't dare take his gaze off his opponent. Keeping a tight grip on his sword, Kerrick pushed to his feet.

"I see you, Magic Man," Noak said as he settled into a fighting stance.

Kerrick released the magical camouflage; he had a bad feeling he'd need all his energy.

Noak's dadao shot forward. Kerrick countered the thick sword just in time. Fear shot through him. Yep, this wasn't going to be pretty. Noak struck again and again. Kerrick scrambled to protect himself. His actions switched to pure survival mode as Kerrick countered Noak's lightning-fast attacks. Kerrick blocked and dodged, but the big man had more speed, strength and endurance. The leader was relentless, and Kerrick's skills inadequate.

As the cuts multiplied on his arms, legs and torso, Kerrick wondered why Noak didn't press his advantage when he had the opportunity to deliver a killing blow.

Panting with effort, Kerrick swept his sword too wide and Noak's dadao sliced a deep gash across his stomach. Kerrick stumbled back, and Noak followed, knocking the sword from Kerrick's hand. Then Noak reversed his sword and punched Kerrick in the ribs with the hilt.

The sickening crunch of bone accompanied an explosion of pain. Kerrick dropped to his knees, gasping for breath. Noak gestured to the skirmish nearby. The tribal warriors fought with a fierce intensity. Blood stained their white uniforms, but Kerrick doubted it was their own blood as they cut easily through his soldiers as if reaping hay. Outnumbered and outmatched, his army lay broken and bloody. Grief and rage filled him, erasing his pain. Kerrick shook the trees with his magic, signaling a retreat before they all died.

With a surge of energy, he hopped to his feet and charged Noak. The leader raised his dadao and struck Kerrick hard on his temple. Blackness claimed him.

Intense pain shot through his arms, waking Kerrick. Sunlight stabbed. He squeezed his eyes shut as the throbbing in his head caused nausea to swell. Kerrick drew in deep breaths. Each one caused a sharp stab of misery. How many of his ribs were broken? His foggy memories swirled with fear and death—a nightmare that refused to fade.

He needed to remain calm, so he concentrated on his present situation. Lying on his side on the ground, every muscle ached and the sting of multiple cuts flared along his arms and legs. His shirt, still damp with sweat and blood, stuck to his skin. A gash on his right temple burned, and a deep slice along his stomach pulsed with pain.

Trying to relieve the cramps in his arms, Kerrick discovered his wrists had been tightly secured behind his back. And his ankles had been lashed together. With a quick glance through stilted eyelids he confirmed his dire situation. The tribesmen had captured him. He sought his army with his magic. A few of his soldiers fled south. Otherwise, the pale northerners occupied most of the forest. He hoped the rest of his men had obeyed his signal and retreated.

Despite his list of woes, he was alive. But for how long? At least Danny and Zila had gotten away. He hoped his brother, Izak, would heed their warning and evacuate Orel in time.

He recalled his fight with the tribal leader. Even though Kerrick had fought with every skill he possessed, it hadn't been enough. On the positive side, he still had access to his forest magic. He opened his eyes and surveyed what he could with his limited view. It appeared as if the tribesmen were preparing for travel.

No guards stood near him, so he tapped into the forest's energy and camouflaged his body. When a shuffle of boots approached, he struggled to his knees, hoping to catch the man by surprise.

Instead a hand clamped around his neck. The instant Noak touched him, Kerrick's magical connection to the forest was severed and replaced with a cold that gripped him in icy fingers, freezing him to his core.

Two more tribesmen arrived. They yanked him to his feet. His injuries burned with pain. Kerrick was now eye-level with Noak, who still grasped his throat.

"More soldiers coming?" he asked Kerrick.

He refused to answer. Noak pressed his thumb into Kerrick's windpipe as the cold intensified. Kerrick felt as if his entire body had turned to ice. Part of his mind wondered what type of magician could do that, while another screamed at him to fight back. But he couldn't move. He couldn't breathe.

Noak eased his grip. Kerrick swayed in relief as the cold receded enough for him to pull air into his lungs.

Touching one of the scars on Kerrick's neck, Noak said, "Magic Man, you will help us."

"Not a chance," Kerrick said.

A fleeting smile twisted his lips. "You understand we never take prisoners, yes?"

Fear traveled through him like a crack snaking along a frozen pond. "Yes."

"Do you know why?"

"No."

"It is a...kindness to kill." Noak let that sink in, before adding, "If you don't help, you will wish to be dead."

Kerrick's back burned with remembered pain. Estrid's men had whipped him, trying to get him to divulge Avry's location. It hadn't worked then, and it sure as hell wouldn't work now. He stared at the man, refusing to be intimidated.

Another spark of amusement flashed in those ice-blue eyes. "I like a challenge, Magic Man." He squeezed.

A bone-aching, teeth-chattering chill raced through Kerrick's body. His muscles stiffened into immobility as his extremities burned with cold. Kerrick's heartbeat slowed, and taking a breath required an immense effort, as if icicles had formed inside his lungs.

Noak released him, but Kerrick remained frozen.

"Winter's Curse. You understand?" Noak asked.

"No." Kerrick forced the word out.

"Slow cold death. So slow winter'll be here and gone before you. Cold like fire, consuming you as you turn to ice from the inside out. Your magic gone." Noak poked him in the chest. "Nothing like it."

Noak gestured to the two men standing next to Kerrick. They removed his bindings, dragged him over to a tree, sat him down and, even though he couldn't move, they secured his wrists behind the tree's trunk. The metal pinched his skin. And he noted that the pain felt greater than it should.

Squatting next to him, Noak said, "We hunt what is left of your—" he half smiled "—army. When I return, you will help."

By the time Kerrick could say the word *no,* the leader had
strode away. A brief spark of worry for his soldiers gave him
a momentary distraction, but soon the bite of cold deep in
his body made the pain from his other cuts and bruises fade
to nonexistence. He would have yelled if he had the breath.
Instead he fought the slow suffocation with sips of air.

It didn't take long for Kerrick to agree with Noak. This
was a torture like no other. Being whipped seemed pleasant
in comparison. And the thought it would continue for months
almost sent him over the edge. But he refused to give in. He
concentrated on Avry, recalling her kind sea-green eyes, her
stubborn pout that he loved but would never admit to her,
and her determination.

He wondered if her touch would break this curse. But
would she be dying a slow, cold death in his place? He didn't
know enough about Noak's magic to answer that question.
Either way, he'd never endanger her.

As the hours, days, maybe even weeks passed, Kerrick's
existence shrank to the cold misery feasting on him and the
endless effort to draw a breath. When a familiar pair of snufa-
skinned boots came into his limited view, Kerrick didn't know
if he could refuse Noak again.

The tribe's leader knelt next to him. "Ready to cooperate?"

Kerrick's body screamed in agreement, but he couldn't be-
tray his people. "No." Through frozen lips, the word was
barely a whisper.

Noak met Kerrick's gaze. He nodded as if he'd been expecting that answer, then glanced to his right and gestured.

Shuffles of feet and a muffled shout reached Kerrick before
two tribesmen carried a squirming bundle into sight. Bound
and gagged, Danny's expression showed more anger than fear.

"How about now?" Noak asked.

CHAPTER 11

The dead soldiers had completely disappeared. We had spent the rest of that day and most of the next searching for them, or for signs of their passage in the forest. Nothing.

When the sun touched the horizon, Thea said, "That's enough. Time to report back to the major, and let him decide what to make of it."

As we hiked toward Zabin, Flea stayed by my side, asking questions. Well aware that Thea and Saul could hear, I deflected the ones that I thought Jael shouldn't know about.

We had been away for six days, and it took us another two days to reach the outskirts of Estrid's main army. Two days without encountering anyone—friend or foe. But as soon as we heard a patrol around midafternoon on the third day and determined it was one of ours, Thea flagged them down.

They hadn't seen any of Tohon's troops in this quadrant, but a couple of his patrols had attacked their lines to the southwest, drawing Estrid's men to that area. Thea warned them of a possible ambush, then we moved on.

She stopped a couple more patrols before we arrived at the rather tranquil base. Most of the buzz was over the skirmishes to the southwest. The soldiers thought Tohon was testing their response since the clashes hadn't lasted long before Tohon's soldiers retreated. While Thea and Saul reported to Major Granvil, I headed straight for Ryne's tent with Flea in tow.

I burst through the tent flaps with a huge smile on my face, but the place was empty. Flea yawned—it had been a long day.

"Stay here, and I'll see where everyone's at," I said.

Flea plopped onto Ryne's cot near the back of the tent and was soon fast asleep. I hesitated at the tent's entrance, afraid to leave him alone. I wondered if it was just my nurturing instinct or something deeper. Examining my feelings, I felt this odd attachment to Flea that went beyond friendship. Like that of a mother bear—fiercely protective. Was it due to his death or because we shared a bond since we'd both been revived by a Peace Lily?

Had Kerrick felt this way when we parted? He'd seen me without life. And then I'd walked away, claiming it was for the best. Not nice—almost cruel. Had he suspected the real reason I'd ran? Did I?

I glanced at Flea. He looked so young and peaceful. No nightmares disturbed his sleep, unlike with me. Most nights Tohon visited my dreams. Most nights Tohon's kiss lingered long after I woke breathless with desire. His touch so vivid, I worried my dreams of him would erase my memories of lying with Kerrick.

Pulling the sheet over Flea, I tucked him in. Even though I knew he was safe, I just couldn't leave.

I settled in one of the chairs and waited. My thoughts returned to past decisions and mistakes. Had Tohon claimed me? Is that why I dreamed of him every night?

Familiar voices woke me from a light doze. Night had fallen, and Quain carried a lantern. He held it high in one hand and clutched a sword in the other as he entered the tent. I called to him to avoid being skewered.

Quain's defensive posture didn't relax. "What are you doing here?"

Equally armed, Loren slid in behind him, followed by Ryne. Of the three, only Ryne appeared happy to see me. And in that moment, it hit me.

"Quain, I'm sorry," I said.

Caught completely off guard, he just stared at me.

"You're right. I didn't trust you. Any of you. Because I'm terrified," I said.

"Of what?" Ryne asked, stepping closer.

I drew in a deep breath and then the words gushed forth. "Of being captured by Tohon again. Scared of what he'd do to me. Not of being tortured or even being experimented on, but losing myself. Also if he found out about Kerrick and me…" I swallowed. The thought of Tohon's wrath shook me to my core. "I can't resist his life magic. The contract I signed was the only reason he didn't press his advantage before. Next time, there won't be negotiations. I'd rather die again than be his."

The three men gaped at me as if uncertain what to make of my confession.

But for me, once I'd said the words aloud, admitting my fears, I felt much better. Odd. And I realized I couldn't hide forever. I'd let the fear drive me away from Kerrick, and he might be killed fighting the tribes. I vowed, if I got another chance, I wouldn't let Kerrick out of my sight.

Quain sheathed his sword, handed the lantern to Loren and pulled me into a Belen-sized hug. Loren put the light down and wrapped his arms around us both, making an Avry sandwich.

"Don't worry about Tohon, Avry," Loren said. "We'll protect you."

"He's not getting near you," Quain said. "You'll be safe with us."

I let myself believe them as I leaned my forehead against Quain's shoulder.

"Avry died, too?" Flea asked. "When did that happen?"

In a flash, I was tossed aside as the monkeys whooped and pounced on Flea.

"Why didn't you tell us? Was he hiding, too?" Quain demanded.

I explained how I found Flea.

"Wait. A Death Lily *told* you to go there? Is no one else suspicious?" Quain asked.

"I asked it to help me with the Peace Lilys, and it sent me there. I'm not complaining."

After another round of hugs and slaps on the back, Loren introduced Flea to Ryne since they hadn't met. The prince shook his hand and thanked him for helping to save him. Flea stammered and gave him one of his lopsided grins.

And then I remembered what else the Lily had given me. I fished them from my pack and held them out.

"What are those?" Ryne asked.

"The Death Lily's poison sacks."

Loren and Quain shrank away, but Ryne picked one up and examined it in the lantern light.

"That's interesting," Ryne said. "Why would it give them to you?"

"I don't know," I said.

"Maybe it wants us to inject it into Jael," Quain said.

"I'd second that," Flea said. "I missed a lot of cool stuff because of her."

We glanced at each other. *Cool* wasn't the word I'd use to describe the past six months.

"What do we know about this?" Ryne asked, holding up a sack.

"It kills people and its own plants if you pour it around the base of the Lily's stem," I said.

"But it doesn't kill everyone," Ryne said. "Healers survived the poison, and Danny and Zila."

"Maybe there is another use for the toxin," I suggested. "Maybe it wants us to figure it out." I remembered when Tohon had injected the toxin into me. My consciousness had floated above my body, which was similar to being inside a Death Lily, but when Tohon had touched me, I'd merged with his thoughts. I'd wondered if he had used the toxin to create his dead soldiers but had dismissed the theory since he froze the dead bodies in a magical stasis so they didn't rot. Perhaps I'd been too hasty.

"Here." Ryne handed it back to me. "I'll let you figure it out."

"Gee, thanks."

"Tell me what else you learned while you were gone," Ryne said.

I filled him in on the disappearing troops.

Ryne stared at the wall for a long moment before declaring, "We have five days to prepare."

"To prepare for what?" Quain asked.

"For war."

"Why five days? He could attack tonight," Loren said.

"That's midsummer's day," Ryne said as if we should all know the significance of that day. When no one commented, he continued. "When we were in school, that was always the last day before our annual break. And the last-year students always crown their elected king on that date, during graduation."

Now it made sense. Tohon had wanted to be king but hadn't been elected, and now he was determined to be king of the Fifteen Realms.

"Estrid's forces have been training for months. Are they strong enough to stop him?" I asked.

"I'm not sure," Ryne said.

"You don't *know?*" I asked. "You're supposed to be a military genius!" My voice turned shrill.

Ryne put his hands on my shoulders and leaned close, capturing my full attention. "Jael commands this army. They are loyal to her and to Estrid. Not me. I have four hundred soldiers and that's it. I can only give advice. Plus Jael hasn't confided her real plans to me. She's been feeding me the same bull she's been telling her mother-in-law."

"What about your troops?" I asked.

"When Tohon attacks, they'll be in the forest divided into small tactical units."

"Like your elite squads you used to help Kerrick in Alga?"

"Yes. They'll harry Tohon's soldiers with quick, short strikes. I wanted to divide all of Estrid's forces into squads because I don't think we can win using more traditional warfare methods."

"But what about the dead soldiers?" Loren asked. "None of your elites returned from scouting missions in Sogra."

Ryne released me from his piercing gaze to glance at Loren. "We were unaware of Tohon's abominations then."

"But they have neck armor now," I said.

"My troops have been training to deal with that. Estrid still isn't convinced."

Alarmed, I asked, "Haven't Belen and Ursan returned?"

"It's only been ten days," Ryne said. He squeezed my shoulders as if consoling me, then let go.

We had five days until Tohon attacked. "Tell me what you're doing, and I'll start training my squads."

Ryne raised an eyebrow. "*Your* squads?"

"Sergeant Irina's squads. I'm sure she'll help."

He promised to send one of his men over in the morning to demonstrate the technique.

Once again I hesitated before leaving. Flea stood between Loren and Quain. "Do you have an extra cot for him?" I asked.

"Yes," Ryne said.

"You'll need to find him some clothes that fit, and—"

"We'll take care of him," Ryne said.

I pointed at the monkeys, getting their attention. "Don't let him out of your sight. Understand?"

"Hey," Flea said. "I can take care of myself."

We all ignored him.

"Yes, Sergeant," Loren said, smiling.

"Good." I nodded.

As I left, Quain said, "She said *I* was right, Loren. Did you hear her?"

"I don't recall."

"Liar, you just don't…"

Their bickering faded as I strode through the camp, heading toward my tent. If only Belen and Kerrick were here, it would be perfect. Until Tohon attacked. With that sobering thought, I sought out Thea. She talked to a group of lieutenants, and by their intense gazes I guessed she discussed the disappearing soldiers.

I hovered on the edges, hoping to catch her eye. She noticed me and waved me over.

"Sergeant Irina estimated over two hundred in a squad," Thea said, including me in the conversation.

The others looked doubtful.

I made a quick decision. "Prince Ryne is pretty confident Tohon will attack on midsummer's day." Before they could dismiss the news as hearsay, I continued, "We'll need special

training to counter them. All your squads that are not on patrol are to report to the main training area in the morning."

The lieutenants gaped at me, then glanced at Thea. She
met their outraged expressions with her typical calm. "All my
squads will be there, Sergeant," she said without looking at me.

One by one, they nodded and left to inform their platoons.

She turned to me. "Go tell Liv, and I'll find Saul and Odd.
Wynn's out on patrol."

"Thanks," I said.

A brief smile. "You haven't led me astray. Besides, nothing
wrong with more training."

We parted to spread the news. It was well past midnight
when I crawled into my cot. Exhaustion had one benefit—
no nightmares.

Liv shook me awake at dawn. "Come on, Baby Face, wake
up."

I groaned and tried to roll over, but she yanked my sheet off.

"You're evil," I mumbled.

"This was your idea, not mine." She crossed her arms and
studied me.

I ran my fingers through tangled hair. Still no lice. "What?"

"Your hair is getting darker, and your lips aren't as fat."

There had been no free time for me to reapply Mom's various dyes. "So?"

"So, there have been rumors about you."

Oh, no. It had started. "What rumors?" I asked with what
I hoped was a mildly curious tone. Getting up, I pulled on
my shirt.

"That you're working for Prince Ryne. You were spotted
heading straight to his tent when you returned from your secret mission. And you've been in his tent a couple times since
he has arrived."

Thinking fast, I said, "Since the exercise in the forest, he's been consulting me on a few things. Lieutenant Thea is well aware of my activities."

"Consulting you? A sergeant? Yeah, right."

"Okay, I confess."

Liv waited.

"We're lovers."

She burst out in a high-pitched semigasping laughter. So amused by my comment, she doubled over and collapsed onto her cot. I debated between being offended and glad I entertained her as I finished dressing.

After waiting for her to calm, I said, "What's so funny about that?"

"Come on, Baby Face. First, he's a prince, and second, everyone knows there is only one man for you."

That surprised me. "Really? Which man?"

"We've no idea. But you're the prettiest sergeant around and you've been so oblivious to the interest from the other guys that we've figured you had to be in love with someone else. Did he die from the plague?"

"No." My reply just popped from my mouth.

"Then why isn't he with you?"

"It's complicated." Before she could ask any more questions, I brushed past her. "Let's go, we're late."

A sizable group had already gathered in the training yard with more arriving. Saul and Odd joined us as soon as we entered the area.

"More games of hide-and-seek?" Odd asked me with a smile. "Or do you have a new game to play?"

"A new one."

"Oh? What's it called?"

I remembered Thea's comment about the dead soldiers. "Fighting the impossible."

Odd's humor died as his gaze slid past my shoulder. "I think I'm going to like hide-and-seek better."

Ryne, the monkeys and Flea approached us. Quain carried the neck collar along with a burlap sack that clinked with each step.

"I thought you were sending someone else," I said to Ryne.

Liv and Odd shared a look, and I realized too late that my tone and demeanor had been inappropriate for a sergeant talking to a prince.

Ryne ignored my insubordination. "This will be another chance for me to get acquainted with Estrid's troops. It'll be important when we're fighting together. Please ask all the officers and sergeants to come over. We'll demonstrate the technique to them first, and then they can teach their squads."

I waved Thea over and relayed Ryne's request. Soon we were surrounded, and even Major Granvil joined us. He nodded to Ryne, gave me a look that would pierce armor, but didn't say a word.

Prince Ryne explained to the group that when Tohon attacked, the soldiers wearing the metal collars would be Tohon's special forces. "They will come at you with a mindless determination in utter silence. They will be unaffected by injuries to their bodies."

A ripple of unease tinged with amusement rolled through the audience.

"Yes, I know what you've been told. And you probably think I'm crazy right now. But I'm not here to convince you, just to teach you a skill that might save your life in battle." Ryne gestured to Quain.

Quain set the sack down. It clanked. He clamped the metal collar around his throat, drew his sword in one hand and a dagger in the other. He advanced.

Ryne pulled his own weapons. "First step is to unarm your opponent."

They engaged in a sword fight. Metal rang and clanged as they fought. Even though I wasn't an expert, Ryne's superior skills with a blade were obvious. He used a number of quick and efficient moves. Quain's cheeks turned red as he struggled to defend himself. I scanned the faces watching the match. The others appeared to be impressed. I suspected that was another reason Ryne decided to lead this training exercise—to gain the soldiers' respect.

Quain grunted, and I turned in time to see his sword fly from his hand. Blood welled in a bright red line from his thumb to his wrist. I fought the desire to rush to him and check the severity of the cut.

"Once your opponent is unarmed, don't hesitate to take the next step," Ryne said. "Plant your sword." He shoved the tip of his blade into the hard ground. "Move in close. As you advance, change the grip on your dagger like so." He spun the hilt in his hand so the blade now pointed to the ground. "With your free hand, grab his head and pull down. Then aim the blade for the base of his skull. The collar protects the neck and prevents decapitation, but if you can jam the blade into the spot between the cranium and spine, you'll stop him."

Murmurs of shock and disbelief sounded. Comments and questions erupted all at once.

"That's brutal."

"It's an impossible place to reach in a fight."

"What if he's taller than you?"

"Why can't we just chop their arms off instead?"

Ryne explained with a strong calm voice. Even when he repeated the same answer multiple times, he never lost his temper. He demonstrated the strike many times, as well. Each repetition soothed the ripples. They quieted and finally really listened to him. When they started repeating back his instructions, Ryne appeared satisfied.

Quicker than I'd expected, the lieutenants and sergeants practiced finding the kill spot on Quain, Loren and Flea. The burlap sack held more collars. Although they didn't quite match the one stolen from Tohon, they proved adequate for the training. When Ryne was happy with their efforts, he distributed collars to the sergeants so they could teach their squads.

As they disbursed into smaller groups, I walked over to Quain. "Let me see."

He flexed his hand. "It's just a scratch."

"Scratches can get infected." I grabbed his wrist, but he broke my grip.

"No. I'm not letting you blow your cover."

I huffed. "We're four days away from war. I'm not going to hide when I'm most needed."

"You still have four days," Quain said. "If it isn't better by then, I'll be first in line."

"All right, but go wash it with soap right now and cover it with a clean bandage. Keep it dry and—"

"Av—Irina, don't worry, I know how to take care of a cut."

"Sorry. I'm just…"

"Overprotective? Overly cautious? Smothering?" He smirked.

I crossed my arms and gave him my best stern look. "You didn't seem to mind my tendency to nurture when I healed Belen and Loren."

Unaffected by my comment, he said, "They're a bunch of wimps."

Just then Loren joined us. "Who's a wimp?"

"According to Quain, you are," I said.

Quain's smirk died. He sputtered.

"Care to explain?" Loren asked him, putting his hand on his sword's hilt.

"Go ahead." I waved jauntily and left the monkeys.

Ryne moved among the squads, assisting when needed. Flea also helped. I watched a few bouts and answered questions. Eventually, Loren and Quain joined the training.

By the end of the day, word of the special strike training had spread to the other companies. Major Granvil organized with his colleagues and scheduled more practice and teaching sessions for the next couple days.

As the groups finished for the night, Ryne approached me. "Sergeant Odd's team picked up the technique the fastest. Can you ask him if they'll help demonstrate it tomorrow?"

"Sure."

"And we need to discuss what we're going to do about the Peace Lilys," he said.

"How do you mean?"

"First, we need to decide if we're going to give the information to Estrid. Also if war breaks out, we'll have fatalities. Do we try to feed one to a Peace Lily?"

He had followed the same logic that Thea had the first night we found Flea. I scanned the area, searching for Flea. He joked with Loren.

"Thea and Saul know what happened. I was so excited about Flea, I didn't ask if they planned to report it to Major Granvil." If they had, it would explain Granvil's nasty look earlier.

"Can you find out?" Ryne asked.

"Yes. And as for the Peace Lily, I think we owe it to the soldiers to try it at least once."

"I agree. I'll see you in the morning." He touched my shoulder before heading to his tent with the monkeys and Flea in tow.

I caught Odd and Liv staring at me. Liv's lips were pursed in thought, and Odd gave me a knowing look. Sighing, I decided it would be a relief when I no longer had to pretend to be Irina. But, for now, I had to talk to Thea. I found her near her tent.

"Yes, I told the major everything," Thea said. "It was too big for me to keep secret."

"Will he report it to his commanding officer?" I asked.

"If he wants to cover his ass, then, yes, he will." She considered. "He was pretty pissed off when I explained, but he was at the training today. That's a good sign."

I guessed I'd have to talk to him. The thought was far from enticing, and I decided to put it off until the morning. Instead, I washed up, filled a tray of food and joined Liv, Odd and Saul around the sergeants' fire.

As soon as I sat next to Liv, the discussion switched to Prince Ryne. Liv and Odd asked me a bunch of questions about him.

"Liv, I was kidding this morning. You know that," I said.

"Yeah, but you were so chummy with him today that I thought it might just be possible that he's the one you're pining for," Liv said.

"He touched your shoulder," Odd said as if that proved everything.

"Tell them," Saul said.

I hesitated.

"They'll understand," he said. "I did."

Still I paused. Telling them would be the start of the end of Sergeant Irina. I liked her. She was safe. And she'd earned her place as a member of Axe Company. But it would be better if they learned who I was from me and not through the rumor mill.

It didn't take long. After I finished, the silence stretched to an uncomfortable length.

Then Odd said, "Ursan's going to gloat. He's suspected since you arrived."

"He already knows," I said.

"Are we the last?" Liv asked.

"No. Only Lieutenant Thea and probably Major Granvil know."

"Not Wynn?" she asked with a gleam in her eyes.

"Not yet."

"Ho boy! Can I tell her?"

Then I remembered what Thea had said about Liv and Wynn. How they couldn't resist passing along juicy gossip. I figured by tomorrow night the entire camp would know. At least I'd have one night of peace.

Except I was wrong. In the middle of the night, I was woken by a hard shove. Noelle stood over me. She held a small lantern in her hand. At least it wasn't a knife. Progress.

"General Jael wants to see you," she said.

Half-asleep, I was more confused than afraid. Silly me. "Now?"

"Now."

KERRICK

Noak held Danny in one hand as if the boy weighed nothing. Danny looked like a fragile toy next to the big man. Pulling a knife from his red sash, Noak pressed the tip to Danny's neck. The ice growing inside Kerrick seized his heart.

"Cooperate, or he dies," Noak said.

Danny's muffled protests were clear. Brave boy. But Kerrick couldn't let him die. Could he?

Breaking his frozen thoughts, he considered his options. If he refused, they'd be killed and the tribes would continue to advance south, except they would move with caution. If he agreed, Danny would live, and the tribes would continue to advance. However, they wouldn't be as cautious, and the noise of their passage might alert those pockets of people who hadn't moved to Orel, perhaps saving them.

Ah, hell. Logic aside, he couldn't let the boy die.

Still fighting Winter's Curse, Kerrick summoned every bit of strength and pushed, sliding his torso up the tree. The skin on his arms scraped along the rough bark as the manacles clanked. Noak watched, impassive, as Kerrick stood.

"He…goes…free…" Each word burned his throat.

"No," Noak said. "He lives as long as you cooperate."

"Free…him…I'll…give…my…word."

Noak scoffed. "No. You cooperate. No magic against us. He lives."

"Curse?"

"Lifted. For now. Agreed?"

Kerrick had no choice. Danny might get an opportunity to escape. "Yes."

Handing Danny over to a tribesman, Noak grabbed Kerrick's throat. The ice inside Kerrick melted, releasing him. He drew in a deep breath, luxuriating in the ability to breathe.

"No trouble or—"

"Keep the boy close to me, and there won't be any," Kerrick said.

Noak slammed him against the tree. "You do not give orders, only follow. Understand?"

"Yes."

The tribesman tied Danny to a tree near Kerrick. Satisfied the boy was safe for now, Kerrick sank back to the ground and fell into an exhausted sleep.

An ufa stalked him through the tall grass. The long thin blades rustled slightly and were the only sign of the beast's movements. Kerrick's magic couldn't sense the dead creature, and he had lost his sword. His heart slammed against his chest as he backed away.

With a roar, the animal broke from the grass and pounced on him, knocking him down. The pure-white ufa opened its huge maw, flashing razor-sharp teeth made of ice before they ripped into his throat. A freezing-cold pain pierced his body.

Kerrick jerked awake, gasping for breath. He glanced at Danny, checking that he was safe. The boy had curled up against Kerrick's legs and was sound asleep. After that first night, they hadn't bound Danny to a tree, and he'd actually listened to Kerrick and kept close.

He leaned his head back, trying to work the kinks from

his shoulders and arms. His ribs protested with painful jabs, and the rest of his body ached. The tree's rough bark rubbed against a raw spot on his spine. Every night since he'd agreed to help Noak to save Danny's life, the tribesmen had secured Kerrick to a tree. The irony of his situation was not lost on him. He'd done the same to Avry, so he couldn't complain. At least Danny was alive and well. For now.

Damn boy was too much like Avry. He couldn't follow a simple order. Instead of fleeing with Zila, he'd stayed behind to rescue Kerrick. The fact that he hadn't a clue how to go about it hadn't stopped Danny.

Remembering the deal he'd made with Noak five days ago, Kerrick closed his eyes briefly before he scanned the sleeping northerners. The tribesmen had hunkered down for the night. Their discomfort at being in the forest continued, despite knowing there would be no more attackers. No more *human* attackers. From the comments made by a few of the warriors, Death Lilys had grabbed a couple of them. And ufa packs had tried to surprise them, but the tribesmen were skilled hunters and had dispatched them as easily as Kerrick's army.

Grief consumed him. So many dead. And he'd been forced to tell Noak that his tribes would face no resistance this side of the Nine Mountains. The northern realms would be decimated. Kerrick wondered what would happen if the tribes clashed with Tohon's dead army. It would be interesting. Maybe they'd kill each other. A nice thought, but in battle there was always a loser and a winner. Who would Kerrick root for? Or even fight for? Tohon or Noak?

He hated to admit it, but Tohon would be his choice. Even though he was mentally unbalanced and a megalomaniac, Tohon wasn't trying to commit mass genocide. In Tohon's warped mind, he believed his efforts to unite the Fifteen Realms were of the purest intentions.

Kerrick spent the rest of the night drifting in a half doze. Noak woke him at dawn. He had a couple of his "generals" with him. Danny roused but was smart enough to keep quiet.

"Tell me of this…sickness that killed your people," Noak ordered.

"What do you want to know?"

"All."

"It began five years ago." Kerrick told him how it had spread and killed two-thirds of their population. Over six million people gone. "The last known case in the Fifteen Realms was three years ago."

"Your magic healing not enough?" Noak asked.

"No. Our healers couldn't cure it. Not without dying themselves."

Noak considered. "Will it sicken my people?"

"I hope so."

The leader kicked Kerrick in the ribs. Intense pain radiated through his chest. He panted with shallow breaths, hoping to ease the daggers of agony. Distantly, he heard Danny yell.

By the time Kerrick recovered, Noak held Danny in a tight grip. Noak didn't need to say a word. Just touching the boy was enough of a threat.

"I don't know if your people will get the plague," Kerrick said. "We think it spread from person to person by touch. But some of us, like me and Danny, never sickened. We don't know why."

"How did it kill?" Noak asked.

An odd question. Kerrick described the symptoms. Memories of Avry suffering through the final stage still haunted him. He'd give Izak his realm if he could just see her one more time.

Noak exchanged a glance with one of his men. "Did your magic healers die?"

"Yes."

"All?"

"All."

Noak left with his warriors, dragging Danny along. Kerrick shouted, but they ignored him. The leader handed the boy over to another, and Danny disappeared.

Fury burned deep inside Kerrick. The branches of all the nearby trees shook with his anger. The tribesmen cried out in alarm, ducking and covering their heads with their arms. Except for Noak. He stared at Kerrick as if waiting for him to break his word. Kerrick wouldn't. The branches stilled as he wilted.

He'd save his strength for later. If they harmed Danny, he'd bring the trees down on them all.

CHAPTER 12

I followed Noelle outside my tent. Four soldiers waited to escort me to Jael. No one said a word as we walked. Instead of going to her tent, they led me to the manor house. Noelle disappeared. Still surrounded by the guards, I sat in one of the parlors, nervously waiting. The minutes turned to hours, and the sun rose. After a while, I dozed in the chair.

Tohon's laughter followed me as I ran through the dark corridors of his castle. Sweat poured from my skin as I flew around the corners in a complete panic.

"I'm coming for you, my dear," he called.

The soles of my feet stung, and pain stabbed my side, but I didn't slow.

"You can't escape."

I turned left and slammed into a wall of the dead. They grabbed me. The feel of their cold flesh sickened me as I shuddered in horror. Caught in their trap, I couldn't move. They turned me so I faced Tohon.

Flushed with anger, Tohon slapped me.

I woke with a jolt. My right cheek burned with pain. But I didn't have time to interpret my dream. In the hallway, Jael barked orders and discussed plans, but when she entered the room, she waved everyone out, including my guards. From the fire that burned in her eyes, I guessed she didn't want any-one to witness my murder. I jumped to my feet.

She studied me for a moment. "I'm not quite sure what to think about you, Avry. Are you a miracle, a liar, an oath-breaker, a traitor or a spy?" She held up a hand. "Don't an-swer. I already decided that you're all of them in one package. Impressive. Very impressive."

"I can explain."

"Oh, I'm sure you have plenty of excuses. I have no de-sire to hear them, but I do need to decide what I'll do with you. My instincts tell me to kill you now before you become a bigger problem."

Fear curled in my stomach. I braced for her attack.

"However, as Sergeant Irina you have made quite the im-pact, both good and bad. Your disappearance would cause some ill will, and I'm sure that brat Ryne knows who you really are and would make a stink." She paused. "Plus, we'll need your healing magic once Tohon strikes. Did you forget the promise you made to my mother-in-law?"

"No. I said I'd return to help, and I've been training your soldiers since I've arrived."

She laughed. "Estrid meant your help in the *infirmary*."

"And she will get it as soon as the fighting starts. You can't deny that I've been an asset to your army."

"Regardless, you're working in the infirmary as of now. You're also under house arrest. I'll have Noelle fetch your belongings and tell your lieutenant you've been reassigned."

I was in midprotest when she pulled the air from my lungs in one quick gesture. Fighting to stay conscious, I used my magic to counter hers and was able to take a few breaths. Until she increased her power. My legs gave out, and I flopped back in the chair.

"You're not strong enough, and Kerrick isn't here to help

you." She tapped her fingers on her full lips. "I'm tempted to finish this, just to upset Kerrick, but your death would cause problems for me right now."

I grabbed the chair's arms to keep from sliding to the floor. Black-and-white spots swarmed in my vision.

Jael leaned close. "Don't ever relax. There will be a point where it won't matter if you live or die, so I'd suggest you do everything you can to keep me happy."

The desire to wipe that superior smirk off her face swelled. I gathered all my energy and concentrated on breathing, managing to suck in a couple lungfuls of air before she shut me off.

"This isn't making me happy," she said.

My grip slipped. I slid to the floor. The need to breathe burned in my chest.

"Jael, stop." Estrid's commanding voice filled the room.

Yes, stop. But the encroaching blackness wouldn't stop.

A magical touch woke me, sending me a rush of energy. Kerrick! I opened my eyes and met Flea's concerned gaze. Disappointment pierced my soul, and I squeezed my eyes shut and rode out the wave of heartache.

"Avry, are you all right?" Flea asked in a high-pitched squeak.

Once again I looked at him. He cradled my head and shoulders in his lap. His fingers pressed on my neck as if he'd been feeling for a pulse. Voices argued from somewhere behind him.

"I'm fine. It's just… Flea!"

"What?"

My cry silenced the others. I glanced over his shoulder. Estrid, Jael and Ryne stared at me. Not wanting to share my realization about Flea with Estrid and Jael, I said, "How did you know I was here?"

He blushed. "I...uh...had a bad dream. You were in trouble and well...I—"

"He woke me up and insisted we come here," Ryne said. "And a good thing, too, or she would have killed you." He glared at Jael.

"That was not my intention," she replied.

"And just what was—"

"It doesn't matter," Jael snapped. "Avry's mine." She glanced at Estrid. "She's ours. She made a promise to return after healing you and work for us in the *infirmary*. She's an oath-breaker, and I was exercising my right to punish her."

Ryne turned to me. "Is that true?"

Flea helped me to stand. "I did promise to return."

The prince gave me a significant look. One that said he could work something out. I shook my head slightly.

"Why this elaborate ruse, Avry?" Estrid asked, gesturing to my sergeant's uniform.

I explained what I'd been doing and my reasons. Jael tried to interrupt, but Estrid shut her down with a clipped "Let her speak."

"And I planned to start working in the infirmary when Tohon attacks," I finished.

"It doesn't matter what you—"

"Jael, I'll handle this," Estrid said. "Attend to the army."

Wow. Estrid treated Jael like a troublesome daughter-in-law. Didn't she fear her power? The air seemed to vibrate with Jael's fury, but she reined in her emotions, nodded to the High Priestess and strode from the room.

"She's dangerous," Ryne said into the silence.

Estrid agreed. "We need her."

"And she needs you to defeat Tohon. Once he's no longer a threat, she'll—"

"Come after me. I'm well aware of her plans, Ryne. The creator will protect me from harm."

"And if the creator doesn't?"

"Then it is my time to go."

I studied Estrid. Did she really believe that? Was her fervent demeanor and the passionate glint in her eyes all an act or true devotion? I couldn't say for sure.

"What about Avry?" Ryne asked.

"She stays here."

I clamped down on my protest when I saw Ryne nodding in agreement.

He caught my look. "You'll be safer here."

"Safe from Jael?" I asked. That was hard to imagine.

"*Safer,*" he corrected. "And safer from Tohon's soldiers, as well."

"I feel *so much* better."

Despite my sarcasm, he smiled. "Good." He turned to Estrid. "Can I assign a guard to protect her?"

"She's secure inside this house. It's well guarded," Estrid said.

"I can defend myself," I said, annoyed.

Ryne waited.

"All right. Avry, you're welcome to stay in the same guest room as before, or there's a smaller room next to the infirmary that's not in use."

"I'd rather stay closer to my patients."

She nodded, as if expecting that answer. "Good." She left.

I rounded on Ryne. "Why did you insist on a guard? You know he can't protect me from Jael, and if Tohon's soldiers get this close, we're done."

"It's for my peace of mind."

"About what?" I asked.

"That you won't take off, for one."

"That makes no sense. Where would I go?"

"What if there's news of Belen? Someone spotted him in enemy territory. Would you stay here or go search for him?" He saw the answer in my expression. "We can't risk you encountering Tohon's soldiers again, Avry. You're too valuable."

I'd heard that before. "And your other reason?"

"Tohon's spies. They're here, and we've no idea who they are. When Tohon learns the truth, you'll be too tempting for him to resist. The way this camp is set up, a couple men wearing Estrid's uniform can easily get to you."

"They can try."

"And they'll know all about your defenses. Why take the chance?"

"All right, I'll stay put for now, but Flea—"

"Stays with you. I agree," Ryne said.

"Hey!" Flea said. "I'm not—"

"Going to let anyone sneak up on Avry," Ryne finished. "I need you to protect her."

Flea stared at Ryne as if seeking his true intentions. I also wondered if Ryne really believed Flea could guard me or was he protecting the boy from battle. Despite his reasons, I was glad for Flea's company.

"But I faint at the sight of blood," Flea said.

Then again... "Nice try, but I know better. You helped with Belen. His blood was everywhere, and you didn't even flinch."

The boy pouted. "Why can't Loren or Quain baby...er... guard her? And I'll stay with you."

"Because you know when she's in trouble," Ryne said. "If you didn't wake me..." He didn't need to finish.

But his comment reminded me about Flea's touch. Striding to the doorway, I glanced out, looking for eavesdroppers. Satisfied we had enough privacy, I returned and pulled Ryne and Flea close to me so they'd hear me.

I explained about the energy from Flea and how I'd thought Kerrick had returned. "The Death Lily said Flea had potential, so he might be developing magical powers."

Ryne frowned. "But you said you fed Flea to a Peace Lily."

"Not that Lily. The one that tried to eat him before."

"The one you saved me from?" Flea asked.

"Yes."

"But magicians are born with their powers," Ryne said.

"Except healers. He could become a healer." I paused as another thought bubbled to the surface. "If you think about it, Flea's resurrection can be considered a birth, so he could become a mage."

"Well then, there's another reason to keep you two together," Ryne said. "You can figure out what's going on."

Flea's pout had turned thoughtful. "I don't feel any different."

"Did you experience anything when you touched me?" I pointed to my neck. "Skin on skin. It doesn't work through clothes."

"I…" He bent his head so his hair covered his eyes. "I dreamed you were in trouble, and when I woke up, I couldn't breathe." Flea played with the bottom of his nightshirt. "But I knew exactly where you were. Now that I think about it, that's really weird."

"What type of magician has that kind of power?" Ryne asked me.

"I don't know. Not a healer or a forest mage, as we're inside a building. An air magician? Perhaps he was drawn to Jael."

"Ugh, I hope not," Flea said.

"She did kill you. Perhaps her magic stayed with you," I said, thinking about how Tohon's magical taint must still be lingering inside me.

"Can you move the air?" Ryne asked Flea.

He lifted his head and scrunched up his nose. Nothing happened.

I mulled over what he'd said about knowing my location. "What did you feel when you touched me?"

He shrugged. "Your skin was cold, but I felt your pulse and was relieved. Other than that...tired."

When two magicians shared energy, both felt the exchange. One was strengthened while the other weakened. Usually the link could only be between two of the same magicians, but Kerrick and I could share. This puzzle would have to wait. My head ached, and my throat burned from Jael's attack.

"Ursan might be able to sniff out his magic when he returns. In the meantime, we can do a few experiments." I rubbed my neck. "But not now. I should grab breakfast before reporting to the infirmary. Flea, do you want to meet me there after you get your stuff?"

"I guess. Where is it?"

"I'll show you," Ryne offered.

"And can you extend my...regrets to Lieutenant Thea and her sergeants?" I asked Ryne. I was already missing the sergeant's fire.

He agreed, but before he left, I asked about Belen. "When do you expect him to return?"

"Soon. Don't worry about Belen."

But the flash of concern in Ryne's brown eyes was hard to miss.

I spent the rest of the day working in the infirmary, reacquainting myself with the staff and the layout. Most of the staff remembered me. The young woman in charge of the caregivers, Christina, took a little more convincing. She tucked a strand of long black hair behind her ear as she eyed me with suspicion. I had to demonstrate my magic in order for her to cooperate.

Only a few patients occupied beds. I visited each one, assessing injuries and sicknesses. All would heal on their own.

Satisfied no one needed me, I scanned the infirmary. Estrid had converted a ballroom to take care of her soldiers. The four long rows of beds would hold a significant number of injured. She also spared no expense with the supplies. The cabinets were well stocked with clean bandages, basins, sponges, needles, thread and medicinal herbs.

My pleasure at returning to my job was tempered with the fact that these beds and supplies would be needed in three days if Ryne was right about Tohon. Plus worry for Belen, Ursan, the jacks and especially Kerrick never faded from my heart.

Flea's arrival distracted me from my morbid thoughts. We moved a bed into the small room next to the infirmary. Flea insisted it be stationed along the right wall near the door so an intruder would have to trip over him before reaching me. My trunk had already been delivered. It sat at the bottom of the other bed in the back left corner. The room also contained a desk, chair, night table, couch and an armoire. I offered the armoire to Flea since I had the trunk.

He touched the sword he had taken from the ambush. "Aside from this and the trio of juggling stones, I've nothing but the clothes on my back."

"Well then, tomorrow we'll go—"

"No. Prince Ryne told me to make sure you stay in the manor."

"It's just into town to buy you a few things. Surely there won't be any danger at the market." I sensed a softening. "And we'll take along Saul or Odd."

"No. We'll send one of the caregivers with a shopping list," Flea said.

"Hey, that's…"

He waited.

I huffed. "A good idea. But don't be so smug. You're not going to win every argument."

"Oh, yes, I am."

"Oh, no, you're not."

Flea straightened to his full height. When did he get so tall? He rested his hands on his hips. "I am. Prince Ryne trusted *me* with the task of keeping you safe. And I'm not going to disappoint him."

I crossed my arms. "You sound like Kerrick."

"Thank you."

"Uh-huh. You do know I disobeyed almost all of his orders. Right?" I suppressed a grin.

"I do. But I'm smarter than Kerrick."

"You are?"

"Oh, yes. I know the magic word."

"And that would be?"

"Please."

Over the next two days, I worked in the infirmary. The injuries I treated were mostly minor. The first day, I healed a soldier who had sprained his ankle because it would have taken him weeks to recover, while it would only take me a couple days.

Liv and Wynn visited me on the morning of the second day. They hovered in the doorway, eyeing the room as if seeking evidence of an ambush. Flea juggled for a young patient who had hit her head. She giggled as he pretended to lose control of the stones and pratfell into another bed.

I limped over and waved them in.

Wynn pointed to my ankle. "What's the matter, Baby Face? Can't hack it without us?"

"It's one of the perks of my new job," I said. "So what can I do for you?"

Liv held out her right index finger. "I've got a splinter that I can't get out. It's killing me and affecting my duty."

"Uh-huh." I examined the minuscule speck that could be dirt. "Let's go into my examination-slash-treatment room."

They followed me to the alcove that had been built for a full-sized orchestra back when the owners of this house had hosted balls. I was in the process of converting it into a place where I could heal without everyone watching. Flea had rounded up a number of privacy screens that I had used as walls. But the best part was the oversized windows that allowed in the bright sunlight.

I washed Liv's hand, taking care of the problem.

She rubbed her finger. "Wow, you're a miracle worker, Baby Face."

"Did Lieutenant Thea send you to check up on me?" I asked.

"I'm insulted that you're unsympathetic to my pain," Liv said with a smile.

I patted her shoulder. "Poor baby."

Wynn looked around. "Nice digs. Do all the rooms in the house have their own entertainer or are you just special?"

"I've been blessed by the creator."

Liv snorted. "Just don't let the Purity Priestess's goons catch you, or you'll be begging his forgiveness in a two-by-four foot cell in Chinska Mare for the rest of your days."

"Now I'm insulted." But her comment reminded me of Melina. Too bad I couldn't do anything to help her right now.

"Are you saying I'm wrong? Maybe I should go find Miss Purity..." Liv stood.

"Sit down," I said, laughing.

But she remained on her feet. Concern filled her eyes despite her smile. "If I leave the infirmary, could you follow me?"

Ah, the real reason for their visit. "Of course. I'm here because this is where I belong."

Liv and Wynn glanced at each other.

"We get that you're a healer, Baby Face," Liv said. "But you're also a teacher. We've already learned so much from you. Why can't you do both?"

I gaped at her. I'd never been called anything other than a healer. But as I thought about it, I realized she had a point. I could do more than heal. How nice to have another skill. Another purpose.

"Uh, Avry? We're waiting." Wynn swiped her hand in front of my face.

"Sorry. I could do both, but you don't need me anymore. Odd's taken over the silent training, and Ryne's teaching that skull jab."

"But what about your healing knowledge?" Liv asked. "It's not all about magic. I've heard there are plants that can help. I'm sure you know all about that."

"I do, but there's not much time."

"True." Liv sat. "There have been more skirmishes along our front lines. It's like Tohon's testing our defenses. And reports have been coming in that more of Tohon's patrols have been spotted before they disappear. Poof!" She snapped her fingers.

"Creepy," Wynn added.

"Is there a magic that can turn them invisible?" Liv asked.

"A forest mage can camouflage them, but as far as I know, Tohon doesn't have one."

I considered the nine other magical powers—earth, water, fire, air, life, rock, death, moon and sun. Tohon's army included a death, fire, rock and earth magician. Of those four,

I knew the most about Sepp's death magic and how he could freeze life in a fake death. If I ever encountered Sepp again, that pompous traitor would wish for death by the time I was done with him. However, what little I knew about the others hadn't included invisibility. Could an earth magician also camouflage them, as well? Even before the plague, magicians had kept the extent of their abilities to themselves for fear of kidnapping and coercion.

Another round of giggles erupted from the infirmary followed by Flea's chuckle. From the tests we'd tried so far, Flea hadn't been able to influence air, water, fire or heal anyone. Strange talents did manifest from time to time. But the only thing Flea could do so far was give me energy. We needed to do more experiments.

"Do you know if the soldiers that disappeared wore neck armor?" I asked Liv.

"Yeah. A couple sergeants reported seeing them. And one guy said he spotted ones that had been painted green."

"It makes sense to camouflage them," Wynn said. "We'll be fighting in the woods."

Thinking about the dead soldiers, I tried to figure out what would be the best way to employ them in a battle. They didn't need food or water or sleep or air. They mindlessly followed orders. They were disposable. Tohon could have been hiding his dead soldiers all around us for weeks or months. I straightened in alarm.

"What's wrong?" Liv asked, staring at me.

I needed to talk to Ryne to see if I was way off base or not. If he agreed, Estrid's troops would need to be warned. But would they listen? They had learned the skull jab, but not because they truly understood the nature of the enemy. Unless Belen arrived with proof.

Instead of answering her, I asked, "Have Ursan and the jacks returned?"

"Not yet."

"What's wrong? Come on, Baby Face, spit it out," Wynn said.

"It's crazy, and I doubt you'd believe me," I said.

"Hey, we've been with you from the beginning. And we're here with you now," Liv said.

True. In a low voice, I explained my suspicions.

"It's not crazy," Wynn said. "It's insane!"

"And just the thing to catch us completely off guard." Liv rubbed her hands over her face. "Lieutenant Thea and Major Granvil might understand, but our company is just one of many."

"It's impossible, Liv!" Wynn said. "Even assuming they're camouflaged and able to sit still for days, one of our numerous patrols would have stumbled over at least one of them. It's statistically impossible!"

She made an excellent point. We sat in silence for a moment.

"Ulany is an earth magician, and she's working for Tohon," I said. "Perhaps she can do more than find good soil for crops and worms."

"You think she buried them?" Liv asked.

"Not possible. We'd have seen the signs," Wynn said, dismissing the idea.

I wondered if her resistance to this line of thought stemmed from fear or her skeptical nature. "Magic is woven into the fabric of our world, Wynn. I've seen what a forest mage can do with his powers, and it's impressive. And I think anything is possible, including the ability of an earth magician to conceal soldiers in the dirt."

"All this speculation isn't getting us anywhere. Wynn and I can ask around, see if any of the patrols have spotted Ursan.

Everyone's already on edge because of the skull jab and rumors that Tohon is going to attack on midsummer's day. We can keep that energy up just in case Tohon has another magical trick up his sleeve."

"I'll talk to Prince Ryne and have my workers put together care packages," I said.

"Care packages?" Liv asked.

"It's your idea. I'm going to have my caregivers put together a few medicinal herbs that might come in handy when the squads are out on patrol or after a battle."

"See that?" Liv punched Wynn on the arm as they headed out. "I helped. And you said I wouldn't amount to much."

"No. I said you talk too much." Wynn swatted her on the shoulder. "You never listen to me."

After they left, I checked on my patients and asked Christina to have her staff fill pouches. "Put the crushed herbs in the ones made of oilskin to protect them from getting wet, and include a set of quick instructions."

"We're not going to have enough pouches or herbs," Christina said.

Since I'd been working with her, I'd learned she had been born in Quaia Mare near the southeast coast of Ozero. Her honey skin tone and cat-shaped brown eyes matched the others from that region.

"Then send someone to the market," I said.

"Uh, the High Priestess must approve all purchases."

"Not if I give you the money."

Since I'd been a soldier in Estrid's army, I hadn't needed to buy food or clothing, and Kerrick had given me more than enough. A pang of longing hit me. I allowed an image of him smiling at me to fill my thoughts for a moment before I retrieved the coins for Christina.

Once I was satisfied with the progress Christina and the others were making, I headed toward the door.

Flea blocked my path. "Where are you going?"

"To talk to Ryne." When he didn't move out of my way, I added, "It's important."

"Send him a message."

"Too risky, I need—"

"To stay put like you promised Prince Ryne. I'll send a message to the prince, requesting his presence in the infirmary so you can talk to him." Flea kept his expression neutral, but a smugness gleamed from his eyes.

Not much I could do. "As long as you *stress* to him that it's *vital* and *time sensitive.*"

"Of course." A hint of a smirk curled as he turned to find a messenger.

"Flea."

He looked over his shoulder. "Yes?"

"Kerrick would be proud."

I was rewarded with one of his full-blown smiles before he hurried away.

I helped pack herbs and write instructions while I waited for Ryne. With every slight noise or scrape of a boot, I glanced at the entrance. What was taking him so long?

When he finally arrived a few hours later, I couldn't miss the commotion that heralded his approach. At first, I thought a fight had broken out in the hall. Flea pulled his sword and stood by the door. Voices called, and a big group of men burst into the room followed by Ryne, Thea and Major Granvil.

It took me a heartbeat to recognize a couple jumping jacks among that first clump. They carried an injured man. I pointed to a bed. And only when they laid him down did they allow me to get close.

Ursan. One part of me cried out in dismay, but another cat-alogued his injuries. A deep gash on his head bled profusely. He hugged his stomach, and his right leg bent at an impossible angle. Broken. His eyes were squeezed shut, but they opened when I touched his neck, feeling his rapid pulse and sweat-slick skin. Pain-filled eyes met my gaze, and I knew there was another deeper wound.

Magic bloomed from my core, but I held back while I sought the injury. It wasn't hard to find as his men had tried to bandage it. A huge chunk of flesh had been gouged from his side as if an ufa had taken a bite out of him, damaging his spleen and a kidney. Fatal for him. I wasn't sure about my chances, but I didn't hesitate.

When I reached to touch him again, he grabbed my arms with surprising speed, wrapping his fingers around my sleeves.

"No," he gasped, stopping me. "Don't."

"Don't what?" I asked.

"Save me."

"Not your decision." I tried to move my hands closer to make skin contact, but he held on with all his considerable strength.

"Listen." He hissed in pain. "It stinks…"

"Let me—"

"Listen! It…all stinks…every…where." He shuddered, but he wouldn't let go. "Under…stand?"

"Yes. It stinks. Now let me heal you."

"No."

I glanced at the others hovering nearby. "Help me."

Ryne stood next to me. "Will you survive?"

"It doesn't matter."

"Yes, it does," Ryne said in a soft voice.

"She…won't." Ursan convulsed again. "I…know…" He met Ryne's gaze. "Don't let…her."

Ursan's grip relaxed as he passed out. Before I could touch him, Ryne grabbed me and yanked me back. I yelled and struggled, but he wouldn't let go. Stronger than he looked, Ryne trapped my arms so I couldn't zap him.

All I could do was watch as Ursan drew in his last breath. Utter sadness washed through me. I sagged against Ryne until I remembered he had prevented me from healing Ursan.

"Bastard," I said, jerking from his embrace.

Ryne didn't reply. Silence blanketed the room. I closed Ursan's eyes. No life sparked under my fingertips. He was beyond my reach. I glanced at the others. Three jumping jacks, Thea, Major Granvil and Flea stared at Ursan with various degrees of grief. My gaze lingered on Flea, and a bit of hope pushed against the gloom inside me. Perhaps a Peace Lily would bring Ursan back to life.

But something was missing. I scanned the faces again until I reached Flea. Then it hit me. Not something but someone. Belen.

"Where's Belen?" I asked one of the jacks.

He dropped his gaze and stared at the floor. "He's gone."

Terrified, I rounded on him. "What do you mean by *gone?*"

His buddy answered for him. "Belen disappeared."

KERRICK

"Are they going to kill us?" Danny asked.

The boy had hooked his arm through Kerrick's as they walked toward Krakowa with the tribesmen. Unlike Kerrick, Danny's hands were free, and he had his backpack. Kerrick considered his response carefully. He didn't want to scare Danny, but he didn't want to lie to him either.

Was it better to be prepared for death or surprised? Kerrick had no idea. His ribs throbbed with every step, and the rope they'd used to bind his wrists behind his back stung as blood dripped down his hands. His sluggish thoughts felt as if they'd been soaking too long in pickle juice. The combination of not enough sleep and food over the past seven days had taken a toll on him.

"They'll keep us alive as long as they have a use for us," Kerrick said. He glanced over his shoulder.

Noak followed the warriors. Since they'd started the trek north, Kerrick had been racking his brain trying to figure out why Noak was returning instead of conquering the rest of the northern realms. Perhaps he was scared of the plague. Kerrick almost laughed at the notion that something good might happen because of the plague.

"How do we know when they don't need us anymore?"

Danny asked. His fingers dug into Kerrick's arm as he gazed up at Kerrick with eyes wide.

Poor kid was terrified. Kerrick lowered his voice. "Danny, I want you to do something for me."

Danny's grip tightened, but he kept steady. "What is it?"

"I want you to make friends. Be helpful. Ask questions and learn about their ways and beliefs."

"Like a spy?"

"Yes. But you need to be genuine about it."

"Why?"

Kerrick took a moment to form a reply. It would be so much easier to just order Danny, but the boy would resist. "If they…like you, they'll always find a use for you."

"You mean they won't kill me?"

Too smart by far. "Yes."

"What about you?"

"Don't worry about me."

Danny gave him a long look. "Yeah, right."

Over the next day, Danny took Kerrick's advice. At first the warriors rejected the boy, but he persisted, trying different tactics.

That day—their third on the road—Kerrick estimated they'd reach the outskirts of Krakowa by midsummer's day. And then what?

Not long after they stopped to prepare for the night, Kerrick dozed until shouts and curses rang out nearby. One of the warriors dragged Danny along by his arm. The warrior talked to Noak in a rapid-fire burst, gesturing wildly.

Kerrick caught the words *poison, sneak* and *kill.* Not good. He summoned his strength in case he needed to help Danny. The boy held a plant in his hands. Dirt still clung to the roots.

Danny tried to explain, but Noak clipped him on the ear.

Kerrick pushed to his feet, sliding his back and scraping his arms along the tree's trunk until he stood. He yelled at Noak. All three turned toward him.

Noak snatched the plant from Danny and strode to Kerrick. The warrior pulled Danny with him as he followed his leader. The boy pressed a hand over his left ear, but held back the tears that threatened to spill over his eyelashes.

"What's this?" Noak asked, waving the green leaves.

Kerrick glanced at Danny. "Are you all right?"

"Yes."

Noak grabbed Kerrick's throat. "I asked a question."

Icy daggers shot through his neck, but Kerrick kept his gaze on Danny. "I don't know. Danny, what's going on?"

"It's a fonswup plant," Danny said in a rush. "It helps with infection. I wanted to give it to Onion. He has a bad cut on his leg."

Noak released him and turned to Danny. "How do you know this?"

Danny looked at Kerrick as if seeking permission. Kerrick nodded.

"It's in Avry's book. She gave me her notes before she died."

"Show me," Noak ordered.

Danny fetched his backpack. He pulled Avry's journal out and flipped through it. When he reached the page he sought, he turned the book so Noak could see. He pointed to a drawing of a fonswup plant and the explanation written in Avry's neat hand. "It says it right here."

Kerrick was impressed by the artwork. Avry's picture appeared so lifelike with the delicate leaves and blue veins.

Noak stared at the page with his brow creased. Suspicion or confusion, Kerrick couldn't tell. Perhaps the leader couldn't read.

"Danny, how does it say to prepare it?" Kerrick asked.

"Boil the leaves in hot water and drink the broth."

"Noak, let him brew the...tea and I'll drink it first. He's trying to help...Onion? Is it?"

Danny nodded.

"He won't hurt Onion," Kerrick said.

"Why would he help?" Noak asked.

That was an easy question to answer. "Because the woman who gave him that book was a healer. And she'd heal anyone, friend or foe, without hesitation. He honors her memory by doing the same."

"With magic?"

"No. With plants."

Noak still didn't look convinced, but he allowed Danny to brew the medicine. Kerrick swallowed a few mouthfuls. It was bitter but had no ill effects. Danny was eventually allowed to treat Onion.

When Danny reported that the warrior's cut looked better, the tight fist that had been clamped around Kerrick's heart since he'd seen Danny in Noak's hands eased a fraction. The boy had found a way to be needed.

CHAPTER 13

The day after Ursan died dawned with bright sunlight in a cloudless blue sky. The temperature rose as the hour of his funeral approached. Last night I had wanted to search for Poppa Bear and would have left in an instant, except that bastard Ryne prevented me from leaving the infirmary. He had promised to investigate.

As I'd waited for news, one horrible scenario after another ran through my mind. I couldn't concentrate. Each hour that Belen failed to return upped my agitation level tenfold. If Tohon had taken Belen… I shied away from those thoughts. Instead, I focused on planning my next move. If I could bypass my keepers, then I could…what? Offer myself in Belen's place? Yes, I would, despite the sheer terror that gripped me when I imagined myself back with Tohon. Belen was worth it.

Eventually, I'd gone to bed heartsick and exhausted.

Ryne arrived at midmorning. He wore a blue silk tunic and black pants. And for the first time since I'd known him, he looked regal. Loren and Quain followed him in. They, too, wore formal clothes.

"Are you ready?" Ryne asked.

Too worried about Belen, I had forgotten about changing into proper attire for a funeral. I hurried to my room.

My nicest clothes were the green skirt and light yellow shirt Kerrick had bought me long ago. I debated between that and my dress uniform and decided that, for Ursan, my dress uniform was more appropriate. After I changed, I joined Ryne, and we walked to the burial grounds east of the manor house.

Estrid's creator promised life after death, and her religion insisted on a proper burial in hallowed ground. I stood between Quain and Loren as the High Priestess performed the ceremony—an unexpected honor. Jael's absence wasn't a surprise. Major Granvil, Lieutenant Thea, the sergeants and the remaining jacks were also in attendance.

Only three jacks had returned from the mission. According to the report, they had encountered a troop of dead soldiers but hadn't been able to capture one. Instead, they'd been attacked and then pursued when they retreated. Belen and Ursan each had taken five jacks and split up to confuse the enemy.

Ursan's group had run into another ambush, which they'd barely escaped alive. Unfortunately, one of the jacks had died before they could reach me. And Ursan… I shied away from those thoughts, only to brood about Belen's whereabouts.

When Ursan's coffin was lowered into the ground, Loren leaned close and whispered, "It's empty. We have his body."

"When?" I asked. Hope replaced my grief for a moment, but I tucked it away. There was no guarantee that the Peace Lily would take Ursan, let alone revive him.

"Right after the service."

"I need to be there."

"That's why I'm telling you. Do you still have the Lily location map?"

"No." I glanced at Saul. He stood with Liv, Wynn and Odd. They all bowed their heads as Estrid asked the creator to welcome Ursan's soul into her peaceful embrace.

After the High Priestess finished, she grabbed a handful of

dirt and threw it into the open grave. Then as custom dictated, each person in attendance would add another handful. A line formed as Estrid moved away from the burial site. I followed Quain, and Loren stepped behind me, ending the queue.

"I'll talk to Saul," I said to Loren in a low voice as we waited for our turn. "If he doesn't have the map anymore, I'm pretty sure I can find the Peace Lily again," I said.

"Good," Loren said.

"How do you plan to move—"

"Horses."

"But it's been a day, and with this heat…isn't he…" I couldn't finish.

"We have him on ice."

"Where did you find ice?"

Loren glanced around and then whispered, "Marisol, the water mage. Prince Ryne is acquainted with her and the specifics of her power."

"Does she know why you needed it?"

"Probably not. Prince Ryne made the arrangements. The wagon and horses are ready. They're over by the woods next to the POW camp. We'll meet there an hour after the service. Prince Ryne wants us back tomorrow."

Which was midsummer's day. "But what if the Lily doesn't spit him out right away?" I asked.

"Then we'll return on another day."

I faced forward as we drew closer to Ursan's grave. When it was my turn, I grabbed a fistful of moist earth. It hadn't rained at the camp in weeks, but the grass out here was a lush green. Was Marisol's or Jael's power keeping it watered?

Leaning over the open grave, I let the dirt pour from my hand onto the top of Ursan's coffin. My emotions swirled into a confusing mix of sadness, guilt and dread if our plan didn't work. I closed my eyes and made a silent promise to do all that I could for him.

After the ceremony, the sergeants approached me. Although time was an issue, I wouldn't hurry away. No humor sparked in Odd's gaze, Liv and Wynn looked glum, and lines of grief creased Saul's face.

"I'm sorry," I said. "I tried—"

"We heard," Liv said. "The jacks told us."

"Typical of Ursan to think of the bigger picture even when dying," Wynn said.

The others agreed, and silence descended as each of us mourned our colleague.

"Any news about Belen and the others?" I asked.

"No. Not even a rumor," Wynn said. "We'll let you know if we hear."

She squeezed my shoulder before she, Liv and Odd headed back to camp. Training and preparations continued despite the loss. If anything, Ursan's death was an added reminder to be extra diligent.

Saul lingered behind. He waited until the sergeants had moved out of hearing range. "When?"

"When what?" I asked.

He pulled out a paper from his pocket and handed it to me. I unfolded it, revealing a rough sketch of the area around Zabin marked with the locations of the Lilys. He had copied the original.

"That obvious?" I asked.

"For those of us who know." Saul glanced at Flea, who hovered a polite distance away. "Major Granvil requests that you take me along in exchange for his cooperation."

Interesting. "His cooperation for what exactly?"

"For keeping his mouth shut about your young friend. He

wants to be kept in the loop regarding any future attempts to duplicate the…incident."

Saul was uncharacteristically verbose. I suspected he had quoted the major word for word.

"That's rather brave. Isn't the major worried about Jael eventually finding out?" I asked.

"The major is taking a wait-and-see approach. If this doesn't work, then he won't look like a fool for believing you."

"Me?"

He smiled. "Yes, you. Now that your true identity has been revealed, you're not trustworthy, so we can blame you for lots of stuff that goes wrong."

"Great. What if it works?" Again a swell of hope threatened to push the sadness away.

"Then he has some good news and proof for his commanding officer."

"I see. I'll consult with Ryne and let you know." And then it hit me. I'd never discussed with him my theories regarding Tohon's dead soldiers. With everything that had happened with Ursan and then Belen, it had slipped my mind. I spotted Ryne talking with Estrid. The monkeys stayed close to him.

Saul nodded and returned to camp. When Ryne broke away from Estrid and her retinue, he joined me. The monkeys trailed behind with Flea.

Ryne gestured to the sea of tents below us. "No time to waste."

We headed back.

"Did Loren tell you where to rendezvous with them?" he asked.

"Yes, and Saul wants to accompany us." I repeated my conversation with the sergeant to him.

"Major Granvil is putting a great deal of faith in us," Ryne said. "Saul can come, but he'll have to ride with you."

"I'll tell him. And I also need to talk to you regarding those disappearing soldiers."

His full attention focused on me. "What about them?"

"This is pure speculation." I explained my theory about the buried soldiers. "Feel free to tell me I'm crazy. I won't mind."

Instead, he stared at me with shocked horror as if I'd just plunged my stiletto into his heart.

"Please tell me I have an overactive imagination," I said.

"Give me a minute." Ryne's voice cracked.

Uh-oh. I wondered if he was also acquainted with Ulany, the earth mage, and the extent of her powers.

"It sounds impossible, but I…" He sucked in a deep breath. "I need to…"

Ryne flabbergasted? Fear shot through me. "Need to what?"

He straightened, pulling himself together. "Check my books. I brought a few with me. In school we had learned about the abilities of various magical powers in depth."

"But I thought they kept that to themselves?"

"As future leaders of the Fifteen Realms, we were privy to more sensitive information than regular students."

When we reached the edge of the encampment, Ryne rushed off. Loren and Quain hurried after him, leaving me and Flea. The restless energy of the camp pressed against me as we walked through the tents. A buzz filled the air, and the soldiers in the training sessions sparred with a fierce determination.

I found Saul and told him where to meet us. Then Flea and I hustled back to the manor house to change and pack. I informed my staff we were going to collect herbs and I'd return tomorrow, leaving Christina in charge. We cut through Ryne's army, heading north to the POW camp. Loren waited with Saul on the edge of the woods.

"There's been a change in plans," Loren said when we approached. "Since Saul is going with you, Prince Ryne wants me and Flea to stay in camp. The horses are within the forest about a quarter mile straight north of here. Ursan's body is already secured to one horse, and there are two others for you. Their handler is with them, but he'll return once you're under way."

I exchanged a glance with Flea. Something was wrong. "What's going on, Loren?"

"I'm not sure. Honest. Whatever you told Prince Ryne earlier has agitated him. He said we needed to concentrate our forces at the border."

Which meant he believed my theory was possible. A horrified dread churned in my stomach. "Why does he need Flea? He's been so adamant that I'm protected." And Flea, as well.

"He knows you'll be safe with Saul. And he said, 'Tell Avry to trust me regarding Flea.'"

I might not understand Ryne's motives, but I trusted him. "All right."

Loren's shoulders relaxed, and I almost smiled. The poor guy must have been prepared for a fight.

"Don't dawdle. Be back early tomorrow. The horses are fast and can be ridden after dark," Loren said.

"Got it," I said.

Saul and I said goodbye to Loren and Flea. Despite Ryne's assurances, I felt a twinge of worry for Flea as we entered the woods. It was probably something I'd have to get used to. Flea couldn't be by my side all the time after all. I wondered if this was how mothers felt with their children. At least Danny and Zila were safe at Ryne's castle. Unless the invasion of the tribes wasn't stopped, which would mean Kerrick... No. I wouldn't even consider the possibility.

Before we reached the horses, Saul made a noise and called out in a soothing voice so we wouldn't startle them. When we approached, the three horses had their heads raised with one ear perked forward and the other cocked back. Their handler—a young man—murmured to them and stroked their necks until they relaxed.

Ursan's body had been wrapped in oilskin and draped over the back of a chestnut-colored mare. Saul talked to the handler. The young man bobbed his head, gestured to the saddlebags and then took off. Saul grabbed the reins of the big brown-and-white horse before swinging into the saddle.

"Hand me the reins of Ursan's horse," Saul said. When I hesitated, he shot me a concerned look. "Do you know how to ride?"

"Uh...sort of." I moved closer. "My mentor, Tara, taught me the basics back when I was an apprentice." She had insisted, claiming we might be needed in an emergency and would have to travel fast. Horses were expensive, and my family hadn't been able to afford to own or even hire one.

"How long ago?" Saul asked.

"Five years."

"Heck of a time to get reacquainted."

I agreed, but since I'd promised Ursan to do all I could for him, I swallowed my anxiety and untied the reins of Ursan's horse, handing them to Saul. The last horse was all black except for the white on the bottom half of her legs. She looked as if she wore socks. I secured my pack on my back, freed her reins and hopped up into her saddle. She cocked her head to peer at me as I patted her neck.

"You need to lead," Saul said. "My hands are full."

I pulled the map from my pocket and studied it a moment before spurring my horse into motion, which almost unseated me. With her bumpy, jarring gait, it took effort to gain my balance. Once I felt more secure, I urged her into a faster, smoother rhythm along a footpath.

Traveling via horseback might be quicker but it certainly wasn't quieter. Our passage through the woods could probably be heard miles away. Another drawback was locating paths big enough to accommodate the horses. Our route wouldn't be direct, but at least we were heading northeast, away from enemy lines.

Soon after we'd set off, the horse broke her stride and stumbled before recovering. Behind me, Saul and Ursan's horses also shied before settling. I shrugged it off; horses were skittish despite their size.

As we traveled, I consulted the map from time to time and made adjustments. When we reached the clump of Lilys northeast of Zabin, the sun hung low in the sky, casting long shadows.

We dismounted. Taking Ursan's horse close to the Lilys, I helped Saul untie the body, and we lowered him onto the ground. Now I understood the term *deadweight*. Saul cut the bindings around the oilskin. Even though I was no stranger to death and cadavers, I braced myself as I peeled the cloth back.

Bone-pale despite the hours he had trained in the sun, Ursan's skin was damp from the melting ice. Pain throbbed deep inside me. Anger flared. Stupid, stubborn man should have let me heal him. If this worked, I had a few choice words for him.

"Can you carry him?" I asked Saul.

"With your assistance."

I helped Saul lift Ursan, but once he straightened and settled the body in his arms, he didn't need me. We walked to the Lilys. Only a single Death Lily grew among three Peace Lilys. We approached the closest Peace Lily and stood underneath its petals. The faint scent of vanilla wafted in the air. Biting my lip, I waited for the giant flower to move.

Nothing happened.

"Come on, you helped Flea," I cried.

Not even a twitch.

I grabbed the Lily's stalk and tried to shake it. The thick green stem didn't budge.

Yanking my stiletto from its sheath, I lunged for the Lily, aiming the tip at a petal. But vines snaked around my ankles before I could reach it, tripping me. They continued up my legs and along my arms, stealing my weapon.

I thrashed, yelled and cursed, but the plant held me tight. Eventually I ran out of steam and wilted.

Saul had watched my antics with a queasy expression. But he'd remained in place with Ursan.

"Now what?" he asked.

The ground around us rumbled alarmingly. The earth heaved, and Saul stepped back as a mound of loose soil grew as if a very energetic dog dug for a bone.

When the noise died and the dust settled, a deep rectangular hole had opened up at the base of the Peace Lily. Oh, no.

"You're supposed to take him, you overgrown weed," I shouted. "Not bury him."

"Wow," Saul said. "That's not subtle. Should I...?"

"No. We'll find another Lily. Cut me loose."

Saul set Ursan down and pulled his sword. But as soon as he came close, the Lily ensnared him in its vines, as well. His sword disappeared into the foliage.

"Got any more ideas?" he asked.

"I'm thinking."

As I considered, roots from the cavity flowed over the edge, wrapped around Ursan and drew him toward the grave.

"Think faster," Saul said.

But no matter how hard I thought or struggled, there was nothing I could do but watch. After the Peace Lily pulled him in and covered him with a lattice of roots, the dirt mound reversed, filling the hole. Within minutes all that remained was the smooth ground.

The vines released Saul, but they carried me to the base of the Death Lily, letting go just as its petals encircled me in darkness. The barbs pierced my skin, and I connected with the flower's soul.

I demanded answers to Ursan's rejection. Instead of a reply, memories came to my mind unbidden.

It was strange to remember past incidents not of my own choosing. Images from my time with Tohon, conversations with Sepp, the death magician, being held by the dead, Danny, Zila and Kerrick all flickered in front of me.

One memory wasn't mine. A vision of Kerrick sitting on the ground, cradling me in his arms. My lifeless eyes stared at nothing. Kerrick closed them and then squeezed his own shut as he hunched over me in utter misery. Then my eyes opened. This view had to be from the Death Lily, but why show me? Was it significant?

Touch.

The answer hit me. The Peace Lily hadn't brought me back to life, Kerrick's touch had. It was the same with Flea. He hadn't been breathing until I touched him. And why us? Because we had Peace Lily serum in our veins. However, one wouldn't work without the other. A person needed both the serum and a touch. But could anyone touch them?

I asked. No answer. What about Ursan? I could touch him, too.

Gone too long. The Lily withdrew its barbs and expelled me onto the ground. It took me a moment to gather my wits. I glanced around in the semidarkness. The sun had set, and Saul had built a small fire.

He hurried over and knelt beside me. "Are you all right? You're bleeding." He pointed to my upper arms.

Blood stained my sleeves. "I'll be fine."

"What happened?"

"I'm not sure."

Saul stood and reached his hand out. I would have grasped it except I held an orange sack in each hand. More of the Death Lily's toxin sacks. Why? There must be a reason the Lily wanted me to have them. I hoped I'd figure it out.

"How long was I in the Lily?" I asked.

"Long enough for me to feed, water and groom the horses," Saul said. "I also cooked us dinner. You must be starving."

"I'm sorry about Ursan. We didn't get him here fast enough."

"At least there's hope for another."

Suddenly exhausted, I sank down next to the fire. "I've no idea about the timing. Flea had been dead a couple hours." According to Kerrick, I'd died inside the Peace Lily. "I don't think I'll be able to figure out these Lilys."

"Don't give up. It's too important."

I nodded.

"We need to leave at dawn. Tomorrow's midsummer's day." Saul handed me a steaming bowl.

After I ate, Saul offered to take the first shift. I gratefully accepted and fell asleep next to the fire. Tohon's dead hunted me through my dreams. Saul woke me before they could drag me back to Tohon. I spent my shift pacing around the Lilys, mulling over the significance of its toxin.

Midsummer's day dawned with another cloudless sky. My horse seemed to understand we were returning home. She chose the path before I could direct her.

As we neared the camp, we crossed the area that had spooked the horses. This time, the horses broke into a panicked run, bolting as if chased. I took the hint and kept going.

When we rode into the camp, the horses automatically headed to their barn behind Estrid's manor house. Something seemed odd, but it wasn't until after we dismounted and left the horses in the care of their handler that we discovered the reason.

We rounded the corner of the house and stopped in our tracks. A section of the camp appeared…different. Tents remained, but some of them had toppled and others had rips in their fabric. Trash littered the ground, and the fire pits had been doused. The abandoned area appeared as if a strong storm had swept a path right through it. After a moment, I realized the section was where Ryne's army was bivouacked.

I rushed over to Ryne's tent and entered. It was empty.

KERRICK

Midsummer's day used to be special. It had been the last day of school, and after the graduation ceremonies the students returned home for a two-month break. For Kerrick, it had been a bittersweet day for a number of years—the ones where he'd been in love with Jael. It had meant sixty days without her, but it had been balanced with being home with Belen and his father. His father... Kerrick wondered what King Neil would think of his son's present circumstances—captured and cooperating with the northern tribes on this glorious mid-summer's day.

King Neil had always shown Kerrick how to lead by his own example. His father had him attend as many meetings, rulings and visits to the other realms as possible. Kerrick would observe the proceedings. After the session, his father would sit with him and they'd discuss the day's events, and he would answer questions. That time together had been Kerrick's favorite. He had his father all to himself, and even when Kerrick disagreed with his father, King Neil had never raised his voice in anger. Kerrick had gotten his temper from his mother.

The warriors escorting Kerrick and Danny relaxed once they exited the forest and entered the farm fields surrounding Krakowa. Kerrick felt his connection to the living green weaken with every step. When they reached the outskirts of the town, their progress slowed. The tribes had set up tents, and their passage drew a crowd. They stared at Kerrick and Danny with both hostile and curious expressions. Blond-haired children ran alongside them.

When they reached the edge of the town proper, a warrior waited. He was a head taller and thicker than Noak. He wore a necklace made from jagged snufa teeth, and his long, pure white hair had been braided into two ropes. Despite the age difference, there was no mistaking the resemblance between the two. Father and son.

Without a word, the older warrior pulled his dadao, strode toward Kerrick and swung the sharp blade. Kerrick braced for the blow, but Noak grabbed his father's arm, stopping the weapon from slicing into Kerrick's neck.

"No prisoners," the older man said.

"Come." Noak led his father away from the others.

Unable to hear them argue, Kerrick watched their expressions. Noak had saved his life, if only for the moment. His and Danny's continued existence would depend on who won the discussion.

Danny wrapped his fingers around Kerrick's arm. "He's scarier than Noak."

Kerrick glanced down at him. "Hard to believe, isn't it?"

A brief grin, then it was gone. "But he's not scarier than Tohon."

"Really?"

The boy nodded. "The tribesmen are straightforward. They kill their enemies, not turn them into an army of dead soldiers."

"True. But if you surrender to Tohon, he won't kill you."

"I'd rather be dead than help Tohon."

"Me, too. But what if he threatened to harm Zila?"

Danny shot him a surprised look.

"It complicates things, doesn't it?" Kerrick asked.

"Yes." Danny swallowed. "I'm sorry, Kerrick. I shouldn't—"

"Stop. Don't apologize. It's my fault you're here. *I* made the mistake of not sending you back to Orel right away. Do you understand?"

"Yes, but—"

"And I want you to promise me something." He didn't add *if we live through the next hour.*

Danny let go of his arm and turned to him with a wary suspicion mixed with fear. "What?"

Kerrick lowered his voice. "While I gave my word to co-operate, you didn't. At some point there will be an opportunity for you to escape. I want you to promise me you'll take it."

The boy's eyes were as wide as an ufa's just before it pounced. "Where would I go?"

"South. Cross the Nine Mountains and find Prince Ryne. He needs to know what's going on." Kerrick waited a few heartbeats. "Will you do that for me?"

Danny met his gaze. "Yes."

"Good." Another knot in his chest eased just a bit. However, it didn't last.

Their conversation finished, Noak's father approached Kerrick with his dadao still in hand. He pointed the dangerous weapon at Danny. "You betrayed your people for this boy. Why?"

Just the same question Kerrick had asked himself a week ago.

"What you learn from me won't make a difference in the end. My people have already been warned of your arrival. I failed to stop you from invading my land, but if I can save one boy…then I will."

Noak's father relaxed his arm. The dadao's tip no longer

threatened Danny. He glanced at Noak. "All right. The boy lives."

"Do you give your word?" Kerrick asked.

The man's full attention slammed into Kerrick. It felt as if he'd been pierced with a thousand daggers of ice.

"You dare question me?" In a blur of motion, his thick sword cut toward Kerrick's neck, then stopped. The man lowered his weapon, stepped closer and peered at him. He pointed to the scars on Kerrick's throat. "Who marked you?"

"An ufa." Kerrick's voice remained steady, despite his racing heart.

He grunted and sheathed the dadao. Glaring at Noak, the tribesman turned and strode away. Kerrick blew out the breath he'd been holding. Had his scars just saved him? That would be a bizarre twist of fate, but he'd gladly take it. He knew it was just a matter of time before they killed him. In the meantime, he would do all he could to ensure Danny's survival.

Noak barked orders at his men. One dragged Danny away. The boy shot him a terrified look.

"It'll be all right," Kerrick called to him. "Just remember what I've told you."

Then two grabbed Kerrick and led him deeper into town. The tribes had moved into the abandoned houses and businesses of Krakowa. Their pale skin and clothes stood out among the dark wood and red bricks. It almost seemed fitting. The plague had killed this town and now ghosts lived here.

His escorts brought him to the jailhouse. They untied his wrists and shoved him into a cell. The door clanged shut behind him. When he turned around, they were gone. Kerrick scanned his surroundings—iron bars, a pallet to sleep on and a slop pot. The place smelled of mildew and musty sweat. Only a few cells occupied the space—all empty except his. He examined his raw and bleeding wrists. A wave of dizziness hit him. He sat on the thin straw-filled mattress. Rubbing his hands over the week's worth of growth on his cheeks, he wondered how long he'd be incarcerated.

The last time, he'd been locked up for two weeks. Two miserable weeks worried about Avry. He still was concerned about her, but by now Ryne and the monkeys should be with her and protecting her—if she'd let them. Had the war with Tohon started? Kerrick stretched out on the bed. Better to recover his strength than to fret about things he couldn't control.

Danny woke him later that afternoon. Sunlight streamed in through the one barred window. The boy stood between two warriors. He held Kerrick's pack along with his own.

"What's going on?" Kerrick asked Danny.

"They're letting us get cleaned up. Your cuts need to be washed or they'll get infected."

The guards unlocked his cell, and for the first time since he'd been caught, they didn't secure his hands. Kerrick followed them to the bathhouse and washed away almost ten days' worth of grime and blood. All his weapons had been taken from his pack, but there was a rustle of consternation when Kerrick pulled out his razor. His guards grabbed the hilts of their dadaos, but he ignored them and shaved, feeling better with every stroke of the sharp blade along his skin.

His razor was confiscated when he finished, but he was allowed to keep his pack. It felt like a luxury to wear clean clothes. And the set of lock picks hidden within them was a nice bonus. Kerrick wasn't sure if or when he'd use them; it was just nice to have the option.

Danny smeared the cuts on his wrists with a sweet-smelling goo and covered them with bandages. The boy seemed jumpy. When they returned to the jailhouse, Kerrick asked Danny where the tribes had taken him.

"I'm in a house with other boys," Danny said, darting a glance at the guards. "I'm to take care of you. Bring you food and stuff like that."

"Good, then I'll know you're well."

Danny nodded, but he gnawed on his lower lip.

Kerrick knelt next to him and took his hands. "Tell me what's upsetting you." Besides the obvious.

Danny dropped his hands and threw himself at Kerrick, wrapping his arms around his neck, hugging him tight. "It's the other boys in the house," he whispered in Kerrick's ear. "They're not from the tribes. They're from Krakowa."

CHAPTER 14

Saul glanced at me. His shocked expression matched mine. "Did you know Prince Ryne was leaving?" he asked.

"No." I glanced around the abandoned tent, searching for a note or clue as to where Ryne had gone. "Maybe he repositioned his army as part of a military strategy to counter Tohon."

"Who are you trying to convince? Me or you?"

"Let's find Thea."

She pounced on us as soon as we drew close. "You're back," she said with a note of accusation in her voice.

I bristled. "Of course we're back. You and Major Granvil knew our mission."

"In light of what has happened, your task could have been an elaborate ruse. Everyone believes you snuck away to meet up with the prince."

"With Saul along?"

She shot him a glance. "He could be an accomplice."

"Ouch," Saul said.

"What exactly has happened?" I asked.

Thea swept her hand out, indicating the empty tents. "It's midsummer's day. Ryne's cowards left last night without a word, so they wouldn't have to face Tohon's attack."

Maria V. Snyder

"How do you know why they left if they didn't say a word?"
I asked.

"Why else? If it's a strategic move, Prince Ryne would have
notified General Jael of his plans."

Not if he didn't trust her. But I wasn't going to add fuel
to Thea's anger. "Perhaps he did tell her, and she's keeping
it quiet."

"I might believe that if she hadn't sent a whirlwind through
their camp."

That explained the mess. And then it hit me. "Did you tell
Jael where I was?"

"No. She thinks you've left, too. You're going to have to
explain it to her."

Lovely. "Look, Thea. I don't know where Ryne went or
why. I'm just as surprised as you. However, I do know he did
it for a reason. A very good reason, and I trust him."

Unconvinced, she said, "Uh-huh. Let's see how you feel
about him when Tohon's soldiers are sending you a steady
stream of injured and dying. Prince Ryne abandoned you,
too."

Thea's words didn't sink in until I reached the infirmary.
I stopped in my room to drop off my pack and froze. Flea's
scant belongings were gone. Ryne had taken Flea with him. A
memory tugged—Loren relaying a message from Ryne about
trusting him regarding Flea.

I sat on the edge of my bed, remembering. Ryne had
changed the plans after I'd told him about my theory of Tohon
burying his dead. What if he'd returned to his tent and read
that book on magicians and learned something horrifying?
Had he spooked? He'd certainly acted like it, and Loren mentioned he'd been agitated. Then why didn't he confide in
me? Maybe he didn't have time or maybe because he knew I

wouldn't break my word to Estrid by leaving. And it was safer for me if I didn't know.

Quain and Loren had promised to protect me from Tohon. Not that they could, but still…I felt forsaken, despite knowing there had to be a good reason why they had left.

My door flew open. It banged against the wall as a blast of air slammed into me, knocking me down. Jael stormed into my room. The air around me thickened like syrup. It picked me off the floor and held me suspended in midair. My legs dangled.

"Where is he?" Jael demanded.

"I don't know."

With a whoosh, I hit the wall hard enough to rattle my teeth.

"Tell me."

"I don't—" The air pushed me up until I banged my head on the ceiling. Hard. Pain flashed, dimming my vision.

"Where were you?" she asked.

"Collecting medicinal…herbs." I gasped. Her power still held me aloft. "Ask Sergeant Saul."

"You're lying."

My air support disappeared, and I plummeted. Crashing to the ground, I rolled until I stopped flat on my back. My wrists burned with agony, and my knees and right hip hurt. Before Jael could pick me up again, I asked, "Why else would I return?"

"A guilty conscience," she said.

"I'm not a glutton for punishment, Jael. He left me behind. I'm sure he has an excellent reason. I just don't know it!"

"I do. He's been scheming with Tohon all this time, feeding him information. It explains how you managed to escape Tohon, cure Ryne and live through the plague. I don't believe that nonsense that Kerrick's magic saved you. Tohon, yes. Kerrick doesn't have that ability." Jael considered. "Now all I need to decide is if you're in collusion with them or if you're a patsy. Tohon can be quite…persuasive when he applies his full power."

She revealed quite a bit in her comments, but I focused on the problem at hand. I caught movement behind her. Noelle hovered near the door. Great. All I needed was Tohon to complete this little get-together.

"I'm—" A gust swept me toward the ceiling. Fast.

"Jael, stop," Noelle said.

I hovered in midair as Jael rounded on Noelle.

"The harder you push her, the harder she'll resist," Noelle said before Jael could respond. "Besides, she's a coward. If she knew Prince Ryne was leaving, she would have gone with him."

Jael hesitated.

"And you should know better than anyone that Ryne and Tohon would never team up," I said. "Tohon hasn't forgiven him for what happened when you were in school with him."

"Boarding school for brats" is how Kerrick had described it. Where Ryne had been crowned king in their final year, Jael broke Kerrick's heart and Tohon turned into a monster.

Jael set me down hard. Pain shot through my arms as I sat up. My wrists were either broken or sprained. Jael stepped back.

I continued to poke holes in her argument. "You're also well aware that Kerrick and I can share our magical energies. Or have you forgotten that day you attacked us and *we* stopped you?" I glanced at Noelle. "I haven't." Nor would I forget Noelle had asked Jael to stop hurting me. Progress!

Jael pressed her lips together—a warning sign that I ignored.

"Plus, if Tohon had…claimed me with his life magic, I'd be…well, I wouldn't be here, that's for sure." I shuddered. I'd been a complete mess. His touch had been like an elixir, and each time I'd grown more addicted.

Jael's gaze turned contemplative. I hoped she remembered those six years. Even though she and Kerrick had been friends with Tohon, she had to have seen the rot below the surface of his mind. As I thought about the stories Belen and Kerrick had told me, I recalled a comment.

"Did Tohon use his magic on you when he attempted to steal you from Kerrick?" I asked her.

She smiled. "The bastard tried and failed. Like you, he needs skin contact to work his magic. I wouldn't let him near me." Her grin turned sinister. "As you've just learned, air is a powerful force."

"Handy."

"Indeed. Estrid believes we need Ryne and his army to stop Tohon. I'm here because of her panic." Jael shoved a long golden strand of hair behind her ear, expressing her exasperation. "My mother-in-law doesn't put any faith in my abilities during a battle."

Odd. I hadn't considered her magic either. My pain forgotten, I scrambled to my feet. "Can you knock a company down?"

"I can send a whirlwind to distract and keep them off balance."

"Just one?" I asked.

"Yes."

Too bad. "How many soldiers can you neutralize by suffocation?" I asked.

"About a dozen."

Not enough. And it wouldn't even work on the dead troops. I wilted.

"Why the sudden interest?" she asked.

"I'm looking for some hope."

"And?"

"We need Ryne."

I lay on the floor long after Jael left. She hadn't appreciated my comment and had knocked me flat before leaving
my room. At least she no longer considered me a threat. Of
course, it would be temporary.

My wrists ached, my head throbbed and my knees stung.
When the pain lessened, I climbed to my feet. I wasn't going
to spend the rest of midsummer's day lying on the ground.

A ripple of surprise rolled through the caregivers when I
entered. I wondered if they'd heard Jael's attack or were just
shocked to see that I'd returned. Christina helped me splint
my wrists, and I did what I could to fill the herb pouches for
the troops. A few soldiers visited the infirmary for cuts and
abrasions. I questioned all who entered, seeking news. Nothing
about Tohon's troops engaging ours or Belen's whereabouts.
Or Ryne's, for that matter. Jael had ordered double patrols for
tonight, and her first-wave soldiers guarded Pomyt's border.
She must have trusted Ryne's prediction that Tohon would
strike today more than she let on.

The sun set and still no word about an approaching army.
I doubted anyone would be able to sleep tonight. I couldn't.
As I tossed and turned, images flashed in my mind—Tohon
and his dead, Kerrick and Belen, Ursan and the jumping jacks.

During the night, Tohon's troops attacked. It wasn't what
I'd imagined the start of a war would be like. I'd expected
battle cries, the ring of metal against metal and the crash of
two forces colliding. I'd expected to be roused from my restless sleep. Instead the assault happened with utter and complete silence.

In fact, nothing appeared to be any different in the morning. As my first shift of caregivers arrived, they reported all was well. But as the day progressed, reports filtered in. The patrols that were due back failed to return. And when the second-wave soldiers arrived at Pomyt's border to relieve the others, the first wave had disappeared.

Tension permeated the camp. Everyone was on high alert. Rumors reached us that Jael had sent a company of soldiers to the north and one to the south to flank the enemy, she'd doubled the troops at the border and she'd remained with them.

In the middle of another sleepless night, loud voices and yells of pain drove me to my feet. I raced to the infirmary and roused my staff just as the first injured arrived, followed by a steady stream. My world shrank to cleaning and bandaging stab wounds, splinting limbs, treating concussions and dispensing medicines. So far, no one had sustained an injury that needed my healing magic. A good thing, considering my wrists hadn't fully healed and I needed to save my strength for someone on the edge of dying.

Those who could talk kept repeating the same thing about the enemy. Silent, deadly and without life or mercy. They shuddered in revulsion.

"We are the lucky ones," a sergeant said to me as I stitched a deep slice on his arm.

"How so?" I asked.

"We escaped. The others…" He fisted his hands. "The others…" The sergeant closed his eyes. "The others were dragged down into the earth."

Although I wanted to dash out and find Noelle so we both could hide under the bed, I kept calm, finishing his stitches. As I checked on other patients and gave instructions to the caregivers, I overheard more horrible descriptions.

"…the ground opened up, and they poured out like fire ants."

"Two grabbed Helen and snapped her neck…"

"…didn't give chase, but most of my team couldn't run…"

"Our squad climbed through the trees, thinking to get behind them, and they swarmed after us."

Within a few hours, the stream of casualties stopped. Jael had called a temporary retreat.

I wasn't surprised when Jael arrived later that afternoon. Haggard and bloody, she clutched a map in one hand and a dagger in the other.

Without a word, I led her back to my examination room. Then I turned to her. "Where's my sister?"

"She's running messages for me. Don't worry. She stays well away from the zone."

"Zone?"

Jael sheathed her weapon and unrolled the map. A bright red arc slashed a long curve around the western side of Zabin. She tapped it with a dirty finger. "This is where they're hiding. Approach this area, and they…swarm, but back off and they stay in this combat zone." She took a breath. "How do we stop them?"

I resisted the urge to be petty. "Are they wearing metal collars?"

"Yes."

"Then you have to use the skull jab." I explained the maneuver. "We were training your troops before…" *Ryne left,* but I was smart enough not to say his name.

"Who knows this technique?"

"Major Granvil's Axe Company." None of his soldiers had come into the infirmary, and I didn't know if I should be worried or glad by their absence.

Jael cursed. "Figures."

I waited.

"I put them on suspension due to too many unanswered questions about their involvement with you and Ryne."

"They're loyal. Ryne taught them the skull jab. I taught them to move silently in the forest. Their involvement with us prepared them for this."

"Then they're unsuspended as of now." Jael gathered the map and strode away.

It wasn't until after she left that I realized I'd just condemned my friends by defending them.

The next three days passed in a blur. Casualties arrived in waves as Jael tried different tactics. I healed only a couple soldiers who had more severe wounds. Most of my patients suffered treatable injuries. It seemed the soldiers who could walk away from the combat zone had a better chance of escape.

Noelle came to the infirmary every night to write down the names of the injured. Her face appeared more drawn each time. She looked very young and frightened. I wanted to comfort her, but I was afraid she'd spurn my efforts—although she did drink a tonic I mixed for her to help restore her energy. She thanked me with a tentative smile.

The soldiers in my care remarked that Tohon's dead stayed within the combat zone. They didn't advance nor retreat. Jael stopped sending patrols, since none of them returned. Also no one encountered a living enemy, which made sense for Tohon and had the added benefit of unnerving our army.

When Odd arrived carrying a limp Wynn in his arms, I rushed over. Blood covered half her face, the other half was pale. Fear lumped in my throat as I gestured him to the examination room. He laid her down on the table with a gentleness I didn't know he possessed.

"What happened?" I pulled her eyelids up to check her pupils.

"Her opponent tried to decapitate her," Odd said stiffly.

While there was plenty of blood, it wasn't spurting or gushing. I grabbed a wet cloth and cleaned the skin. A deep cut ran from the tip of her chin, along the jawbone and sliced through her left ear. The gaping skin exposed teeth and bone. I examined the laceration, running a finger along the inside of the injury.

"Well?" Odd asked.

"She'll live."

He blew out a breath.

"It'll heal, but..." I pushed the skin together.

"But what?"

"Infection could be a problem, but...this is going to heal ugly."

"So?" Odd asked.

"It could affect her hearing and her mouth. Like her smile and maybe interfere with chewing." Magic swelled in my core. "Or I could heal her, and she won't even have a scar."

"But you will," Odd said.

I shrugged. "I won't develop the other problems."

"And she might not either. Besides you'll be useless for a while." Odd scanned the full infirmary. "You're in high demand."

Wynn opened her eyes. "Stitch me up and send me back out, Baby Face," she slurred. "Gimme something for the pain first." She squeezed her eyes shut.

I hesitated.

"What would you do if she wasn't your friend?" Odd asked.

No need to answer. He'd made his point. Giving Wynn a dose of pain medicine that also put her to sleep, I assembled the supplies. Odd hovered as I stitched her skin back together. I made the stitches small and close together, hoping the scar wouldn't look as bad.

As I worked, I asked Odd about the battle. "Is the skull jab effective?"

"When we can get in tight, it works just fine. But those... things are hard to disarm." Odd sank down into a chair next to me. "I never realized how much pain factors into a fight."

"What do you mean?"

"Usually when you slice a person, he backs off or at least hesitates. And he's more cautious when you have drawn his blood. But these things just keep coming. Their intestines can be falling out, but it doesn't matter."

Unfortunately, I remembered when Kerrick, Belen and the monkeys had fought them.

"Too bad we don't have more soldiers," Odd said. "That skull jab works better when we can double up on one."

"How?"

"One distracts the thing, while the other sneaks up behind it and pow!" Odd stabbed the air with his hand. "Although I wonder why we bother. They're not moving closer, and we can't punch through their line. So why fight?"

An excellent question. "Any signs of..."

"Your boyfriend?" Odd smirked.

I resisted the desire to correct him. At least he hadn't called Ryne a coward. "Of Prince Ryne or his army?"

"Nope. And before you ask for the millionth time, no sign of Belen either."

I finished bandaging Wynn's cut. Odd carried her to an empty bed and then sat with her until she woke.

The flow of injured stopped the next day. When Odd came to visit Wynn, I asked him what had happened.

He puffed up his chest. "General Jael took my advice."

"Uh-huh."

"We ceased engaging the enemy. Now we're keeping a distance, watching and waiting for them to make the next move."

I wondered how long it would last. Two days passed with no new casualties. I was able to concentrate on my patients and discharged a number of them, including Wynn, who promised to follow all my instructions in caring for her wound.

"I want to see you back here in a week to take those stitches out," I called as she hurried out the door.

At the end of the third quiet day, Noelle arrived with a couple soldiers. She looked haggard with dark circles under her eyes.

"The High Priestess requests your presence immediately," Noelle said to me in a thin voice.

I left Christina in charge and followed Noelle to Estrid's study. Not as elaborately decorated as her receiving room, it had a huge desk crafted from a dark wood. Estrid stood behind it, and Jael and a few high-ranking officers were standing in front. They turned as soon as I entered. The tension in the room pressed against me with such force I almost stepped back into the hallway.

Estrid's expression remained serene, but Jael's gaze burned with fury and indignation. Not good.

"Avry, please come in," Estrid said, gesturing me closer.

When I approached, the officers made room.

"I won't lie to you, Avry," Estrid said. "We're in trouble, and it's hard not to believe that Prince Ryne abandoned us. Did he say anything to you before he left?"

I recalled our conversation after Ursan's funeral. "He didn't give me any indication that he was going to leave, but I told him something that might have been the trigger."

"I knew she was keeping secrets," Jael said.

"Jael, let me handle this," Estrid said. "What did you tell him, Avry?"

I explained my theory about Ulany burying the dead. "I thought it was crazy, but Ryne said he'd look into the possibility."

"And why didn't you tell us about this before?" Jael asked.

"What would you have done?" I asked. When no one answered, I said, "You didn't believe us about Tohon's dead, so there was no chance you'd consider my speculation without proof."

"Ryne figured out what Tohon was up to, and he took off without warning us," Jael said.

Again, I asked, "And if he warned you, what would you have done? Nothing!"

Estrid smoothed the sleeves of her robe. "That is true. Then he was smart to leave. Otherwise he'd be stuck in this trap with us. At least we have some hope he'll continue to fight Tohon." She sank into her chair.

It took me a moment to catch up. "Trap? What trap?"

"Show her," Estrid said.

Jael unrolled one of the maps on the desk. I recognized it as the same one she had shown me before. Except instead of just a red arc west of Zabin, a big red circle marked the map with Estrid's camp right in the middle.

"We're surrounded," Jael said.

KERRICK

Kerrick was beyond bored. Locked up in his cell for the past seven days, he had nothing to do except brood over his situation and worry about Avry and his friends. Danny visited twice a day, bringing him food and information. The boys Danny shared a house with had lived in Krakowa before the tribes had invaded. Some had watched their parents murdered in front of them, while others had been separated by the chaos and confusion. A few had already lost their parents to the plague. Either way, the fact that the warriors hadn't killed the boys outright was unexpected and worrisome. Kerrick wondered what else about the tribes the history books had gotten wrong.

When Danny arrived with his evening meal, he had more news. "There's a house of Krakowan girls, too." He slid the tray through the slot. His two guards waited by the door. "We had...lessons with them today."

"Lessons?" Kerrick asked. The food was the standard fare—bread, cheese, a corn mash and a cup of water.

"Yeah. They're teaching us how to read their...pictures." Danny settled on the floor next to Kerrick's cell. "They don't use letters and words like us. They string pictures together to form sentences."

"Is it hard to learn?"

"A few are tricky, but the others make sense, like a tree is a picture of a tree. As long as you can draw, it's not hard."

"And if you can't?"

"Then you have to stick to verbal communications." Danny smiled.

Kerrick was glad to see him smile. And the fact the tribes were taking the time to teach the children was an excellent sign.

"Did you learn anything else?" Kerrick asked.

"Yeah." He glanced at the guards, but they appeared uninterested. "There are only two tribes left. I guess there's not much food in the wildlands, or as they call it, Vilde Lander. They had joined together before attacking Krakowa. But they still refer to themselves as either a Sokna or a Jevnaker."

Interesting and potentially useful. "Which tribe does Noak belong to?"

"Sokna. His father, Canute, is the leader and his sister, Rakel, is going to marry the Jevnaker's leader, Olave, to bind the two tribes together."

The word *bind* stood out to him and made him realize he hadn't seen too many women in town since he'd arrived. Then again, he'd only been to the bathhouse a couple times. "Is that why Noak returned? For the marriage?"

"I don't know."

Too bad. The fact that Noak had traveled to Krakowa and not gone south to conquer had been bugging him since they'd headed north. Although there was no reason to hurry on the warpath. Thanks to Kerrick's information, the tribes were well aware that there wouldn't be an army gathering to stop them. At least the more time they spent here meant more time for Izak, Zila, Great-Aunt Yasmin and the rest of Orel to escape over the Nine Mountains.

The next morning, Danny arrived with Noak instead of his guards. The boy clutched Avry's notebook to his chest.

"Are you all right?" Kerrick asked, stepping close to the bars between them.

"Yes." He cleared his throat. "A couple tribesmen have developed fevers, and I need you to help me find the venite plant in the forest." Danny showed him a sketch of a bush with narrow drooping leaves. "Can you do that?"

Kerrick considered. Through his magic he sensed the difference between trees, bushes and the Lilys. But a specific plant might be beyond his abilities. "I can try."

Noak stared at Kerrick as if he still couldn't figure him out. Good.

"We go now," Noak said. "No trouble or I'll—"

"Curse me, I know. Isn't my promise worth anything to you?"

"No. Your people chased us from our homeland and forced us to live in the cold Vilde Lander."

"You crossed the mountains first, invading and killing my people."

"We did not go past the Ni Fjell. You came like flakes in a snowstorm. Few at first, then more and more until you roared down the Ni Fjell like an avalanche."

"That's not what our history reports." Kerrick crossed his arms.

"Our ancestors do not lie. Our stories are told from old to young so we all remember."

"We should go," Danny said into the heated silence. "Hilmar is very sick."

Before Noak could unlock his cell door, Kerrick yanked it open and stepped through. "Which way?"

Noak grabbed the hilt of his dadao but didn't pull the sword free from the scabbard. Kerrick waited as the man sorted through the logic. He had just shown Noak he was more than capable of escaping, but he hadn't. In fact, he just risked losing his set of lock picks—the ones that had been tucked inside his clean clothes.

"How long?" Noak asked.

He shrugged. "Couple days."

"You're holding to your promise?"

Kerrick rested his hand on Danny's shoulder. "Yes. As long as you keep yours, I'll keep mine." He wasn't sure why it was so important to him that these warriors understood that his people were capable of honor. It just was.

Noak gestured. "This way."

Two of Noak's men fell into step behind them. When they neared the woods, Kerrick's connection to the living green flowed through his body. He inhaled the moist, sweet scent of the earth, feeling a surge of power. Before entering the forest, he studied the picture again, reading Avry's description. The thick roots had small pebble-sized knots that could be ground into a paste and used on itchy bug bites.

With the image of the venite in his mind, Kerrick strode through the bushes and trees, touching the leaves. As his magic spread throughout the forest, it revealed a map of the area as acknowledged by the living green—more felt than seen. Mild irritations, such as animals and insects, barely registered, but unwanted intruders caused an intense reaction. Kerrick ignored the group of tribesmen hunting about a mile southwest of them. Instead, he concentrated on that one specific plant.

The map changed texture, going from smooth to hairy. Each strand represented a living extension of the green, like a tentacle. Kerrick sorted through them, seeking the venite. He walked with his eyes closed. With this full immersion, he didn't need to see.

The variety of plants growing in a small area surprised him.

And the specific details of each one eluded him. Before he admitted defeat, Kerrick switched his efforts to the roots underground. He crouched and laid his palms on the cool loam, sending his magic to twist and turn through the earth as he searched for the venite's unique—he hoped—knots.

Kerrick found a possible match, but he couldn't walk with his hands on the forest floor. Remembering Avry's trick when they had played hide-and-seek, he pulled off his boots and socks. When his bare feet touched the soil, energy sizzled up his calves. He fingered a leaf, and a picture of the surrounding forest, both above and below the ground, formed in his mind.

After a moment of dizziness, he zeroed in on a patch of venite and led Danny there. On the way, he wondered why he hadn't ever gone barefoot into the forest before. With this intense connection, he could easily avoid the stinging plants, poison ivy and Death Lilys.

Once they reached the patch, Kerrick stumbled as his strength waned. Finding the venite had used up all his energy. He rested against a tree trunk as Danny pulled and then bundled the plants together.

With bunches of venite in hand, they headed back to Krakowa. Noak led since Kerrick had nothing left. They stopped to pick up his boots and returned to the city by midafternoon. Kerrick collapsed on the bed in his cell. He didn't care if Noak locked the door or not as he surrendered to his exhaustion.

The smell of beef woke him. Danny stood next to him holding a tray with a steaming bowl of stew. It took Kerrick a few moments to realize that his cell remained unlocked and the quality of his supper had improved.

Danny sat on the end of the bed as he inhaled the food. The boy worried his lower lip and squirmed.

"Isn't the venite working?" Kerrick asked.

"It's great. Hilmar is coherent and Yok is eating again."

"So what's wrong?"

Danny glanced at the door. Despite the small measures of trust, two guards flanked the jail's exit. He lowered his voice to a whisper, "Since the venite worked so well, they brought me to an old warehouse. And there are lots more sick people."

"How many?"

"Hundreds." Danny stared at his hands in his lap.

"Do they have fevers like Hilmar?"

"No."

"Plague?" The word left a bad taste in his mouth.

"No."

"How bad is it?"

"They're dying."

Dread lumped in the pit of his stomach. Was this another killing disease? "Can you heal them?"

"I've studied Avry's book." Danny laced and unlaced his fingers together.

"And?"

Danny met Kerrick's gaze. Confusion creased his young face. "I think I can help them."

Kerrick waited.

"But should I? They're killing our people, invading our land. Why should I help them?"

CHAPTER 15

Not a rustle of movement. Not a sign of activity. Not even a cry of a bird. Nothing all day. As each hour passed, the anxiety level rose along with the temperature until we sweated through our uniforms. The news of our situation spread through the camp as fast as a stomach flu.

When would Tohon spring his trap? The question hung over our heads like the sharp blade of a guillotine.

I remained in the infirmary, concentrating on my patients to avoid thinking about the inevitable. And the few times I stopped to consider my future, fear ripped through my heart. By late afternoon, I needed to be with my friends—the ones who hadn't abandoned me. I clamped down on that line of thought right away.

Even if Ryne had warned me and invited me along, I wouldn't have gone. At least, I hoped I would have refused. And that my terror over being Tohon's prisoner again wouldn't have made me break my promise to Estrid.

I left Christina in charge of the patients and sought Saul. Strained faces and haunted gazes followed me as I wove through the eerily quiet camp. Saul and Lieutenant Thea's other sergeants huddled together near his and Odd's tent.

Their intense whispered discussion consumed their attention, so I waited.

"...we're to team up with Dagger Company," Saul said.

"Everyone is to have a partner," Liv said.

"No, Wynn. The only way you are going is over *my* dead body." Odd thumped his chest with his fingers.

Too curious to wait until they noticed me, I asked, "What's going on?"

"We're organizing for one last desperate offensive," Odd said.

"What's the plan?" I asked.

"A concentrated attack of all our forces in one area," Saul said. "General Jael is hoping we can break out of the encirclement."

Not a bad idea. "Will it work?"

"We hope so. Otherwise, we're screwed."

I would need to prepare for casualties. "When?"

Saul lowered his voice. "Late tonight."

"Where?"

"Only General Jael knows," Odd said. "But I'm thinking to the northeast since there's a stream there that we could use to get past their line of horror. Plus, Marisol can use her water magic."

"Even with her, we'll need every single person," Wynn said.

Odd appealed to me. "Avry, tell her she can't go."

I examined her wound. She had kept the cut clean, and small scabs dotted her jawline. Her stitches could be taken out in a few days. "As long as she doesn't rip open the sutures or reinjure the area, she should be fine."

Odd growled. Wynn smirked. I wished them all good luck before returning to the infirmary. So much for spending the evening with my friends. Calling in all the caregivers, I organized our supplies and rearranged the beds.

★ ★ ★

The first wave of wounded arrived just after midnight. The injuries matched what I'd been treating since midsummer's day. However, the mood was…different. Not as glum or defeated.

Stitching up a sergeant's leg, I asked about the battle.

"We're getting through," he said. "It's not easy, but we're making progress for the first time since we encountered those blasted things."

The second group of injured acted almost buoyant. They laughed and joked. My fear eased a bit. Perhaps we would break out of Tohon's trap.

A private with a broken arm arrived with the third batch. "We punched a hole!" he announced to the entire infirmary. Cheers rang out.

The jovial atmosphere continued. Happy patients healed faster, so I encouraged the optimistic comments. A few more casualties trickled in as the night progressed. By dawn, no more soldiers had arrived for the past couple hours. We took it as a positive sign. I sent half of my caregivers to get some sleep.

Saul entered the infirmary as I was checking on my patients one more time before heading to bed. Blood dripped from a nasty gash on his shoulder, and deep lines of exhaustion etched his face. Hurrying over, I guided him to my exam area, sitting him down on the bed.

When I tried to remove his chest armor, he grabbed my arm. "Liv and Thea are gone."

His words stabbed deep into me, igniting horror. "Dead?"

"No idea." Saul let me go to rub his bloodstained hand over his face. "They disappeared during the fighting, after we punched a hole in their defenses." His unfocused gaze stared through me as he remembered.

This time when I yanked on his chest plate, he let me pull it over his head. "Maybe they are free of the trap."

"There was another line of defenders beyond the ring, waiting for us."

I stopped. "More of Tohon's dead?"

"No. Living soldiers, but plenty of them." He shuddered. "They surged forward and the hole closed soon after. We were forced to retreat."

Fear and grief churned together, forming a lump in my stomach. "Do you think Tohon was tipped off?"

"Yeah. No doubt. And when I find that bastard who has been spying on us, I'm gonna rip out his entrails and strangle him with them."

And I would cheer him on. After I cleaned his wound, I examined it. Deep, with ragged edges and still bleeding, it snaked from his left shoulder down to his bicep. I could stitch the skin together, but it wouldn't heal well. Magic grew, expanding from my core.

Before healing him, I glanced at the door. "How many more wounded are coming?"

"I'm it. Those dead things chased down anyone not quick enough to escape."

Which was why he was so certain Liv and Thea were gone. I bit my lip to keep from crying. Instead, I concentrated on mixing a sleeping draft for him. Saul's obvious pain stemmed more from the loss of his friends than the gash on his shoulder. He drained the cup without question.

It didn't take long for him to lie back on the mattress. When his eyes drifted shut, I traced his injury with my finger, letting the magic inside me flow into Saul before returning to me. A line of fire carved into my left shoulder and down my arm. Blood welled, soaking my sleeve as the pain gripped me in its hot talons, matching the burn of sorrow in my heart.

★ ★ ★

A pounding on my door woke me. Bright sunlight filled the room, indicating midafternoon. My shoulder throbbed, and the memories of why it hurt came flooding back. Ah, hell. Then the deep voice attached to the ruckus penetrated my grief. Saul.

I jumped to my feet and paused for a moment to weather the sharp pains that shot down my arm. My correct assessment of Saul's injury being difficult to heal didn't make me feel any better.

Yanking my door open, I almost ran into him. He scowled and crossed his arms over his chest in the classic pissed-off man pose.

"What's wrong?" I asked.

"You drugged me."

"No. I *healed* you. Big difference."

"Avry, you didn't need to—"

"Excuse me. Are you a healer now? 'Cause that would be very helpful." I waited.

His shoulders drooped. "Ursan was right."

"About what?"

"You."

"And?"

"He said you were the most vexing person he has ever met."

Remembering Kerrick's similar comment, I grinned. "I'll take that as a compliment. Now, unless you want to assist in cleaning out bedpans...?"

Saul stepped back, wrinkling his nose. "I should report in."

"I thought so." Then I sobered. "Tell Wynn and Odd I'll stop by later tonight."

"Will do." Saul left.

Since I was awake, I checked my patients. A few needed their bandages changed. One young soldier thrashed in his sleep. Sweat dampened his hair, and his forehead was hot to the touch. I gestured Christina over and instructed her to administer him a dose of fever powder. Then I discharged a handful of soldiers. I'd been pleasantly surprised there hadn't been any serious cases so far, but Saul's remark about the dead chasing down anyone not quick enough to retreat explained the reason and killed any optimism I'd felt.

Saul returned. A strange half scared, half queasy expression creased his face. He barreled through my caregivers as if he didn't see them, heading right to me.

"What's—"

He clasped my wrist and pulled me to my feet. "You've got to see this."

Without waiting for my response, he tugged me along, almost dragging me from the infirmary.

"Is someone hurt?" I asked.

"Not yet."

"Saul, what—"

"You'll see in a minute."

We left the manor house by a side door. Questions piled up in my throat, but I followed Saul. He led me to the same shady spot I'd used to spy on the activity around Jael's tent. Except this time, all the action was happening in the courtyard.

A white flag of truce drew my attention right away. It fluttered above a woman on horseback, but as soon as my gaze dropped, it riveted on the ring of ufas surrounding the horse. I braced, expecting the creatures to leap onto the line of soldiers blocking the manor house's steps. But the ufas remained in position as if they'd been ordered like dogs to stay.

When Jael exited the house with her entourage of officers, I moved closer, keeping to the thin line of trees. No one would notice me with a dozen ufas drooling on the cobblestones.

"What are you doing?" Saul asked from behind me.

"I need to hear."

I crept as far as I dared. As expected, none of the people even glanced my way, but a few of the ufas swung their huge heads in my direction. Sniffing the air, they stared at me with dead eyes. I clutched a tree trunk to keep on my feet. Dead ufas. Tohon was beyond insane.

Recovering from the shock, I considered how effective that pack would be in a fight against the living. Ufas were already hard to kill, but now they'd be impossible to beat. Probably why Tohon used them to protect his emissary. I wouldn't trust Jael to abide by the protocols of a truce flag either.

Jael stopped midway down the steps behind the line. "I see not much has changed since school, Cellina. You're still Tohon's lackey and he still treats you as well as his mongrels."

Her tone was derisive, but I caught an edge of fear in her voice. Had Cellina noticed?

"Go fetch your mother-in-law, Jael," Cellina ordered. "My message is for her and not some underling playing dress up." She sat straight in the saddle, looking down her pudgy nose at Jael. Her blond hair had been braided and wrapped around her head like a crown. She didn't appear intimidated, even though she was in the middle of the enemy's camp. Then again, with a pack of ufas at her feet, I wouldn't be worried either. Plus she had her sword—

I stared at the hilt of the sword hanging from her belt. Blinking, I squeezed my eyes shut for a moment, hoping I was mistaken. No, it couldn't be. But it was. She had Kerrick's sword. Which meant…

A wave of dizziness washed through me. I sank to the ground and buried my face in my hands. To never see him again… To never feel his magic again… To never touch him again… I lay there in utter and complete misery.

"What's wrong?" Saul asked in alarm.

I couldn't answer.

"It might not be that bad. We haven't heard any terms yet." Saul tried to console me even though he had no clue why I'd collapsed. "No sense getting upset before anything is confirmed."

His logic pierced my fog. Kerrick might still be alive. Tohon might have ordered Sepp to freeze him in a magical stasis or locked Kerrick in his dungeon. Or turned him into one of his dead soldiers. I shuddered.

Saul rubbed my arm. "Come on, Avry, pull it together."

With considerable effort, I reined in the crushing despair. I needed to be able to function. I returned my attention to the courtyard. Estrid had arrived.

"...I will not discuss terms with you," Estrid said. "Tohon—"

"King Tohon will accept nothing less than unconditional surrender," Cellina said, causing a shocked silence. "In exchange for your lives, you and your entire population will swear loyalty to him and accept him as your king. Your army will be incorporated into his."

"And if we don't surrender?" Estrid asked.

"Then you will be slaughtered. Every single one of you."

The ripple of voices from those within hearing distance soon turned into a loud outcry with everyone talking at the same time. Cellina gestured with both her arms. The ufas all howled at once. Silence descended.

"You have one day to decide," Cellina said. "I will return tomorrow." She turned her horse and nudged it into a walk toward the border. The ufas followed.

Without thought, I sprinted after her. I had to know what had happened to Kerrick. The ufas snarled when I approached. Not caring, I called Cellina's name. She glanced back and then stopped the horse. I slowed, keeping my distance from the creatures.

"Well feed me to a Death Lily," Cellina said. "She lives."

"You didn't know?" I asked in surprise.

"We've heard rumors, of course, but you had the plague. How did you survive?"

"How did you get Kerrick's sword?"

She smirked. "You answer my question and I'll answer yours."

I almost growled in frustration. Instead, I stuck to the explanation I'd given Estrid and Jael. "Kerrick shared his magical energy with me, and I recovered. Now it's your turn."

Cellina studied me. "Kerrick had a nasty run-in with my mutts." She swept a hand out, indicating the ufa pack. "Unlike you, he didn't survive."

KERRICK

Kerrick had spent a sleepless night wondering what Danny would decide and a restless day worrying about him. One of his guards had brought him his breakfast, claiming the boy was busy with lessons.

Last night he had told Danny it was his decision to heal the tribespeople or not. Kerrick would support him either way.

Danny hadn't been happy with his reply. "Why would you let me decide? It's my stupid fault that you're cooperating with them!"

Ah. Kerrick had knelt next to Danny and waited until the boy met his gaze. "No. You're wrong. Remember what I told Noak's father, Canute? My information isn't going to make any difference in the end. In fact, we're helping our people right now. Since Noak and his warriors are here and not on the warpath, they'll have more time to evacuate." Kerrick considered the situation. "Plus, Noak could have easily killed me during the battle. He planned to take a prisoner. Probably because of his sickened tribe members." Now it made sense why Noak had returned to Krakowa.

Kerrick had touched Danny's arm. "Okay?"

He'd nodded, and the deep crinkles between his eyebrows

had smoothed for a moment before puckering again. "But what should I do about the sick tribespeople?"

"Look deep within yourself. I can't order you one way or another. Avry taught me that. This is something you will live with for the rest of your life. Can you do nothing and let them die? Think about it."

Danny had agreed to sleep on it and Kerrick hadn't seen him since.

When another guard brought him his evening meal, Kerrick decided to search for Danny in the morning if he didn't show. Since no one had locked his cell door or confiscated his lock picks despite being well aware he had them, Kerrick figured they wouldn't object. And if they did, he'd deal with it then.

After the guard left with the remains of his breakfast, Kerrick strolled from the jail with confidence. If he acted as if he knew what he was doing, perhaps no one would question him. Danny had pointed out the house he stayed in during one of their trips to the bathhouse. He headed to it. Kerrick was surprised guards hadn't been posted outside the jail, but within a few blocks he spotted a couple tails. Noak had probably planted them.

The tribespeople he passed gawked and scowled, but he ignored them. Danny lived in a narrow two-story row house in the middle of the street. Unlike dozens of others, this town had survived the plague with little damage. The Krakowans hadn't burned down the homes of the plague victims in panic. Living so close to the border, they tended to be rather unflappable.

Kerrick didn't bother knocking on the door. He pushed it open and called Danny's name, startling a group of boys in the living room. Some jumped to their feet, while others remained rooted in place, gaping at him. Danny wasn't among them. He questioned the boys, and they told him Danny had been spending all his time at the library. He managed to get directions before their guardian bustled in from another room and shooed him out.

His tails followed him across town, but he didn't care. It felt good to be moving. He wished he could get some real exercise. What would the warriors do if he joined one of their practice sessions? With their expert skills on the battlefield, it stood to reason that they trained constantly.

Or was that part of their magic? Did they all possess magic, or only Noak? There had been no record of anyone else with his ice magic in the Fifteen Realms. But he was beginning to distrust the history books. Kerrick wondered if Noak's father or sister also possessed powers. And, if so, what would they be?

Danny sat at a table just inside the library's entrance. Bent over an open book and making notes in another, Danny didn't even glance up when Kerrick entered. Rows of full bookcases extended to the back of the room and along the walls. Kerrick moved closer and read the titles, impressed by the extent of topics. His father would have been ecstatic by the collection and would have badgered the poor librarian for hours. Kerrick glanced around, but no one else occupied the other tables and reading chairs. Then he remembered the tribes didn't read words.

Kerrick returned to Danny's table and cleared his throat. The boy jerked at the sound but then relaxed.

"They let you out?" he asked.

"Not exactly. I was concerned about you," Kerrick said.

"Oh. Sorry, I found these great books about herbs and medicines." He gestured to the piles on his table. "They were brought here after the town's healer died of the plague. And there are some of his journals in here, too. I guess I just lost track of time."

"Does that mean you decided to help them?"

Danny met his gaze. "Yes. It was an easy choice once I thought about it." He tapped his stylus on the book he'd been writing in. "Well, once I considered what Avry would have done. She healed Tohon's soldiers. And they're probably attacking Estrid's army right now."

"True, but she was his prisoner at the time and had to cooperate." A horrible situation—it had taken all of his willpower not to storm Tohon's castle and rescue her before she could find and heal Ryne.

"But Tohon didn't care about his wounded soldiers. To him, they are just as useful dead. Avry could have made a token effort, but she didn't. She cared, and I do, too."

And her patients had thanked her by pretending to be asleep when Kerrick and Loren had finally reached her. He couldn't call it a rescue since she'd stayed behind after they had escaped with Ryne. It had been a miserable ten days, but she'd broken out on her own and had saved Danny and Zila from Tohon.

"Can you cure them?" Kerrick asked.

"I thought so, but the plant Avry mentions in her journal doesn't grow this far north." Danny pointed to a drawing of a plant with large heart-shaped leaves. "So I'm trying to find another that will work as well before the disease spreads."

"Any luck?"

"Not yet, but there are plenty more books to look through."

"Want help?"

Danny beamed at him in relief, which meant the boy had been worried Kerrick would object to his decision.

"Sure." Danny explained the specific healing properties he was looking for.

Kerrick pulled a book off a pile and settled next to Danny. They worked for a while in silence, but it didn't take long for

Noak to enter the library with an equally tall man by his side and a few guards behind him.

Disgust creased the stranger's sharp face. He resembled a bird of prey with his hooked nose and his blond hair hanging loose like feathers over his wide shoulders. He wore a warrior's uniform and held his dadao at the ready. The powerful muscles along his long arms were as thick as Quain's. Kerrick stood and braced for trouble.

"It is just as I expected," Noak said to the man. "He is with the boy."

"So they can conspire against us," he snapped.

No one else had taken that tone with Noak except his father, so this must be the Jevnaker leader, Olave. His bright blue gaze swept Kerrick with contempt.

"He keeps his promise," Noak said.

"To lull you." He pointed the sword at the books. "We can't read that. He's probably going to poison us all."

"I don't have to," Kerrick said.

Olave swung the blade's tip toward him. "Explain."

Kerrick glanced at Noak as if seeking his permission just to anger Olave. When Noak nodded, he said, "The sickness will kill you all. Good riddance, as far as I'm concerned."

With a cry, Olave lunged at him. Kerrick sidestepped the thrust and grabbed a chair just in time to block the next attack. The dadao was primarily a chopping weapon, and Olave hacked the wooden chair to pieces as Kerrick dodged and ducked.

Eventually Kerrick was left with a single spoke. But he used it like a sword. Avoiding the sharp edge of Olave's weapon, Kerrick countered along the flat of his blade. Kerrick snaked in past his defenses a few times, rapping him on the arm and poking him in the stomach. Olave didn't have Noak's skill or finesse. Each touch increased his fury. A part of Kerrick knew this fight wouldn't end well for him, but he was having too much fun goading him.

Despite Kerrick's skills, a sword beats a wooden stick every time. Olave unarmed him and pressed the dadao's tip into the hollow at the base of his throat.

"Olave, my father has him under *our* protection," Noak said.

"He should die," he said.

"That is not your decision."

"Nor yours, princeling. You shouldn't have brought him here." Olave traced the four scars on Kerrick's neck with the blade's tip. "These marks mean he's lucky. Nothing more."

"Even so. He is protected." Noak put his hand on the hilt of his dadao.

Olave stepped back. "Not for long. Once I marry your sister, I will challenge your father, and take his place."

Noak laughed. Kerrick stared in amazement. The man did know how to smile.

"It will be your right to test my father," Noak said. "But consider, a man armed with only a chair almost defeated you."

"I spared your pet dog. For now. Once I'm leader, he'll be the first to go, followed by you." He left without saying another word.

Kerrick touched his throat. The cuts burned, and blood coated his fingers, but they didn't seem deep enough to worry about.

Danny stared at his neck with a strange expression. He reached toward Kerrick with an intense focus. Kerrick recognized the significance of it. He had seen that same avid gaze on Avry's face before she healed someone with her magic.

Kerrick grabbed Danny's arm, making sure he didn't touch the boy's skin. If Danny healed him in front of Noak, then they'd never let Danny go free.

CHAPTER 16

Estrid had a day to decide to either accept the unconditional surrender or to condemn us all to death. The atmosphere sizzled with tension and fear. But for me, that day passed in a watery blur. As I checked on my patients, tears leaked until they built up so much pressure I had to run to my room to muffle my sobs. Most of the people in the infirmary believed I was upset about the potential surrender, and I didn't bother to correct them as I stumbled through the day like one of Tohon's dead.

My thoughts kept returning to what Cellina had told me. At first, I had thought she lied just to be cruel. But she had described Kerrick's death with such horrific detail. Plus she had his sword. The one his father had gifted to him. Kerrick would never part with it willingly.

Sleep was impossible. Every time I closed my eyes, I saw an image of Kerrick being torn apart by a pack of ufas. Grief and guilt filled me until I thought I'd burst into a thousand pieces. Giving up, I returned to the infirmary. I hadn't had a good rest in days, and I doubted one was in my future.

While my patients slept, I organized the supplies and prepared the morning's round of medicines. When I exhausted all those tasks, I returned to my room, settled on my bed and sorted through my meager possessions. If Estrid surrendered, I had no doubt I would be claimed by Tohon and would need my pack.

The gloves Belen had given me caused tears to flow. I crushed them in a fist, hoping he was still alive. Perhaps I could ask Cellina if he'd been captured when she returned for Estrid's answer.

I found the Death Lily's toxin sacks as I dug deeper in my pack. Why had the Death Lily given them to me? The toxin wouldn't work on Tohon's dead soldiers, and I wouldn't use it on anyone living. Well…I'd love to inject it into Tohon, except he was immune. I placed the sacks on the night table, considering.

Tohon would have no qualms about using these to threaten and/or torture his enemies since almost everyone pricked by the poison suffered a long, horrible death. And those few who survived turned into healers. That was the theory. Tohon had been trying to create more healers, but I had destroyed his garden of Death Lilys and rescued Danny and Zila—the only survivors of his horrendous experiment—before it could be proven. It might be years before we'd know for sure.

I should destroy the sacks so Tohon couldn't confiscate them. Yet, the Lily had wanted me to have them. I mulled over what else I'd learned about the toxin. When Tohon had injected it into me, my body had reacted as if I was inside a Death Lily. My consciousness had floated free from my body, but my body had obeyed Tohon's commands. When I'd witnessed Tohon creating his dead soldiers, he'd injected something into them before freezing them in a magical stasis, keeping their bodies from decomposing.

Rolling one of the sacks along the table, I remembered believing he had used the Death Lily toxin to animate the dead, but they had no consciousness to detach. Plus he froze them so the toxin wouldn't work. Except the substance he'd injected had worked despite the stasis.

The Death Lily had also made a point to show me that the Peace Lilys didn't bring me and Flea back to life…well, not technically. That it had been a combination of the serum and a touch.

Tohon had hundreds of Peace Lilys growing all around his castle in Sogra. What if Tohon had injected Peace Lily serum into someone who had died? Horror welled. Were they really alive?

No. With a shudder I recalled their lifeless gazes, black blood and rotting smell when they'd been decapitated. Not alive, but able to understand and follow orders. Why? Tohon had touched them after administering the serum. I'd assumed he was putting them into a stasis to keep them from decomposing, but what if it was the serum that kept them from rotting? Flea had been inside the Lily for six months and had been perfectly preserved!

So then Tohon's touch revived the dead. But they weren't truly living. Tohon's magic must not bring the dead all the way back. Or else he manipulated his magic so he'd have these obedient, unstoppable creatures. That made the most sense.

I considered. Perhaps if his dead were injected with Death Lily toxin it would counteract the effects of the serum and stop them. I picked up the sacks and was halfway to the door when I remembered we were under a flag of truce. Estrid would never agree to break that for my crazy theory. If it failed, the consequences would be her entire army's lives.

I could treat my throwing knives, sneak out to the eastern edge of the combat zone and trigger the dead to test my hypothesis. Of course, that was assuming I could keep out of their reach. What if it didn't work? And what if Tohon found out? He could say I'd been acting under Estrid's orders and use it as an excuse to kill everyone.

Why hadn't I thought of this before? I returned to my bed. Setting the sacks back on my night table, I lay down. If I couldn't test my idea, then who could? Ryne. He wasn't working for Estrid. Tohon's encirclement prevented me from searching for him. Although if Estrid surrendered, there would be no need for the dead. Perhaps I could slip away then.

No. Tohon would never allow me to leave. I could ask Saul or Odd. Would they be able to find him? He had to be nearby. I refused to believe he'd abandoned us. Once again I hopped out of bed. I needed to talk to Saul before Tohon arrived, which would be anytime after Cellina reported Estrid's answer back to him.

Grabbing the sacks, I placed them in my pack. On my way out, I passed Flea's bed and paused. Flea and I had a connection. Could I use that bond to find him as he had found me when I'd been in trouble?

Flea had said he'd been dreaming. Since there was no way I'd be able to fall asleep, I would need to take a sleeping draft. I glanced out the window and hurried to the infirmary. Dawn was about an hour away.

After giving one of the caregivers instructions not to disturb me unless it was an emergency, I poured a small dose of the draft and returned to my room. Hiding my pack under Flea's bed, I slipped between his sheets, hoping his scent of earthy vanilla would help me. I swallowed the draft in one gulp.

With my thoughts firmly on Flea, I lay there until my body relaxed. My limbs felt heavy, and then a numbing nothingness pressed down on me.

"Avry, wake up," an annoyed voice said.

A hand shook my shoulder. I batted at it. "Go away."

"You don't want to miss this," Saul said, pulling me up.

"Miss what?" My groggy thoughts couldn't keep up, and I stumbled.

Saul caught my arm. "Cellina's back."

"Oh." The fog in my mind disappeared with a cold realization. I had slept the morning away and hadn't dreamed of Flea's location.

With disappointment filling my chest, I followed Saul from the manor house. Cellina and her ufa entourage waited in the courtyard. Estrid's army had gathered close, but not too close to the ufas.

Soon Estrid and her staff arrived. One look at the High Priestess's defeated expression and everyone knew her decision. Jael stood to the side. The wind gusted with her anger.

"What shall I tell King Tohon?" Cellina asked.

"We…" Estrid paused. "We surrender."

The truce flag fluttered. The flaps of the tents snapped. Tree limbs bent and shook. Otherwise, not another sound pierced the air.

"Unconditionally?" Cellina asked.

"Yes."

"Wise choice." Cellina unrolled a scroll and read from it. "Tomorrow morning a company of King Tohon's soldiers will come to confiscate all your weapons. You will also release all your POWs. After both are secured behind our lines, King Tohon will arrive. You will prepare a royal feast for him and his retinue. The High Priestess, her staff and all her high-ranking officers, including Jael Ozero and Healer Avry, are required to attend, along with Prince Ryne and his staff. After—"

"Prince Ryne isn't here," Estrid interrupted.

Cellina covered her surprise quickly. She lowered the scroll. "Where is he?"

"We've no idea. He and his little army disappeared the night before midsummer's day."

Scanning Estrid's soldiers around the courtyard, Cellina didn't appear convinced. "I will inform the king." She resumed her instructions. "After the feast, King Tohon will conduct the fidelity ceremony. Every single soldier in your army, every priest, priestess, staff member and member of your family shall kneel before King Tohon and swear loyalty to him."

Cellina rolled up the parchment. "Failure to comply with his wishes or any attacks on those under his protection will be considered a violation of your surrender and will result in the total annihilation of your people. Until tomorrow…" She swung her horse around and spurred it into a gallop. The ufas kept pace.

After that little speech, I'd leave quickly, too. The murmurs from the soldiers increased to an angry buzz. Estrid returned to the manor house without addressing her troops, which caused even more consternation.

"I guess that's it," Saul said. "All that training for nothing. General Jael was right—we should have gone on the offensive months ago."

"And you would have lost many more lives," I said.

"Better than being forced to fight for Tohon."

I paused as a terrible thought welled. From what I knew of Tohon, he didn't seem the type to trust an entire army to keep to their word. Would he do something to ensure their cooperation? Just when I thought I couldn't feel worse over this situation, I was proven wrong.

"Your training wasn't wasted," I said to Saul. "I'm going to need your help."

Saul hesitated. "I won't break the truce."

"This won't."

After stopping in the infirmary for a few supplies, he followed me back to my room. I wrote instructions and then wrapped them, a couple syringes and all but one of the Death Lily sacks in bandages, making a soft package that I tied tight.

I handed it to Saul. "Since Tohon didn't know about Ryne's disappearance, that means the prince hasn't been captured. I need you to find Ryne or one of his men—doesn't matter who—and give this to them."

"How will I find them?"

"They have to be out past the encirclement. Probably to the north."

"Why north?"

"If it all goes wrong for Ryne, the Nine Mountains would make a nice temporary barrier." That was if the tribes hadn't invaded that far south. "Also, if Tohon doesn't keep his word, I want you to open the package and follow the directions inside."

"Do you think he'll kill us anyway?" Saul didn't act surprised. Guess I wasn't the only one with terrible thoughts.

"I hope not."

"You didn't answer my question."

"My gut feeling is he'll either turn you into his dead or drug you or use his magic to influence you."

"Thanks for putting it to me gently."

"You asked."

"And we won't have any weapons."

"You have your silent training," I said. "And you could get creative with the definition of *a weapon*."

"Gee, thanks."

"At least you haven't been invited to the feast." A shiver raced over my skin.

"It sucks for all of us." Saul put his hand on my shoulder. "Come to the sergeant's fire tonight."

"All right."

After Saul left, I checked on my patients. The news of Tohon's terms had spread throughout the camp at lightning speed. The mood in the infirmary was downright glum. My caregivers tried to remain upbeat, but I told a few of them to take a break to compose themselves. I wondered how many people would try to escape tonight. They wouldn't get far, but desperate people do desperate things.

I, on the other hand, felt eerily calm. Considering how terrified I had been of being Tohon's prisoner again, I had settled into a detached state. I'd done what I could. The rest would be inevitable. Plus, with Kerrick gone, life seemed lackluster.

Not that I'd given up. If Tohon made a mistake, I'd be the first one to take advantage of it. Despite his powerful magic and keen mind, he had made them before. In fact, Tohon's army hadn't spotted Ryne's leaving.

I mulled over the implications. Four hundred soldiers were hard to hide. And the encirclement had to have been in place before midsummer's day. The image of Jael's map with the red circle came to mind. Saul and I had crossed it on our way back from feeding Ursan to the Peace Lily. Then I remembered the horses spooking. Was that where the dead had hidden underground? Ursan had used his last breath to warn us about it.

I was an idiot. But Ryne wasn't. Oh, no. He'd figured it out long ago. Combined my theory about Ulany's magic with Ursan's message, and he'd known. I hoped he also had a plan to stop Tohon.

When my patients were settled in for the night, I joined Saul, Odd and Wynn next to our fire. I gave Wynn and Odd each a long hug before sitting next to Saul. No one said much at first. We stared at the dancing flames, lost in our own thoughts.

"Remember when Liv liked Sergeant Kol?" Wynn asked.

"Yeah, the entire camp knew she was sweet on him," Odd said.

"She wasn't the most subtle," Saul agreed.

"Then when he finally invited her into his tent for dinner, she bolted." Wynn laughed.

"It's hard to believe she'd be scared of sharing a meal," I said.

Wynn laughed harder, gasping for breath. "Oh! Baby Face... you're so..."

"What did I say?"

"When you invite a woman into your tent for dinner, that's code for inviting them into your bed," Odd explained.

"Oh. Does the Purity Priestess know this?" I asked.

"She hasn't bothered our platoon since Ursan invited her for dinner," Odd said. "She said it was the sweetest—"

"Odd, that's enough," Wynn said. "Ursan was just yanking your chain." She looked at me. "Every guy in the army claims he'll be the one to take the pure out of the Purity Priestess."

Our conversation didn't improve after that. It was raunchy, irreverent and silly. Our neighbors probably thought we were drunk. We talked about everything and nothing. We all knew it was the last time we'd have the sergeant's fire, but no one wanted to acknowledge it. No one wanted to say goodbye either.

Instead, when it grew late, we said good-night as we had all those times before. We pretended we'd see each other in the morning.

Deep sleep remained elusive. I drifted in and out, dreaming of being locked inside a familiar jail cell. The same one I'd occupied back when I'd lived in Jaxton. Tohon's dead surrounded the building, but Kerrick stood on the other side of the bars.

"Come on," Kerrick said, opening the cell door.

Unable to move, I said, "I can't. I'm trapped."

"It's not so bad," Flea said. He was lounging on a mat in the next cell.

"Flea, what are you doing?" Kerrick asked.

"Hiding. This is a great spot. No one will think to look for me here."

"Who are you hiding from?" Kerrick asked.

"Tohon."

"We need to go, now." Kerrick held out his hand to me.

Feeling as if my legs were mired in mud, I took a step toward him. Our hands almost touched.

"Not so fast, my dear," Tohon said. He breezed pass Kerrick and snatched my hand. "You have a lot of explaining to do."

Pain shot up my arm, waking me. The fingers on my right hand tingled, and my heart thumped in my chest. My sheet was tangled around my legs. Giving up on sleep, I rolled out of bed and changed.

A loud and fast knocking sounded as I buttoned my shirt. Muffled words, "…an emergency…the High Priestess…" reached me. I sprinted for the door. Christina stood with her fist raised in midknock. Her red cheeks and messy hair indicated her distress.

"You're needed in the infirmary now," Christina said.

We ran the short distance. Estrid waited with two of her priests. She didn't appear to be sick or injured, but she was clearly upset.

"What—" I started.

"Wake her." Estrid pointed to a prone figure on a nearby bed.

Recognition spurred my steps. Noelle was unconscious, and her face was as pale as snow. She had no visible injuries, but blood stained the pillow.

"What happened to her?" I demanded.

"That's what we want to know," Estrid said.

I gasped. "Did someone attack her? Where's Jael?"

"Wake her and we'll find out."

When I placed my hand on her forehead, her eyes fluttered open. My magic sought her injury. There was a serious gash and lump along the back of her skull. She must have hit her head pretty hard. She also had a few bumps and bruises on her limbs, but nothing serious.

As I drew her injury into me, she blinked. "Avry?"

"Who hurt you?" I asked.

"Jael."

Pain exploded in my head. I would have to wring the bitch's neck when I recovered. Groping for an empty bed, I collapsed onto it, squeezing my eyes shut against the searing lantern light. I teetered on the edge of consciousness.

"Where's Jael?" Estrid asked.

"I tried to stop her, High Priestess," Noelle said.

"Stop her from what?"

"From leaving."

KERRICK

His dream seemed so real. The tips of Kerrick's fingers tingled and Avry's scent lingered on them. Longing and fear filled him. She was in trouble. But he couldn't do a damn thing about it. Probably why Flea was in the dream, as well. Another he couldn't save.

As he lay in bed, he concocted an escape plan and calculated how long it would take to reach Avry. Thirty days if he was on foot, ten by horseback if he managed to find a horse and it didn't balk at crossing the Nine Mountains. Either way too long.

Giving up on sleep, Kerrick rose and headed downstairs to the library. Danny had discovered an apartment on the second floor when he'd collected the books. Noak had allowed them to use it while they researched.

Kerrick lit a lantern and opened a book on herbal remedies. He read through the descriptions, but his thoughts returned to Avry. Lately, anything he did reminded him of her. The bone-deep ache never left him. To avoid slipping into a self-pitying sulk, he concentrated on the list of green ferns, which had different properties than the yellow variety. No surprise, his mind wandered again.

Kerrick and Danny had spent the past two days researching a possible cure for the sick tribespeople. After Kerrick had stopped the boy from healing him, Noak had questioned them on what they'd been doing with the stacks of books.

Although seeming to be perplexed that they would put so much effort in finding a cure for their enemy, Noak had allowed them to work together.

When Noak had left, Danny had grabbed his own stomach. "Avry was right. The desire to heal just…grew from my core and then tugged hard, pushing to get out. Why did you stop me?"

"I don't want the tribespeople to know. Not yet. They could force you to heal this disease, and it might kill you. We need to learn more about it." Kerrick rubbed his neck. The cuts had already stopped bleeding. "Besides, you don't need to heal minor injuries."

"But I'd like to experience how it works before I need to save someone. What if I do it wrong?"

"I don't think there's a wrong way, but when we have some privacy, I'll cut myself someplace that's easy to cover and let you heal me. All right?"

Danny had agreed to keep his new healing powers under wraps. Over the next two days Noak had stopped by from time to time to check on their progress. Otherwise, he left them alone.

Kerrick felt better having the boy close to him, but his dream about Avry still haunted him. Danny joined him after dawn, and by the time Noak arrived late in the morning, they had a list of possible plants that might work as a substitute.

Noak and two of his men escorted them into the forest to collect samples. Kerrick had seen the first plant when they'd searched for the venite, so he didn't need his magic to find it. A slight breeze blew through the trees, and he breathed in the comforting scent of the living green.

As they hiked, Kerrick asked Noak about his ice magic. "Can anyone else in your tribe do the Winter's Curse?"

"My father. That is why he's our leader. Only those touched with power can lead."

"Does Olave have magic, as well?"

Noak scowled. "No. His tribe is different."

Kerrick considered. "Then how can he challenge your father?"

"When he marries my sister, he will control her power. She's been touched by summer."

"And she'll let him?" Kerrick couldn't mask his surprise.

"She has no choice. When they marry, they will be bound during the ceremony. This allows him to…use her power despite her wishes."

"Is that how it works for all your people?"

"No. Only those who have been touched by one of the seasons."

"So you would—"

"Yes. Only if my wife does not have power. If she has been touched, we would be able to use each other's power equally. It is the ideal situation."

"Is Rakel happy about the arrangement?"

"It does not matter. It is done."

Kerrick marveled at Noak's cold response. "If your father knows Olave will challenge him, why would he promise his daughter to him?"

"For our people. We are divided and need to be one. Father will either prove his right as leader of all, or die, proving Olave is the one to lead us."

"Why do you need to join together?" Kerrick asked.

Noak scanned the forest, but his gaze grew distant. "We've endured too many harsh winters in the Vilde Lander, and my people can no longer survive on our own."

That would explain why they were on the warpath. "My people are also struggling to survive. If you're willing to share resources with Olave, then why not share with us?"

Noak stopped and turned to him. He huffed with amusement. "And who are you to offer such a thing?"

Ah. Kerrick considered but decided Noak would more likely kill him than try to ransom him. "I'm Prin..." No. It was time to face the truth. "I'm King of Alga Realm."

If Noak was impressed, he didn't show it. "Your people forced us off our land. We will not share."

"That happened a long time ago. I had no part in it, nor did my people. I'm not going to apologize for the decisions made by my forefathers. But I can offer you land of your own where no one can chase you away again. In exchange for peace."

"And I am supposed to trust—"

"I would give my word."

"Why would you do such a thing?"

"To stop the killing." He gestured to Danny, who hadn't said a word the entire time. "So he can grow up, find love and have a family."

"Weak sentiments. It is why you lost."

Kerrick shook his head. Why did he even bother? The tribes were looking for revenge. But when they crossed the Nine Mountains, they might view his offer differently. Especially if Tohon and his army of the dead waited on the other side.

Letting out a breath, Kerrick concentrated on finding the plants, using his magic to discern the location of a few. They spent the day gathering leaves and roots. By twilight he stumbled with exhaustion. Danny grabbed his hand. A zip of energy flowed up his arm. Avry had been able to share her strength with him, but he thought it had been an anomaly. Perhaps it was just a part of the healing magic.

When he felt a little better, he released Danny's hand. He

didn't want the boy to use all his energy. They returned to the library after full dark. Lantern light blazed from the windows. That was the first clue something was wrong.

Inside, Noak's father, Canute, and Olave waited with a dozen armed men. Another clue.

"Where is she?" Olave demanded.

Kerrick thought he referred to Avry. But the man had addressed Noak.

"Rakel is in seclusion as is proper," Noak said.

"Not anymore. She is gone," Canute said.

"Escaped?" Kerrick asked.

Olave glared. "Not without help." His tone dripped with accusation.

"I would not aid her," Noak said. "It is not proper."

"Then she has been taken by another suitor," Canute said.

CHAPTER 17

I stood and fidgeted with the sleeves of the long beaded pink gown that had been Jael's, feeling naked without my weapons. I had surrendered my throwing knives and stiletto to one of Tohon's soldiers that morning. It had taken them all day to collect and pile the army's weapons into wagons, which then disappeared.

Estrid's servants had been frantic to prepare a suitable feast and decorate the grand dining room. Word had just arrived that Tohon's procession approached. Torches lit the path up to the manor house, and the invited "guests" lined the steps, waiting for his arrival.

The wind pressed the silky material against my legs. I kept my arms down at my sides despite the shivers that raced along my skin. My fingers curled into fists to keep my hands from shaking. Noelle's injury throbbed in my head. Christina had pulled my hair back and arranged it to cover the gash.

As Tohon's horse stepped into view, I focused on the single hope I held on to. When I had recovered from the blinding pain from her head wound, I had lain in bed thinking about all that had happened in the past couple of days.

My thoughts had snagged on my dream with Kerrick and Flea. Kerrick's presence had been pure wishful longing. The jail had been the same one he'd rescued me from ages ago. Or so it had felt. More had happened to me in the past three seasons than the three years before.

However, Flea's presence in the dream might not have been wishful thinking. He had been at my rescue last fall but hadn't been hiding. I had clutched the sheet tight. Perhaps Flea was sending me a message. There was a jailhouse in Zabin. In fact, Flea, Quain and Loren had spent time there when I'd been detained by Estrid. That was where they'd been hiding!

Unable to contain my excitement, I had asked Christina to fetch Saul. He'd arrived quickly. Concern had creased his forehead. I'd spent more time assuring him I was okay than I wanted.

Lowering my voice, I'd pulled him to me and said, "Remember when I said Ryne would be close by?"

"Yes."

"He's still inside the encirclement."

"Wow. That must have been some blow to your head. Do you want me to get Christina?"

"Not funny, Saul." How did I explain about my dream? And how I put the clues together. I didn't. "They're hiding—"

"In Zabin. We already thought of that. The town's been searched. Plus all nonessential civilians have been evacuated well before midsummer's day."

"What about the jailhouse?"

"It's too small to fit more than a dozen."

He'd been right. I sunk back. What had Flea meant? I'd racked my brain. What else was located inside the encirclement? They could be hiding in the training forest, but that wasn't a—

I'd sat up, startling Saul. "What about the POW camp? It's big enough to hold them all. And who looks too closely at faces when they're all wearing that bright yellow jumpsuit?"

Saul had stared at me. "That's...that's...genius! And they all left this morning."

"How many?"

"I don't know. But now that I'm thinking about it...more than we had. What if they're all gone?"

"That would be too risky. Tohon's army might accept a few they don't recognize but not four hundred. Probably just a handful so they had a bridge to the outside. You need to deliver that package I gave you before you swear loyalty to Tohon."

He had agreed to check the camp before hurrying away. All day, I'd had mixed feelings about it. If Tohon suspected I knew Ryne's location, it wouldn't be hard for him to extract that information from me. But I couldn't help clinging to that one bit of hope as I waited for the start of what was sure to be a horrible evening.

The procession entered the courtyard. Tohon wore a huge crown that sparkled with diamonds. I wondered if he had pried the gems from his father's throne. In comparison to the crown, his silk tunic and pants were elegantly tailored without decoration. His gaze swept over the steps with a possessive glint. At least he wasn't smirking outright. His smile was closer to smug.

When he spotted me, his demeanor changed for an instant, and I caught a glimpse of molten anger before he hid it. His face smoothed back into his handsome and charming expression. With his black hair, long eyelashes and deep blue eyes, he looked every bit a prince.

Only after he passed me did I notice Cellina. She wore a dark purple gown, and amethyst flashed from her hair. Sepp walked with her. His hair had turned all gray since I'd seen him last. And his resemblance to Kerrick still seemed creepy.

Sepp didn't hide his displeasure at seeing me. The feeling was mutual. Sepp had betrayed us when we'd rescued Ryne.

I wondered why Tohon brought him along. To intimidate Estrid? Or for something more sinister?

A few of Tohon's generals and a couple bodyguards followed Sepp and Cellina. Behind them marched Tohon's living army in perfect step. When they reached the bottom of the stairs, they fanned out into rows, filling in all the space between the tents and Estrid's army. The numbers were overwhelming.

Tohon waited at the top of the stairs for his soldiers to get into position before turning to Estrid. She wore her High Priestess gown. Curtsying, she invited him in for the feast.

He said something to her that I couldn't hear. Her face turned bright red as she knelt in front of him. Tohon waited. Slowly the rest of Estrid's party knelt, and then those on the steps did, as well. Except me. I just couldn't do it.

That anger he'd hidden earlier rushed to the surface as he gestured to two of his guards. They grabbed my arms and dragged me up the stairs.

"You must kneel before your king, Avry," he ordered.

"You're not my king, Tohon." The terrified part of my mind squeaked at me to shut the hell up.

"I will be, once you swear loyalty to me."

"I can't do that." And it seemed I couldn't keep my mouth shut either.

"Why not?"

"I'm sworn to another king."

"Kerrick's dead, my dear. Cellina's ufas chased him down on his way to Ryne's. I think it was a fitting end for him, don't you?"

His words twisted inside me like a dagger, shredding my already fragmented heart. I refused to answer. Instead, I said,

"You are mistaken. I gave my life for King Ryne. That act is akin to swearing loyalty."

"And he has abandoned you, my dear. Therefore he has rejected your fidelity." Tohon grasped my wrist. "You will kneel."

Pain burned up my arm and spread through my body. My head pounded with renewed fury as my muscles trembled. It didn't take long for my legs to give out, and I fell to my knees. The pain faded, but he didn't release his grip.

"Better," Tohon said. He scanned those kneeling in front of him. "Where's Jael?"

"She ran away last night," Estrid said.

Tohon's fingers dug into my wrist, drawing blood, but his voice remained even. "We will discuss this later." His gaze met mine. "Including your little adventure, my dear." He gestured for everyone to rise with his free hand. Yanking me to my feet, he towed me along as he entered the manor house.

When we reached the grand dining room, the group paused as everyone took in the elaborate decorations. Platters laden with cold meats, cheeses and fruits lined the tables. A string quartet played softly as servers waited to seat the guests. Tohon dragged me up to the head table, and I sat on his left with Estrid on his right. Sepp and Cellina joined us.

Tohon released his grip on me after the wine was poured. He grasped his glass and stood. The low buzz in the room ceased as he raised his wine, proposing a toast.

"Now that our conflict has ended, it is one more step to peace and prosperity. Here's to the unification of all the plague survivors into one realm."

Everyone clinked glasses and drank.

Cellina hopped to her feet. "Here's to the man who will lead us to peace, King Tohon!"

More clinking and drinking. I went through the motions

but only touched my lips to the edge of my glass. No doubt I would need a clear head for later. Also my thoughts had snagged on a comment Tohon had made about Kerrick. He had said the ufas tracked him down before he reached Ryne's, but according to Ryne, Kerrick had not only arrived, but then was sent to the north.

Why would Tohon lie about the timing? Unless Ryne had been lying all along to save my feelings. Perhaps he thought I'd be too upset over Kerrick's death to function. As much as I'd like to curl into a ball and sob, I knew Kerrick wouldn't want me to give up. Tohon had to be stopped. And if the op-portunity to do him harm presented itself, I wouldn't hesitate.

The feast seemed endless. Servers brought out so many courses, I lost track. The tables filled with steaming bowls of soup, spicy beef, buttered potatoes and sugar beets. Unable to eat, I pushed the food around my plate.

Tohon appeared to be enjoying himself. He talked to Estrid during most of the meal. From what I could tell, he was pump-ing her for information. Not that it mattered. I wondered if Ryne was indeed hiding in the POW camp. Would he attack tonight? It would be quite the surprise. But when I remem-bered Ryne's troops only numbered around four hundred, the odds wouldn't be ideal.

Perhaps I shouldn't try to guess Ryne's plans. Tohon would eventually turn his full attention to me, and I didn't know if I could refuse to answer his questions.

Tohon reclaimed my wrist after the dessert course had been cleared away. He ordered Estrid to lead him, Sepp, Cellina and all his bodyguards to her study. Tohon also requested that her top-ranking officers accompany us, as well. Dread lumped in my stomach as he pulled me along. This was it. He would demand all of us to swear our loyalty.

Settling behind Estrid's massive desk, he pushed me to my

knees next to him. I considered rebelling, but he still had a tight grip on me. Then he asked the High Priestess to explain Jael's absence.

"She failed to attend our morning meeting, and when I sent a runner to fetch her, he found her page unconscious on the floor and Jael was nowhere to be found," Estrid said. "When we revived her page, the girl said Jael had left during the night."

"Did Jael tell her page where she was going?"

"No."

Tohon pressed his lips together. "Bring her page here. I wish to question her."

Oh, no. Not good. "She doesn't know anything," I said.

His annoyance transferred to me. "I didn't ask you. But don't worry, you'll get your turn soon enough."

Estrid sent one of her officers. While we waited for Noelle, Tohon questioned Estrid on her staff and troops. How many, who was in charge of the companies, and who had been left behind in Ozero.

When Noelle arrived, I held my breath, hoping she wouldn't mention being my sister. Aside from a quick look at me, she kept her gaze on Tohon. He stared at her for a full minute before asking her to recount the events of the previous night.

Noelle glanced at Estrid.

"Tell him everything," Estrid said.

She repeated the story. "I blocked the door, hoping to keep her from leaving, but she used her magic, and the next thing I knew I was in the infirmary." Noelle also confirmed that she didn't know where Jael was hiding.

Tohon leaned forward. "What is your name?"

"Noelle, sir."

"It's *sire*. Or you can say *your highness* or *my king*."

"Yes, sire."

"Do you know what happens to people when they lie to me, Noelle?"

She stammered. "No, sire."

He raised his hand, showing her that he held my wrist. "This is what happens."

Although I braced for the pain, I still gasped as the wave hit me. Stronger and faster than what he'd sent me before, every part of me felt as if it were on fire. My world shrank to a pinpoint of agony.

When the onslaught stopped, I came to my senses. Lying on the floor, I panted as sweat dripped down my back.

Noelle's panicked voice pierced my fog. She swore she hadn't lied.

"I know," Tohon said. "I just wanted to see your reaction. Very conflicted, and not quite what I expected. Come here." He reached a hand to her.

I scrambled to my feet and blocked her. "Don't touch him."

Tohon grinned with pure delight. "Now, that's what I'd hoped to see. My dear, why didn't you tell me you had a younger sister?"

He was quite aware that his question destroyed any hope that I might make trouble for Tohon. "The topic never came up," I said. "Besides, her loyalty is with Jael."

"I see." He focused on Noelle. "And now Jael has flown the coop, leaving you behind. Where do your loyalties lie?"

She hesitated. I felt a bit of comfort from that. And as much as I would have loved for her to throw her lot in with me, I knew that'd be the worst thing she could do right now.

"With you," Noelle said to him.

Tohon laughed. "I like this girl. I'm going to keep you close. You can be the first to swear allegiance to me."

After Noelle took the oath, Tohon presided over Estrid, her staff and the high-ranking officers' vows.

When everyone but me had sworn their loyalty, Tohon asked Noelle if there was a ballroom in the house. "We need to celebrate this momentous occasion."

"There's one on the second floor," she said.

"Good. Please escort everyone there, and then bring the rest of the dinner guests to me. Once they take the oath, they can join in the dancing. Cellina, will you talk to the string quartet about relocating from the dining room?"

They all hurried to obey. Before Sepp left the room, Tohon caught his attention by tapping his fingers against his thumb. Sepp nodded. The death magician had a smug gleam in his eyes. The smugness wasn't unusual, but the gleam…

When they were gone, I rounded on Tohon. "They're not going to dance. Sepp's going to encase them all in a magical stasis, isn't he?"

"Would you rather I kill them?"

"Of course not, but—"

"I'm far too smart to trust their pledges. However, Estrid and her staff might prove useful in the future, so I'll keep them alive. For now."

"Including Noelle?"

"Don't worry about her, my dear. She won't be harmed."

"As long as I cooperate, right?" I verbalized the unspoken threat.

"No. She's interesting. Out of all the people here, her emotions are the most complex. A puzzle to figure out."

I didn't like the sound of that. "Won't you be too busy ruling your new kingdom?"

"There's always time for a few side projects, including your little miracle, my dear. I'm sure there's more to it than Kerrick sharing his energy with you. But that's a discussion for later." He stroked my arm.

A shudder ripped through me.

Noelle arrived with the remaining dinner guests. Tohon enjoyed watching them kneel in front of him and swearing their allegiance. Once everyone had had a turn, he sent them to the ballroom with most of his bodyguards.

"You will attend me like you had Jael. Understand?" Tohon asked Noelle.

"Yes, sire."

"I will be in Estrid's suite. I expect you there at dawn."

"Yes, sire." Noelle bowed and made a quick exit without glancing at me.

Tohon stood and made a show of stretching. He gestured to me. "Shall we retire for the evening, my dear?"

For a moment I froze in pure terror. Then I said, "I need to check on my patients."

"All right. Lead the way."

Oh, no. I avoided Tohon's outstretched hand, breezing past him as I headed toward the door. Trailing four bodyguards, Tohon followed me to the infirmary and waited while I made my rounds. A few patients teased me about my gown. Others asked about my companions. Not many of Estrid's soldiers had actually met Tohon before. Fear swirled in their gazes when I told them. No help for it, they would have to swear allegiance to him eventually. I wondered when Tohon would force me to take the pledge. All he'd have to do was threaten Noelle, and I would do it.

I prolonged my interactions with my patients. However, Tohon caught on and ordered me to finish. I was amazed that he was being rather...well, pleasant for him. Considering all that I'd done to ruin his plans—killed his Death Lily garden, stolen Danny and Zila and rescued Ryne—I'd expected him to punish me as soon as we were alone.

Unfortunately, the night was still young. I didn't spend as much time with my last couple of patients. And before he could say anything, I said good-night, shot out of the infirmary and strode to my room.

"Not so fast," he said, catching up to me at the door. "You're staying with me tonight. I want to hear about your adventures."

Numb with horror, all I could say was, "I need to change."

"No need. That dress suits you far better than your usual clothes." He scanned my body as if appraising a gemstone. "However, if you want to collect your things, I will allow it."

I entered my room. Tohon leaned against the door, letting in the lantern light from the hallway. Pausing near my bed, I gathered my courage. I'd expected this, and even had my pack ready to go. Yet now that my fears had turned real, I balked.

"Avry." His tone warned.

I pulled my pack from underneath the bed. Clutching it to my chest, I followed Tohon. He chatted about…I'd no idea. All my energy was focused on moving my feet forward despite the panic building inside me.

Estrid's expansive rooms had been decorated in the same elaborate and ornate style as the rest of the manor house. Oversized furniture filled the space, and rich drapery covered the windows.

A serving girl waited in the receiving room. Tohon ordered her to fetch us some tea. Then he circled the room, examining the décor. "Not bad if you like gold and gaudy. Good thing we won't be here long."

"Where are *you* going?" I asked.

He ignored my implication. "I need to establish my rule in all the towns that have been previously occupied by Estrid, set up my people and soldiers to keep them in line. I also need to find Jael. That little whore *will* kneel before me and acknowledge me as her king."

Good luck with that, I thought, knowing better than to say it aloud.

When the girl returned with a tray, Tohon waved me into one of the armchairs. "Sit and relax, my dear." He waited until the tea was served before dismissing the girl.

I perched on the edge of the chair, holding my tea. Tohon's mood could change in an instant. In my experience, his friendly act wouldn't last long.

Tohon lounged in the chair opposite mine, sipping his tea. A brief hope that someone might have poisoned his drink died when I remembered his life magic kept him healthy, counteracting poisons, plagues and other sicknesses.

"So, my dear. What did you think of my little trick?"

"With your dead soldiers surrounding the camp?"

He nodded.

Best to stick to the truth. For now. "It was brilliant."

"It was," he agreed. "But you figured it out before I could spring it, didn't you?"

"I…" I considered.

"Be honest, my dear." A hard edge sharpened his tone.

"I found the clues, but Ryne put them together in time to escape your trap."

"And he left you behind." He tsked. "The woman who saved his life."

If he was hoping to hurt me, it wouldn't work. I shrugged.

"Just how did you survive the plague?" Tohon leaned forward.

Time for some creative stretching of the truth. "I didn't. I died and Kerrick brought me back."

His body tensed at Kerrick's name. "Impossible."

"You need to change your definition of *impossible*. I once thought that about your dead soldiers. Yet they're here."

"My magic—"

"Keeps them from rotting, but you inject something into them that animates them. What is it? Death Lily toxin?" It was the wrong guess, but I wanted to see his reaction.

His teacup clattered when he placed it back in the saucer. "I'm impressed by your effort to trick the answer from me. No one knows the substance, and that's the way I intend to keep it." Tohon relaxed back. "And you managed to change the subject. I believe you were going to tell me the *real* reason you survived the plague."

"Does it matter? The plague is gone."

"No more stalling."

"A Death Lily saved me." I explained how I'd been in excruciating pain and sought the release only the Death Lily's toxin could give me. All true, except I failed to mention the Lily had spat me out within seconds, and a Peace Lily took me. "I died inside its petals. When it ejected me, I woke in Kerrick's arms."

"That's more believable than Kerrick saving you. I'm sure he was happy about your recovery." He crinkled his nose. "I can smell his scent on you. Good thing he's dead. Otherwise, I'd be jealous."

Without thought, I brought my arm up to my nose, hoping to catch a whiff of spring sunshine and living green. Nothing. Fresh grief tore through me.

Tohon paused with his teacup inches from his lips, which curled into a smile. "Too bad the ufas ripped him to pieces. I would have liked to display his body in one of my glass coffins."

I stared at my hands, struggling to keep the burning tears locked tight.

Sensing my emotions, Tohon kept going. "Handy creatures, those ufas. Alive, I can only control one, but dead…they're so much easier to work with. Cellina has been training them to track by scent. Kerrick was their first kill."

The desire to run away pulsed in my chest. I glanced at the door. Two of Tohon's bodyguards blocked the exit. Perhaps I could zap them before Tohon reached me.

"You won't get far, my dear."

Sagging back in the chair, I acted as if defeated. But I plotted in my mind. Too bad all my ideas for escape ended the same way—recaptured. I needed to keep him talking. Plus, there was a question I had to know the answer to. "Did you send your ufa pack after Belen?"

Tohon laughed. "No. That big oaf stumbled onto them on his own."

"Did he... Did they..." The words clung to my tongue, refusing to be spoken.

"Belen is in one piece."

I straightened as hope sprang inside my chest. "Then he's—"

"Dead."

Shocked, I gaped.

"It's not all bad news, my dear. I rather liked Belen, so he's still lumbering around. Once he's finished with his training, I can have him be one of your...escorts. How's that?"

Worse than death! I jumped to my feet and lunged at him, intent on wrapping my hands around his throat. He caught my wrists. But instead of pushing me away, he pulled me closer as heat raced across my arms and through my body, liquefying my muscles.

I sank to my knees before his chair, leaning over his lap. His face was inches from mine. An intense expression—cruel and mocking—darkened his gaze. His magic pulsed through me. The sensation teetered between pain and pleasure, robbing me of speech.

"I should blast you until you scream for mercy, then take

your life," he said. "You have wrecked my plans, slept with Kerrick and have been actively helping my enemies. Both Cellina and Sepp strongly advised it. It's sound advice. I should heed it."

Sharp daggers of pain pierced my skin. I yelped.

His expression softened. "Yet…when Cellina informed me you still lived, joy touched my heart. Not only did you survive the plague with the help of a Death Lily, but you're also smart. And you react to my touch like no other."

The pain turned into desire in a heartbeat. Goose bumps tickled my skin as a warmth spread along my stomach and between my legs. He slid his hands under my loose sleeves, up my arms and around my back, pulling me closer. Tohon kissed me, sending a blaze sizzling along my spine. I groaned and climbed into his lap, straddling him and deepening the kiss.

The smart side of me acknowledged that my healing magic made me far more susceptible to his life magic than any other woman. That I still despised him despite the part of me that wanted to yank his pants down and ride him. Too bad logic had no control of my body.

He broke off the kiss. The force of his magic eased a bit.

"As much fun as it would be to have you quivering under me every night, you would no longer be you. You'd be a… what did you call it before?"

"A drooling mess?" My voice sounded husky. "Scatterbrained?"

"Yes. And I don't want that. I want to woo you."

I leaned back in surprise. "You do?"

"Yes. Kerrick was nasty to you and you forgave him. Ryne's rumors and accusations caused the death of every healer in the Fifteen Realms except you, and you died for him. It's only a matter of time before you see me as I truly am and fall in love with me."

Biting my lip, I kept from saying that his actions—using the dead and experimenting on children—were unforgivable. He took my silence as...I'd no idea.

"This is how it's going to be," Tohon said. "I can't trust your word, so I won't ask for it. I also won't force you to make love to me. However, you will stay by my side. And—"

"What about my patients?"

Annoyance creased his brow. "Wait until I'm done. You can work in the infirmary, but you will be guarded at all times."

Still shocked, I mulled over his words. "What if I try to run away?"

"What happened when you tried to run away from Kerrick?"

"That was different."

"How? He basically kidnapped you so you could heal Ryne. When you tried to run, he chased you down and dragged you back. Right?"

"How did you know?"

"When you were in my dungeon, my guards paid close attention to your conversations with Ryne."

"So you'll do the same? Drag me back?"

"Not me personally, but one of my men."

"What about my sister?"

"What about her?"

I huffed. "Aren't you going to use her to ensure my cooperation?" Not that I wanted to give him any ideas, but it needed to be said.

"I told you before that I won't."

"Then you'll let her go?" I tried to keep the hopeful tone from my voice.

"If she wants to leave, she can. But where would she go, Avry? She'd be alone."

True. I thought quickly. "I know a lady who owns an inn

in Sectven Realm who would gladly take her in." And Mom would heal her in ways that I couldn't, maybe even earn her trust.

"Fine. We'll ask her in the morning."

I slid off his lap and stood. "Just like that?"

"Yes."

"Uh-huh. Is this part of that whole…wooing thing?"

He didn't answer, just smiled that killer smile.

Cellina arrived without knocking. She strode in still wearing her purple gown but stopped when she spotted me and Tohon.

"Should I escort her up to the ballroom? She's missing all the fun, and Sepp's been waiting to dance with her," Cellina said with a touch of malice.

"No. She's staying with me."

"She's dangerous and you know it."

Tohon stared at her.

"At least have Sepp freeze her. There's too much—"

"You've made your point. Did you want something?" he asked in an icy tone.

She shot me a poisonous glare before answering. "The dinner guests have all been…taken care of. Do you want me to help with the…uh, swearing in of Estrid's soldiers in the morning?"

"No. I need you to gather your ufa pack. You're going on a hunt."

Cellina's anger slipped a bit. "Who are we hunting?"

"Ryne and Jael."

"Which one first?"

"Avry? Who should we find first?" Tohon asked me.

"Jael." Her magic could probably handle the pack. And if not…oh, well.

Tohon chuckled. "I see there's no love lost between you

two. However, she's bound to be farther away and will be tricky to capture. While Ryne is probably quite close."

Ryne might be closer than he thought. Fear swirled in my heart.

"Do you want me to bring him in?" Cellina asked.

"Oh, no. Let the ufas tear him apart, just bring me a souvenir."

KERRICK

The night insects buzzed and trilled. An owl called for a mate. A raccoon rustled, foraging for food. Kerrick detected no sounds of a person moving within the forest.

He fingered the stem of a tuble flower. One of its blue-green petals had been bent back, indicating someone had brushed past it on his or her way east.

Kerrick paused a moment as a wave of exhaustion swelled. He'd been searching the forests around Krakowa most of the night for Rakel and her captor or captors. Noak, Canute and Olave waited for news at the edge of town. Danny had been sent to bed.

It had taken Kerrick nearly an hour to convince the tribal leaders to let him search alone and not with hundreds of warriors bumbling around the woods. Not only would that many people interfere with his magic, but they might ruin any trail signs left behind. It had been a difficult concept for them to understand, having lived all their lives in the flat wildlands.

And asking for his sword had caused another intense debate. The last thing he wanted was to run into a couple rogue warriors and be unable to defend himself. Kerrick rested his hand on the hilt of the sword, its familiar weight a comfort.

Pushing his magic as far as he could to the east, he connected with the living green, seeking any irritations or sore spots that would indicate another person walked among its home. Nothing, except the hollow void that meant a cave about a mile away.

He smiled, remembering Avry's aversion to them. Unlike Kerrick, who held a certain fondness for them since they had made love for the first time in one, and the second time and the third… Before he could wallow in his memories, he returned his attention to the problem at hand.

They weren't hiding in this section of the forest, but they might be overnighting in the cave. Better check and make sure. Kerrick jogged through the underbrush without causing a sound. After tonight, he'd probably sleep for a week. When he drew close to the entrance, he slowed, then stopped about fifty feet away. Once again he scanned the area with his magic, but no one guarded the entrance.

He crept closer. The faint scent of wood smoke reached him. The first positive sign since the tuble petal. Kerrick parted the vines, revealing a three-foot-wide by four-foot-high crack in the rock face. A flickering, orange-yellow glow reflected off the jagged wall just inside. No voices murmured, only the small pops from the fire.

If he was lucky, they would be asleep. If not…

Crouching down, he entered. A few flames clung to the dying fire. Stretched out next to it was a woman. She was asleep. Kerrick glanced around the small cavern, seeking others. But it was empty.

He studied the woman—no doubt Rakel. Long limbs, lean and a powerful build like her brother, Noak. Her white-blond hair had been braided into one long plait. It took a moment for him to notice her split lip, the purple bruises on her right cheek and her ripped shirt. Still-wet blood stained the front of her white tunic. A dadao rested next to her within easy reach. Dried blood coated the edge of it.

It appeared Rakel might have fought off her captor. Kerrick inched closer. Was she injured? A sheen of sweat glistened on her brow. She also looked flushed, but it was hard to tell in the dim light.

He took another step. Rakel jerked awake. In one smooth move, she hopped to her feet, grabbed her weapon and pointed it at Kerrick.

"Don't come closer," she ordered.

"Easy," he said, holding out his empty hands.

Her gaze slid past him. The vibrant green of her eyes matched the forest. Since all the other tribespeople had blue eyes, Kerrick wondered if the color was due to her summer magic.

"I'm alone."

She huffed in disbelief. "Noak sends his dog to track me down, fetch me home. And he's all alone?"

"He asked me to find you. He thought you'd been taken against your will."

A harsh laugh. "Everything has been against my will."

Even though her comment could be interpreted many ways, Kerrick guessed it had to do with her upcoming marriage. "Did you escape from your seclusion?"

"I will not go back."

And that would be a yes. "But—"

"I will die before I marry. I will not be bound!" She charged.

Instinctively, Kerrick twisted. The dadao's sharp tip narrowly missed his stomach. He trapped her weapon against his chest and stepped back, pulling her off balance. She released her grip, recovered her footing and pulled a dagger.

Kerrick clasped the hilt of her dadao, but she aimed the

blade at her own neck. He dropped her sword and tackled her. The dagger flew from her grasp on impact. She stilled under him, panting as if she'd run for miles. Kerrick rolled off her but kept alert for any sudden movement.

Rakel squeezed her eyes shut for a moment. Fresh blood soaked the front of her shirt.

"You're injured," he said.

"Leave me to die, then."

"I can't."

"You are afraid of Noak."

"With good reason. His Winter's Curse is unlike anything I've experienced before, but I'm more terrified of a certain healer I know who would kill me if she ever found out I left you to die." And Belen wouldn't be happy either. He leaned back on his heels. "May I?" He gestured to her stomach.

With resignation, she pulled the fabric up, revealing a long deep slice all the way across her waist. Kerrick wasn't an expert, but he'd seen his share of battle wounds, and this one didn't look good.

"You need care. Won't your father reconsider your marriage to Olave since you're unhappy?"

"He cares not for my...happiness. Only for the tribe."

"Is there another you wish to marry? One who can challenge Olave or your father?"

Pain creased her expression. "Arkin. But...my father...killed him."

Hell. Kerrick knew he couldn't take her back to the tribe. He considered his only option—help her escape. Double hell.

Bandaging her wound with strips he cut from her pants, he tied the ends tight. He brought her water and a handful of those fuzzy plant's orange berries to eat. Danny had pointed them out earlier and said they helped with blood loss. Kerrick added wood to the fire, made her comfortable and promised to return.

He staggered from the forest an hour before dawn. No need to act exhausted. Canute, Olave and Noak didn't visibly react when he informed them that he'd searched the forest and found no signs of Rakel.

"They must be hiding in the city," Kerrick said. "Or have gone north. Maybe back to Vilde Lander."

"We wasted time with your dog, Noak," Olave said.

"Send warriors door to door," Canute ordered his son. "Olave, take Oya—she's the fastest horse—and go north."

If he had any energy, he would have been surprised by Canute's trust. Instead he trudged to the library and woke Danny. The boy squinted at him, his hair sleep tousled.

"Wake me in four hours," Kerrick said.

"Why? What happened?"

"It's better if you don't know." Kerrick collapsed in his bed, hoping his scheme wouldn't get Danny killed.

CHAPTER 18

Tohon stood and held his hand out to me. "Time for bed, my dear."

His words sliced through my grief over Belen and worry for Ryne. I stared at him without moving.

He twitched his fingers in annoyance. I glanced at the guards stationed by the door.

"Go ahead," he said in a tight, dangerous voice. "Give me a reason to heed Cellina's advice."

She had told Tohon flat-out to kill me. I considered my options. Sleep with Tohon or be killed.

"Can I sleep on the couch?" I asked.

"No." And when I didn't move, he said, "You really try my patience. What do you think is going to happen?"

"Uh…"

"I already told you I won't force myself on you."

I couldn't trust him and his ridiculous plan to woo me, but I didn't have much choice. So I took his hand, and we entered Estrid's bedroom. The huge canopy bed occupied almost the entire area. The two night tables next to it seemed tiny in comparison. There was a small washroom in the back. I ducked inside and changed into my uniform. Even though

I was on the fourth floor and surrounded by guards, an opportunity to escape might present itself. A girl could hope.

Tohon snorted in amusement when I rejoined him. He lounged on the right side of the bed under the covers. I slid in on the left side, staying as far away from him as possible.

"Good night, my dear." Tohon leaned over, gave me a chaste kiss on my cheek, then extinguished the lantern.

I stared at the darkness, reeling from the events of the day. Tohon's breathing slowed as he fell asleep. My emotions see-sawed from grief over Poppa Bear to pure rage at Tohon for turning him into one of his dead. Tears gushed, and I muffled my sobs with the pillow.

In order to pull myself together, I concentrated on how I could send a message to Ryne about the ufa pack. I could enlist one of my caregivers to alert him, but Cellina planned to leave in the morning. By then it would be too late. Too bad no other solutions came to mind. Eventually, I drifted off.

And for the first time in months, Tohon didn't invade my dreams.

Cellina barged into the bedroom around dawn. Tohon roused next to me, scowling at her. He had been a perfect gentleman all night.

Before Tohon could say a word, Cellina blurted, "They're gone."

"The pack?" he asked.

"No. Estrid's soldiers. They're not in their tents."

"Did you search the town?"

"Of course."

Tohon sat up. "Well, they couldn't have gotten far. The encirclement is still in place."

"Maybe they heard how you planned to ensure their co-operation."

"Doubtful. Only you and Sepp know."

Cellina glanced at me. The force of her hatred slammed into me.

"Avry doesn't know. Estrid's troops are probably hiding within the encirclement. Go find Ulany," he ordered.

"Ulany hasn't checked in," Cellina said.

She was the earth magician who had buried the dead to trick us. I almost cheered but kept my emotions in control. For an area that was supposed to be secure, there were quite a number of missing persons. I hoped Ryne and his men were among them.

"Send a squad out to find her," he snapped, getting out of bed. He wore a pair of black silk pajama bottoms and nothing else. Tohon caught me staring at his muscular chest and leered. "Like what you see, my dear?"

I didn't answer, but Cellina made a sound that could have been a growl.

"Cellina, go. I'll be out shortly."

She shot me another lethal look before leaving.

"Don't mind her, my dear. She's jealous." He seemed unconcerned.

While I was glad Estrid's troops were missing, I worried over Cellina's comment about Tohon's plans for them. It wasn't a surprise as I'd already theorized a few nasty outcomes to Saul. And the one that made the most sense caused me to shudder.

"You're going to kill all of Estrid's troops," I said. "And turn them into your dead."

Tohon paused as he dressed. "Is that a guess?"

"No."

"Dead soldiers are loyal and obedient. I have more realms to conquer, and since I have to leave some of my men and officers to keep the peace in my new realms, I need to expand my army." He shrugged, as if murdering thousands of men

and women was of little consequence. Tohon must have noticed my horror. "I promise they won't suffer, my dear. As
each one enters to offer his allegiance, I'll pluck his life with
my magic. It's usually quick and painless."

"Usually?"

"If I'm annoyed, then I can make it quite painful." He gave
me a significant look.

I clutched the blanket in tight fists, wishing I could wrap
my hands around Tohon's neck and zap him. Too bad once I
touched his skin his magic overpowered mine. Maybe I could
warn Estrid's soldiers. If they were still here. That thought
helped ease my anger.

Tohon said, "You can work in the infirmary today while
I find the missing army." He left the room.

Tohon didn't appear concerned over the new developments
and seemed quite confident he'd locate Estrid's troops. He had
a good reason for his attitude. Estrid's army had tried to break
through the ring of dead and failed.

When I joined him in the receiving area, I stopped short for
two reasons. One—Noelle waited for her orders. Two—four
dead soldiers waited with her. Three men and one woman.

Noelle stood as far away from them as possible. She stared
at them with a combination of utter revulsion and fear. Ah,
her first encounter with them. Unfortunately, I understood
too well how she felt. The dead wore grubby and tattered uniforms. Protective metal collars ringed all their necks. Lifeless
eyes gazed at nothing. At least I didn't recognize any of them.

A terrible thought swelled. What would I do if I encountered Belen? Or even worse, if I were in a position to stop
him? He'd want me to release him from the horror. Could
I? Or could I "wake" him like Flea? Would my touch counter Tohon's?

Tohon pointed at me and addressed his dead. "She is not allowed to leave this building. Understand?"

They all nodded in unison. Creepy.

"You go where she goes. Do not let her out of your sight. Understand?" he asked.

Once again, they nodded.

He turned to me. "Sorry, my dear. I know how much they repulse you, but I also know that you can't use your magic on them. When you're not with me, you'll be with them." Tohon snapped his fingers at Noelle. "Come, girl."

Noelle hurried after him. But before she left, she shot me her blech face. When she was little and had tasted something awful, she'd stick out her tongue and squeeze her eyes shut. Despite the prospect of spending the day with the dead, I smiled.

I worked in the infirmary for the remainder of the morning. My dead bodyguards stood next to the door, watching my every move. Their presence made my patients uneasy, but I couldn't do anything about it. I wondered what would happen to those in my care. If Estrid's troops had escaped, leaving them behind, would Tohon make an example out of them? Probably.

If he killed them... My legs trembled and I sat down as reality caught up to me. I couldn't bear more deaths on top of Kerrick, Belen, Liv, Thea and Ursan's. The additional grief would crush me. I let my morose thoughts run rampant. My muscles shook with the effort to keep from bawling. Taking deep breaths, I recovered my composure one inhalation at a time. Now I understood why my mentor, Tara, hadn't talked about her healing experiences on the battlefield.

I checked on Sergeant Enric. The knife wound on his thigh had healed, but I wasn't sure what to do with him. His squad had left without him. Enric reminded me of Ursan—tall, muscular, with his brown hair cut bristle-brush short. His desire for action was evident in his restless agitation.

"I need you here," I said to him.

"For what? I should be…doing something. Anything," Enric said.

Gesturing to the other patients, I said, "Eventually Tohon's going to decide what to do with them, and you might be needed to help me."

"With what? They took my sword."

"I have a few…medical instruments that might come in handy. Relax for now."

He agreed. I finished my rounds. In order to stall another episode of wallowing in misery, I concentrated on organizing the supplies. Later, a few of Tohon's soldiers arrived with various injuries, mostly minor. Assessing one man's infected toe, I lectured him on proper foot care before letting Christina clean the wound and apply salve.

My next patient had to be helped onto the examining table by his buddy. A piece of broken wood had pierced his left thigh. All color had fled his face, and he bit his lip to keep from crying out when his leg bumped the table.

Once he was settled, his friend said, "Nice to see you again, Healer Avry."

I turned. "I wish it was under better circumstances, Lieutenant Fox."

"At least we're both still alive."

"True," I agreed.

"The rumors claimed you'd died of the plague," he said.

"You know better than to believe camp gossip. How's the leg?" I'd healed his broken leg back when I'd been at Tohon's castle.

"Never better. I'm hoping you can work your magic on Sergeant Steward."

I examined the man's injury. "How did it happen?"

"He fell through a floor," Fox said. "We were in an old wooden barn, and the section he was standing on collapsed under his weight."

"You were smart to leave the large slat in. If you'd have pulled it out in the barn, he might have bled to death."

Magic grew and expanded deep inside me. I placed my hands on his arm, seeking other problems. He also had a sprained wrist, bruised back and fractured elbow. All secondary in comparison to his leg. The wood and all the splinters would have to be carefully removed before I could heal him.

Christina helped me mix the sleeping draft. Steward gulped it down. After he fell asleep, I cleaned the wound, grabbed the tweezers and then began the slow and arduous process of removing all the little slivers before tackling the biggest piece.

"Why were you in the barn?" I asked Fox as I worked.

"Searching for the enemy. They snuck away last night." His tone held disbelief.

I paused, glancing at him. "How can that many soldiers get by all of you?"

"Last time we checked, they were sleeping in their tents and the barracks. We didn't have many patrols out. The noose held all this time so we figured we didn't need to worry."

"The noose?"

He grimaced. "That's what we call the encirclement."

Ah. Overconfidence was one of Tohon's weaknesses. "What if they managed to break out of the noose?"

"They won't get far. King Tohon has plenty of troops. The companies that aren't here are moving to position themselves all around the perimeter."

My hopes died. "Encircling the encirclement?"

Fox huffed. "Yeah."

I returned to plucking fragments.

"That tactic with those…things." Fox lowered his voice. "We all thought it was a nasty trick, but it saved lives. And this way we'll all get a little closer to peace."

"Do you really believe that?" I asked, meeting his gaze.

"I have to."

"I don't. As long as Tohon's in charge and the dead obey him, there will never be peace."

Fox didn't reply, but he assisted me when I removed the largest piece from Steward. He held his leg as I yanked it out. Relieved it wasn't gushing blood, I examined Steward's wound. The muscle wasn't as badly damaged as I'd first thought, and the wood hadn't pierced anything vital. He'd live.

I debated if I should wrap it and see what happened, or heal him. If Tohon's troops found Estrid's, there could be more casualties today. And some could be life-threatening. In the end, I stitched his skin closed and bandaged it.

Satisfied his sergeant had been taken care of, Fox left to return to his unit. I checked on a few patients until all those sleepless nights caught up to me. Not even bothering to go to my room, I napped on an empty bed for what felt like three seconds.

A ruckus woke me. I sat up and faced a nightmare. Tohon strode toward me with Sepp right behind. I'd never seen him that angry. A numb horror spread through me. When he reached me, he grabbed my neck and yanked me to my feet.

Without a word, he dragged me from the infirmary and into my room where he slammed me against the wall. Pain shot through my skull. Then he wrapped both hands around my throat and squeezed, cutting off my air. In a panic, I latched on to his forearms and blasted him with my power.

He yelled and dropped me. I landed in a heap, marveling that my attack had worked.

"You dare fight back!"

When he leaned over me with murder in his eyes, Sepp said, "You might want to question her before you kill her."

Tohon hauled me up and pinned me to the wall. This time he put a hand on my cheek and sent white-hot agony straight into my head. The pressure was so intense, I screamed in an effort to expel the pain. And just when I was about to slip into unconsciousness, Tohon eased up a bit before making me scream again. Then he repeated it.

Hours later, or so it felt, Tohon tired of the torture and released me. All I could do was collapse onto my bed. I curled into a ball, gasping for breath.

Tohon sat on the edge. "Get her a glass of water," he ordered.

Only after I recovered and drank the water did Tohon reveal what had set him off. He pulled out a familiar cloth and unwrapped a syringe.

I was too spent to react.

"Estrid's troops escaped through a number of holes in the encirclement last night. My special soldiers in those areas were neutralized. Not by decapitation or that strike to the base of their necks. No, they had been shot by a single dart. This was found near one of the breaches." He held up the syringe. "Do you recognize it?"

"Yes." My voice rasped. "I use them all the time."

"What substance did they use to stop the dead?"

"I don't know. I was with you all night."

Tohon touched my cheek again. I braced for the pain, but this time a warm tingle spread and I felt as if I had been drugged. Then the feeling intensified, and the room spun as my body flushed with desire. I gasped.

His magic filled me, seeping into my brain and wrapping around my heart like roots. Logic packed a bag and left me. My clothes rubbed over my sensitive skin, and I plucked at them, wanting them off.

Tohon's voice sounded in my mind. *I'll claim you, Avry. Then you'll tell me everything just to please me. Just to be rewarded by my touch. Cooperate or I'll take you.*

His words had the opposite effect. After all the grief and pain over the last few days, I'd be damned if I'd let the bastard claim me. Concentrating on my magic, I viewed the heady feeling as a disease. As something that needed to be healed. Slowly my body cooled as the desire subsided.

"What was in the syringe?" he asked.

"I don't know."

"You're lying." His surprise didn't last. "Which means you're resisting me." Now he sounded like a petulant child.

Except he was far from a child. Tohon increased his magic. My body responded. Shivers chased each other over my arms and legs. But I imagined that they were bugs, and my healing powers sought each out and squashed it.

I fought Tohon, planning to expend all my energy. But Tohon stopped before that point. Red splotches covered his cheeks as if he'd run a race. Pure fury burned in his eyes.

He glanced toward the door. "Girl, come here."

Noelle stepped into my view. Ah, hell. Had she been here the entire time? I studied her expression. Yep.

Tohon picked up the syringe and examined it. "There's a couple drops left."

Fear spurred me into a sitting position. "No."

He ignored me. Instead, he grabbed Noelle's wrist and rested the syringe on her forearm. "Shall I test it?" he asked me.

"It's Death Lily toxin," I said.

My answer threw him. "Really? How did you figure that out?"

"It was a guess."

He waited.

And since he still held my sister, I explained part of my theory. "I knew you'd been experimenting with the toxin, but then I remembered you were helping the Healer's Guild to develop an antidote for the toxin before the plague. Maybe during those experiments, you discovered that substance you used to create the dead. So I guessed the toxin might counter your mystery medicine."

"Impressive. Good thing only you and I can harvest the toxin. How many sacks did you give Ryne?"

"Three."

Tohon considered. "Not many then. And he probably used them all to rescue Estrid's troops." He frowned. "Now we'll have to hunt them down. You do realize that you've condemned her soldiers to death?"

"You already planned to kill them."

"But it would have been orderly and painless. Now they'll be killed on the battlefield, and I won't be able to turn all of them. Such a waste."

Hard to feel guilty over that. If I had a choice, I'd choose to go down fighting than on my knees, swearing allegiance to Tohon.

"You've interfered again," Tohon said. "Killing you is the smartest thing I can do right now. Yet, I hesitate because I'm still hoping that you'll use that intelligence in my favor."

"That wooing thing?"

"Yes. Although I no longer believe that tactic will work. No, it's time to try one last strategy with you before I admit defeat."

I didn't like the sound of that.

"Every time you upset my plans or go against my wishes, I will kill someone close to you. You will bear witness to a very painful death, knowing it's all your fault."

Oh, no. "As of now?"

"No. Starting today, which means—" Tohon pricked Noelle with the needle and depressed the plunger, sending Death Lily toxin into her body "—she's the first."

KERRICK

Four hours had passed by in a heartbeat. No dreams of Avry or Flea had disturbed his short sleep. A pang of disappointment filled him. He lay there, summoning the energy to move.

Danny reached for his hands. "I can help."

"No, thanks. Save your strength."

"Why?"

"You're going to need it." Kerrick put a hand up to stop the next question. "Put together a pack with the medicinal herbs that are good for lacerations and that bread from yesterday. I'll explain once we're away from here."

"Are we escaping?"

"Yes and no."

"Kerrick, you're not making any sense." Danny rested his hand on Kerrick's forehead as if checking for a fever, his serious expression at odds with his young face.

"I'm fine. Now go." He shooed the boy. Not really a boy any longer. He'd been forced to grow up quickly, but Danny had risen to the challenge.

Once he returned with the pack, Kerrick showed Danny the opening he'd made in the wooden wall of the other bedroom. The library didn't have a door to the back alley, but its neighbor did.

Danny raised an eyebrow before climbing through.

"It is always a good idea to be prepared for anything," Kerrick said.

They crept downstairs, and Kerrick checked the alley for Noak's men. By now he knew them all by sight.

"Once we're out in the open, I want you to act like you're on a mission. Don't glance around, don't stare at the ground and don't avert your gaze if we pass anyone. Understand?"

"Yes."

"Good. Let's go."

Kerrick strode into the alley with Danny by his side. He headed to the bathhouse. Halfway there, he changed directions and aimed for the forest west of Krakowa. His back burned as he imagined all of Noak's warriors following them, ready to pounce as soon as they stepped outside the city.

He relaxed only when they reached the outer edges of the woods. Once they traveled deep enough to be hidden by the trees and bushes, Kerrick took Danny's hand and tapped into the living green, using his magic to camouflage them both.

Danny held his free arm out. "I'm green!"

Kerrick put a finger to his lips.

"You're green, too," Danny whispered.

He smiled.

"Even your teeth!"

Keeping a hold on Danny's hand, he turned east toward Rakel's cave. The boy matched his step, cutting down on the noise of their passage.

They reached the entrance an hour later. Kerrick called softly so he wouldn't scare her. She was still armed after all. But when they entered, she didn't stir from her prone position next to the fire.

Danny dropped Kerrick's hand and knelt beside her. "Where—"

"Waist."

He lifted her shirt. Blood had soaked through the bandages. He peeled them back. Rakel didn't move.

"It's bad. None of the herbs will work for this. I need to—"

"Can you survive?"

"I...don't know."

Conflicted, he paused. Danny's life meant more to him than his own. How could he risk him?

"It's not your decision, Kerrick. Remember? It's mine, and I'm going to do it."

Spoken like a true healer. "Then I'll help you like I did with Avry. Go on."

Danny placed both his hands on her exposed skin. Nothing happened. Then Danny yelled, clutched his stomach and doubled over, passing out. Kerrick picked him up. He turned to take the boy into the forest.

Noak blocked the entrance.

"Step aside," Kerrick said. It wasn't a request.

Without changing his expression, Noak backed from the cave. Kerrick followed, and as soon as he reconnected with the living green, he plopped onto the ground with Danny in his lap.

He tried to channel energy into Danny. Except Kerrick had nothing left. He'd used all his strength. All he could do was hold Danny tight and hope his healing powers would save him.

"Will the boy live?" Noak asked. He stood nearby.

"I don't know."

"You lied about Rakel." Noak's tone was matter-of-fact.

Kerrick couldn't believe he was bringing this up now. "I did."

"You gave your word to cooperate."

"And I cooperated by searching for Rakel and her abductor

as requested by members of your tribe, and I found her. But you never told me what to do *once* I located her."

"It did not need to be said."

"In this case it did. She asked me to keep her location hidden, and since she's a member of your tribe, I had to cooperate." Technically she hadn't asked, but he doubted she'd correct him.

Danny groaned, and Kerrick remembered the pack full of herbs. Perhaps one of them would help him heal faster. Kerrick gently laid Danny on the ground and staggered to his feet.

Rakel exited the cave. She scowled at her brother but didn't say a word. Instead she stepped into the sunlight, closed her eyes and turned her face toward the sun. Her pale skin darkened to a honey color. After a few minutes, she strode toward Danny. When she reached the shadows, her skin glowed as if she'd swallowed a piece of the sunlight.

Kerrick intercepted her. Heat and magical energy pulsed off her.

"I will not harm him," she said.

He moved aside. Rakel knelt next to Danny. Placing her hands on his chest, she stared at him. The glow spread over the boy. He moaned.

"Wait," Noak said as Kerrick stepped closer.

Danny shuddered, then relaxed. When the glow faded, Rakel stood, her skin pale once more. Kerrick checked on the boy. The wound had disappeared. Not even a scar marked Danny's stomach.

Confused, Kerrick asked Rakel, "Did you take it back?"

"She used summer's touch to heal him," Noak said.

"Then why didn't she heal herself?"

"My magic only works for others."

"Then why aren't you helping your people? They're sick."

"I was in seclusion." Rakel shot Noak a nasty, hate-filled

look. "No interaction with anyone but my intended during the course of four seasons."

Kerrick put a few clues together. "Olave abused you."

Rakel turned to Noak. "I will not marry him." She placed her hand on the dadao hanging from her belt.

"Father—"

"It is time for you to challenge Father, Noak, and take your rightful place over both tribes."

Noak's expression didn't change.

Rakel pointed to Kerrick. "You were right about this one. I will act as second for you."

He remained silent.

"If you won't, then I will challenge him," Rakel said.

"It is not how it is done."

"Neither is bringing back a prisoner. We need to adapt, Noak. Father is old."

"He is still strong," Noak said. "And no one in the tribe will defy tradition and agree to be your second."

Rakel glanced at Kerrick. Oh, no.

"Will you be my second?" she asked. When he hesitated, she added, "If I am successful, I will release you and your boy. You will be free."

"And if you're not successful?" Kerrick asked.

"Then you both die," Noak said.

CHAPTER 19

Noelle lay on my bed, sweating and shivering as the Death Lily toxin poisoned her. At least she hadn't died right away, so there was hope she'd survive. Not much, as only ten percent lived. Tohon left me to watch her die, taking Sepp with him. My four dead bodyguards remained crowded inside my small room.

Pacing, I considered my meager options. I couldn't heal her, which was why the healers at the Guild had been experimenting with the toxin—to find a cure. And I couldn't bear to see her suffer. Guilt squeezed my chest. All this was my fault.

What if she died? I stopped. She couldn't. I wouldn't allow it. But what could I do? I could take her to a Peace Lily. Provided I was able to slip past my bodyguards, escape the manor house and break through the encirclement. Almost impossible to do on my own, but add in one sick girl and we wouldn't get far.

I sat on the edge of Flea's bed and put my head in my hands. If she died… No. Surging to my feet, I continued to pace. There must be a way. I just needed to think harder. My foot kicked something. I glanced down and halted. The syringe.

A plan formed. Not a very good one, but it was better than

doing nothing. I checked on Noelle, mopping her brow and helping her to lean forward to sip water.

She clutched my sleeve. "Avry…"

"Shhh. Save your strength. I need—"

"They're waiting for you." Her body convulsed, and she curled into a ball.

"I know. Tohon—"

"East. Go east. Leave me."

"No way, little shadow."

"Stupid."

"I disagree. Now I need to fetch a few things before it's full dark. Rest, I'll be back."

My bodyguards followed me to the infirmary. I pulled Christina aside and asked her to sit with Noelle. When she left, I found Sergeant Enric. He played cards with a private from Halberd Company, keeping the boy occupied.

"Enric, can I talk to you a moment?" I asked.

"Sure." He tossed the deck to the boy. "Shuffle them good, Bronson. I'm tired of losing."

We stepped out of hearing range of the other patients.

"I need your help," I said. "I—"

"Sure, anything."

"I didn't even explain. And it's dangerous."

"I'll take action over inaction no matter how dangerous it is."

I told Enric my plan.

He glanced at the dead soldiers waiting by the door. "What about your new friends?"

"I'll take care of them. Are you in?"

"Yes."

I grabbed a few supplies and headed up to Estrid's suite, trailing my guards. Hoping Tohon hadn't returned, I slipped inside. The servants were lighting the lanterns as I dashed to the bedroom, grabbed my pack and hurried back down to my room.

Christina jumped when I entered. The four dead crowded in behind me.

"How's she doing?" I asked.

"Sleeping now," she whispered. "But she was vomiting." Christina pointed to the floor next to Noelle. "I brought in a few more clean bedpans for when she wakes. Does she have the plague?" Fear laced her voice.

"No. She has a stomach flu." The plague symptoms closely matched the toxin's. Except the plague's victims lived longer— about eleven days, compared to an average of seven for the Death Lily's. "Thanks for staying with her." I escorted her out.

I placed my supplies from the infirmary on the night table and then dug through my knapsack. Unable to find what I was looking for, I upended my pack, spilling the contents on Flea's bed. Frantic, I searched.

"Looking for this?" Tohon asked.

He stood in the doorway, holding a Death Lily toxin sack. Or to be more exact, *my* sack.

"You made this one easy, my dear." Tohon strode over to the bed, gazing down at Noelle. "The Lilys make two sacks per flower. So if you gave Ryne three of them, then there has to be one left. And sure enough…" He tossed it into the air and caught it. "I found it in your bag, and I knew you'd want to use it on your special companions."

Tohon turned to me. Behind him Noelle stirred, sitting up. I kept my gaze on him.

"However, not all your schemes will be this easy. So, I'm afraid—"

He staggered forward as a loud clang echoed. Noelle had hit him over the head with a bedpan. I rushed forward and caught him. He looked at me with a dazed expression. Taking advantage, I found the spot on the back of his neck and zapped him before he could counter me. Tohon collapsed.

Dumping him on the ground, I yanked the toxin sack from his hand and swiped the syringe off the night table. One of the dead soldiers wrapped his arms around my waist, picking me up. His buddy grabbed my legs.

Noelle brandished the bedpan as the other two advanced on her. I shoved the needle into the sack and drew toxin, then pricked my captor.

Nothing happened.

A clang sounded as Noelle's bedpan connected. I tried to fight, but the two held me tight, and soon Noelle was captured, as well.

As they headed to the door, the man I'd pricked lurched once, then collapsed. A horrible stench filled the room. But I didn't hesitate to stab the dead holding my ankles. The other two recognized I was the bigger threat and dropped Noelle to come after me. Noelle reclaimed her bedpan, distracting them just enough so I could inject them.

We ducked and dodged, trying to keep out of reach long enough for the toxin to work. Once they fell over, Noelle and I grinned at each other, panting in the foul air.

"Way to go," I said.

"Not too bad yourself." She paled. "Ewww! I'm going to be…" Noelle heaved over the bedpan. When she recovered, she pointed to Tohon. "How long will he be out?"

"Not long. His life magic will counteract mine soon."

"Kill him before he wakes."

I balked at first. I was a healer, not a killer. However, killing him would save thousands of lives. I glanced around, looking for a weapon.

The door burst open, and Tohon's guards rushed in. They paused in horror, gagging on the fetid stench. Without thinking, I tackled the man closest to me, knocking him down into the hallway. I wrapped my hands around his neck and zapped him before he could shove me off.

Grabbing his dagger, I spun in time to see the other guard advance. He had pulled his sword. I threw the knife, embedding the blade in the man's stomach. With a gasp, he fell to his knees.

The sound of drumming boots echoed to my right. Enric raced down the corridor with Private Bronson right behind him.

"There's a bunch of guards looking for Tohon. They're in the infirmary, so we need to leave right now," Enric said.

I yelled for Noelle. She stepped over the man slumped in the threshold, carrying my pack. She set it down next to me as Enric stripped the guards of all their weapons. He handed a sword to Bronson.

Before I could protest, Enric said, "He knows how to use it. We need him." Voices and the pounding of boots emanated from around the corner.

"Go!" Enric pulled me to my feet.

We ran, dashing into the stairwell near my room. I led them downstairs and out a back entrance of the manor house.

"Which way?" Enric asked when we reached the fresh air.

Farm fields stretched out in all directions. Not much cover, but since the moon hadn't risen we wouldn't be as visible.

I glanced at Noelle. Bronson supported her since she hadn't been able to keep up.

"East?"

She nodded. East also offered the quickest route to the forest. Where we'd find concealment, but then we'd have to deal with the encirclement. I dug into my pack—Noelle had shoved everything back in. I found two syringes and filled them with toxin. I handed one to Enric.

"East it is," I said.

Enric took point, followed by Noelle and Bronson, then me. We bolted for the woods. I expected to hear sounds of pursuit any second, but we reached the woods without incident.

We stopped for a minute. Noelle needed to rest. Moving away from the group, I listened to the forest, seeking those off notes and telltale noises. A light breeze rustled the trees, but nothing else indicated intruders.

I sniffed the air. Were we close to the encirclement? The sweet scent of moist earth rode the air currents. I inhaled, filling my nose with the comforting aroma. Automatically I touched the leaves on a nearby bush, but no magic tingled under my fingertips. Grief burned deep inside me at the thought I'd never feel Kerrick's magic again.

Returning to the others, I outlined our next move. "Once we reach the dead, just keep moving. Enric and I will inject them." I gestured toward his weapon belt. "Give me the daggers." He passed them over, and I treated each of the blades with the toxin. Then I squirted a few drops on Enric and Bronson's sword tips before refilling the syringe.

I handed one of the knives to Noelle. "Just in case the dead get close to you."

"Do you know how to use it?" Bronson asked her.

"Oh, yes," I answered for her, grinning. "She's quite capable. And she swings a mean bedpan, too."

A howl sliced the silence, followed by another. The distant sound sent a shudder down my spine.

"That's our cue to leave," I said. "You two stay close to me and Enric."

With me in the lead, we headed deeper into the woods. After a few more steps, the ground under our feet rumbled. Tremors rolled along the soles of my feet.

"Don't stop," Enric ordered.

Shadows stood up around us. The hiss of dirt rained to the ground. The clang of a sword meeting another sounded as Enric parried a thrust. I'd forgotten Tohon had armed his dead.

Bronson shoved Noelle at me so he could fight. "Go, go, go!" he yelled, countering a swing and dodging another with the grace of a much older soldier.

Noelle wrapped her arm around my shoulder. I dragged her forward. One of the dead charged right at us. I pushed Noelle to the ground as I spun, avoiding the point of a knife. Jabbing his arm with my needle, I injected the toxin.

But he didn't stop, and I cursed the delay. It might just be the death of us. He stabbed again, cutting my upper arm. I backpedaled, moving out of his reach just before he toppled to the ground.

"Keep moving," Enric shouted.

However, the dead surrounded us like bees defending their hive. All I could do was stand over Noelle as another dead soldier attacked me. This one was a woman, and her blade pierced my left shoulder as I nicked her with my knife. Pain shot down my arm. She yanked the sword out and drew back for another strike.

I braced for the thrust. She stumbled and went down but was immediately replaced by another. I held my hands up in the universal sign for surrender. The dead man paused.

Voices called behind the line of dead. And in a flash, living soldiers joined the fray. Since they fought the dead, I didn't bother to ask any questions. Tucking my dagger back into my belt, I helped Noelle to her feet and wove around the clumps of fighters, pricking the dead whenever I had the chance.

When we broke through the encirclement, I slowed. But two men waved us on, guarding our backs. We kept moving even when the sounds of fighting died. My shoulder burned, Enric had a nasty cut on his cheek and I'd lost sight of Bronson. Enric just shook his head sadly when I asked about the private.

The moon had risen, and dim light shone through the trees. Our escorts/rescuers wore leather armor over civilian clothes, so I had no idea who they worked for. I counted ten of them— six men and four women. They didn't talk but signaled each other from time to time, which meant they've been together for a while. However, they didn't know how to walk in the woods without making noise.

After an hour, I stopped. Noelle needed to rest, and I needed answers. She plopped down on the ground.

"It's not safe," one man said. He had short brown hair and carried a saber.

"She's sick." I pulled my pack off. "If you can keep your squad quiet for a minute, I'll be able to tell you if anyone is chasing us."

He agreed. Concentrating on the sounds of the forests, I closed my eyes. No sour notes or strange sounds reached me.

Opening my eyes, I said, "We've either lost them or they've given up."

"It's still not safe. Tohon's other patrols—"

"Are nowhere near us."

He squinted at me. "How do you know?"

"Tohon's troops crash through the forest like blind deer. They haven't learned how to go silent. Neither have you."

He bristled. "Yet we managed to rescue you."

"Thank you, Mr...."

"Gilson."

"Avry."

He inclined his head.

"While I'm grateful for your help, you have to admit your appearance was rather...timely. Were you in the area, or..."

"We were waiting for you," Gilson said.

Alarmed, I wrapped my hand around the hilt of my knife. "How did you know we would be coming?"

Gilson glanced at Noelle. She had told me to go east. The pain from my shoulder spread to my heart. Noelle had betrayed me again.

KERRICK

Willing to do anything to ensure Danny's freedom, Kerrick had agreed to be Rakel's second when she challenged her father. If they failed, Kerrick and Rakel would die. In that case, Noak had promised to take care of Danny.

The boy woke soon after Rakel healed him. Noak helped him to his feet.

"You have been touched by summer, and now are tribe, little brother," Noak said.

Danny craned his neck back to stare at the big man. "Kerrick's been touched by winter, does that make him tribe, too?"

"No."

"Why not?" Danny asked.

Kerrick suppressed a chuckle at Noak's uncomfortable expression.

"She gave you a gift in exchange for your sacrifice."

Danny didn't look convinced, but he kept quiet. As they walked back to Krakowa, Rakel explained his duties as a second. He would fight Canute's second, who would probably be Olave, and share magic and energy with her if she needed it. Since Olave hadn't been touched, it would be her power against her father's.

When they reached the edge of the forest, Rakel gripped

his hands to test if they were compatible, just in case. Her warmth soaked into his hands, traveled along his arms and spread throughout his body. His exhaustion lessened, and he leaned toward her like a sunflower following the sun.

That feeling of longing reminded him of Avry. An image of her rose in his mind. Tohon touched her cheek and she writhed in pain. He cried out, and Rakel released him.

"You are bound to another," she said.

"I…"

"Your challenge will fail," Noak said to Rakel.

"It is not like ours. He can still aid me. But you must focus on me, and not let another claim your thoughts. Can you do that?" she asked.

Kerrick glanced at Danny. "Yes."

Olave and Canute waited for them on the steps of the library. They demanded answers and insisted Rakel return to seclusion. Kerrick left Noak and Rakel to deal with them, going to bed. He would be useless unless he rested.

Something bumped into his bed. Kerrick rolled over, grabbing for a weapon he no longer possessed. Danny stood next to him holding a tray full of food. Darkness filled the windows, and lantern light flickered in the hallway.

Kerrick groaned. "It's not even morning."

"You're right. It's actually evening. You slept the entire day."

He sat up in alarm. "The challenge?"

"The big fight is scheduled for tomorrow." Danny set the tray on the night table. "Kerrick, you don't have to do this. I'm tribe now. They won't hurt me."

"Don't you want to go home?"

Danny stared at his feet. "I never had a home. Well…not one I remember." He played with the hem on his shirt. "You're my…home, and I don't want to be alone again." Plopping down on the edge of the bed, he grunted. "That sounded so… selfish! What I meant was…I'm fine with how things are."

"But then you'll never see Zila or Ryne again."

He shrugged, putting on a brave front. "Zila's annoying, and Prince Ryne's too busy. Besides, he'll come find us eventually. Right?"

"We can't count on that. There's a very good reason why Ryne's busy." *And it might be Tohon and his army that finds us first,* Kerrick thought. He'd better warn Noak before the challenge.

"Don't fight. Please."

Ah. Kerrick considered his next words carefully. "Danny, there's more than one reason I agreed. Rakel doesn't wish to marry Olave. I can't stand by and let that happen, even though she's my enemy. Besides, Avry would kill me if she found out."

"Uh, Kerrick. Avry's—"

"No, she's not. She made me promise not to tell anyone, but if I die tomorrow…I want you to know."

Kerrick watched as a combination of emotions rolled through the boy. Joy, anger, fear and back again.

Danny hopped to his feet. "Avry's alive! You can't fight now. If you lose, she'll be devastated."

He took the boy's hand. "There's another reason." Kerrick waited until he had his full attention. "If Rakel is forced to marry Olave, he will eventually become the leader of the tribes, and getting rid of me is the first thing on his to-do list. Better now than later."

"Do you really believe that?" Danny asked.

"We both know it's just a matter of time. And don't forget, if Rakel wins, we'll have our freedom."

"Isn't there any other way?"

"Not that I can think of."

Danny stared at him for a moment. "You've given up. But I won't." He left.

Kerrick debated going after him but decided to let Danny have some time to accept the inevitable. Suddenly ravenous, he devoured the food and then lay back on the pillow.

Despite what Danny believed, he hadn't given up. Not at all. And he planned to fight as if his life depended on it. Because…well, it did.

The next day Kerrick stood at the edge of a large circle that had been etched into the ground. The tribespeople surrounded the area, all hoping to get a good view of the action. According to Rakel, they'd been told that a challenge had been presented, but not by whom. They also didn't know the circle had been located near the forest so Kerrick could access his magic.

Danny pressed against him as they waited for the ceremonial challenge to be called and accepted. Rakel strode into the middle of the circle and formally announced her intention to assume leadership of the tribes. A ripple of disapproval rolled through the crowd.

The murmurs ceased when Canute stepped into the circle, accepting the contest.

"I call my second," Canute said, gesturing to the edge. "My son, Noak."

By the shocked gasps, Kerrick wasn't the only one expecting Olave to be named. Pulling his dadao, Noak joined his father.

Kerrick's hopes sank. This would be a short fight.

"Who will defy tradition and be your second, girl?" Canute asked.

Before Rakel could answer, Danny dashed into the circle. "I'm her second."

"No!"

Kerrick moved to chase him, but the people around him

held him back. He fought them, but the man next to him said, "Cross the threshold and her attempt will be forfeit, and the boy will die."

He was going to die anyway. Unless Noak refused to fight. No expression showed on the man's face. Not good.

Jeers, hisses and angry words rose from the crowd.

Canute silenced them all with a glare. "What is this? A farce?"

"No," Danny said. "As her second, I request you concede the match in our favor."

Laughter ringed the circle, and even Canute cracked a smile. "Why would I be so foolish, boy?"

"Because if you don't, your tribe will cease to exist."

The noise level dimmed in an instant.

"You're sick and dying. Half your tribe lies abed." Danny strode to the edge. He jabbed a finger at a man. "He's coughing up blood. This other man is hours away from collapsing. And she can't stop bleeding. Without Rakel and me to heal them, they'll all die."

Kerrick beamed with pride. Well played. But would Canute heed the wisdom of Danny's words?

CHAPTER 20

"No," Jael said. "I'm not falling for your tricks. I know nothing cures Death Lily toxin. She'll either die or survive."

"But if Noelle dies, this will prevent Tohon from turning her into one of his dead," I said.

"He won't." Jael's hard expression softened. "I'll ensure she has a proper burial."

Anger surged. If my hands hadn't been secured behind my back, I would have lunged for her throat. Instead, I said, "Tohon's not going to agree to your terms, Jael. He doesn't want me that badly."

"And I've had enough of your whining." She waved a hand. "Take her back to the barn."

Gilson grabbed my upper arm. He escorted me to the old barn. All the windows had been boarded over and the door locked from the outside. At least he removed the manacles before pushing me inside.

The door clicked shut behind me. Sunlight glinted through the wooden slats and streaked the straw with yellow lines. Having already explored every inch of the one-story structure this morning, I sat on a pile of hay bales, considering my limited options, which included actions such as should I lie down or bang my head against the boards?

Enric had been happy to discover Gilson and his squad reported to General Jael and had quickly joined their ranks. Jael had the foresight to send her loyal troops away before Tohon could tighten his noose. The squad had ushered us to Jael's hideout at a rapid pace. Noelle had to be carried and it had taken us a full day to reach the small abandoned settlement southeast of Zabin.

Noelle had then been whisked away as soon as we had arrived, and, except for my brief audience with Jael in the farmhouse, I'd been locked in the barn. Enric actually believed I had been incarcerated for my own protection.

Although I knew I should be angry at Noelle for betraying me again, I couldn't produce the feelings. She was dying, and she was my sister. Everything but anger pulsed in my chest. I needed to get her to a Peace Lily. Maybe this time it would save her as it had saved me, but Jael wouldn't listen.

My shoulder ached, and a bone-deep fatigue pressed on me. I dug through my pack. Gilson had confiscated my dagger and syringe, but I still had the toxin sack. Too bad I couldn't do anything with it, as I'd never inject it into a living person.

One side of the sack was dented, but liquid squished inside. Not as much as before, but enough to take out a few dead soldiers. The fibrous material hadn't leaked despite being pierced a number of times with a needle. Impressive.

Down near the bottom of my pack, I found the Lily map. It had been in there since Saul and I had delivered Ursan. Spreading the map out on my lap, I located my current position and deduced the closest clump of Lilys. It was approximately one day east of here. So close!

Frustrated, I tested every wooden slat for weakness again. Solid. Building a pyramid of hay bales, I climbed into the rafters and pushed against the roof with my hands, hoping for a soft spot. None.

Finally exhausted, I stretched out on a pile of loose straw.

I jerked awake. Surrounded by darkness, I listened. Only the thumping of my heart reached my ears. But an uneasy feeling stirred in my chest. I jumped to my feet. The barn door remained locked tight. What had roused me? I peeked out through one of the small knots. No moonlight or lanterns lit the farmhouse. No movement. No—

An ufa howled, which would have been creepy if it had been a distant keen. But when the noise sounded on the other side of the wall, it went straight past creepy and right into terrifying.

A loud thud shook the barn's wall. The boards creaked. Alarmed, I backed away. More howls pierced the night. Shouts and screams followed them. Cellina's ufa pack had found us.

Another thud vibrated. Cracks snaked through the wooden slats. I grabbed my pack and scrambled up the hay pyramid. When I reached the rafters, I kicked the bales, knocking them down.

With a crash, an ufa broke through the wall. It paused as if stunned. Crouched on a rafter, I knew I wasn't high enough to stay out of its reach. The creature might not see me, but it could smell me.

Through the hole in the wall, I spied a fire. Ufas usually shied away from flames, but I doubted anything could scare the dead ones. The beast below me turned its head, sniffing the air. Smoke and the scent of burning wood wafted inside the barn. Just when I thought it couldn't smell me, the ufa slunk in my direction.

I pulled the toxin sack from my pack. Perhaps I could rip it with my fingernail and squirt the toxin in its face. But when the creature lunged into the air toward me, I panicked and tossed the sack at it. The ufa snatched it with its teeth, popping it before slamming into the rafter.

The beam shook, and I lost my balance, falling to the ground. The good news, I landed on a pile of straw. The bad, the ufa landed next to me. Before I could move, the creature was on top of me, pinning my shoulders down with its huge paws.

Bracing for its teeth to rip into me, I shut my eyes. But it didn't. Instead the ufa remained over me as if waiting for further orders. It had been on a seek-and-find mission, not seek-and-kill. Good to know.

The stench hit me a second before the ufa collapsed on top of me. I would have gagged if my lungs hadn't been crushed under its weight. Using my arms, I pushed on the beast's chest and wiggled sideways enough to make some breathing room. However, getting the dead weight off me would be impossible.

While I debated calling for help, a thud vibrated the floor boards of the barn, then a second. I froze as snuffling sounded quite close. Long sharp claws scraped at the ufa on top of me. It rocked, threatening to uncover me. I clung to its fur as the other ufa pushed its nose under my ufa's belly.

My throat burned with the need to breathe, and I was on the verge of passing out when the ufas padded away. After waiting a few more seconds, I sucked in the foul air in relief. Still trapped, there wasn't much I could do.

Eventually a voice hissed my name.

"In here," I said.

"Thank— What died?" Enric asked, coughing. "Where are you?"

"Stuck under the ufa."

He grunted and I pushed. Together, we moved the ufa's body enough for me to squirm free.

Enric helped me to my feet. "You stink."

He gave me an idea. I rubbed my back along the ufa's fur, hoping to cover all my body with its scent.

"Now what? There are ufas all over the place," Enric said.

"Thanks for the help, but this is where we part ways." I picked up my pack and ran for the broken wall.

He followed. "I had to pretend to support General Jael, Avry. Otherwise I would have been locked in here with you."

"Just don't get in my way." I'd decide later if I should trust him or not.

Climbing through the gap, I pressed against the barn, scanning the area. A few of Jael's soldiers fought ufas. The tobacco shed burned, and the house appeared dark.

"The general fled south with most of her men," Enric whispered.

"Noelle?"

"I didn't see her with them."

Jael probably left her behind. Again. Keeping to the shadows, I headed to the farmhouse. An ufa streaked pass, but didn't stop. Broken furniture, splintered doors and other evidence of a fight littered the first floor. I ran up the steps to the bedrooms, calling Noelle's name. She answered. Tracking her voice, I found her in a small room at the end of the hall.

Noelle lay on a single bed in an otherwise empty room, her hair tangled and sweat-soaked.

"Avry, I— You smell awful."

"Come on," I said, pulling her up.

She resisted. "I didn't—"

"Tell me later." I yanked her to her unsteady feet.

"No."

"Enric, help me."

"Here." He handed me his sword, then crouched down and tossed Noelle over his shoulder before standing.

"Let's go," I said.

"Where?" he asked.

"East."

We rushed down the steps and crept out the back door. I pointed to the forest. Enric nodded. With my heart jumping in my chest, I led him across the open yard, expecting to be attacked at any moment. Behind us ufas howled, but I didn't hesitate.

When we reached the outer edge of the woods, I said, "Go silent."

The rest of the night we pushed to cover as much distance as possible. My goal was to reach the Lilys before Cellina and her ufas found us. I guess I should have been grateful for the ufas as they helped me escape Jael, but it was only a matter of time before they picked up my scent.

We rested briefly in the morning. Enric laid Noelle down. Her skin tone was one shade darker than death's pallor.

She waved me over. I knelt beside her.

"I didn't...trick you," she said, tapping her chest with a closed fist. She held something. "Jael..." A violent shudder shook her. Noelle curled into a ball, panting. "Jael...set me up. I'm sorry I..."

"Shhh. It's okay." I pressed my hand on her forehead. The skin burned my fingers.

"No. Jael said...Prince Ryne was hiding in the east." Noelle grabbed my wrist with her other hand. "I wanted you to... find him...to be...safe."

A nice sentiment, but I was beginning to think he'd used me to keep Tohon occupied so he could rescue Estrid's troops. Which was a great plan for them, but not so much for me. Plus I was tired of being a pawn.

Noelle noticed my expression. "Prince Ryne asked me." Another convulsion struck her.

When she recovered, I asked, "What did he want?"

"Me to go with him."

"When?"

"Right before...he disappeared."

"So you knew he was leaving, and you didn't say anything to Jael?"

She nodded.

"Why?"

She looked away. "He said something...about family...and you."

"Are you going to tell me?"

"Ask him." All her muscles trembled, and she gasped.

"He's not here. And I doubt I'll find—"

"He said..." Blood ran from her nose and streaked her cheek. "Said...when you've escaped...to go..."

I pulled her into my arms and rocked her as I used to do when she was little.

She thrust something hard into my palm. My fingers closed around it, but I leaned closer as she struggled to talk.

"To go...home." Noelle exhaled but didn't inhale.

I glanced at what she'd given me. My necklace with the hands pendant. As much as I wanted to cry and carry on, I couldn't. Time was more an issue now than ever. I didn't want the Lily to reject her because she'd been dead too long, like Ursan.

Enric crouched next to me. "Ah, hell. I'm sorry."

"Can you carry her?" I asked.

"But—"

I explained about the Peace Lily. "It's her only chance."

Although he didn't appear to be convinced, he said, "All right."

I looped the necklace around my neck and then set a fast pace, heading straight for the clump of Lilys. Even though the odds were in our favor, I still worried and hoped there was a Peace Lily in the bunch.

We reached the area by late afternoon. After a few moments of frantic searching, I found one Lily tucked behind a row of trees. Death or Peace? I approached the flower. Nothing happened.

Relieved, I gestured Enric to join me. He held Noelle in his arms. Stopping under the plant's huge petals, he waited.

Nothing. I sank to my knees. "Please?"

The flower dipped toward us. I had a brief moment of joy before the Lily snatched me.

"No!" I screamed and kicked, but its barbs soon wrapped around my arms, holding me tight while it injected serum into me. A chilly numbness spread throughout my body, robbing me of emotion. The crushing weight of grief lifted, the worry and anxiety about Belen, Ryne, Flea and the monkeys disappeared. I relaxed for the first time in months. Enjoying the sensation for a moment, I breathed in deep, smelling vanilla. Then I returned to the matter at hand.

"My sister?" I asked.

The Lily's sadness washed through me. *No magic.*

Surprised that the Lily spoke to me, I floundered for a moment. "But—" Another blast of serum shot through me.

Rest.

I woke on the ground. Through the tree's canopy, stars flashed like diamonds. For a moment I felt at peace, until the memories rushed back in one awful wave. I groaned as my grief returned, gnawing on my heart with its sharp teeth.

Enric leaned over me. "Are you all right?"

No. "I'll live. How long—"

"A couple hours."

I pushed up on my elbow and looked around. A small fire

burned. A blanket covered my sister, and Enric had dug a grave for her. No, I'd never be all right again.

"What happened?" he asked.

I told him. My second attempt at using the Peace Lilys had failed. It seemed it would only save someone with magic or the potential for magic and only if they were freshly dead. Bitterness threatened to consume me.

He listened with sympathy.

When I finished, I lumbered to my feet and knelt next to Noelle, pulling the blanket down. I smoothed her hair and closed her eyes.

A whole list of I-should-haves bubbled to the surface of my mind along with the I-shouldn't-haves. Mistakes made, regrets and wrong decisions popped up, as well. The I-wishes and if-onlys had their say, too.

In the end, all that wouldn't change a single thing. And while I had hoped to change her future, the Peace Lily couldn't. I leaned forward and kissed her forehead, whispering goodbye. Glad for this chance, wishing I had the same opportunity for Kerrick and Belen.

Together, Enric and I picked her up and laid her in the grave. We covered her with the loose soil, packed it down and added a thick layer of rocks so the animals wouldn't dig her up.

I gestured to the grave. "How did you dig a hole so fast?"

"A collapsible shovel—standard equipment for a foot soldier."

"Thank you for doing that." Grief ate through my insides like acid. A burning pain ripped through me with every breath. Better for her to be buried than part of Tohon's dead army was the only positive aspect.

I searched for a stone to mark her grave and found one along a small stream. Planning to return someday to carve her name into, I positioned it.

Before Enric could ask, I said, "We'll camp here tonight and get an early start."

"What about the ufas?"

I shrugged. "They're after me. You can climb a tree and wait until they leave."

"Just like that?"

"Yep."

I grabbed my pack and went back to the stream. Scrubbing the foul odor of dead ufa from my skin and hair with soap, I tossed my stained uniform into a pile. Then I dressed in my travel clothes.

When I returned, Enric offered me some jerky. Unable to eat, I huddled by the fire, lost in memories.

"Where's home?" Enric asked the next morning.

According to Noelle, Ryñe said for me to go home when I escaped. However, I doubted he meant Lekas in the Kazan Realm. My hometown was southeast of here and at least a thirty-day walk. I fingered the pendant under my shirt as I unrolled the Lily map. The place that my heart now recognized as home was Galee. Where I'd apprenticed to Tara before the plague. Although that cave outside Grzebien where we'd hidden... No, I wouldn't think about Kerrick and the boys.

Galee abutted the Nine Mountains and was about fifteen days away. However, the Healer's Guild, or rather, the ruin that had been the guild's headquarters, was only seven days northwest. And looking at it from Ryne's point of view, it made the most sense. I told Enric our destination.

"Wouldn't Tohon guess that?"

"Probably."

"You're not concerned he'll ambush us along the way?"

Not really. "Do you have a better idea?"

"What if we encounter one of Prince Ryne's patrols?"

"Then we'll hook up with them, although I doubt it, since I plan to stay well to the east and skirt Zabin." I tapped the map. "But I need to make a stop first."

"More Peace Lilys?" Enric asked.

We had found another clump of Lilys about three days into our trek north. I sniffed the air, hoping to catch the light odor of anise among the sweet smells of lemon and honey. "I think that one's a Death Lily."

When I moved toward it, Enric yanked me back. "Are you crazy? I know you're upset about your sister, but that's suicide."

I explained about my immunity. "I need better answers. Wait here, I'll be back."

The Death Lily hissed as I drew closer. Its petals parted, and in a flash, it scooped me up. Thorns pierced my arms, and my consciousness joined with the Lily. Through the connection, I saw Enric pacing nearby, and farther along the roots, I saw soldiers fighting, units creeping through the forest and others waiting in ambush.

It welcomed me. I imagined the scene with Noelle and the Peace Lily. It confirmed my guess that a Peace Lily could only revive those with magic or magical potential and freshness. "What about Tohon's dead?" I asked. "He used the Peace Lily's serum and then touched them."

Stolen. No grow.

An image of Tohon placing his hands on a Peace Lily filled my mind. The Lily's petals parted abruptly as if he had pushed a button. He grabbed the sacks before the petals snapped closed. I remembered how the Death Lily reacted to Sepp, pulling away. Was this the Peace Lily's reaction to Tohon's touch?

Yes.

That explained how Tohon harvested the serum. And he

had plenty of Lilys to milk. But why did it work on those without magic?

No grow.

It didn't. Not as it had with both me and Flea. We were alive and thriving…growing in plant speak, not like the dead.

Yes. Stop it.

I need more toxin, I thought.

Yours.

A glimpse of other Lilys dropping sacks came unbidden before the Death Lily retracted its barbs and deposited me onto the ground. I held its two bright orange sacks. Two more lay on the ground nearby.

"Are you okay?" Enric called.

I rubbed my arms. Grief's claws gripped me again, squeezing my chest. Perhaps someday a Death Lily would keep me forever. But not today. Today I held the antidote to Tohon's dead, and I would see this through to the bitter end.

We traveled roughly north for the next several days before we turned to the west, reaching the edge of the Healer's Guild compound on the eighth day. Our slower pace was due to finding all the Death Lilys en route to collect their toxin. Also, we avoided any patrols and skirmishes. We'd decided to stay away from everyone just in case. Other than the creepy howling of ufas, no one bothered us.

Crouched in the bushes nearby, we scanned the complex, seeking ambushers. The Healer's Guild had once been comprised of three magnificent buildings with marble pillars and smooth stone blocks. Smaller buildings that housed the healers, apprentices and staff had been scattered around the complex. All had been destroyed during the plague years. Their pillars broken, the stones blackened from the flames that had engulfed the interiors.

During the height of the panic, the people had blamed the healers for the disease and had vented their anger and fear on us. Only I had survived by hiding and running for three years. A wasted life until Kerrick and his companions had found me. All that time I'd thought the healers had been the scape-goats, but Tohon confirmed that the Guild did indeed start the plague when they experimented with Death Lily toxin, crossing it with another plant to produce what they'd hoped was an anti-venom. Instead, it had turned into a deadly and incurable disease.

Now vines covered most of the ruin. Small saplings and other plants grew between fallen blocks and cracks. A slight breeze blew. Nothing else stirred. However, there could be ambushers buried under the ground.

"There's no one here. Are you sure this is the right place?" Enric asked.

"No, but there's an underground records room that we'll need to check before moving on."

Even though the place appeared empty, we waited until twilight to venture out in the open. I led Enric to the unre-markable pile of debris that covered the doorway to the room. Clearing off the detritus, I unearthed the door.

"Doesn't look like anybody's been here in a long time," Enric said.

"It's supposed to look that way." I pulled the door, and it opened without a squeak. A lantern with a new wick and oil hung just inside the entrance.

"You were right."

Lighting the wick, I held the lantern aloft, illuminating the steps that spiraled down into the records room. When we reached the bottom, the area was just as I remembered—rows of dusty shelves filled with musty-smelling wooden crates.

However, a stack of crates had been piled in the walkway with a paper resting on top.

Enric picked it up and said, "It's for you."

It had been folded in half with my name written on the outside. I opened it.

There's a big storm coming. Seek shelter.

I must have groaned aloud because Enric grabbed the hilt of his sword. Waving the paper, I said, "Relax. I know where they are. Let's go before it's full dark." I hoped I remembered where that cave was. The one we sheltered in during the blizzard.

It wasn't far, but there had been snow on the ground and no leaves on the trees. I headed east. Concentrating on finding familiar landmarks, I didn't notice the off notes until too late.

Two men sprang from the underbrush with swords in hand. Enric yanked his weapon free, but I put my hand on his arm, stopping him.

"Have you guys gone feral?" I asked the monkeys. "What kind of welcome is that?"

"One concocted due to boredom. What took you so long?" Quain asked.

"The usual—dead ufas, Tohon's evil schemes, Jael's evil schemes, Death Lilys. You know. Same old, same old. You?"

"About the same," Loren answered, smiling.

"I'm guessing they're friendly," Enric said.

"That depends on who you are." Quain studied him.

"Down, boy." I swatted his arm. "He helped us escape."

"Us?" Loren asked.

"Long story. And I only want to tell it once. Are Flea and Ryne here?"

"Yes."

Relief that they had all survived coursed through my body.

I hurried inside the cave, seeking Flea. My need to hug him far outweighed all other considerations.

"I missed you, too, Avry," Flea said, patting my back. "You should have known Prince Ryne would make sure I did all the dull jobs."

"I know…it's just…" I squeezed him again. He was close to Noelle's age.

Eventually, I let him go, and we all sat around the fire and exchanged information. Ryne had made this cave his head-quarters, and messengers interrupted us from time to time.

Ryne also kept glancing at me as if checking my mood while he recounted what they'd been up to. He confirmed they had been hiding in the POW camp and had been har-rying Tohon's soldiers ever since they'd rescued Estrid's army.

"Are Saul, Odd and Wynn—"

"They're still alive and working together in the western quadrant," Ryne said. "We don't have as many personnel as Tohon, so I've split everyone into small, mobile units. Even so, we're losing ground every day," Ryne said. "That Death Lily toxin was genius and made such a difference, Avry, but we've run out."

I opened my pack and dumped the contents into a pile on the floor. "Does this help?"

Ryne stood up. "You're beautiful!" He scooped up a bunch of sacks and raced over to his runners.

"Was he complimenting the toxin sacks or Avry?" Loren asked.

"Well, you have to admit, there's something special about… bright orange," Quain quipped.

When Ryne returned, I told my tale.

At one point, Ryne said, "Jael's gone south. Hmm. Inter-esting choice." But he kept quiet during the rest of the story.

It was difficult to recount the Peace Lily's refusal over

Noelle, but Ryne needed to know how the Lilys factored in Tohon's dead. Flea slid closer to me and put his arm around my shoulder. Having all survived the plague and now a war, no one was a stranger to loss.

Later as we prepared to retire for the night, Ryne pulled me aside. "Avry, I wanted to explain about—"

"Don't." I held up a hand. "I don't want to know the reasons why you left me behind. I've assumed it was a tactical decision based on strategy and am fine with that."

"Uh-huh." Ryne failed to sound convinced.

"What I want to know is why you didn't tell me Kerrick was killed by Cellina's ufa pack?"

"He wasn't. He gave Cellina his sword to convince Tohon of his death." He paled. "Didn't I tell you?"

"He's not…" I swayed, and Ryne grabbed my arm to keep me from falling.

"Sit down, Avry."

My legs gave out, and I plopped down. Joy wanted to explode from my chest, but Ryne's expression kept it locked inside.

"He took a battalion north just like I said. According to my most recent messenger, he continued up to Krakowa and engaged the tribes." Ryne glanced down.

"Tell me," I ordered.

He met my gaze. "Only a couple soldiers returned. The attack was unsuccessful."

The tribes didn't take prisoners. Everyone knew that.

The cave spun. The firelight turned into streaks and swirled around my head. I had believed Kerrick died and had been living with the knowledge for two weeks.

Except for that brief instant where I thought…

And just when I didn't think I could feel any worse…

I did.

KERRICK

He clicked his tongue, urging Oya along the narrow ledge. The horse had done so well crossing the other eight ridges of the Nine Mountains, but even Kerrick had to admit this last one was daunting. A two-thousand-foot drop was mere inches to their left while sheer rock lined the right. Instead of riding, he dismounted and led her by the reins.

They had been on the road for the past nine days and were farther along than even his most optimistic estimates. Canute had been right, Oya was their best horse. The only problem—since she had been bred to live in the ice-covered Vilde Lander, she was pure white. Granted, he could camouflage her when they rode through the forest, but it required more energy. Plus, she drew too much attention in the few towns they had encountered.

Kerrick had spread the news about the tribes as they'd traveled. Many of the town officials invited him to spend the night and share more information. Anxious to find Avry and Ryne, he hadn't lingered long. Just enough to ease their minds about the tribes and to inquire about any news from the south. No one had heard anything regarding the conflict between Tohon and Estrid.

After coaxing Oya around the tightest bend, the ledge widened. An hour later, he mounted and spurred her into a trot as they entered the foothills. Once they reached the tree line, Kerrick reconnected with the living green, seeking ambushes or intruders. He needed to be more careful on this side of the Nine Mountains.

As the day turned into night, Kerrick sensed activity to the west. Pulling power, he camouflaged them both and headed west. After a few miles, Kerrick knew he'd have to leave Oya tied to a tree. She made too much noise.

Once they got close to Peti, he dismounted, fed and watered her. Even in the dark, her white coat was visible. Kerrick encouraged the surrounding vines to weave into a blanket that covered her. She watched the living cover with one ear cocked back but otherwise didn't seem to mind the strangeness. Her personality matched the tribes to a tee—unflappable.

A ring of watchers guarded the town, but Kerrick slipped by them with ease. By the time he reached the burned-out edge of Peti, he relaxed and strode out into the open. For once, his brother had heeded his warning and actually evacuated Orel.

It didn't take long before someone spotted him. They led him to Izak and his Great-Aunt Yasmin amid happy cries and lots of questions. He promised answers after he talked to Izak. His family had moved into the first floor of one of the old abandoned factories. Inside, a kiln roared, pumping out heat in the corner. Great-Aunt Yasmin sat right next to it. Nestled under a blanket, she rocked in her chair.

"Ah, Kerry, I knew you'd return," she said, gesturing him closer.

He took her hand in his and leaned down to give her a peck on her cheek. Deep lines of fatigue marked her face. Her fingers felt like toothpicks. But her gaze remained sharp as always.

"It's a miracle," Izak said as he entered the room, his sarcasm clear. "Your messengers proclaimed the demise of your entire army. What did you do? Hide and let them fight to their deaths?"

"Kerry," Great-Aunt Yasmin warned, squeezing his hand.

He drew in a breath and ignored his brother. "Is Zila safe?"

"The dear child is with Berna."

One worry down, a hundred more to go.

"But I'm afraid her brother didn't make it." She shook her head sadly. "Zila said he ran off to rescue you. She was quite upset, poor child."

"Then I've good news for her. Danny did indeed rescue me." Many times, but he wasn't going to go into details now.

Her face lit up, and she looked twenty years younger. "Where is he?"

Back with the tribe, helping Rakel heal their people. But again it was too much to explain. "He's safe. Did anyone get hurt when you evacuated?"

"Of course," Izak said dismissively. "It's a strenuous climb over those mountains. We had heart failures, twisted ankles, altitude sickness and broken bones. But you seem to have survived your adventures unscathed."

Kerrick turned to Izak. Great-Aunt Yasmin kept a firm grip on him.

"Aren't you going to regale us with your exploits, brother?" Izak gestured to the dadao hanging from Kerrick's belt. "Or have you gone tribal?"

He placed his free hand on the hilt of his new weapon. "This was a gift. And considering the best way to stop Tohon's dead soldiers is to chop their heads off, this will be quite useful. Unless *you* made another deal with Tohon?"

"Boys," Great-Aunt Yasmin scolded. "Behave."

Experience had taught them not to argue with her. They both mumbled, "Yes, ma'am."

She waved Kerrick into one of the empty chairs and sent

Izak to fetch tea. Once he returned with a tray and settled into the other chair, she ordered Kerrick to start at the beginning.

A quarter of the way in, Izak interrupted. "They don't take prisoners. Everyone knows that!"

"Are you calling me a liar?" Kerrick demanded.

"Hush now, Izak, let your brother speak."

Kerrick continued until he noticed movement behind Izak. He was halfway out of his chair when a small figure slammed into him, sending him back down. Zila clung to him, her arms wrapped so tight around his neck, he had trouble breathing.

"Easy," he squeaked.

She relaxed her arms, but her face was pressed into the hollow of his throat. She sobbed. "I tried to stop him...Danny wouldn't listen..."

He quickly reassured her, telling her Danny was fine. No surprise, she wanted to know more, so he tucked her into his lap and let her stay to listen to the rest of his story.

"There's no way I'm letting them live in our realm," Izak declared after Kerrick had finished. "They're—"

"Honorable people. And you don't get to decide. I do."

"So you're going to come back with us? Deal with the thousands of details of the journey? Be King Kerrick?" Izak didn't wait for his reply. "Of course not. You're going to run south to help your friend."

Kerrick clamped down on his temper. "Okay, Izak. I'll take charge. I'll go back to Alga with Great-Aunt Yasmin and Zila, deal with all the details and get the tribespeople settled in the northern territory. And you will meet up with Ryne. I'll even lend you my dadao because you're going to need it."

"Cute, Kerrick. But you know what I meant."

He did, and he realized he was being unfair. "You did a great job getting everyone here in such a short time, Izak." Kerrick gazed at Zila for a moment. One thing he'd learned during the last few months was the importance of family. "How about a deal?"

Surprise mixed with suspicion, but Izak said, "Go on."

"If you handle the return to Orel, promise to let the tribes settle in Alga, then I will abdicate the throne to you."

"What about you?"

"I'll still be Prince Kerrick, and once Tohon is defeated and the southern realms are on their way to recovery, I'll act as a consultant for Alga, be a liaison with the tribes and spend time playing chess with Danny and reading books with Zila."

Zila beamed at him along with Great-Aunt Yasmin, who asked, "And get married? Have babies?"

"Izak first," he quipped.

And for the first time since he'd arrived, his brother cracked a smile. "I'll be king, so I can arrange a marriage for you."

"Good luck with that."

They laughed, but then Izak grew serious. "What happens if Tohon isn't defeated?"

"Then you won't be king."

"Why not?" Zila asked.

"Because Tohon will be."

CHAPTER 21

"No. It's too dangerous," Ryne said.

"I don't care, I'm going—"

"Avry, be reasonable, please." Ryne spread out a map of the area. He pointed to the multiple clusters of red Xs to the south, west and east of the Healer's Guild. "Tohon's units are marching north, doing a sweep. Each X represents approximately four hundred soldiers, both living and dead."

"But I can—"

"Finding Belen among all those soldiers would be impossible. Besides, you don't even know if Tohon was telling the truth. It's typical for him to lie just to upset you."

"Then we *need* to make sure. Maybe he's hurt or—"

"And every one of my patrols has orders to search for him when they do their sweeps. Avry, we're roughly half the size of Tohon's army. We're losing more each day. We *need* you to heal the injured."

Ah, hell. He was right.

Ryne put his hand on my shoulder. "I know you've just lost your sister, and Kerrick." He paused, swallowing.

I wasn't the only one suffering.

"And I fully understand the temptation to find Belen, but

we need to be smart. Plus, if you go, then the monkeys and Flea will follow. Would you want to risk their lives, as well?"

"All right. You made your point."

"Have I? Kerrick warned me you're stubborn. Do I have your word?"

"Yes, I won't go off searching for Belen…for now."

"Thank you."

I glanced around the cave. "Where are your injured?"

"There's another cave southeast of here. We've been using it as an infirmary. It's well hidden, easy to defend and has a back entrance. I also would like you to keep harvesting those toxin sacks."

"If the Death Lilys keep giving them to me, I can."

"I'll have the monkeys and Flea escort you to the cave and stay there for future toxin runs and help with defense."

"Shouldn't they stay with you?"

"They'll be safer with you."

I smiled sadly. He understood if I lost another friend, I'd dissolve into a puddle. A morbid thought crossed my mind. I didn't have any more family members to lose. At least I'd spent the last minutes of Noelle's life with her. And that reminded me…

"Ryne, what did you tell Noelle?"

"What do you mean?"

"When you tried to get her to come with you before midsummer's day. You said something to her about me?"

"Oh. Well, you might not like this."

"Why not? It made her stop hating me."

"I told her those letters she wrote to you when your family was sick hadn't been delivered."

"How do you know that?"

"That's the part you're not going to like."

"Spit it out."

"Remember, this was *before* we knew what was going on with the plague and I had just lost my sister." He paused as if summoning the courage. "In my quest for information, I stole a bunch of papers from your mentor Tara's office. I grabbed what I could and left. When I went through them, I found a stack of opened letters addressed to you." He cringed with guilt. "I read through them, but since they didn't have any relevance to me, I threw them away."

"You're right."

"About what?"

"I don't like it." Not that my irritation could change anything. Tara had hidden the letters from me, so I should be mad at her. Except if I hadn't been so self-absorbed, I would have noticed that I hadn't gotten a letter from home in a while. "Thanks for telling Noelle. Bad enough she's gone, but it would have been torture if she'd died without forgiving me."

"Babysitting duty," Quain muttered with disgust for the third time in the last hour.

"That's enough," Loren snapped. "This is just as important as fighting. Besides, it's *Avry*. Trouble follows her."

"Hey," I said, acting indignant. Acting, because…well, it was true.

Unmollified, Quain huffed.

We ignored him. He'd been bellyaching since we'd left the Healer's Guild cave. Ryne had assigned the monkeys and Flea as promised. He'd also sent Enric along. We'd left in the morning, and it would take us all day to reach the "infirmary." We didn't expect any trouble as the route to the cave didn't have any red *X*s on Ryne's map.

Sunlight shone through the trees, heating the air to an almost uncomfortable level, despite being twenty days away from the end of summer. In the fall, Kerrick's eyes had been a lovely russet color with flecks of orange, gold and red.

To keep from crying and to stop Quain from whining, I asked Loren about the skirmishes. "You're a small unit, how have you been faring against Tohon's larger army?"

He flashed me a grateful smile. "We rely on ambushes mostly, drawing the enemy into the kill zone before attacking. Then we don't linger. By the time the enemy unit changes from pure reaction to action, we're already leaving."

"How about the dead soldiers?" I asked.

"We've been using blow guns and darts filled with the toxin until our supply ran out." Loren grinned. "So we are really really really glad to see you, Avry."

Now it was my turn to mutter. "I guess if you'd have known about the Death Lily toxin before, you wouldn't have left me to deal with Tohon alone." I rubbed my cheek. Even when compared to Belen's stab wounds, Kerrick's whipping and Noelle's knife to the gut, that onslaught remained the most pain I'd ever experienced.

Loren and Quain wouldn't meet my hard gaze. Guess I wasn't as fine with them leaving me as I'd claimed.

"The one thing I won't miss about the attacks is the smell," Flea said. "Those dead reek so bad I about throw up every time I get a whiff."

"They don't reek as much as your socks," Quain said.

"My socks are sweet compared to your sh—"

"Gentlemen," Loren warned.

And just like that, the mood returned to normal. As we hiked, I mulled over Loren's comments.

"What happens if something goes wrong when you're engaging the enemy?" I asked Loren.

"Prince Ryne has given us contingencies for every possible outcome. If our primary attack runs foul, we switch to another tactic, and if that doesn't work, then we have three more options to try before we retreat."

"Every possible outcome? I find that hard to believe," I said.

"I've been leading our small unit for the last ten days and haven't used more than two options. Kerrick was right. Prince Ryne has a gift for strategy." Loren glanced at me in concern. Probably worried that mentioning Kerrick's name would upset me.

It did, but I kept control of my emotions.

"What about communication between units and with Prince Ryne?" Enric asked. "His map had Xs all over the place. You don't have any magicians, so how do you know you're not ambushing yourselves?"

Loren studied Enric as if impressed with his questions. "Prince Ryne assigns each unit a series of tasks. When those tasks are complete, we return for another set of directives. He knows which unit is doing what at any given time. He has loads more maps with diagrams."

"Where did he get them?" I asked.

"He drew them when we were in Estrid's camp."

"And when we were in hiding. He had plenty of time then," Flea added completely unaware of Loren's signal to shut up.

"Good to know he was putting that time to good use. I'd hate to think he was relaxing while Estrid's soldiers were dying as they tried to break the encirclement." The bitterness in my voice surprised even me.

Loren and Quain glanced at each other. Quain made a go-on gesture to his friend.

"Avry, we're sorry we had to…to deceive you," Loren said. "But no matter which angle we looked at the problem, Tohon would have torn the encampment apart, searching for you. It would have ruined our entire strategy, and all of Estrid's and our soldiers would have died. 'Cause you know as well as we did that Tohon wasn't going to 'incorporate' the armies."

Ryne's tactics made sense. I hadn't doubted that.

"Plus, you were needed," Flea said. "You healed lots of people while we couldn't help anyone."

Another valid point.

"And we were worried you might let our…surprise slip."

Perfectly reasonable.

"And you figured it out. Which really impressed Prince Ryne," Quain said.

Which made me ask, "How did you plan to get past the encirclement before I sent the toxin?"

"We sent a bunch of our people out as the POWs to help on the outside," Loren said.

"That wouldn't have been enough."

"You're right." Quain's eyes lit up. "We had axes."

I waited.

"Made from liquid metal," Loren said. "We…er…raided Zabin's arms merchant's supply of liquid metal axes. They cleave right through those collars Tohon put on his dead. But we didn't have many, and it would have been an out-right, dragged-out fight with many casualties. Your way was much better."

"Glad I could help." Again with the sarcasm—what was wrong with me?

"Avry, we've explained and apologized," Loren said. "You let us believe you were dead for months, and we forgave you. What more do you need?"

"I don't need—" And then it clicked. "What bothered me wasn't that you left, but that you left without asking me to come along." I held up a hand. "All those points you made were excellent reasons for me to stay behind. But you didn't think I would have made them, too. That I would have said, no, go on without me and don't tell me anything. You assumed I'd want to run and hide with you."

"But you admitted to being terrified of Tohon," Quain said.

"I did. But I wouldn't have compromised you guys because of my fear. I guess I'm upset because you think I would."

"I understand now," Loren said. "Okay, so we've made a mistake and so have you…so, we're even?"

I smiled. "We're even."

"And you escaped from Tohon," Flea said. "Does that mean you're not afraid of him anymore?"

"I'd be an idiot not to be, but I'm not terrified that he'll claim me any longer."

"Why not?"

"Because he can't."

"Woo hoo! Score one for the healer!" Quain pumped his fist in the air.

"Oh, grow up, Quain," Loren said.

"Lighten up, Loren. You make an acolyte seem fun in comparison."

"I do not. You're like an overeager puppy—all drool and unable to hold your bow—"

"Boys," I said. "That's enough. Besides, we should be encouraging Quain in his efforts to be housebroken, not—"

"Hey!" Quain rushed me.

I held up my hands and wiggled my fingers. "Beware the touch of death!"

He tackled me anyway. We rolled on the ground together, laughing.

"Great. Just great," Loren said. "Now the entire realm knows exactly where we are."

Quain jumped to his feet. "Bring them on! I'm ready for a fight."

The rest of us groaned. I stood and brushed dirt from my clothes.

Enric pulled a leaf from my hair. "Is this…?"

"Typical behavior?"

He nodded.

"Yes. Now you know why they're called the monkeys."

"Lovely," he deadpanned.

"That's what I thought as first. Don't worry, they'll grow on you."

"Or I'll kill them?"

"Pretty much. It's either a love or hate type of thing."

"Lovely."

We arrived at the cave without encountering another unit or any Death Lilys. The outer guards led us inside. A large cavern had been converted into an infirmary. There were cots instead of beds, but it was better than the patients lying on the cool, hard floor. Medical supplies had been stacked along the right wall, and there were other, smaller caverns being used by the four caregivers who had been helping the wounded.

I quickly assessed the patients. Battle wounds and broken bones. Nothing dire or infected yet. The caregivers had done a good job. After setting up an examination area, I added the herbs I had gathered on our way to the pile of supplies. Then I unrolled my bedroll, smoothing it out near the monkeys', Flea's and Enric's in an otherwise empty area.

The boys were added to the guard duty rotation, but they had the first night off. We sat around a fire, eating dinner and talking about nothing in particular. It felt like old times.

When Quain started to complain about babysitting again, I offered him a new job.

"Anything would be better," he said.

"Okay, then that nice young caregiver…Valorie…can patrol and you can clean bedpans."

"I…"

"And suture wounds, set bones and wash patients. You're not squeamish, are you?"

"I…"

"Great comeback, Quain." Loren smirked. "Or should I call you lord of the bedpans?"

"Lord B.P., for short," Flea chimed in, causing a ripple of laughter.

Enric stood. "I think I'll volunteer to work a shift tonight. Good night."

When he disappeared from sight, Quain leaned forward and asked, "Where did you find *him?* He's as dry as jerky." He waved the piece he'd been gnawing on.

"Be nice, Lord B.P."

Working with patients and hanging out with the boys, I started to feel stronger. Grief still hit me at odd times, crashing over me with an unexpected fierceness. At those times all I could do was stagger to an empty cavern and curl up into a tight ball, letting the waves of misery flow until spent.

As the days progressed, new casualties arrived as I released others. One man had a nasty cut on his calf that had become infected on the long trip here. There had to be a better way to get to the injured, but I couldn't think of it.

It was a steady stream but not overwhelming. I'd assumed Ryne's tactics must be working, but on the sixth day we received bad news with the latest batch of patients. The red Xs had advanced, and we might have to evacuate within the week.

Sergeant Odd arrived the next afternoon with his Odd Squad. He didn't have any injured, but he had heard I'd escaped and stopped by for a visit. While his unit visited with the patients, cheering them up, Odd and I talked.

"We're back in business," Odd said with a huge smile. "Finally using all that training. Me and my Odds are silent as ghosts thanks to you."

Glad to see him, I asked, "How are the others doing?"

"Saul has what's left of the jumping jacks and a few of his original unit. I've heard they're doing major damage to the west. Wynn has a young squad, and they have been mostly running messages."

"But it isn't enough, is it?"

Odd waved away my concern. "It's like chipping away at a huge rolling boulder. Eventually, we'll carve it down into a tiny pebble."

"By then, we might be up against the Nine Mountains."

Odd shrugged. "If that's what it takes."

I admired his optimism. And maybe he was right. After all, he'd been out on the field of battle, engaging the enemy. Which reminded me. "Have you seen Belen?"

He sobered. "No sign of him. There have been rumors he was turned, but I don't believe them."

"Why not?"

"'Cause it's *Belen*. Come on. Do you really think he'd get caught? No way. He's just lying low somewhere, waiting for an opportune moment to strike." Odd curled his fingers into claws and growled.

It sounded more like a cat in pain than a bear, but he succeeded in making me smile. "Maybe that should be our secret signal."

"Oh. I like. With or without the roar?"

"Without. Since you're the ghosts of the forest now."

"Ah, yes. But what would it mean? We found Belen? Or

we found a huge man-eating bear? No, wait, that could be confusing."

I laughed. "How about it means it's time to strike."

"Perfect." And then Odd's eyes lit up, and he growled, dashing to the cave's entrance.

For one heartbreaking second, I thought Belen had arrived, but it was Wynn. Odd pulled her into a hug, then led her over to me.

"Look who's back," Odd said to Wynn. "Avry escaped the big bad."

"I'm the one who told you, you idiot." She elbowed him in the ribs. "Good to see you, Baby Face."

"It's so nice to see you both. Here. At the same time. What a *coincidence*," I said.

Odd leered and Wynn elbowed him harder this time.

"How's the scar doing? Are you having any trouble eating?" I stepped close, examining the jagged line along the left side of her jaw.

"It doesn't bother me at all. In fact, it's actually useful."

"How?"

"All I have to do is snarl and scowl at the kids in my unit, and they about wet their pants." She laughed. "Youth can be wonderful when we're trekking through the woods for twelve hours at a time, but, man, they can be pretty dense at times."

"Are you staying tonight?" I asked.

"Yep, I even brought supper. Coll, get in here," she yelled.

A very young man—younger than Flea—scurried in carrying four dead rabbits.

"Fresh meat," Wynn said.

"The rabbits or Coll?" Odd asked.

She smirked. "Both."

The poor boy blanched. I took the rabbits from Coll, and he bolted for the exit.

"I'll give these to the cook," I said. "He makes a delicious stew, but it'll be a few hours."

Odd turned to Wynn. "In that case, would you like to have an early supper with me?"

Confused, I said, "The stew won't be *that* long."

They exchanged grins.

"Oh."

"Ah, Baby Face, you're finally growing up." Wynn took Odd's hand.

They left to find a private place to…er…dine. Various emotions tumbled in my chest—happy for them and sorrow that the one I'd like to have an early supper with was gone.

The next morning a rare summer rainstorm drummed outside. I worried that Jael might have sent it, but the steady sound and lack of wind eased my mind. Before breakfast, Wynn pulled me aside. "Forgot to tell you last night. Prince Ryne needs more of those toxin sacks. Have you collected them?"

"Not yet. He said he'd send word."

"Well, this is the word." She put three fingers up and widened them so they looked like a W.

"You're chipper this morning. And here I thought you'd be tired from all that…sleeping you were doing last night." Jealous? Who, me?

Wynn winked.

I retrieved the Lily map from my pack. Spreading it out, I searched for the nearest Lily cluster. Small checks marked the ones I'd already taken the sacks from. According to Tohon, the Lily would regenerate the toxin in two months' time.

Tapping on the map, I said, "There's a patch about a day and a half east of here."

Wynn leaned over. "I saw a bunch of them to the southeast and only a couple hours away."

"It's not marked."

"Must have missed it. And there was a Death Lily, as it tried to snatch Coll. Poor kid almost soiled his pants."

"Coll? Really?"

"Well, he is young."

"No, I meant the Death Lily. They go after those they think have potential for magic. Has he shown any other signs?"

"No, but if you want, my unit can accompany you today."

"That would be great. Plus, Quain will be happy. Not only about staying dry, but he's been fussing about this assignment every chance he gets. Keeps calling it babysitting duty," I said.

"Quain? Is he the cute bald guy?"

"Yes, but don't *ever* let him know that."

"About being bald?"

"No, the cute part. He would be insufferably smug forever."

"Got it."

After we ate, I grabbed a few supplies, borrowed a wide-brim hat to keep the rain off my face and headed out with Wynn. Even though it was late morning, the air was still chilly, and it smelled of moist earth.

Her team followed us, but their progress through the woods made nary a sound. And they kept well hidden, so I didn't see them at all. Though we weren't technically in enemy territory, it was still prudent to be as quiet as possible.

"They're good," I whispered to Wynn.

She beamed. "I've been training them."

After a few hours, she led me into a clearing that was just the right size for the Lilys. They liked the sunlight but also liked being protected by trees.

I glanced around but didn't see any. "Are they deeper in?"

"No."

"Where are they?"

"There're all around us. Can't you see them?"

I looked again. Instead of Lilys, dead ufas stood among the trees. Fear kept me rooted to the spot, but I yanked my knife out and threw it at the closest ufa, burying the blade into its shoulder.

I shouted at Wynn. "Run! They're after me."

"Well, of course they are, Baby Face. Why do you think I invited them?"

KERRICK

He had left Oya back in Peti. It was far easier to travel on foot through the forest, but slower. Agonizingly slow, in his opinion, as he wanted nothing more than to hold Avry in his arms again. But the pace was prudent. Through his magical connection with the living green, he sensed many groups of soldiers moving in all directions. A battle raged to the west and southwest. And Kerrick wasn't sure who was who. Plus, he couldn't sense the dead soldiers or any dead ufa packs, which increased the level of danger.

After a week, he reached the Healer's Guild and discovered Ryne's location in a nearby cave. It was quite the reunion since Ryne thought he'd died.

"Three miracles in one summer," Ryne said after pouncing on him. "This is a sign!"

"Three?" he asked.

"You, Avry and Flea."

His heart skipped a few beats. "Flea?"

"I forgot you don't know. So much has happened. Sit down, sit down, I've lots to tell you."

Kerrick glanced around the cave as strong emotions slammed into him. Flea alive? "Where's Avry and Flea?"

"Not to worry. They're both safe and with the monkeys in the infirmary."

"Which is...?"

"About a day east of here."

Another delay. It took all of Kerrick's willpower to stay and listen to the events over the summer. At one point, he jumped to his feet. "You left without her." His hands curled into fists, but he kept them by his sides.

"A tactical decision that worked *exactly* as I'd imagined. Well...except for her sister dying."

"Noelle died?"

After that, it was a very long night.

"And no one knows where Belen is?" he demanded.

"Tohon claims he turned him into one of his dead, but I find that hard to believe," Ryne said. "We'll find him."

Much later, when Kerrick tried to sleep, his mind whirled with all the information Ryne had divulged. But three events kept snagging: Flea being saved by a Peace Lily, Avry believing he was dead and Belen's disappearance. He gave up on sleep a couple hours before dawn, told Ryne he couldn't wait any longer and took off in the rain for the infirmary cave.

Wishing he'd brought Oya, Kerrick jogged through the forest, concentrating his magic on the immediate vicinity only. Ryne had assured him no enemy patrols lurked in the woods to the east, and he didn't want to waste his energy scanning the entire area.

He arrived at the infirmary cave around midafternoon. Not recognizing any of the guards outside, he bypassed them. Then he slipped inside and stopped, searching for Avry and Flea. His heart jolted, banging against his rib cage when he spotted Flea joking with Quain and Loren.

When he approached them, they stared at him for a moment in confusion. His gaze focused on Flea. He'd believed

Ryne, but some things you just needed to see for yourself. And this was one of them.

"Kerrick!" They all jumped to their feet.

Their words and questions jumbled together. Kerrick ignored the noise as he grabbed Flea's shoulders and pulled the boy into a hug, reveling in the fact that he held real solid, living flesh. Flea had grown, and a spark of magic reached Kerrick.

He pulled back. "Are you a healer now?" he asked Flea.

Flea's smile went from ear to ear. "No. I'm something, but we haven't figured it out yet."

"Gee, Loren, I'm beginning to feel we're being left out." Quain pouted. "No one cares about us since we've done the boring thing and stayed alive all this time. No miraculous return from the grave for us, so we're not worth hugging."

"Sorry," Kerrick said, pulling in each one and thumping them on the back. "And I didn't die."

"So there's another reason you look like a drowned oversized rat?" Quain asked.

"I'm hoping there's a good reason you managed to get past my men," a man, wearing Estrid's uniform, said. "Otherwise, they're in trouble."

"You can't fault them. This is Prince Kerrick, he's a forest mage," Loren said.

The man studied him with a keen interest. "Sergeant Oddvar." He held out his hand.

Kerrick shook it.

"Oddvar?" Quain asked.

"You don't really think my parents named me Odd, do you?"

"Uh, no. Of course not."

"Where's Avry?" Kerrick finally asked as he scanned the room again.

"She's going to flip when she sees you!" Quain said.

His patience was about to end. "Where—"

"She went out to harvest toxin sacks," Loren said.

"By herself?" he demanded.

"No. Sergeant Wynn and her squad accompanied her," Odd said.

"When?"

"A couple hours ago. She'll be back in another two or three hours," Odd said.

In order to find her faster, he asked, "Which direction?"

"Southeast."

"I'm not in the mood to wait. Gentlemen, I'll see you later." Kerrick hurried from the cave. Flea called after him, but he wasn't going to waste another moment.

As soon as he connected with the living green, he sent his magic to the southeast, searching for Avry and her companions. He found a cluster of irritations about eight miles away. Breaking into a jog, he headed in that direction.

Avry was going to be surprised.

CHAPTER 22

Wait. Did Wynn just say she'd invited them? Perhaps the noise of the rain hitting my hat had garbled her words. I kept my gaze on the dead ufas—eight…no, seven now, as one collapsed from the toxin on my blade. They surrounded us, so I turned in a slow circle, wishing I had more weapons. They kept their positions at the edge of the clearing.

"Wynn, did you—"

"Yes. I led you into this trap. Surprised?" she asked.

If her revelation had been before my sister died and the confirmation of Kerrick's death, I would have been devastated by her betrayal. But at this point, I had nothing left. "You did catch me off guard. I mean, we knew someone had to be spying on Estrid's army, but you were the last person I'd expect to rat us out to Tohon."

"Not Tohon. I hate him just as much as you do," Wynn said.

"Then who— Oh. You're working for Cellina?" That was more of a shock.

"Yep."

"Why?"

"She's my sister."

Understandable. "And you hate Tohon."

"Exactly, I knew you were smart, Baby Face."

"Not smart enough," I muttered under my breath.

She laughed. She could.

"Where is she?" I asked, certain Cellina would want to gloat.

"How boring," Cellina said as she stepped from behind a tree. "I'd thought Avry would at least shed a few tears over your treachery, sister dear."

"I'm tapped out right now, but if you'd like to come back tomorrow, I could probably shed a couple just for you." I should be scared, but I was actually having fun. Plus, a few off notes sounded to the south, indicating two people were quite close, and a distant rustling might be a squad farther behind them. Perhaps the monkeys had decided to follow me and brought the Odd Squad. I glanced at Wynn. Did she hear them?

"Amusing, but I'm here to—"

I stopped her. "Let me guess. Hmm… Drag me back to Tohon? No. You wouldn't have bothered with the ruse. You'd have sent the ufas." I considered. "You want sister dear to keep her cover, but you want me dead, so she lures me out here and I'm attacked, she survives and runs back to the cave to report on my demise." I turned to Wynn. "What about your unit?"

"I sent them on another mission. They didn't accompany us."

"Ah. Nice."

"Too bad you didn't figure this out a couple hours ago," Cellina said. "Do you know why I wish you dead?"

"You're jealous that Tohon is so smitten with me." I let that sink in. "I hope you know that getting rid of me is not going to make him love you, Cellina. That man is incapable of loving anyone other than himself."

"Nice try. He is obsessed with you, and it's causing him

to make poor decisions, and he won't listen to reason. Once you're gone, he'll be easier to manipulate."

"Interesting word choice, Cellina," Tohon said. He stepped into the clearing. "However, I already suspected you had your own agenda regarding Avry. In fact, I was just discussing this *at length* with Sepp as we followed you here. Wasn't I?"

Cellina's face paled as Sepp joined Tohon. We were having quite the party.

Sepp's queasy expression suggested he was uncomfortable being here, and he stared at the ground. "Yes, you were."

Tohon's arrival confirmed that I'd no chance for rescue. Unlike Cellina, he might keep me alive for old times' sake. Tohon strode over to me and took my hand in his. His fiery gaze promised pain. Perhaps not.

"You'd be proud of me, my dear," Tohon said. "I also deduced Sepp's involvement with this little plot. Should I kill them both?"

A few slight sour notes sounded to the northwest. "No," I said, hoping this time it was someone who could help me. Of course, the person needed a couple squads with him or her to be of any use.

"Why not?"

"You can use them."

"Ohhh, I like. Go on."

"Well…Wynn's in tight with Ryne's army. She runs messages for him and is privy to all his plans. But I'm thinking if you kill her sister, she won't be as accommodating for you. And Sepp…this one is harder since he's a whiny, nasty man who betrayed me before." I paused. "You know…I've changed my mind. You can go ahead and kill him. He has no redeeming value."

Tohon laughed as Sepp whitened. Interesting that the death magician was terrified of Tohon. And for the first time *ever,* I wasn't. At this point I had nothing left to lose. Tohon might try to claim me again, but I was quite confident he couldn't.

"I agree with you about Sepp, but not Cellina and her sister. It is tempting to use them, but I'm too pissed off."

"Tohon, I—"

"No begging, Cellina, you know how much I hate it."

"In case you didn't realize it, your royal asshole," Wynn said, "you're surrounded by Cellina's ufa pack with no allies nearby. Even Baby Face would side with us on this one."

Tohon gasped in mock horror. "Is that true, my dear?"

"No. I'm good."

He blinked at me in surprise. "Why?"

"You've always been straight with me. Unlike them. Two are traitors, and Cellina killed Kerrick. Ooh… Can I kill her? With Kerrick's sword?"

Tohon didn't need to know the whole truth about Kerrick. At least, not yet. I gave her a pointed look.

"That would be fun to watch. Cellina, give Avry his sword."

"You're insane," Cellina said, gripping the hilt. She backed away a few steps. "Attack!" She pointed at us.

The ufas surged forward as one. I grabbed Tohon's arm with my free hand, bracing for the impact.

"Heel," Tohon said in a loud and commanding voice.

And just like that, they halted their charge and aligned themselves behind Tohon.

"I'm disappointed in you, Cellina. Do you really think I'd train them without a way to stop them from attacking *me*? And I'd never stray too far away from reinforcements. I've a squad stationed nearby." He glanced at my hand clutching his arm. "I see you didn't trust me either."

I let go, but he kept my other hand. Before I could comment, he turned his head to the northwest as if listening to something. A succession of muted forest noises sounded. His cheeks reddened in anger, and his grip tightened painfully. Uh-oh.

Instead of blasting me, he said, "Cellina, you bitch. Just how long have you been lying to me?"

"Uh…" Cellina exchanged a glance with Sepp.

"Although I'm surprised he gave you his precious sword. That was quite the coup."

"What are you talking about?" she asked.

"Kerrick, come on out and join the reunion," Tohon called.

Ah. He thought Kerrick hid in the forest. I said, "Kerrick never returned from the north. He died fighting the tribal warriors."

"Then you're in for a shock, my dear."

Pain burned up my arm and stabbed into my chest. I yelped.

"Kerrick, the longer you wait— Ah, there you are."

The agony ceased. What game was Tohon playing now? Everyone stared to the northwest. Guess my would-be rescuer just got caught. I followed their gazes and gasped.

The world around me faded. It blurred into blotches of colors—greens, grays, browns. Kerrick stood in the center of the big blur, clear and sharp. His gaze met mine, and the hard shell that had formed around my heart crumbled. Emotions I thought had died sprang to life, flowing through me until I was dizzy and sick.

Unlike Kerrick. His face showed no emotion. He held a strange curved blade in one hand and a sword in his other. The rain had plastered his hair to his head and soaked through his tunic. Dark circles marked his eyes. He'd lost weight.

When he released me from his intense gaze, only Tohon's tight grip kept me on my feet. I'd accepted my fate, but Kerrick's impossible arrival had changed the game in one instant.

Tohon's evil smile meant he'd figured it out, as well. "Such passionate emotions, *my dear.*"

"She's not yours," Kerrick said, striding forward.

"Protect," Tohon ordered.

The ufas rushed to position themselves between Tohon and Kerrick. He didn't hesitate. He chopped the closest ufa's head off with one mighty swing of that curved sword.

Tohon stepped behind me and put his free hand on my neck. "Kerrick, stop or I'll take her right now."

"You're going to do it anyway." However, he checked his second swing, waiting.

"I'd hoped to play with her first, but you're right. And now I get the pleasure of watching you while I pull her life force from her body."

"Don't, Tohon. What do you want?" Kerrick asked. Fear shone on his face.

"This. I want to take something from you. The man who had it all. Petty, I know, but I don't care."

Magic tingled along my throat. I concentrated on blocking it.

"Nice try, my dear, but I'm afraid our courtship is at an end."

"No!" Kerrick yelled.

A powerful wave of Tohon's life magic slammed into me. Inside, an ice-cold sensation grew from my core, countering it. Not my healing magic, but something else—different yet familiar. The freezing agony reminded me of the Peace Lily serum and how it had frozen the plague. But this time, it prevented Tohon's magic from plucking my life from my body.

He threw me to the ground in frustration, then gestured to his ufas. "Attack them."

Gray brindled fur leapt into action, obscuring my view. Six ufas against four, they might have a chance.

Tohon yanked me to my feet. "Time to go." He whistled shrilly as he dragged me away from the fray. "You lied to me, too, my dear. A Death Lily didn't save you from the plague, did it? It was a Peace Lily."

"Yes."

"And the serum is preventing me from plucking your life. No matter, a sword through your heart will work just the same."

If Tohon dragged me back to his squad, whose crashing through the underbrush sounded quite close, I'd never see Kerrick again. Turning around, I caught a glimpse of Kerrick beheading another ufa. I stumbled. Pretending to swoon, I collapsed into Tohon.

He pushed me away. "You're not the fainting type, Avry."

When I staggered back, I grabbed his sword's hilt and drew the weapon, pointing the tip at his chest.

"What do you plan to do with that?" he asked in that smug tone.

"Put it through your black heart."

He scoffed. "You can't kill. You're a healer."

I paused. He opened his arms wide. "Go ahead."

Images of the dead soldiers and the children he'd experimented on flashed through my mind. He'd done such terrible, awful things to thousands. I drew my arm back and lunged. He jerked in surprise so the sword's tip pierced the right side of his chest instead of the middle. It slid through his ribs, and I pushed until the bloody tip poked out from his back.

He stared at me with horrified shock.

"Overconfidence has always been your downfall, Tohon," I said.

He dropped to his knees with a gurgle. Cellina screamed and rushed over. I stepped away, noting that she was unarmed and splattered with black ichor. She gathered Tohon in her arms.

Then Tohon's men burst onto the scene.

Cellina didn't waste time. She gestured to the ufa pack. "Help Sepp, bring him here now!" Cellina pointed at me. "Kill her."

The sergeant in charge sent his men to fight the ufas while he drew his sword and advanced toward me. Oh, no. Unarmed, I backed away. He kept pace. I stumbled into a bush. The branches scratched my arms, but I didn't care. Kerrick's magic zipped along my skin. I glanced down. My body now blended in with the forest.

"What the hell," the sergeant said.

Taking advantage, I dove to the side and went silent, finding a hiding spot. The sergeant chased after me but soon lost me. He eventually gave up and returned to join his men.

I crept closer to the fighting. Sepp argued with Cellina over Tohon's body. Dead or alive, I couldn't tell. When the last ufa was killed, Wynn and the eight armed soldiers turned on Kerrick.

He didn't hesitate. The colors of the forest snaked up his body, and he disappeared. Seeing my chance, I snuck up on one of the soldiers, touched his neck and zapped him. I hit a second man, adding to the confusion. Then Kerrick attacked.

We had the advantage for a minute, but they rallied. Kerrick grunted as a sword bit into his leg. A soldier caught a handful of the back of my shirt and dragged me closer.

"Don't be shy, gentlemen," Kerrick called.

Huh? The man wrapped his arm around my neck. I touched his hand, sending a blast of pain. He yelped and pushed me away.

Suddenly, Loren, Flea and Quain joined the fight. It didn't take them long to disarm the rest of Tohon's soldiers. Kerrick dropped the camouflage, revealing us both.

Grins all around until Sepp stepped out from behind a tree.

Before we could react, the death magician wrapped his hands around Quain, who was the closest to him.

"Drop your weapons, or I'll freeze him," Sepp said.

Kerrick, Loren and Flea obeyed, but Quain yanked his dagger out and stabbed Sepp in the leg. Sepp yelled but kept his grip and froze Quain. He toppled to the ground.

"No," I shouted.

Kerrick rushed Sepp, knocked him over and sat on him, pinning his arms down. He yanked Quain's knife from Sepp's leg and pressed it to the mage's throat.

"You can't kill me," Sepp gasped. "You need me to wake your friend."

Kerrick paused.

Taking advantage of the commotion, Tohon's men rearmed themselves, and Cellina joined them, now grasping Kerrick's sword.

"Kerrick, let him go," Cellina said with an edge of desperation in her voice.

Kerrick glanced at me. "Did you kill Tohon?" he asked.

"I missed his heart, but his injury is fatal," I said.

He turned to Loren and Flea. "I'm sorry, but I can't let Sepp wake Tohon."

Which meant Quain would be frozen forever.

"But they don't have a healer," Loren said.

"They know how to create one," I said, hating the words as I spoke them. "Kerrick's right."

"You need me to wake Belen!" Sepp cried.

Kerrick leaned on the knife at Sepp's throat. "Explain."

"Tohon lied to Avry about him," Sepp said. "Belen was captured but not killed. Tohon had me freeze him in a magical stasis until he decided what to do with him. I swear!"

My insides twisted tight. The joy of knowing Belen lived was balanced by the pain of knowing Sepp still had to die.

By the haunted look etched in Kerrick's face, he felt the same thing. Suddenly a knife struck Kerrick's shoulder, and in a blink of an eye, Wynn tackled him. She sprang to her feet and stood between him and Sepp with her sword in hand.

Without looking away from Kerrick, she said, "The Odd Squad is coming. We need to retreat."

Shocked over what had just happened, it took me a moment to understand. But sure enough, the faint sounds of a squad emanated from the northwest. Too focused on Kerrick, I hadn't heard their approach.

Cellina gripped the sword tighter, then relaxed her arm. "Remember, Kerrick, just because Tohon's out of commission, doesn't mean the war is over. I'm just as qualified to run his army. Understand?"

"Queen Cellina?" Kerrick mocked from his position on the ground. Sitting cross-legged, he held his left arm close as a bloodstain spread on his shoulder. He gripped Wynn's knife in his right hand.

"That does have a nice ring to it," she mused. Then her demeanor changed. "Get up," Cellina ordered Sepp. "Grab Tohon, we're leaving," she said to the soldiers. Cellina gestured toward me with her sword. "Next time, healer."

Sepp dusted himself off and stormed off.

As they retreated, Wynn saluted me with another knife—where did she stash them all? And without warning, she turned and threw it at Kerrick. He twisted so the blade just sliced his upper right arm.

She grinned. "That was a fresh knife, Baby Face."

Which meant the blade had been treated with Death Lily toxin. I cried out and rushed to Kerrick, ripping off his right sleeve.

"It's not deep," he protested. "The left one is worse."

Ignoring him, I sealed my lips around the wound. I sucked

the blood and spat it on the ground. Then repeated. He stilled, finally understanding, as I worked to pull as much of the poison from his body. Because the blade had been treated, I tasted anise along with the coppery bite of blood. I kept doing it until I no longer detected the anise.

"Here." He handed me his flask of water.

I rinsed my mouth. "How do you feel?"

"Much better now." Kerrick pulled me in close, wrapping his arms around me. "I've been wanting to do this since the moment we parted." He squeezed tighter.

"Easy," I said. And as much as I wished to scream with joy and lose myself in this moment in Kerrick's arms, I couldn't.

"We'll figure out how to wake Quain," he said.

I glanced over. Loren knelt next to Quain, and Flea stood nearby. He gripped his stomach and twisted his lips as if he was about to vomit.

"That's not the only problem," I said.

"We'll find Belen."

Poppa Bear. A shudder ripped through me. Taking in a deep breath, I controlled the emotions that threatened to send me into hysterics.

Kerrick leaned back to search my expression. "What's wrong?"

"The blade had Death Lily toxin on it."

"I figured it had been poisoned, but it couldn't have been very much."

I jerked away from his grasp. "It's very powerful. A few drops killed my sister."

He pulled me closer. "I'm sorry about Noelle."

"The point is, you might die, and…if you do…I can't… can't…do it again." Uncontrolled sobs racked my body. I clung to Kerrick and didn't try to stop them. The tears gushed, then slowed to sniffles as Kerrick murmured soothing words.

"What's Avry bawling about?" Quain asked.

I opened my eyes and gaped. Quain stood between a grinning Loren and a happy but still queasy-looking Flea.

"What...?" My throat burned.

"I did it," Flea blurted. "I... There was this...weird feeling in my guts, and I just had to touch Quain, and...well, he woke up."

"Flea, that skill's going to come in handy," Loren said, slapping him on the back.

Flea's face turned green, and he dashed away to vomit in the weeds.

Kerrick and I exchanged a concerned glance. Flea's magic was a wonderful discovery—the only thing to go right all day—but if anyone found out, he'd be a target.

Before we could question him further, Odd and his squad arrived.

"What an incredible stench," Odd said, covering his nose with his sleeve. He scanned the piles of dead ufas and unconscious soldiers. "Where's Wynn?" he asked in alarm. "Did she..."

"She's alive and well." I disentangled from Kerrick and stood. Time to break Odd's heart, but I hesitated.

"We should head back before Cellina returns with more soldiers," Kerrick said. He winced slightly when he lumbered to his feet. "We'll exchange information as we go."

I took Kerrick's hand, then released my magic. He smiled until he felt my power surge through his body.

"Avry, don't," he said, trying to shake me off.

"Too late." Pain stabbed into my shoulder as blood soaked my shirt.

"You shouldn't have."

I gave him a flat look.

He sighed but kept my hand. We trudged to the infirmary,

taking turns explaining what happened in the clearing with Tohon, Cellina, Sepp and Wynn. After hearing the news about Wynn, Odd clammed up and listened in stony silence. One of his men told us that after the monkeys and Flea had left the cave, Sergeant Odd decided to follow just in case.

"And why did you follow me?" Kerrick asked Loren.

"Flea had one of his bad feelings." He glanced at Flea. "We've learned to trust them."

Looking better, but still uncharacteristically subdued, Flea shrugged.

After we ran out of explanations, I noticed that instead of tiring, I had more energy with each step. The pain in my shoulder settled into a dull throb. It took me a moment to detect the subtle flow of magic from Kerrick.

I yanked my hand from his. "Save your strength. If even a drop of toxin is in you—" I swallowed "—you'll need it."

He recaptured my hand, lacing his warm fingers through mine. "I'll be good, I promise."

"Will you promise not to die from the toxin?" I half joked.

"If it will make you smile, then I will solemnly swear not to die from Death Lily toxin." He made an *X* across his chest with his finger.

I couldn't suppress a grin.

Kerrick squeezed my hand and smiled back.

When we reached the cave, we endured another round of questions before we could collapse by the fire and inhale supper.

The monkeys discussed Tohon's semideath and Cellina's possible courses of action.

"Will she wait to make a healer or try to capture Avry?" Loren asked.

"Cellina knows I won't cooperate, and there may be children who have survived the toxin at Tohon's castle," I said.

"Plus, she really liked the sound of Queen Cellina," Kerrick added. "She might be content to let him stay in that state."

"Well, she'll have all those troops to command, but only a limited number of dead. And once we hit them with the toxin, she won't have them anymore. So she'll need Tohon," Quain said.

"But we're still outnumbered," Loren said. "Even with Prince Ryne's tactics, we're in for a long haul unless we get more soldiers."

"I might be able to find a few," Kerrick said. He told us about making a truce with the tribes. "They know how to fight. One of them is worth three of us."

The monkeys teased Kerrick about going tribal until Flea interrupted them with, "First we need to rescue Belen so I can...wake him, then get more troops and restore the Fifteen Realms."

All humor fled. When listed like that, it was daunting. And I didn't add freeing Melina or dealing with Jael or deciding what to do with Estrid and her staff who might still be frozen in Sepp's stasis.

Poor Odd didn't eat a bite, and he looked devastated. After he mumbled about getting some sleep and left, I followed him. Well acquainted with loss, I pulled him aside to talk to him in private.

"I just feel so...stupid for not figuring it out. Now that I think about it, there were plenty of clues," Odd said.

"Don't beat yourself up. We all missed it," I said.

"Yeah, but you didn't fall in love with her."

He tried to brush past. I grabbed his arm. "Yes, I did. She was like a sister to me. An older, grumpier sister, but I loved her, too."

A quick smile flashed before the haunted expression returned.

"And I *know* she cared for you. That wasn't an act."

He conceded the possibility. Catching movement to the left, I spotted Kerrick hovering nearby. He'd been keeping an eye on me the entire night. And I'd been seeking signs of the toxin, holding my emotions in so tight my muscles ached. He appeared healthy, but I wasn't going to be caught off guard again. I didn't want to hope. I wanted to know without a doubt that he would live before I let myself relax. Before I let myself have that happy reunion.

Kerrick kept his distance from us, but his body language said it all. Odd eyed him for a long moment. "So we guessed you were in love with the wrong prince?"

"Yes," I said.

"At least we got the prince part right. Although I think I prefer Prince Ryne. This one is too overprotective. Doesn't he know you can handle yourself?"

I laughed. "Oh, he's well aware of my abilities. We just haven't seen each other in months."

"Then what are you waiting for, Avry? Everyone expected you two to disappear as soon as we returned." Odd headed to his bedroll.

"What was that about?" Kerrick asked as soon as Odd left.

"Sergeant Wynn. She and Odd were…close."

He took my hand. Warmth spread up my arm. I realized how ridiculous I was being with Kerrick. Every moment counted. Every breath precious.

I led him to the sleeping cavern, thinking to gather my bed-roll to take to a private spot. I stopped at the entrance. Only my things remained by the small fire pit.

"Looks like everyone cleared out for tonight," Kerrick said. "But I'm not letting you out of my sight even if that means I have to sleep on the cold, hard ground."

I turned and kissed him. His surprise didn't last. Wrapping

his arms around me, he pulled me against him as he deep-
ened the kiss.

Fire raced through me, igniting all my senses.

He broke off the kiss and smiled. "Feeling better?"

"Oh, yes." I pushed him toward my bedroll. "You're *not*
sleeping tonight."

KERRICK

Avry snuggled closer as she slept. Lying on his side, Kerrick propped his head up on his hand so he could see her better, still amazed that they had both lived through the day. When he had seen her trapped in Tohon's arms... No, he wouldn't dwell on that moment of pure agony. Unlike any other in his lifetime.

They had so much to catch up on, but he savored the feel of her body pressed against his. He studied every inch of her face. Her hair had grown, and her skin appeared lighter than before. Kerrick resisted the urge to wake her for another round of getting reacquainted. She needed her sleep. And from the new collection of scars on her body, he knew she'd been devoting all her energy to healing others.

He settled his head back onto the pillow. Kerrick never wanted to leave her side. Even if Ryne ordered him to lead a squad and fight, he would stay with Avry. Being apart just hurt too damn much.

Of course, he realized just how selfish that would be. Belen had to be found. And he needed to fetch Danny and find out if Noak's warriors would join them. It was doubtful Avry would agree to accompany him. She was needed here.

One day they'd be like a normal couple, living together with Danny and Zila. Perhaps married with children of their own. Belen, Loren, Quain and Flea acting like uncles and living close by. The war would be a faint memory and recited to the kids as exaggerated tales of epic battles and impossible heroics.

He smiled at his silly thoughts. Although they weren't that silly. That future image gave him more motivation to stop the nonsense. Just thinking about Cellina and Jael turned his stomach.

Another wave of nausea swelled. Perhaps he should have eaten more tonight. So worried about Avry's reaction to his arrival, he'd hardly eaten.

Yes, that was the reason for his sour stomach.

It had to be.

As the night wore on, he grew sicker. Sweat poured off his skin, but he wouldn't wake Avry. It was a little stomach bug and not the Death Lily toxin. Bile pushed up his throat. Clamping down on the need to vomit, Kerrick slipped from the covers, yanked on his pants and bolted outside.

He connected to the living green and felt a bit better. The night breeze cooled him, sending a shiver along his skin. Kerrick leaned against a tree. His respite didn't last long. The forest soon spun around him. Nausea swelled, and he bent over to expel his meager supper onto the ground.

The sickness battered his body. Weak-kneed, he sprawled on the ground as he fought the urge to pass out, concentrating on the tree canopy above him. He had promised Avry not to die.

In his delirium, he must have pulled power. Vines crept over his legs and chest. They twined around his arms. He struggled to free himself. Kerrick had to return to the cave. To Avry.

The living green spoke to him for the first time in his life. *Relax,* it said in his mind. *Be at peace.*

Avry, I'm sorry.
The sickness claimed him.
And he was lost to fever dreams.

★ ★ ★ ★ ★

ACKNOWLEDGEMENTS

For my last book, my acknowledgements spanned two pages. I never want to take my support network for granted because without them, these books would not get written. But this time, I'm going to make it short and sweet. Well, I'm going to try.

As always, I need to thank my editor, Mary-Theresa Hussey, agent, Robert Mecoy, my husband, my daughter and son for their feedback and comments on this book. They spot the holes in logic, the dumb mistakes and, in the case of my daughter and son, yell at me when I kill off favorite characters.

The legions of people at Harlequin who are involved in my books are too many to list individually. They are from every department, from sales to digital to art, and are all over the world. I appreciate all their efforts on the behalf of me and my books. It is always a great pleasure and honor to work with all of you. Thank you so much!

A special thank you to Gabra Zackman, the phenomenally talented actress who reads my audiobooks. You rock! May you never get a sore throat… Ever!

Thanks to Becky Greenly and Amy Snyder for the technical support, and my daughter and son for the inspiration, laughs and support.

My husband, Rodney, gets his own paragraph or else he'll pout. Just kidding. Without him, I wouldn't be a writer. I'd

Maria V. Snyder

still be a miserable environmental meteorologist, working in a cubicle. Now I work in a beautiful office that he built just for me. Thanks, dear!